Book Level ___

AR Points ___ 9/20

GRAYSTRIPE'S
VOW

WARRIORS

SUPER EDITIONS

GRAYSTRIPE'S VOW

ERIN HUNTER

HARPER

An Imprint of HarperCollinsPublishers

Graystripe's Vow

Copyright © 2020 by Working Partners Ltd.

Series created by Working Partners Ltd.

Map art © 2015, 2018 by Dave Stevenson

Interior art © 2020 by Owen Richardson

Comic text © 2020 by Working Partners Ltd.

Comic art © 2020 by HarperCollins Publishers

Library of Congress Cataloging-in-Publication Data

Names: Hunter, Erin, author.

Title: Graystripe's vow / Erin Hunter.

Description: First edition. | New York : HarperCollins Children's Books,
[2020] | Series: Warriors super edition ; 13 | Summary: "During a time of
great turmoil and amid silence from StarClan, respected ThunderClan
warrior Graystripe must break a promise from his past and leave his Clan
behind for a quest to heal his past and uncover his future"— Provided by
publisher.

Identifiers: LCCN 2020018203 | ISBN 978-0-06-296302-4
(hardcover) | ISBN 978-0-06-296303-1 (library binding)

Subjects: CYAC: Cats—Fiction. | Fantasy.

Classification: LCC PZ7.H916625 Gp 2020 | DDC [Fic]—dc23

LC record available at https://lccn.loc.gov/2020018203

20 21 22 23 24   PC/LSCH   10 9 8 7 6 5 4 3 2 1

❖

First Edition

Special thanks to Kate Cary

ALLEGIANCES—NOW

THUNDERCLAN

ACTING LEADER SQUIRRELFLIGHT—dark ginger she-cat with green eyes and one white paw

ACTING DEPUTY LIONBLAZE—golden tabby tom with amber eyes

MEDICINE CATS JAYFEATHER—gray tabby tom with blind blue eyes

ALDERHEART—dark ginger tom with amber eyes

WARRIORS (toms and she-cats without kits)

THORNCLAW—golden-brown tabby tom

WHITEWING—white she-cat with green eyes

BIRCHFALL—light brown tabby tom

MOUSEWHISKER—gray-and-white tom
APPRENTICE, BAYPAW (golden tabby tom)

POPPYFROST—pale tortoiseshell-and-white she-cat

BRISTLEFROST—pale gray she-cat

LILYHEART—small, dark tabby she-cat with white patches and blue eyes
APPRENTICE, FLAMEPAW (black tom)

BUMBLESTRIPE—very pale gray tom with black stripes

CHERRYFALL—ginger she-cat

MOLEWHISKER—brown-and-cream tom

CINDERHEART—gray tabby she-cat
APPRENTICE, FINCHPAW (tortoiseshell she-cat)

BLOSSOMFALL—tortoiseshell-and-white she-cat with petal-shaped white patches

IVYPOOL—silver-and-white tabby she-cat with dark blue eyes

EAGLEWING—ginger she-cat
APPRENTICE, MYRTLEPAW (pale brown she-cat)

DEWNOSE—gray-and-white tom

THRIFTEAR—dark gray she-cat

STORMCLOUD—gray tabby tom

HOLLYTUFT—black she-cat

FLIPCLAW—tabby tom

FERNSONG—yellow tabby tom

HONEYFUR—white she-cat with yellow splotches

SPARKPELT—orange tabby she-cat

SORRELSTRIPE—dark brown she-cat

TWIGBRANCH—gray she-cat with green eyes

FINLEAP—brown tom

SHELLFUR—tortoiseshell tom

PLUMSTONE—black-and-ginger she-cat

LEAFSHADE—tortoiseshell she-cat

SPOTFUR—spotted tabby she-cat

FLYWHISKER—striped gray tabby she-cat

SNAPTOOTH—golden tabby tom

QUEENS (she-cats expecting or nursing kits)

DAISY—cream long-furred cat from the horseplace

ELDERS (former warriors and queens, now retired)

GRAYSTRIPE—long-haired gray tom

CLOUDTAIL—long-haired white tom with blue eyes

BRIGHTHEART—white she-cat with ginger patches

BRACKENFUR—golden-brown tabby tom

SHADOWCLAN

LEADER TIGERSTAR—dark brown tabby tom

DEPUTY CLOVERFOOT—gray tabby she-cat

MEDICINE CATS PUDDLESHINE—brown tom with white splotches

SHADOWSIGHT—gray tabby tom

MOTHWING—dappled golden she-cat

WARRIORS TAWNYPELT—tortoiseshell she-cat with green eyes

DOVEWING—pale gray she-cat with green eyes

HARELIGHT—white tom

ICEWING—white she-cat with blue eyes

STONEWING—white tom

SCORCHFUR—dark gray tom with slashed ears

FLAXFOOT—brown tabby tom

SPARROWTAIL—large brown tabby tom

SNOWBIRD—pure white she-cat with green eyes

YARROWLEAF—ginger she-cat with yellow eyes

BERRYHEART—black-and-white she-cat

GRASSHEART—pale brown tabby she-cat

WHORLPELT—gray-and-white tom

HOPWHISKER—calico she-cat

BLAZEFIRE—white-and-ginger tom

CINNAMONTAIL—brown tabby she-cat with white paws

FLOWERSTEM—silver she-cat

SNAKETOOTH—honey-colored tabby she-cat

SLATEFUR—sleek gray tom

POUNCESTEP—gray tabby she-cat

LIGHTLEAP—brown tabby she-cat

GULLSWOOP—white she-cat

SPIRECLAW—black-and-white tom

HOLLOWSPRING—black tom

SUNBEAM—brown-and-white tabby she-cat

ELDERS **OAKFUR**—small brown tom

SKYCLAN

LEADER **LEAFSTAR**—brown-and-cream tabby she-cat with amber eyes

DEPUTY **HAWKWING**—dark gray tom with yellow eyes

MEDICINE CATS **FRECKLEWISH**—mottled light brown tabby she-cat with spotted legs

FIDGETFLAKE—black-and-white tom

MEDIATOR **TREE**—yellow tom with amber eyes

WARRIORS

SPARROWPELT—dark brown tabby tom

MACGYVER—black-and-white tom

DEWSPRING—sturdy gray tom

ROOTSPRING—yellow tom

NEEDLECLAW—black-and-white she-cat

PLUMWILLOW—dark gray she-cat

SAGENOSE—pale gray tom

KITESCRATCH—reddish-brown tom

HARRYBROOK—gray tom

CHERRYTAIL—fluffy tortoiseshell and white she-cat

CLOUDMIST—white she-cat with yellow eyes

BLOSSOMHEART—ginger-and-white she-cat

TURTLECRAWL—tortoiseshell she-cat

RABBITLEAP—brown tom
APPRENTICE, WRENPAW (golden tabby she-cat)

REEDCLAW—small pale tabby she-cat

MINTFUR—gray tabby she-cat with blue eyes

NETTLESPLASH—pale brown tom

TINYCLOUD—small white she-cat

PALESKY—black-and-white she-cat

VIOLETSHINE—black-and-white she-cat with yellow eyes

BELLALEAF—pale orange she-cat with green eyes

QUAILFEATHER—white tom with crow-black ears

PIGEONFOOT—gray-and-white she-cat

FRINGEWHISKER—white she-cat with brown splotches

GRAVELNOSE—tan tom

SUNNYPELT—ginger she-cat

QUEENS   **NECTARSONG**—brown she-cat

ELDERS   **FALLOWFERN**—pale brown she-cat who has lost her hearing

WINDCLAN

LEADER   **HARESTAR**—brown-and-white tom

DEPUTY   **CROWFEATHER**—dark gray tom

MEDICINE CAT   **KESTRELFLIGHT**—mottled gray tom with white splotches like kestrel feathers

WARRIORS   **NIGHTCLOUD**—black she-cat

BRINDLEWING—mottled brown she-cat
APPRENTICE, APPLEPAW (yellow tabby she-cat)

LEAFTAIL—dark tabby tom with amber eyes

WOODPAW—brown she-cat

EMBERFOOT—gray tom with two dark paws

BREEZEPELT—black tom with amber eyes

HEATHERTAIL—light brown tabby she-cat with blue eyes

FEATHERPELT—gray tabby she-cat

CROUCHFOOT—ginger tom
APPRENTICE, SONGPAW (tortoiseshell she-cat)

LARKWING—pale brown tabby she-cat

SEDGEWHISKER—light brown tabby she-cat
APPRENTICE, FLUTTERPAW (brown-and-white tom)

SLIGHTFOOT—black tom with white flash on his chest

OATCLAW—pale brown tabby tom

HOOTWHISKER—dark gray tom
APPRENTICE, WHISTLEPAW (gray tabby she-cat)

FERNSTRIPE—gray tabby she-cat

ELDERS

WHISKERNOSE—light brown tom

GORSETAIL—very pale gray-and-white she-cat with blue eyes

RIVERCLAN

LEADER

MISTYSTAR—gray she-cat with blue eyes

DEPUTY

REEDWHISKER—black tom

MEDICINE CATS

WILLOWSHINE—gray tabby she-cat

WARRIORS

DUSKFUR—brown tabby she-cat

MINNOWTAIL—dark gray-and-white she-cat
APPRENTICE, SPLASHPAW (brown tabby tom)

MALLOWNOSE—light brown tabby tom

HAVENPELT—black-and-white she-cat

PODLIGHT—gray-and-white tom

SHIMMERPELT—silver she-cat

LIZARDTAIL—light brown tom
APPRENTICE, FOGPAW (gray-and-white she-cat)

SNEEZECLOUD—gray-and-white tom

BRACKENPELT—tortoiseshell she-cat

JAYCLAW—gray tom

OWLNOSE—brown tabby tom

GORSECLAW—white tom with gray ears

NIGHTSKY—dark gray she-cat with blue eyes

BREEZEHEART—brown-and-white she-cat

QUEENS   **CURLFEATHER**—pale brown she-cat (mother to Frostkit, a she-kit; Mistkit, a she-kit; and Graykit, a tom)

ELDERS   **MOSSPELT**—tortoiseshell-and-white she-cat

ALLEGIANCES—THEN

THUNDERCLAN

LEADER

FIRESTAR—ginger tom with a flame-colored pelt

APPRENTICE, BRAMBLEPAW (dark brown tabby tom with amber eyes)

DEPUTY

GRAYSTRIPE—long-haired gray tom

MEDICINE CAT

CINDERPELT—dark gray she-cat

WARRIORS

(toms and she-cats without kits)

MOUSEFUR—small dusky brown she-cat

DUSTPELT—dark brown tabby tom

APPRENTICE, SORRELPAW (tortoiseshell-and-white she-cat with amber eyes)

LONGTAIL—pale tabby tom with dark black stripes

WILLOWPELT—very pale gray she-cat with unusual blue eyes

CLOUDTAIL—long-haired white tom

APPRENTICE, RAINPAW (dark gray tom with blue eyes)

BRACKENFUR—golden brown tabby tom

THORNCLAW—golden brown tabby tom

APPRENTICE, SOOTPAW (lighter gray tom with amber eyes)

ASHFUR—pale gray (with darker flecks) tom, dark blue eyes

QUEENS

(she-cats expecting or nursing kits)

FERNCLOUD—pale gray with darker flecks, green eyes

BRIGHTHEART—white she-cat with ginger patches

ELDERS (former warriors and queens, now retired)

GOLDENFLOWER—pale ginger she-cat

FROSTFUR—beautiful white she-cat with blue eyes

DAPPLETAIL—once-pretty tortoiseshell she-cat

SPECKLETAIL—pale tabby she-cat

SHADOWCLAN

LEADER **BLACKSTAR**—large white tom with huge jet-black paws

DEPUTY **RUSSETFUR**—dark ginger she-cat

MEDICINE CAT **LITTLECLOUD**—very small tabby tom

WARRIORS **OAKFUR**—small brown tom

CEDARHEART—dark gray tom

ROWANCLAW—ginger she-cat

TALLPOPPY—long-legged light brown tabby she-cat

TAWNYPELT—tortoiseshell she-cat with green eyes

ELDERS **RUNNINGNOSE**—small gray-and-white tom, formerly the medicine cat

WINDCLAN

LEADER   **TALLSTAR**—elderly black-and-white tom with a very long tail

DEPUTY   **MUDCLAW**—mottled dark brown tom

MEDICINE CAT   **BARKFACE**—short-tailed brown tom

WARRIORS   **WEBFOOT**—dark gray tabby tom

                      TORNEAR—tabby tom

                      ONEWHISKER—brown tabby tom

                      RUNNINGBROOK—light gray she-cat

QUEENS   **ASHFOOT**—gray queen

                      MORNINGFLOWER—tortoiseshell queen

                      WHITETAIL—small white she-cat

RIVERCLAN

LEADER   **LEOPARDSTAR**—unusually spotted golden tabby she-cat

DEPUTY   **MISTYFOOT**—gray she-cat with blue eyes

MEDICINE CAT   **MUDFUR**—long-haired light brown tom

WARRIORS   **BLACKCLAW**—smoky black tom

                      HEAVYSTEP—thickset tabby tom

                      STORMFUR—dark gray tom with amber eyes

                      FEATHERTAIL—light gray she-cat with blue eyes

QUEENS   **MOSSPELT**—tortoiseshell she-cat

CATS OUTSIDE CLANS

BARLEY—black-and-white tom that lives on a farm close to the forest

RAVENPAW—sleek black cat that lives on the farm with Barley, formerly of ThunderClan

SMUDGE—plump, friendly black-and-white kittypet that lives in a house at the edge of the forest

GRAYSTRIPE'S
VOW

CAT VIEW

GREENLEAF TWOLEGPLACE

TWOLEG NEST

TWOLEG PATH

TWOLEG PATH

CLEARING

SHADOWCLAN CAMP

SMALL THUNDERPATH

HALFBRIDGE

GREENLEAF TWOLEGPLACE

HALFBRIDGE

ISLAND

STREAM

RIVERCLAN CAMP

HORSEPLACE

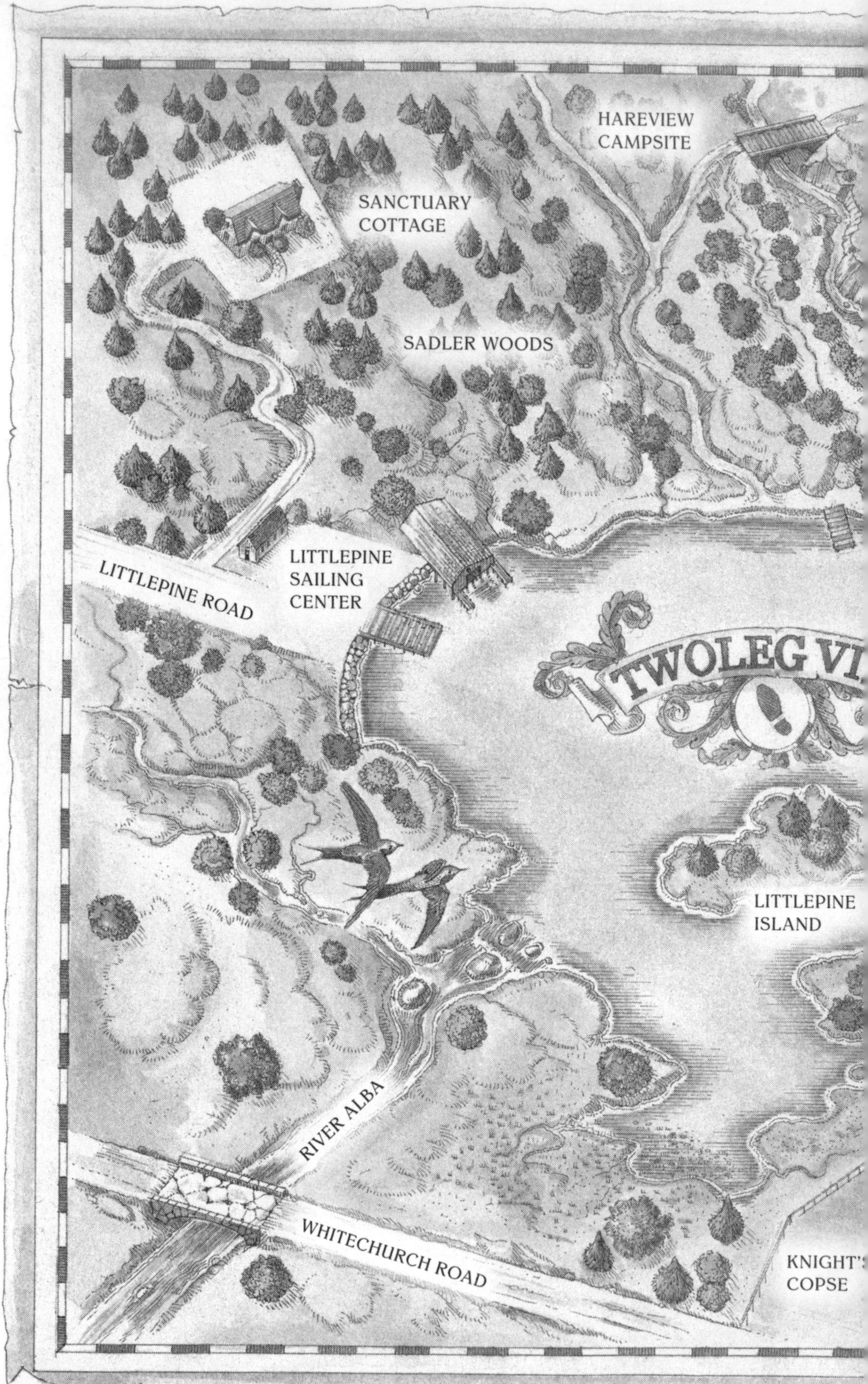
HAREVIEW CAMPSITE
SANCTUARY COTTAGE
SADLER WOODS
LITTLEPINE SAILING CENTER
LITTLEPINE ROAD
TWOLEG VI
LITTLEPINE ISLAND
RIVER ALBA
WHITECHURCH ROAD
COPSE

CAT VIEW

HIGHSTONES

BARLEY'S FARM

FOURTREES

WINDCLAN CAMP

FALLS

SUNNINGROCK

RIVER

RIVERCLAN CAMP

TREECUTPLACE

THE OLD
FOREST
TERRITORIES

CARRIONPLACE

SHADOWCLAN
CAMP

THUNDERPATH

OWLTREE

GREAT
SYCAMORE

THUNDERCLAN
CAMP

SNAKEROCKS

SANDY
HOLLOW

TALLPINES

TWOLEGPLACE

KEY
To The
CLANS

THUNDERCLAN

RIVERCLAN

SHADOWCLAN

WINDCLAN

STARCLAN

NORTH

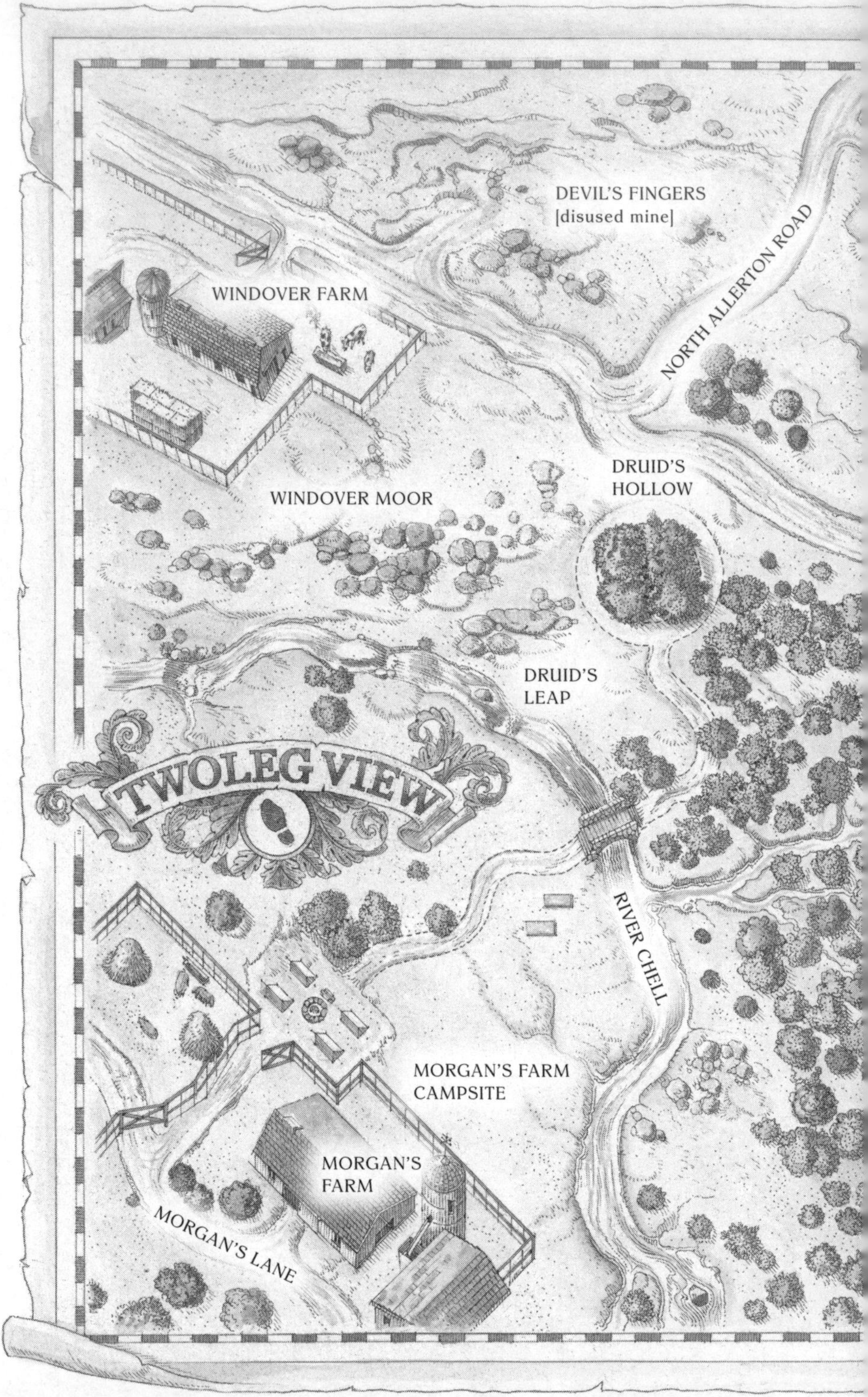

DEVIL'S FINGERS
[disused mine]

NORTH ALLERTON ROAD

WINDOVER FARM

DRUID'S
HOLLOW

WINDOVER MOOR

DRUID'S
LEAP

TWOLEG VIEW

RIVER CHELL

MORGAN'S FARM
CAMPSITE

MORGAN'S
FARM

MORGAN'S LANE

THE OLD
FOREST
TERRITORIES

NORTH ALLERTON
AMENITY TIP

WINDOVER ROAD

WHITE HART WOODS

CHELFORD FOREST

CHELFORD MILL

CHELFORD

KEY To The TERRAIN

DECIDUOUS WOODLAND

CONIFERS

MARSH

CLIFFS AND ROCKS

HIKING TRAILS

NORTH

PROLOGUE

— Then —

Gremlin peered cautiously from the shelter of a holly bush, letting her glance flick from side to side. All her senses were alert, but she could see nothing beyond the dense undergrowth, scent nothing except the lush smell of vegetation, and hear nothing but the rush of the nearby river.

With a sigh, she stepped back into the hollow space of at the center of the bush. "No sign of him," she reported. "Maybe our spies got it wrong."

Her companion, Snake, was crouched down with his black-and-white-furred shoulders hunched. He replied with a grunt. "Maybe."

He took her place, gazing out through the gap between the branches. Meanwhile, Gremlin began to groom her own patchy black, white, and tortoiseshell fur, grimacing at the taste of the chervil she and Snake had rolled in to disguise their scent. Her pads tingled with a mixture of excitement and apprehension at the thought of what could lie ahead— very soon now.

Snake's tail lashed once, snapping past Gremlin's face and startling her so that she had to bite back a squeal of alarm. Snake spoke in a low growl. "He's here."

Gremlin pressed up beside him so that she too could see through the gap. Two ginger cats—a tom with a flame-colored pelt and a she-cat with paler fur—were brushing through the undergrowth, less than two fox-lengths away from the bush where Gremlin and Snake were hidden.

"So the ginger fool is really going," Snake sneered in a whisper. "What is he thinking? He's leaving his Clan leaderless and undefended."

"Who is the cat with Firestar?" Gremlin asked, keeping her voice equally low.

"His mate, Sandstorm," Snake told her. "She's not important, except that now she's one less warrior for us to worry about."

Side by side, Gremlin and Snake watched until the two ThunderClan cats had disappeared, heading in the direction of the Twoleg bridge that crossed the river. When even their scent had faded, Snake turned to Gremlin, a malignant glint in his blue eyes.

"At last!" he hissed. "This is BloodClan's chance for revenge!"

The aggressive note in his voice chilled Gremlin. Though Snake wore a collar, he was no soft kittypet; the narrow pelt-strip was studded with dogs' teeth, and his torn ear told the stories of the many battles he had fought. His claws were flexing in and out, as if he were already imagining the moment when he would sink them into ThunderClan throats.

"Come on," he urged her. "We need to tell Fury."

He plunged out of the shelter of the holly bush and made off downstream toward the Twolegplace, choosing a route that would take him and Gremlin well clear of the ThunderClan camp. Gradually, he picked up the pace, and when Gremlin tried to keep up with him, she felt in her belly the weight of the kits she was carrying.

This is a bad time for me to go to war, she sighed inwardly. *Of course BloodClan still wants revenge on the Clans for killing our leader. But I wish we could wait a bit longer.* What would happen to her kits if she had to fight?

Gremlin and Snake slipped silently through the Twolegplace until they found Fury and the rest of BloodClan gathered on a stretch of ground beside a row of monster dens. Tall buildings on the other three sides cut off the sunlight; the ground lay in perpetual shadow, and the only things growing there were a few clumps of thin, wilting grass.

Fury was sitting on top of a tumbled pile of reddish, squared-off stones like the ones Twolegs used to build their dens. A long-furred tabby with one eye slashed away, her pelt seamed with many scars, she was the latest in a line of cats who had taken control of BloodClan since Scourge had been killed in the battle with the warriors. Gremlin could well believe that she was even more dangerous than the savage black tom, who had almost succeeded in making himself leader of every cat in the forest. But a moon or so before, when

Fury and the previous leader, Claw, had gone to the Twoleg-place to search for food, only Fury had returned, her paws still wet with blood. She'd told the rest of BloodClan that Claw had gotten on "the wrong side of a dog," but Gremlin doubted that was the whole story.

Fury's one remaining eye widened and her tail twitched with anticipation as Gremlin and Snake approached. "Well?" she rasped. "Report."

The other BloodClan cats clustered around them eagerly, their eyes gleaming with anticipation as Snake recounted how he and Gremlin had seen Firestar and Sandstorm on their way out of ThunderClan's territory.

"So ThunderClan is vulnerable," Fury meowed when Snake had finished. Her voice shook with excitement and her shoulder fur began to rise. "We must choose the right time to strike—but believe me, strike we will!"

Her BloodClan warriors broke out in yowls of acclamation at their leader's words.

"Yes! We'll take their territory!" a skinny yellow tom screeched.

"We'll drive them out!"

"We'll take the rest of the forest, too!"

Gremlin listened in silence, feeling unease settle deep into her chest. Her gaze fell on her brother, Scraps, in a huddle with some of the younger BloodClan cats, his eyes blazing with fervor.

"We'll have our revenge!" he growled. "We'll *shred* those ThunderClan cats! They will pay for what they did to Blood-Clan!"

Gremlin couldn't share her brother's enthusiasm. She found it too hard to believe that they could easily take ThunderClan, even with its leader gone. The warriors were well trained, and they outnumbered the remaining BloodClan cats, since BloodClan had been thinned out by the battle the previous leafbare.

Movement in her belly reminded her of the precious burden she was carrying. *I won't let anything happen to my unborn kits,* she mused. *That means I have to find a way out of participating in this battle. I wish I believed we might win, but the truth is . . .*

This fight could be a bloodbath.

CHAPTER 1

❧

— Now —

The sun was going down, casting long shadows over the stone hollow. Graystripe sat in one of the remaining sunny spots, his paws tucked underneath him as he watched his Clanmates coming and going across the camp. His heart was filled with sadness. Everything seemed peaceful as the day drew to an end, but Graystripe was aware of tension stretching like cobwebs among all the cats of ThunderClan.

I'm sure I'm not the only cat who feels the camp is too empty, he thought. So many good warriors had been lost in the battle with the false Bramblestar. And Squirrelflight was doing her best as leader, but the situation the Clan faced now was far from easy.

None of their Clanmates seemed to know what to do—as if they were too distracted to keep up the smooth routine of hunting and patrols. Even Alderheart, the young medicine cat, had just emerged from his den and strode purposefully into the middle of the camp, only to halt abruptly with an irritated twitch of his tail; he bounded back to his den and reemerged a moment later with a leaf wrap of herbs in his jaws.

It's not like Alderheart to forget what he's supposed to be doing.

Glancing aside, Graystripe saw only the empty space where his mate Millie should have been sitting. But Millie was dead, and for moons Graystripe had been suffering the quiet heartbreak of her loss. Now Stemleaf, the son of his daughter Blossomfall, had been killed, too.

That feels even harder than Millie's death, Graystripe thought sorrowfully. *At least with Millie, I had half a moon, as she sickened and grew weaker, to come to terms with the idea that she would soon be gone, and that I would have to get used to being without her.* With Millie, he could at least comfort himself with the knowledge that she had lived a long and full life. But Stemleaf had been so young, and had died so suddenly. . . .

In leafbare, StarClan had suddenly stopped communicating with the Clans. It was the first time in Graystripe's life that he could remember StarClan going so long without sending a single message. At first, the Clan cats had guessed that the frozen Moonpool was preventing StarClan from communicating with them, but when newleaf came and the Moonpool thawed, still no visions came. In the meantime, a ShadowClan medicine-cat apprentice named Shadowpaw had claimed that StarClan had sent him an unusual vision, saying that there was a darkness in the Clans, and naming certain cats who had broken the warrior code. Then, when Bramblestar suffered a terrible illness, Shadowpaw told ThunderClan's medicine cats to leave Bramblestar on the frozen moor overnight. Shadowpaw claimed this was the advice of StarClan again—and indeed Bramblestar died, but returned to life one sunup later, stronger than ever.

ThunderClan had believed that Bramblestar had just taken an unusually long time returning to the next of the nine lives StarClan had given him. But when Bramblestar's behavior became stranger and more cruel—as he insisted on exiling the named codebreakers, and even began naming new cats he believed deserved punishment for breaking the code—ThunderClan eventually realized that he was an impostor. Stemleaf had given his life trying to defeat the false Bramblestar, and though Graystripe wished with all his heart that the young warrior were still alive, he was proud of him. At least Stemleaf had tried, had died fighting for his Clanmates.

Guilt clawed briefly at Graystripe. He wished he had done more himself to face down the impostor. Even though he had given the false Bramblestar a piece of his mind, telling him that not even Firestar had demanded blind loyalty, he had never joined the rebels who had been hiding out on ShadowClan's territory, nor taken part in the battle to defeat the intruder.

But I'm not the young cat I used to be, he reflected. *Not like when Firestar and I would get into all sorts of adventures—and trouble!—and be the first to confront any danger that threatened the Clan.*

But as Graystripe looked around at his Clanmates, he flicked his whiskers in amusement. *Silly old tom—you're retired now, an elder! Isn't that what elders are supposed to do—let the younger, stronger cats fight the battles?* He sought out his surviving kits, and their kits. Bumblestripe was sitting near the entrance to the warriors' den, discussing the warrior code with his sister's kit Shellfur, who had once been his apprentice. Across the clearing, Lionblaze was just choosing a piece of prey from the fresh-kill pile; his golden tabby pelt reminded Graystripe of Sandstorm, who had given her life to help Alderheart on his quest to discover the fate of SkyClan.

Lionblaze carried the prey over to Spotfur, who sat hunched in on herself, still grieving for Stemleaf, who had been her mate. As Spotfur looked up to speak to Lionblaze, an even deeper memory stirred within Graystripe: The shape of her muzzle and the angle of her ears were exactly like those of Frostfur, her distant kin, who had chosen not to make the journey to the lake with the rest of ThunderClan, but to stay in the old forest, the Clans' first territory.

Remembered images of former Clanmates seemed to patrol through Graystripe's mind. Thinking of Frostfur reminded Graystripe of her brother, Ravenpaw, his old friend who had left ThunderClan to live with the barn cat Barley. Sadness rippled through him as he remembered what the SkyClan cats had reported once they'd finally arrived at the lake: that Ravenpaw had visited them in their gorge, where he had died a hero's death.

Surely he must have gone to StarClan, he thought. *He deserved it, if any cat did.*

But thinking of StarClan led Graystripe to remember the current situation in the Clans. The impostor had been overcome in battle, and was being held as a prisoner in ShadowClan in the hope that he would reveal something that could help the Clans reconnect with StarClan. Squirrelflight had taken over as ThunderClan's interim leader. Graystripe could still hardly believe that the impostor had fooled everyone for so long, though he didn't doubt what Squirrelflight had declared, or the report of the impostor's own confession.

Graystripe shook his head, as if that would free it of dark memories. Suddenly Squirrelflight bounded down the tumbled rocks from her den on the Highledge and crossed to a group of younger warriors who were sprawled out near the rock wall of the camp. They fell quickly silent as she approached.

"The fresh-kill pile is getting low," she meowed. "There's time for another hunting patrol before dark."

The warriors stared at her but did not move, and Graystripe's belly cramped with tension. Would they refuse to obey her order? Snaptooth stretched his jaws wide in an insolent yawn, while Thriftear simply rolled her eyes and let her nose rest on her curled-up tail.

Graystripe noticed Thornclaw, a senior warrior, watching from a short distance away. Graystripe stretched his neck to try to catch the tom's eye, but he sensed that Thornclaw was ignoring him. *Say something!* Graystripe urged in his mind. *The younger warriors would listen if you reminded them to respect their leader. . . .*

But Thornclaw wouldn't meet his eye. Squirrelflight stood in front of the younger warriors, her green eyes narrowed, her gaze shifting to each of them in turn. Graystripe could see her muscles grow taut, as if she was finding it hard to restrain herself from leaping at the young warriors and clawing them around the ears. After a moment, Flywhisker muttered, "Okay, keep your fur on." The whole group rose slowly to their paws and trailed across the camp to disappear into the thorn tunnel.

Squirrelflight glared after them, the tip of her tail twitching irritably to and fro. Graystripe felt just as angry on her behalf. *Squirrelflight is our Clan deputy, and our leader until we know whether Bramblestar will return. What's to become of us if our warriors won't accept her authority?*

Once the younger warriors had left, Thornclaw turned and padded over toward Graystripe.

"Why couldn't you back up Squirrelflight?" Graystripe demanded as the tabby warrior approached. "Those young cats should know better than to be so disrespectful to their Clan leader."

Thornclaw halted. "Squirrelflight isn't our leader," he mewed sourly. "She has no right to lead. Bramblestar was made leader by StarClan. But Squirrelflight wasn't our deputy anymore when the truth came out about the impostor. She was in exile—she wasn't even a Clanmate!" He huffed out a sigh. "This is all a complete mess!"

Graystripe's pelt pricked with irritation. "That's a load of mouse droppings!" he retorted. "She was only *in exile* because of the impostor, and he had no right! Now that she's back where she belongs, we should all respect her, and give the same loyalty to her that we did to Bram—"

"Why?" Thornclaw interrupted swiftly, his own shoulder fur bristling. "Just because she was Bramblestar's mate?"

"Of course not!" Graystripe was growing even angrier, his belly beginning to churn. "Squirrelflight has proven she's a good deputy, time after time. And she's a good leader too." Memory caught at him again; he shook his head as he added, "Don't forget there've been other times when ThunderClan was without a StarClan-appointed leader, and we've always done all right in the end!"

Thornclaw turned and stalked off without another word, his tail lashing. Turning back with a dismissive grunt to his contemplation of the camp, Graystripe saw Squirrelflight heading toward him. He could see from the bemused glint in her eye that she'd witnessed his spat with Thornclaw. *At least I was on the right side,* he mused wryly.

"Graystripe, can I have a word with you?" she asked.

"Of course," Graystripe replied. He couldn't read her expression, but he imagined it couldn't be easy for her to see how her Clanmates doubted her.

"Then come up to my den," Squirrelflight mewed with a swish of her tail. "I'd like to talk in private."

Surprised, Graystripe rose to his paws and followed the dark ginger she-cat up the tumbled rocks to the Highledge.

Inside the leader's den, Squirrelflight let herself drop into her nest with a long sigh that told Graystripe how tired she must be, even before he peered closer and noticed the strain in her green eyes, and the way her whiskers drooped. Out in the camp she had kept up the appearance of firm efficiency, but here, with only her oldest friend to see, she could let herself relax. She beckoned Graystripe with a tilt of her head and waited to speak until he had settled down beside her.

"Graystripe, I know you were once deputy, and I'd value your advice," Squirrelflight began. "I believe that we'll be able to get Bramblestar and StarClan back in the end, but as you've just seen, for now I'm struggling with a seriously divided Clan."

Graystripe nodded seriously. *But I don't know why she's asking me*, he thought. *Firestar was much better at giving advice—or at putting his advice into words. I never know quite what to say, or how to say it.*

For a few heartbeats, his mind was blank. He couldn't help wishing that Firestar were there, if only in spirit. Thunder-Clan's previous leader hadn't always known which path to choose, but Graystripe had never felt stronger than when he stood at his best friend's side.

"Squirrelflight," he began at last, "I wish more than anything that I could tell you what to do, but I can't. The false Bramblestar was so good at turning Clanmates against one another—maybe we all just need time to remember that we're on the same side. Those young warriors are a pain in the tail, but they've hardly known what the true ThunderClan was like, before the trouble started. Besides," he added, "I wasn't deputy for very long before the Twolegs took me away."

His time as the Clan's leader, in Firestar's absence, had been even shorter. *And though everything was under control when Firestar returned, that wasn't true for all the time he was away*, Graystripe thought, suppressing a shudder. *I managed to keep the Clan together, but I knew then that I was no leader.*

Now, Graystripe wondered what he could offer Squirrelflight. What could he possibly say to her that would make her impossible job easier?

"You were a good deputy," Squirrelflight meowed, though Graystripe found it hard to believe her.

After a moment, he realized that Squirrelflight was staring at him. "What?" he asked.

She twitched her whiskers. "Where did you go just then? I could see in your eyes that your mind was somewhere else."

Graystripe straightened up in surprise. He'd known Squirrelflight for her whole life, but he hadn't realized she could read him so well. "Oh. I suppose I was . . . thinking about your father," he admitted.

Squirrelflight nodded. "And?"

"And," he went on, "well. It was a different job, being a deputy back then. In some ways, it felt like . . ." He trailed off, suddenly worried that this was the wrong thing to say to Squirrelflight.

But she finished the thought for him. "A different Clan?" she asked.

He let out a breath. "Yes," he agreed, then blurted, "Not better or worse, but . . ."

Squirrelflight shook out her pelt. "You can say it, Graystripe. In many ways, Firestar's ThunderClan *was* better . . . at least, things seemed easier." She sighed.

"You have a difficult job," Graystripe mewed.

She met his gaze. "*You* had a difficult job, when my father left you to watch the Clan," she replied. "I wasn't born yet, but I heard stories about the tough choices you made."

Graystripe took in a breath, remembering. "It was more than I expected," he murmured. "It actually showed me that . . . well, that I never want the job you have now."

Squirrelflight's eyes widened. "Truly? You never wanted to be leader?"

Graystripe shook his head. "Not after that experience. I told Firestar as much, when he returned."

Squirrelflight narrowed her eyes. "But you stayed on as deputy, didn't you? At least . . ."

Graystripe nodded. "I did," he meowed, remembering. "Because I made your father a promise. Even though I would never be leader, I would be a loyal deputy. I would never leave ThunderClan. I would always put the Clan first."

Though Graystripe was looking at Squirrelflight, for a moment his memories clouded his vision. He could so clearly remember the promise he'd made Firestar. He remembered what it had felt like to see his dear friend after so long apart. *I was so relieved. . . .*

But he was brought back to the present by Squirrelflight's voice. "So if that's true—if you'll always put the Clan first—can I count on your help?"

Graystripe blinked, looking almost startled to see Squirrelflight before him. "My help?" he echoed.

Squirrelflight flicked her ear. "I could use your advice, Graystripe," she said. "Things in ThunderClan feel very delicate right now. I could use a warrior to count on."

"Of course," Graystripe declared. But although his voice sounded confident, his mind was whirring. How long ago that promise seemed! A different lifetime . . . possibly even a different Clan. *Firestar's ThunderClan.* He'd left once, to go to RiverClan to be with his kits. But since he'd made that promise—after he'd kept the Clan together while Firestar went on his quest—he'd never questioned his place in ThunderClan. He'd never imagined wanting to leave.

Until now.

The thought made him shudder. *No, surely . . . surely I couldn't leave.* But still, he had to admit that, for the first time in many seasons, his paws were starting to itch. It wasn't so much that he didn't want to be in ThunderClan anymore. It was the worry . . . was the Clan he found himself in now the same Clan Firestar had left? And if not, could it become that Clan again?

Graystripe shook his head, trying to force these thoughts away. *It's absurd. I'm an old cat! Even if I left, where would I go?*

Squirrelflight needed him. Firestar would have expected him to stay, of course.

"Graystripe," Squirrelflight said again, her brusque tone bringing him out of his thoughts. "Are you still with me?"

Graystripe shook out his pelt. "You can count on me," he said simply. *I know that's what she needs to hear right now.* "I promise I'll help you keep the Clan together until we can reach StarClan again . . . and receive their guidance."

Squirrelflight responded with a grateful purr.

Graystripe rose to his paws and dipped his head respectfully before leaving the den and picking his way down the tumbled rocks. He tried to push away the thought that kept repeating in his mind: *What if we can't reach StarClan again?* If there was no StarClan to guide what remained of ThunderClan—no

Firestar, no other ancestors to shape their future—*was* it still ThunderClan?

Exhausted by his own doubts, Graystripe stumbled into the elders' den and lay down. He could catch just a tiny hint of Millie's scent still on the bedding . . . but it was fading every day. Soon it would be gone.

Graystripe closed his eyes. Before sleep took him, one thought took shape in his mind:

I only hope I just told Squirrelflight the truth.

CHAPTER 2

— Now —

Graystripe was padding through the forest; the grass was soft beneath his paws and lightly tickled his pelt as he brushed through it. Sunlight struck down through the trees, the patches of light shifting as the branches rustled in a soft breeze. The forest air was full of the scents of green growth, and the succulent smell of prey nearby.

But as Graystripe glanced around, he couldn't be sure where he was. *Is this ThunderClan territory?* Then he realized that Firestar was walking along beside him, seeming perfectly comfortable in their surroundings.

Firestar! Glancing over his shoulder, Graystripe recognized the barrier of thorns that guarded the current ThunderClan camp. *So this is now,* he thought with some surprise. *We're by the lake. Squirrelflight must be leader. But that would mean . . .*

As the two cats padded along in silence, he suddenly remembered that Firestar should be dead. Graystripe's sense of relief at seeing his friend again was quickly replaced by a restless hope. Graystripe was an elder, a warrior, not a medicine cat or a leader . . . but was it possible that StarClan was trying to contact him directly? The cat beside him seemed solid and real enough. *Maybe Firestar and I were close enough for him to send me a vision. I must pay attention to what he tells me.*

As soon as Graystripe realized that he was dreaming, the forest changed: The sunlight died, and the trees crowded together more densely. The lush scents were replaced by the tang of crow-food. But Firestar still looked real and alive, his flame-colored pelt glowing as if it were still lit up by the vanished sun.

"Firestar, what's happening?" Graystripe asked.

His friend didn't even look at him, heading onward through the trees as if he couldn't hear or see Graystripe. The crushing sense of disappointment was like a massive paw pressing down on him. Dreaming of Firestar—walking alongside him—just made Graystripe miss his friend even more acutely.

So it isn't a StarClan vision, Graystripe thought. *The real Firestar, the spirit who is with our warrior ancestors, would certainly have something to say to me.*

Firestar kept going, and Graystripe followed in his paw steps. Even though he knew this was only a dream, he still hoped that his friend might have something to show him, some final words of wisdom or encouragement before he woke up.

Hope flashed through Graystripe as Firestar finally halted. He bounded to catch up with him, but as he did so, deep darkness flowed around him, blotting out everything except his friend's glowing figure. And though Firestar still didn't speak,

Graystripe felt a strong sense, tingling up through his pads and flowing to every part of his body, as far as his ears and the tip of his tail, that his friend was urging him to do something.

"Why won't you tell me what you want?" he meowed.

For answer, Firestar turned his head, gazing into the darkness, and swept his tail around as if he was telling Graystripe to look, too.

But by now it was too dark to make out anything of the forest; even the nearest trees were covered by the unnatural gloom. When he raised his head, Graystripe realized that a black cloud had covered the sun and all the sky that he could see. And when he looked back at his friend, Firestar's glowing figure had vanished, too. Though the forest around him wasn't cold, a chill settled around Graystripe's heart, and icy claws of terror sank through his pelt.

I have to get out of here. This is not a place I should be. . . .

Graystripe woke, shuddering, to find himself lying in his nest in the elders' den, his paws scrabbling through the moss and bracken as if he was trying to flee. The horror at the end of his dream still clung to him, like dark tendrils of mist seeping through his pelt.

I have to get out of here, he thought, struggling with panic.

Stumbling to his paws, he ducked under the low-growing branches of the hazel bush and emerged into the camp. The sun was shining down on the stone hollow, and a warm breeze rustled the trees above. Puffs of white cloud scudded across the sky. The clearing was almost empty; the patrols must be out, Graystripe realized. The only cats that he could see were Alderheart, laying out some leafy sprigs on a sun-warmed rock beside the medicine cats' den, and his denmates Cloudtail and Brightheart sharing tongues near the fresh-kill pile.

But the sunny, peaceful scene did little to calm Graystripe's fears. His heart thumping as if he had blundered into a fox's den, he bounded across the camp to thrust his way through the thorn tunnel and out into the forest.

At first, as he padded through the trees, he couldn't help turning his head from side to side, his glance flicking into every shadowed hollow and dense thicket. *What am I afraid of?* he asked himself. Then he realized that he was half expecting to see Firestar's flame-colored spirit leaping into the open to confront and challenge him.

"Are you completely mouse-brained?" he growled softly to himself. "There's no need to be afraid of Firestar. I wish he *would* appear. I'd like nothing better than to be able to talk things over with him. Then I might understand what it is he wants me to do."

But no bright spirit appeared. The forest was silent except for the rustling of leaves, birdsong, and the tiny scuttering of prey in the undergrowth. Gradually Graystripe's racing heartbeat slowed, and he expanded his chest to take deep, calming breaths.

But though the terror of his dream had receded, he couldn't entirely dismiss it from his mind. *It wasn't a vision,* he thought, *but all the same, the dream must have meant* something. *I have to work out what that is.*

"Okay, Firestar wants me to do something," he murmured to himself. "And he showed me the forest, so dark that no cat could live there. And I knew in the dream that it wasn't the right place for me." He blinked slowly for a few heartbeats. "Firestar, is *that* what you were trying to tell me? That I should leave the forest—leave ThunderClan?"

Graystripe's heart began to pound again at the enormity of what he was thinking. Even though he'd begun to toy with the idea, the reality of leaving ThunderClan still seemed impossible. Squirrelflight had reminded him of the promise he had once made to Firestar, that he would never leave their Clan.

I'd never break my word, he thought. *But if Firestar was telling me himself that I don't belong . . . does that mean he's releasing me from my promise? But then, why didn't he say so? I wish I had a cat to discuss it with. Oh, Millie, I do miss you!*

Almost as if his silent cry had summoned her, he was conscious of Millie very close to him. In his mind he pictured her: the graceful way she walked, her shining silver tabby fur, the glow of love in her blue eyes. Graystripe almost felt that if he turned his head he would be able to see her, though he knew it was all in his imagination.

"Suppose I tell you all about it, Millie," he murmured, settling himself on a soft cushion of moss and tucking his paws underneath him. "It's so hard for me to make sense of everything, now that I don't have you to talk things over with. You could always help me decide the right thing to do."

Tell me, then, he imagined Millie saying briskly. *And for StarClan's sake, stop dithering!*

Graystripe let the sequence of his dream flow through his mind, as if he were describing what he had experienced. "It almost felt like Firestar was telling me to leave the Clan," he explained. "But how is that possible? Wouldn't he want me to stay here and support his daughter, now that she's acting Clan leader?"

Hardly had the words left his mouth before Graystripe could imagine Millie's response. *Maybe Firestar knows that you could serve the Clan better by leaving,* she would have suggested. *Maybe there's an important task you're meant to carry out.*

"But I'm an elder," Graystripe protested wryly. "We don't do important tasks, not anymore."

With that thought, he began to wonder whether the promise he had made to Firestar so long ago still bound him in the present day. Perhaps that was what Firestar was trying to point out to him. He was an elder; he had no warrior duties now. And ThunderClan had been very different in those far-off days. "Oh, Millie, I wish you could tell me what to do!"

His mate had always been practical. She'd had good sense. *Why not see what other cats feel about it?* she would have advised him. *Or wait and see if anything else happens that might tell you what you're supposed to do?*

"Now you're talking like I'm a medicine cat, looking for signs," Graystripe grumbled.

He could imagine Millie prodding him in the side with her paw, or flicking his ear with her tail. *Warriors look for signs all the time,* she would meow. *Signs that there's a rabbit down that burrow, or a mouse under that bush. Signs that it's going to rain before sunhigh, and you'd better get back to camp. Not all signs come from StarClan.*

"True," Graystripe admitted. "But this is a bit more complicated than a hunting patrol."

Even though he still hadn't found an answer he could trust, Graystripe's heart felt lighter after his imaginary conversation with his mate. When he had left the camp, he had felt as if he were struggling through dense forest with nothing to guide him. At least now, as he rose to his paws and turned back toward the stone hollow, he was able to believe that his paws would find a path forward, even though he didn't yet know what that path would be.

As Graystripe drew closer to the camp, a powerful ThunderClan scent wafted over him from a bank of fern, and a moment later the fronds parted and another elder emerged. Brackenfur was carrying prey in his jaws..

Graystripe called a greeting, and added, "It looks as if the prey was running well."

"Pretty good," Brackenfur mumbled around the two mice he was carrying by their tails. "I felt like a hunt."

He was about to go on when Graystripe raised a paw to halt him. "Brackenfur, can I have a word?" he asked.

Brackenfur blinked in surprise. "Sure," he meowed, dropping the two mice.

"There's something I wanted to ask you," Graystripe began. Now that he actually had to find the right words, he felt awkward, but he knew that Brackenfur was exactly the right cat to tell him what he needed to know. He had once been Graystripe's apprentice, and had grown up in the old forest. He, too, had known ThunderClan when Bluestar, and then Firestar, was Clan leader. "You remember ThunderClan in the old days," he began slowly. "Back when Firestar first became leader, and we had all that trouble with Tigerstar."

"Yes." Brackenfur's voice was mystified. "I remember a lot of stuff. Why are you asking me now?"

"Well, I was wondering . . . Brackenfur, do you feel that it's the same Clan now as it was then?"

Brackenfur stared at him, looking even more confused. "Of course it's the same Clan," he replied. "I know what you mean, Graystripe. When the Clan's in the middle of such a crisis, and especially when we've lost so many of our Clanmates from those times . . ." His voice shook a little, and Graystripe guessed he was remembering his mate, Sorreltail, who had been killed in the Great Battle, or his best friend, Dustpelt, who had worked with him on securing the camp and weatherproofing the dens. "But their kin still live on," he continued more firmly. "And though Bramblestar is a different kind of leader from Firestar, he was still a *good* leader, before the impostor drove him out of his body. You mustn't let these temporary problems get you down," he told Graystripe, resting his tail-tip for a moment on the other elder's shoulder: a gesture that irked Graystripe, even though he knew that his Clanmate meant to be reassuring. "We'll sort it out sooner or later. We always do."

"I'm not so sure," Graystripe responded. "There's so much arguing now, especially among the younger cats. Sometimes I feel like turning my back on the whole lot of them and leaving the whole Clan behind."

"Leave ThunderClan?" Brackenfur's neck fur began to bristle with shock. "Oh, come on, Graystripe, you would never do that! I know I couldn't," he continued after a moment's pause. "Not now, when they need us more than ever."

"I guess you're right," Graystripe murmured. Privately he wished that he felt the same way, or that he could share his Clanmate's certainty. *And if I believe what Brackenfur is telling me, what about my dream? How does that fit in?*

"Of course I'm right!" Brackenfur meowed confidently. "You'll see." He picked up his mice and bounded off in the direction of the camp.

Heaving a massive sigh, Graystripe followed in his paw steps.

A loud yowl startled Graystripe as he approached the camp. Beyond the barrier of thorns, he could hear snarling and hissing from at least two cats.

Great StarClan, what next? he asked himself. *Is the impostor back? Or is it badgers . . . ?*

Graystripe pushed his way through the thorn tunnel and emerged into the stone hollow. Near the center of the clearing he saw Plumstone and Thriftear standing nose to nose, their fur bristling and their ears laid back. They were hissing so angrily at each other that Graystripe was sure that a fight was about to break out.

"Hey," he mewed, bounding across to join them. "What's the problem here?"

Both young she-cats turned toward him with identical expressions of hostility. "She's a traitor!" Plumstone snarled, lashing her tail toward Thriftear. "She's betrayed Thunder-Clan!"

"No," Thriftear growled. "*She's* the one who's a disgrace to our Clan!"

The two cats crouched low, ready to leap at each other. Graystripe thrust his way between them, forcing them apart.

"Slow down," he meowed. "Tell me what happened."

"Ask *her*!" Thriftear hissed. "It's all her fault."

"No, it's not!" Plumstone snapped back, then turned to Graystripe. "Get *her* to tell you what she did."

"I don't care who it is that tells me," Graystripe said, trying not to let his irritation show. "But one of you is going to. Or do we have to take this to Squirrelflight?"

At the mention of the acting Clan leader, both she-cats seemed to shrink into themselves, staring down at their forepaws as they scrabbled in the earth of the camp floor. After a few heartbeats, Thriftear mumbled, "She ate my mouse."

"It wasn't *your* mouse!" Plumstone flashed back at her. "It was *me* who picked it off the fresh-kill pile."

"Well, I was *going* to take it," Thriftear grumbled. "And then *she* pushed her way in and grabbed it, and gobbled it up. She didn't even offer to share!"

"*That's* what all this is about?" Graystripe asked with a sigh. "One stupid little mouse, when the fresh-kill pile is as full as I've ever seen it, in all my many moons? Have you both got bees in your brain? What do you suppose Firestar would have said if he ever saw two warriors ready to come to claws over a mouse?"

"Oh, sure, that was Firestar," Thriftear responded. "That was when ThunderClan had a *real* leader!"

Instantly, Plumstone's shoulder fur bushed up. "Take that back!" she growled. "Squirrelflight *is* a real leader. And she's doing the best job any cat could do."

"Yeah, and it's worked out really great so far, hasn't it?" Thriftear retorted with a contemptuous flick of her tail.

Plumstone slid out her claws and braced her muscles to spring at her Clanmate. Once again, Graystripe hastily stepped between the two furious she-cats before they had the chance to claw each other's fur off.

Graystripe couldn't work out how something so trivial had escalated to the point where two Clanmates were prepared to tear each other apart, accusing each other of treachery. *Is this what we've come to?* he asked himself.

"It's good that you can stand up for yourselves," he continued. "That will be useful to your Clan, but you both need to stop looking for enemies everywhere. ThunderClan needs to unite behind Squirrelflight, or we could fall apart for good." He thought again of his promise to Squirrelflight, and wondered how he could deliver on it. *How can I make them understand that the Clan is more important than any one leader?* His mind flew back to a time at Sunningrocks, when a couple of bickering warriors had been too distracted arguing over prey to defend their Clan from a RiverClan attack. *Our younger warriors could learn something from that.* "When Firestar was leader . . . ," he began.

Plumstone looked up, glaring at him and drawing her lips back in the beginning of a snarl. "That's the problem with elders," she sneered. "They're all stuck in the past! But looking backward won't help ThunderClan now. We don't need advice from some bygone moon. Things worked differently then."

"Yeah," Thriftear agreed, fixing Graystripe with an identical glare. "Firestar isn't our leader anymore. And we couldn't even ask him what he thinks if we wanted to! StarClan has left us. Our ancestors are *gone*, and we need to work out how we're going to survive without them."

"That's right," Plumstone meowed. "We have to look forward. The old solutions won't work, and if we keep on thinking they will, then it's like our minds will be stuffed full of thistle-fluff."

"Are you saying . . . ," Graystripe began, his tail-tip twitching in spite of his efforts to repress his rising anger.

"She's saying that your time is *over*." Thriftear thrust her muzzle toward him. "It's the warriors who make the decisions now, not the elders. Come on, Plumstone. We've better things to do."

The two young cats spun around and stalked off side by side, their pelts brushing as they headed back toward the fresh-kill pile.

"I'll find you another good mouse," Plumstone promised.

Well . . . at least I did stop their fighting, Graystripe thought wryly. But still, his heart ached. Watching them, Graystripe felt a bit like a ghost, an ancestor who just hadn't got around to dying yet. *They think Firestar's days are gone. And which cat is to say that they're wrong?*

It was the same thing he himself felt. It was the doubt that made him question whether he could help Squirrelflight at all. *We're like another Clan now.*

As he let himself sink into a crouch, a cloud passed over the sun and the camp darkened, reminding him of the forest in his dream.

Maybe my advice is too outdated for today's ThunderClan, he thought with a shudder. Perhaps he'd been right about what his dream had been trying to tell him: that this really wasn't the place for him anymore.

Maybe this really is a sign . . . a sign that ThunderClan would be better off without me.

That night, Graystripe barely slept, and he was already awake again when the dawn light began to seep into the sky. But he was so deep in thought, reliving over and over the events of the day before, that it took him some time to realize that some kind of commotion was going on in the camp. He rose to his paws, wincing at the creak of his old bones, and shuffled out into the open.

At first glance, it seemed as though all of Thunder-Clan had gathered in the clearing. As he padded forward, Graystripe spotted Lionblaze and Thornclaw, facing each other, with Bristlefrost, Sorrelstripe, Flipclaw, Snaptooth, and several more of their Clanmates standing around them in a ragged circle. The air was heavy with tension, as if a thunderstorm were about to break.

Lionblaze and Thornclaw stood stiff-legged, their tails lashing and their shoulder fur bristling. They looked like they were about to attack each other. Graystripe's pelt pricked with alarm. Lionblaze and Thornclaw were senior warriors; they shouldn't be scuffling over trivial disputes the way Plumstone and Thriftear had. *They could really hurt each other!*

He glanced up toward Squirrelflight's den, but there was no sign of the Clan leader. *She must be out of the camp,* Graystripe thought. *There's no way she could have missed this racket.*

Pricking his ears, Graystripe heard Thornclaw grumbling, "We're floundering like fish on a riverbank when we should know what to do."

"How *can* we know?" Lionblaze challenged. "No Clan has had a leader stranded between life and death before."

Thornclaw gave a stiff nod. "Exactly. And no Clan should. Our leader should be *here*, leading us."

Lionblaze tilted his head, as if not understanding. "How?"

"A Clan isn't a Clan without a proper leader," Thornclaw snapped, ignoring the question.

"We have Squirrelflight," Lionblaze retorted instantly. "She's our deputy."

A deeper fury lit in Lionblaze's eyes, and he thrust out his muzzle so that he and Thornclaw were nose to nose. "*I'm* your deputy for now!" he snarled.

"Which is why you're so happy with the way things are," Thornclaw flashed back at him. "You were a warrior a moon ago, like the rest of us."

Twigbranch was stepping forward, challenging Thornclaw, but he was growing too angry to pay any attention to her. Graystripe felt his hackles begin to rise. *Thornclaw might be Stemleaf's father, and mate of my daughter Blossomfall, but right now it doesn't matter if he's grieving—he's behaving as if he has bees in his brain.*

Forcing his anger down, Graystripe padded into the crowd of cats. Thornclaw and Lionblaze had chased off Twigbranch, who was now retreating with a frustrated shrug of her shoulders. Bumblestripe too had tried to slip between the quarreling cats, only to be met with two identical glares.

". . . the only reason you're the one making decisions is because you're Squirrelflight's kin," Thornclaw was snarling at Lionblaze.

Uneasiness stirred in Graystripe's belly at that suggestion, and he could see from their ruffled pelts and worried glances that most of his Clanmates shared it.

Lionblaze gave another furious lash of his tail. "Take that back!" he demanded.

"How can I take back the truth?" Thornclaw challenged him. "Since Firestar's time, there's been no question about who ThunderClan's next leader might be."

"ThunderClan's leadership has always passed from leader to deputy," Lionblaze objected, "as the warrior code says it should!"

"So it's just a coincidence that Firestar made his daughter's mate deputy," Thornclaw continued.

Lionblaze dug his foreclaws into the earth. "Bramblestar was the strongest warrior in ThunderClan!"

"And Bramblestar named his own mate deputy. And now—"

"She deserved to be deputy!"

Thornclaw yowled over him. "And *now* Firestar's kin—a cat Squirrelflight and Bramblestar raised as their own kit—is ThunderClan deputy. Are we supposed to believe that only one family in this Clan can raise kits to be leaders? Are the rest of us just here for them to order around? Who will *you* name deputy? Sparkpelt? Flamepaw?"

Graystripe couldn't help feeling that Thornclaw had a point. Perhaps it *was* strange for one family to have had control over a Clan for so long. But he couldn't sympathize with the way Thornclaw was saying it, as if a deliberate choice had been made to exclude other cats.

It was obvious, too, that Thornclaw thought *he* should have been made deputy instead of Lionblaze. Graystripe wasn't surprised: Thornclaw was a strong, experienced warrior, and he would have made a good deputy.

I wish Lionblaze could understand that, and calm down.

But there seemed to be no chance of that. "Why are you trying to stir up trouble in the Clan?" Lionblaze demanded, glaring at Thornclaw. "Don't we have enough to worry about?"

"Should we blindly trust you without asking questions?" Thornclaw's voice was a deep growl from within his chest. "The way we trusted Bramblestar?"

"I'm not asking you to blindly trust any cat—"

Thornclaw thrust his head forward. "It's trusting our leaders that got us into this trouble in the first place. Our faith in Bramblestar allowed the impostor to get away with his crimes for moons! It almost destroyed ThunderClan."

Lionblaze's eyes were alight with fury. "The only cats who might destroy ThunderClan now are featherbrained warriors starting trouble for no reason!" He took a pace toward Thornclaw and unsheathed his claws. "Like you!" he spat.

In response, Thornclaw hissed and arched his back. Graystripe's heart ached with sadness to think that such a thing could happen in ThunderClan: two Clanmates, moments away from attacking each other in the middle of camp. *No, this isn't the Clan I thought I knew.*

But no sooner had he thought it than his sadness was driven out by a burst of anger so unexpected that he had to look away, and grit his teeth against the urge to leap into the argument himself.

These cats will tear the Clan apart because they can't see they're on the same side, he thought. *It's Lionblaze's job as deputy to settle disagreements, not make them worse! Is ThunderClan really coming apart like this?*

When he looked back, he saw that Bristlefrost, desperation in her eyes, had put herself between the two warriors, while Thornclaw was hissing at her to stay out of it.

Then movement drew his gaze to the end of the thorn tunnel. Squirrelflight and her patrol had returned. Immediately, the Clan leader dropped her prey and bounded into the center of the clearing, where Lionblaze and Thornclaw still faced each other.

"What's going on?" she asked, glancing from Lionblaze to Thornclaw and back again.

Squirrelflight will sort this out, Graystripe thought. But almost at once he realized he had been too optimistic.

"Thornclaw is questioning ThunderClan's leadership," Lionblaze growled.

"What does Lionblaze mean?" Squirrelflight turned a cold green gaze on Thornclaw.

"I'm not ashamed to say it," Thornclaw retorted. "If we'd questioned our leader earlier, we might have avoided a lot of trouble," the tabby tom insisted.

Graystripe could see Squirrelflight's irritation rising at Thornclaw's words. She had been Clan deputy when the trouble started, and he was clearly holding her responsible for having let the impostor take control of the Clan. "It's pointless worrying about what we should have done," she mewed firmly. "It's what we do next that's important. And right now, ThunderClan must stick together. Until we can find a way of getting Bramblestar back, we need to trust one another."

Thornclaw snorted. "You didn't seem to think that when you abandoned your Clan."

"I never *abandoned* my Clan," Squirrelflight snapped. "I had no choice but to leave. . . ."

Graystripe's heart sank as Squirrelflight continued to plead her case. He could feel tension and anxiety spreading throughout the Clan like ripples in a pool. *It's because we've been reminded of our lost leader,* he realized. *Bramblestar is stuck between worlds now—no cat knows when, or if, he'll be able to come back! Of course it's hard for us to unite behind a new leader.* He and his Clanmates couldn't even know whether Bramblestar's spirit was still alive. A young SkyClan warrior had seen his ghost prowling around the lake, but that had been a while ago. What had happened to Bramblestar was so bizarre that Graystripe had trouble wrapping his head around it. All he knew was that the loss of their leader was breaking the Clan.

"If we could just get in touch with StarClan," Twigbranch was suggesting to Jayfeather, who stood with Alderheart just outside the medicine cats' den. "Then maybe we would know whether our paws are on the right path. We could all relax a bit."

So far, Jayfeather had taken no part in the commotion. Now he gave his whiskers an irritated twitch. "Do you think we haven't been trying?" he demanded. "What do you expect me to do? Fly up to the stars and drag them down by their tails?"

"There's nothing more we can do until they're ready to share with us," Alderheart pointed out more calmly.

"What's the point of ancestors who only turn up when it suits them?" Snaptooth asked irritably, and soon set off another argument among his Clanmates.

"Yeah, can't you dream yourselves into StarClan or something?"

"What if they never come back?"

Graystripe closed his eyes as more protests and questions swirled around him. Jayfeather's sarcasm hadn't helped matters. But Graystripe had to admit he shared some of his Clanmates' doubts. He didn't want to imagine what could happen if StarClan didn't return.

And yet . . .

"If our ancestors have abandoned us," Flipclaw was saying now, "why bother following traditions they invented? We don't even live in the forests they were born in. We can make up our own codes to suit our new life beside the lake."

Lilyheart stared at him with wide eyes. "Do you really think the warrior code should change?"

Flipclaw shrugged. "I don't know what I think. But isn't StarClan's absence a perfect opportunity to work out what we believe?"

Even though he too had wondered about a future without StarClan, Graystripe was shocked by the young warrior's words. Not only was Flipclaw suggesting that they would never again know the guidance of their warrior ancestors—he was suggesting that they didn't need it.

What stunned Graystripe even more was that some cats seemed to agree with Flipclaw. *That's not right,* he told himself, clinging to the certainty that he had lived by all his life. *A Clan can't live without its ancestors' guidance . . . and it's not what I want. Oh, Firestar, what if I never speak to you again . . . or Silverstream, or all the other cats I've loved and lost? What would ThunderClan's purpose even be?*

He was reminded of the last time he'd seen Firestar . . . or dreamed of him. The unsettling dream came roaring back, along with the doubts it had ignited. *Perhaps I don't belong in the forest anymore. Perhaps that was the last time I'll ever see Firestar. . . . Maybe* that's *what he was trying to show me.*

". . . I love being a warrior," Flipclaw was meowing now. "I would die to protect my Clanmates. But after everything that's happened with the false Bramblestar, I need a chance to think about what being a warrior really means." Turning to face Squirrelflight, he added, "I think we all do."

"I already know what being a warrior means," Squirrelflight growled, her green gaze scorching the young tom.

Flipclaw took a deep breath. "Then perhaps I should go for a wander," he meowed. "Alone. To think things through, and decide whether to come back to ThunderClan. Maybe I can find better, less dangerous territory where we can live. Or maybe it's time we all stopped living like this, in Clans."

Graystripe felt his pelt prickle with shock as gasps of disbelief came from some of the assembled cats. *Did he just say that?* And yet he realized that it was the only logical conclusion to what Flipclaw had suggested earlier. What was the purpose of a Clan if it wasn't guided by its ancestors? Graystripe felt a pain in his chest, as though he'd been pricked by a sharp branch. *It won't matter whether I uphold my promise, if ThunderClan is going to fall apart with or without me.*

"Flipclaw, you don't mean that!" Bristlefrost's voice was outraged as she glared at her brother.

"Maybe he does," Snaptooth retorted from where he stood at the back of the crowd. "And maybe I agree with him."

"Then maybe you should both go," Squirrelflight responded, the tip of her tail flicking angrily to and fro.

Thornclaw padded up to Flipclaw's side. His shoulder fur lay flat again; his rage at Lionblaze seemed to have vanished, and when he spoke, his voice was quiet but clear, carrying to every corner of the camp. "I want to go for a wander too."

Several cats let out yowls of protest, and Graystripe could

understand why. It would be easy to disregard the younger warriors, whatever they decided. But Thornclaw wasn't just a rebellious young cat growing disillusioned with Clan life; he was a well-respected senior warrior.

"Me too," Flywhisker added, stepping up to join her Clanmates. Flipclaw gave her a warm glance and eased himself closer to her.

Snaptooth shouldered his way through the crowd of agitated cats and stood beside his littermate. "And me."

"Can't we all take a while to cool down?" Lionblaze asked, padding up to Squirrelflight and glancing between her and his kits with a pleading look in his amber eyes. "This isn't a decision any warrior should take lightly."

Graystripe could guess how disappointed the Clan deputy must be to see two of his kits prepared to walk away from the Clan he loved so much. But neither Snaptooth nor Flywhisker was prepared to listen to his plea.

"We're not taking it lightly," Snaptooth retorted. "We're taking it very seriously. That's why we need to go—to have the space that we need to think!"

For a few moments, Graystripe stood still, taking in the expressions of his Clanmates and listening to the protests from cats trying to persuade Thornclaw and the others to stay. Bristlefrost in particular looked horrified at the thought that her brother, Flipclaw, had set his paws on a path that led away from their Clan.

Graystripe thought again of his promise to Squirrelflight. He felt a certainty gathering within him that this was his time to speak. Surely he could find words from his long experience of life within his Clan, of times when the world had looked just as bleak as it did now: words that would change the younger warriors' minds and revitalize their loyalty. Surely he could turn things around for Squirrelflight!

He raised his head and opened his jaws to speak, but before any words could come out, he noticed Thornclaw speaking with Blossomfall, who was gazing up at her mate with wide, disbelieving eyes. "If I decide to leave," he murmured, "I'll return to say good-bye."

Graystripe struggled to find words. As he looked around at the confused faces of his Clanmates, he was struck by how very young they all seemed. It reminded him of his argument with Plumstone and Thriftear the day before, and how it had made him question whether he still had any useful part to play in the life of his Clan. *Just another elder, another mouth to feed . . . young cats don't want to hear anything I have to tell them. And maybe I am holding them back with my memories of how it used to be.*

I should leave. As he thought the words, he felt as though the sun had come out from behind a cloud. Along with the shock he shared with the rest of his Clan, he felt a strange sense of relief. He could have told his Clanmates what he thought he *should* feel about warriors leaving the Clan—that it was wrong, a bad idea—but that wasn't how he truly felt. He had been struggling for a while with his place in the Clan, but he had never imagined having the courage to get up and leave, after dedicating so much of his life to ThunderClan. Now, no matter what he had told Squirrelflight earlier, he knew that what

he'd felt in his dream of Firestar had been right: this wasn't
the place for him now. Perhaps it wouldn't be right to leave
permanently—but maybe he had to get away to know for sure.
This new idea of a "wander" could be just what he needed, to
give himself time to work it all out.

Slowly he padded forward, his Clanmates drawing aside to
let him through the crowd, until he stood in front of Squirrelflight. "I'm going to leave too," he mewed quietly.

He was aware of a ripple of shock passing through the
assembled Clan. The older warriors, he knew, would understand what ThunderClan meant to him, and be startled by
the idea that he might ever leave it. Of course they wouldn't
expect Graystripe to want to go. He could hear some of their
disbelieving comments.

"First Thornclaw—not Graystripe too!"

"I thought he would be the last cat to leave his Clan."

Squirrelflight stared into his eyes, mingled shock and grief
and betrayal in her green gaze. "You told me you'd support
me," she responded, her voice rasping in her throat. "You said
I could count on you."

Graystripe bowed his head. Guilt surged through him.
He'd never meant to hurt Squirrelflight, but he understood
something now that he hadn't when he'd made his vow to her.
*I can't sort this out here, surrounded by cats who remind me that things
aren't the way they used to be—and how I wish they still were.* "I'm sorry,"
he choked out. "I can't keep that promise."

Squirrelflight stood frozen like a cat made of ice. "But why?
You made a promise to my father too, that you'd never leave

ThunderClan—or have you forgotten that?"

Graystripe felt another pang of regret. He knew that he was failing his Clan at this moment of crisis: failing his leader, and the memory of Firestar, by breaking that long-ago promise at last. But he knew that it was the right thing for him to do. And perhaps Firestar had released him from his promise, in the dream that he still didn't fully understand.

"Too much has changed," he told her. "I've been through so much with ThunderClan: the destruction of the old forest, being lost and living as a kittypet, then finding you again. But the ThunderClan I see today isn't the same one I served under Firestar. I don't know that I still belong here. I need time to think."

Squirrelflight stepped back, letting her gaze travel over all the cats who had declared that they meant to leave. "If this is your decision," she meowed, "then go with my good wishes. You know your own minds, and I won't try to change them." Her voice grew more ominous. "But remember, a warrior takes care of their Clan. If you go, you are letting down your Clanmates. I will tolerate this for now, but if you do not return within a moon, do not come back at all."

Graystripe dipped his head to her in deepest respect, then turned away and headed toward the thorn tunnel. He could hear the sound of paw steps as the other four cats followed him. Squirrelflight's lament over his broken promises to her and to Firestar was still ringing in his ears, and something in his heart was wailing like a lost kit at the thought of all that he was leaving behind. He took one last glance over his shoulder before plunging into the thorn tunnel.

Is this the last time I'll see my home? Is this really good-bye?

As he emerged into the forest, his thoughts flew like homing birds back to the time, so long ago and far away, when he had made the promise he'd just broken.

CHAPTER 3

— Then —

Graystripe sat at the edge of the camp, his tail wrapped neatly around his paws, and gazed unseeingly toward where Dustpelt was on guard at the opening of the gorse tunnel. He was enjoying the peace of ThunderClan—he was acting leader while Firestar was away, and so far, everything seemed to be going well. There was plenty of prey in the forest, the thorn walls of the camp were strong enough to keep out marauding foxes and badgers, and so far none of the other Clans had decided to cause trouble.

Even so, Graystripe couldn't help wishing that his mother, Willowpelt, could be here to see how peaceful life was now. She had died a noble warrior's death, fighting a badger to protect Graystripe's half brother Sootpaw. Her three youngest kits, all apprentices, were still stunned by her loss.

I think some in the Clan have forgotten that Willowpelt was my mother, too, he thought. But in a way, Graystripe was grateful for the lack of attention. He could grieve quietly for Willowpelt, without having to work through that grief in front of the entire Clan.

The camp was tranquil now; the dawn patrol had returned to report that there was no sign of problems on the borders, and most of the warriors had gone out on hunting patrols. Graystripe looked forward to seeing a well-stocked fresh-kill pile by the time the sun set.

Gazing around, he saw Cinderpelt slipping in and out of her den, laying out some herbs to dry in the sun, while the elders Dappletail and One-eye were lazily sharing tongues at the edge of their den beside the fallen tree-trunk. They were listening to Speckletail, who seemed to be telling them a story with much waving of her tail and forepaws.

Outside the nursery, Ferncloud and the heavily pregnant Brightheart were chatting together while they watched Ferncloud's kits. The two energetic little toms were tossing a scrap of tree bark to and fro, squealing excitedly as they batted at it with their soft paws.

Graystripe was just close enough to hear the she-cats' voices, and a worm of uneasiness began wriggling in his belly as he realized what they were talking about.

"Firestar's scent has faded from the camp," Ferncloud mewed sadly. "It's as if he was never here."

"I know." Brightheart tilted her head to one side. "I never thought he would just go off and leave us like that." She hesitated, then added, "Do *you* believe that he's gone on a mission for StarClan?"

"I don't know what to believe," Ferncloud sighed. "Dustpelt says he thinks Firestar might have gotten tired of leading his Clan, and gone off to be a kittypet again."

Graystripe felt his shoulder fur beginning to rise in mingled outrage and apprehension; he pricked his ears so as not to miss a word of the she-cats' conversation. *Is this what every cat is saying behind my back?*

"Do you really think that?" Brightheart asked, her tone edged with anxiety.

"I don't want to," Ferncloud responded. "And I don't think Dustpelt *really* believes it. But I still want to know where Firestar has gone, and when he's going to come back."

Don't we all, Graystripe thought ruefully. He wondered whether, as acting leader, he should go across and put a stop to the she-cats' speculations. *But that would only cause an argument,* he reminded himself. *Cinderpelt and I know that Firestar is searching for SkyClan, but we're not meant to tell the others. That means there's nothing that I could tell them that they haven't heard already. Maybe in a few heart-beats they'll stop worrying about Firestar and start talking about the kits or something. Then we can have a bit of peace.*

Watching the two she-cats leaning closer together, their mews too soft now for him to overhear, Graystripe realized how swiftly, with how few words, his peaceful mood of a few moments ago had been shattered. Still, he knew that, inevitably, peace could not last for long until the real Clan leader returned.

Even as the thought crossed his mind, Cinderpelt finished arranging her herbs and bounded up to him, flicking her tail over his ears. "Wake up, Graystripe!" she mewed cheerfully. "We have a Clan to run."

Graystripe rose to his paws and arched his back in a long stretch, trying to put what he had heard out of his mind. "I wasn't asleep," he responded mildly, "and in any case, there's no more to do until the evening patrols go out. Look," he added, angling his ears toward the entrance to the camp, "the hunters are coming back, and it seems as if the prey is running well."

Ashfur was just emerging from the thorn tunnel, carrying a plump pigeon. The other members of the patrol, Cloudtail and Mousefur, followed him, also laden with their own catch. Graystripe padded after them as they headed for the fresh-kill pile.

"Good job," he meowed. "The Clan will eat well tonight."

Ashfur dropped his pigeon on the pile and turned to Graystripe with a sneer. "At least we have two fewer mouths to feed. I hope Firestar and Sandstorm are enjoying their kittypet treats."

"Yeah," Cloudtail agreed, ruffling his fluffy white pelt. "After all the fuss he made when *I* went off for a kittypet snack now and again!"

Graystripe stared at them, appalled. "You should all be ashamed of yourselves!" Ashfur and Cloudtail exchanged a derisive glance, as if they couldn't care less what he was saying. Graystripe's eyes then flitted to Brightheart and Ferncloud. Realizing just how many cats were openly questioning Firestar, he knew he needed to act decisively as the Clan's temporary leader. Graystripe tried to force authority into his voice, tried to at least *sound* decisive. "No loyal warriors would gossip about their leader while he's away."

But even while he was speaking, Graystripe saw his

Clanmates averting their gazes and flicking their tails dismissively. He realized that they weren't willing to listen to him in the way they had listened to Firestar.

"He shouldn't *be* away," Cloudtail pointed out. "Then there would be nothing to gossip about."

Graystripe opened his jaws for a stinging rebuke, but before he could utter a word, Mousefur interrupted.

"So where is the great Firestar, then?" Mousefur demanded. "He must be on a very important mission, since he's definitely not living the kittypet life."

"Once a kittypet, always a kittypet," Ashfur muttered. "If he were on an important mission, he wouldn't have had to hide it from the rest of the Clan."

Graystripe knew there was nothing more he could say to satisfy them. Part of him understood how shocked the Clan had been by Firestar's departure, and he could hardly blame them for feeling that their leader had betrayed them. But he had promised Firestar that he wouldn't tell any cat that the mission he had left to carry out was a quest to find the lost SkyClan, which had once been the fifth Clan, until it was driven out of the forest. Only he and Cinderpelt knew that.

"He has gone on a journey at the request of StarClan. *Where* they have sent him is none of your business," he growled.

"Well, the safety of the Clan *is* our business," Ashfur retorted. "And I for one am not sure that you're up to leading it."

For a moment all Graystripe could do was stare in astonishment at the younger warrior. He couldn't believe that any

cat would challenge him like that—or, worse, challenge Firestar, who had left him in charge. He felt his shoulder fur begin
to bristle and forced it to lie flat; he would have liked to claw
the sneering look off Ashfur's face, but he knew he had to
remain calm.

"That wasn't your decision to make," he mewed evenly.
"Firestar chose me as his deputy, and what other cat—"

"Yes, and not every cat is happy about that," Mousefur
interrupted. "A Clan deputy should always be loyal to their
Clan. You left ThunderClan and went to RiverClan. You
have *kits* in RiverClan, for StarClan's sake! If there's trouble
with RiverClan now, who knows what side you would be on?"

"But we don't have trouble with RiverClan," Graystripe
declared.

"That's not the point," Ashfur meowed. "We might. And
in any case, Graystripe, there are plenty of cats in this Clan
who don't think you have what it takes to be leader."

"Yeah, you haven't even appointed a deputy," Cloudtail put
in. "What if Firestar doesn't come back? You couldn't lead the
Clan on your own."

"But Firestar *is* coming back," Graystripe insisted, though
he wondered if he was speaking the whole truth. *Sure, Firestar
intends to come back. But he'll meet a lot of dangers where he's gone—
dangers we can't even imagine.*

"But what if he doesn't?" Cloudtail was clearly unwilling to
let the matter drop. "Honestly, Graystripe, you need a deputy."

Graystripe fixed his gaze upon the white warrior, more
puzzled with him than angry. "I'm not Clan leader, only *acting*

leader. If Firestar had wanted an acting deputy, he would have appointed one before he left." With an irritated riffle of his whiskers, he added, "Why, Cloudtail, do you want the job?"

"*I* think Dustpelt should be made deputy," Ashfur meowed before Cloudtail could reply. "There are some cats who think it would be better if he'd been named deputy in the first place, Graystripe."

Fury swelled inside Graystripe; it took a massive effort for him to stop himself leaping at Ashfur, claws unsheathed. He took a deep breath, and when he spoke, his voice was dangerously quiet. "Who are these cats, Ashfur, who are questioning Firestar's judgment?"

Ashfur hesitated, clearly not wanting, or not able, to respond. In the breathing space, Graystripe glanced across the camp to where Dustpelt still sat on watch at the entrance to the gorse tunnel. He wondered whether the brown tabby warrior had any idea what his Clanmates were saying about him, or could overhear the argument raging around the fresh-kill pile.

Sure, he's a loyal ThunderClan cat, Graystripe thought. *And a brave and skillful warrior. He would make a good deputy.* Briefly his fur prickled with uneasiness. *Better than me?* Then he gave his pelt a shake, banishing the unwelcome thought. *Firestar didn't choose him, and that's that.*

"If Firestar wanted us to respect his judgment, he should have stayed here," Ashfur replied at last. "And I still think you should make Dustpelt your deputy. Then we might have a bit of order around here."

"Order?" Graystripe started at the sound of Cinderpelt's voice; he hadn't realized that the medicine cat had padded silently up to stand at his shoulder. "Ashfur, the only disorder I see around here is you three questioning the decisions of your leader."

Glancing at Cinderpelt, Graystripe saw the fire of fury blazing in her blue eyes. *For such a gentle cat, she doesn't stand for any nonsense,* he thought appreciatively.

Ashfur immediately took a step back. Cloudtail couldn't meet that searing gaze, while Mousefur was suddenly preoccupied with grooming a tangled tuft of fur on her shoulder.

"Firestar is a leader appointed by StarClan," the medicine cat continued. Her voice was as chilly as a wind sweeping across a snowy hillside. "He appointed Graystripe in the proper way. If StarClan disapproved, they've had plenty of opportunity to make their opinion known."

"But I—" Ashfur began.

Cinderpelt ignored his attempt to interrupt. "Meanwhile, Graystripe *hasn't* been appointed by StarClan. He *can't* appoint another deputy. And Firestar didn't seem to see the need before he left. So why don't we all get on with our duties and start minding our own business?"

"Good idea," Graystripe snarled. Without waiting for a response, he turned and stalked away toward the warriors' den.

Before he reached it, he heard his name being called urgently from the direction of the gorse tunnel. "Graystripe! Graystripe!"

He whipped around to see Brackenfur racing across the camp toward him, with Thornclaw and Brambleclaw hard on his paws. Brambleclaw was the Clan's newest warrior, having received his name from Firestar just before he and Sandstorm had left on their quest. This patrol had also gone out hunting, but they weren't carrying any prey. Brackenfur held something in his jaws, but it was too small even to be a mouse.

"What's the matter?" Graystripe asked as the three warriors halted in front of him, and stood panting. "You look as if you've been running all the way across the whole territory."

"We have," Thornclaw mewed grimly.

Brackenfur dropped the thing he was carrying at Graystripe's paws. "Look at that!" he exclaimed.

"Smell it," Brambleclaw added.

Graystripe stared down and saw that Brackenfur had fetched him a scrap of rabbit fur clotted with blood. Stooping, he took a long sniff; as well as the scent of the rabbit itself, the fur was carrying another unmistakable tang.

"WindClan!" he breathed out. "Please tell me you haven't been hunting on their territory."

"We have not!" Brackenfur retorted indignantly, his golden-brown fur beginning to bush up. "We would never. No, we found this on *our* territory, not far from Fourtrees, along with more bits of the rabbit, with the stink of Wind-Clan all over it."

"Those miserable rabbit-chasers have been stealing *our* prey," Thornclaw snarled.

Graystripe gave the fur another sniff. Thornclaw's

conclusion was obvious, and yet he wasn't entirely happy about it. Prey was running well; there was no need for one Clan to steal from another. *It doesn't make sense for WindClan to be crossing our border.*

Meanwhile, Ashfur, Mousefur, and Cloudtail, realizing that something was happening, had padded up and crowded around the bit of rabbit fur to get a sniff. Brackenfur repeated his explanation of how they had found it.

"What are you going to do?" Ashfur asked, turning expectantly to Graystripe, a challenging look in his blue eyes.

"I'm . . . not sure." Graystripe would have preferred time to think things over, instead of being put on the spot like this. It was one of the most difficult things about being the acting Clan leader. He knew Firestar would know precisely what to say in the moment . . . but he was also convinced that Firestar wouldn't want to start any trouble with WindClan unless he was certain that ThunderClan was in the right.

And if I make the wrong decision, Ashfur and the others will say it proves I'm not fit to lead the Clan.

"Well, make your mind up," Mousefur snapped. "You're surely not going to let WindClan get away with this!"

Let WindClan get away with this? The brown she-cat's demand echoed in Graystripe's mind while he paused to think, acutely aware of his warriors gazing at him with a mixture of impatience and accusation. "This might not be as bad as we think," he meowed at last. "Maybe this was a WindClan rabbit, and one of their warriors chased it over the border. Okay, they shouldn't have done that, but it's not as bad as deliberately coming to our territory to steal."

"So you're going to do nothing?" Cloudtail asked him, his white pelt fluffing up in annoyance.

Graystripe stifled a sigh. *Cinderpelt may have stopped the argument, but these cats really haven't changed their minds. How can I decide what to do when they're continually nagging?*

"No," he responded, forcing himself to remain calm. He realized now that patience was one of the most important qualities of a good leader. "But I'm not going to stir up trouble with WindClan over what might be just one minor incident. Instead, we'll step up the patrols on the WindClan border. If we find anything else, we'll discuss this again."

Ashfur let out a snort and turned away toward the fresh-kill pile, flipping his tail at Graystripe as he went. Cloudtail and Mousefur followed. Graystripe heard Cloudtail mutter, "Firestar would never have put up with this."

Ashfur grunted agreement. "Yeah, he may not be perfect, but he'd do something about this."

Graystripe felt his pelt getting hot with anger at his Clan-mates' disrespect, but he tried not to let it show. "Did you catch any prey?" he asked Brackenfur's patrol.

Brackenfur nodded. He was clearly unhappy, but at least he didn't try to argue. "Yes, we buried it. We thought it was more important to let you know about WindClan right away. We'll go and collect it now."

"Good," Graystripe meowed. "And you might freshen up the scent markers on the WindClan border while you're at it."

Brackenfur gave him a brisk nod. "Sure, Graystripe." He

led Thornclaw and Brambleclaw across the camp and out through the gorse tunnel.

Graystripe watched them go. *Is Brackenfur disappointed in me, too? He looked a bit more cheerful when I mentioned the scent markers.* Then he shook off the worry—*I have to be less sensitive if I'm going to be a good leader!* He finished sending out the evening patrols, then headed for his nest in the warriors' den; he didn't feel he had the right to take over Firestar's den underneath the Highrock. Curling up in his nest, he tried to rest and relax, but the tainted rabbit fur, the evidence against WindClan, and his trouble with his own Clanmates swirled around in his mind until he felt as if he were being sucked down into a dark pool.

He had no idea whether he had been able to fall asleep. All he knew was that it seemed as if no time at all had passed before he heard yowling break out somewhere across the camp., the sound of a cat in fear and anguish.

Graystripe sprang to his paws. *What's going on?*

CHAPTER 4

♣

− *Now* −

"*What about a hunt?*" *Thornclaw suggested,* raising his muzzle to sniff the air. "My belly thinks my throat's torn out."

Graystripe and the other four cats who had left Thunder-Clan had halted in the shade of a massive oak tree, not far from their territory's border with SkyClan. Tasting the air, Graystripe could pick out rich aromas of prey, as well as the reek of SkyClan's scent markers, rising from a clump of elder bushes less than three fox-lengths away.

"What, *now?*" Flywhisker responded to Thornclaw. "I thought we were supposed to be leaving ThunderClan. What's the point of hanging around in our own territory?"

Thornclaw let out a hiss of annoyance as Flipclaw and Snaptooth nodded agreement. "Listen," he snapped, "and think about what leaving means. If you continue on in this direction and cross our border, you'll soon come to the Two-legplace. Or you can go that way"—he gestured with his tail—"and cross SkyClan and ShadowClan territory. Your other option is to go back to the lake and cross WindClan territory to leave past the horseplace. Pick one. But good luck finding prey that you're allowed to catch."

The three younger cats exchanged frustrated glances. Fly-whisker in particular was looking annoyed, and Graystripe stepped in before she could start a quarrel with the senior warrior.

"Thornclaw's right," he meowed. "None of us know what we're going to find when we leave the territory. It makes sense to be well fed and well rested before we cross the border."

"I suppose so," Snaptooth muttered.

"Okay, let's do it," Flywhisker agreed. "But I just hope we don't meet any ThunderClan patrols. That would be *so* embarrassing!"

As if her words had called it up, there was a rustling among the elder bushes, but it was a SkyClan patrol, not Thunder-Clan, that emerged. Hawkwing, the SkyClan deputy, was in the lead, followed by Tinycloud and Macgyver.

"Greetings." Flipclaw, who was standing closest to the bor-der, gave a nervous dip of his head.

Hawkwing responded with a curt nod. "Greetings. Might I ask why so many of you are hanging around so close to our border?"

"We're not hanging around!" Flywhisker retorted, her neck fur fluffing up with indignation.

Hawkwing let his yellow gaze travel slowly over the five cats. "It looks like it to me."

Graystripe saw Macgyver slide out his claws, while Tinycloud took a pace forward so that she stood exactly on the borderline.

"It's okay," he began. "We were just—"

"We're leaving Clan territories!" Snaptooth interrupted. "We're taking a break from ThunderClan, and we don't want anything to do with SkyClan either, thank you very much!"

Graystripe gazed in horror at the young golden tabby tom's outspokenness, while Thornclaw snarled, "Mouse-brain!" His lips were drawn back to show his teeth as he glared at Snaptooth.

"Really?" Hawkwing mewed coolly. "How interesting. Well, far be it from me to stand in your way. Just make sure that you don't set paw over the SkyClan border on your . . . travels."

"We won't," Graystripe assured him. Beckoning with his tail, he drew his Clanmates farther away, toward the roots of the oak tree. "You didn't have to tell them that!" he growled into Snaptooth's ear.

"Sorry," Snaptooth mumbled.

"'Sorry' catches no prey," Thornclaw hissed.

The SkyClan patrol was moving away. Graystripe heard Tinycloud exclaim, "Wow! I never would have expected that!"

"Yeah," Macgyver agreed. "I knew things were bad in ThunderClan, but I didn't realize they were *that* bad!"

"And now every cat will know what we're doing," Thornclaw continued savagely as the SkyClan cats disappeared into the undergrowth. "Snaptooth, what have you got between your ears? Thistle-fluff?"

Snaptooth didn't respond, only stared at his paws and let his tail droop at the senior warrior's scathing words.

"Leave him alone," Graystripe sighed. "The damage is done. Let's hunt."

"Okay." Thornclaw gave his pelt an ill-tempered shake. "Flipclaw, come with me." Skirting the oak trunk, he plunged into the bushes; Flipclaw cast a rueful glance at his Clanmates, then followed him.

"Meet back here when you've caught enough!" Graystripe called after him.

Flipclaw waved his tail in acknowledgment before he disappeared into the undergrowth.

"We'll hunt together," Flywhisker declared to her brother, then added, "Graystripe, you can come with us if you like. Or maybe you'd rather rest, being an elder and all. We'll bring you something tasty."

Her tone was so sweetly kind that it made Graystripe want to gag. "Yes, I think I might rest," he responded, flopping down among the oak roots with an exaggerated sigh of exhaustion. "After all, my old bones soon get tired, and my old paws won't carry me very far."

"Er . . . yeah . . . right." Flywhisker seemed to realize she had been less than tactful.

Snaptooth gave her a shove, and the two young cats vanished around a bramble thicket.

Graystripe had no intention of resting. As soon as the scents of his Clanmates had faded, he rose to his paws and headed off in a different direction. All his senses were alert for prey, though it was so long since he had needed to hunt that he was afraid he might have forgotten all his old skills.

"Please, StarClan," he murmured, not sure whether the spirits of his warrior ancestors would be able to hear his prayer, "let me catch something good. Let me show those young fluff-brains what's what."

Graystripe was heading for a place where he had often hunted successfully in the past. The ground fell away into a steep slope covered by mossy boulders, and a small stream meandered around the bottom. Several rabbit burrows gaped among the rocks. Now, as Graystripe approached the top of the slope, he let himself drop so that his belly fur brushed the grass, and he crept forward cautiously, paw step by paw step. He was surprised at how quickly the long-disused movements came back to him.

Checking that the breeze was blowing toward him, he tasted the air and picked up a strong scent of rabbit.

Yes!

As soon as he poked his head out of the cover of a large boulder on the lip of the slope, Graystripe spotted a rabbit down by the stream, drinking and then cleaning its face with its forepaws. A good, fat rabbit, with enough flesh on its bones to feed two or three cats at least. His jaws began to water at the very thought.

Graystripe scanned the slope carefully, trying to work out a route through the boulders, then realized that in the time it would take him to reach the bottom, the rabbit could be alerted and dive to safety down one of the burrows. If he had been hunting with a patrol, he would have sent a couple of his Clanmates to circle around and do their best to cut off the prey's retreat.

Time for action, he told himself.

Bunching his legs beneath him, Graystripe took off in

a massive leap. His paws barely touched a boulder halfway down the slope before he pushed off again. His second leap landed him on top of the rabbit, which let out a startled squeal and went limp.

"Thank you, StarClan, for this prey," Graystripe meowed. Huge satisfaction surged through his body as he picked up his catch and headed back toward the meeting place.

I may be an elder, but I still know a thing or two.

By the time Graystripe returned, the sun was going down, the slanting light among the trees beginning to turn scarlet. At the other side of the tiny clearing, near the abandoned Twoleg nest, Thornclaw and Flipclaw were giving themselves a thorough wash. Graystripe dropped his rabbit onto a meager fresh-kill pile between two gnarled roots of the oak tree and let every muscle in his body stretch and relax. He expected that Snaptooth and Flywhisker would soon be back from their own hunt.

It was strange, making camp with these few cats instead of bedding down in the elders' den. He knew that going on a "wander" was the right choice, and his successful hunt had given him extra confidence, but he still felt adrift, unsure of what it would take to make this a positive experience for himself and his Clan. It didn't help that he had no idea where he meant to go on his wandering. For some reason, his mind kept returning to ThunderClan's old territory in the forest. In some ways, that camp brought back painful memories—of Firestar, Cinderheart, Dustpelt, and countless other Clanmates who had gone to hunt with StarClan. But there were good things to recall, too. Perhaps that was where he should go—to see the old territory again?

But that's mouse-brained, he thought. *It's only because I'm remembering those times.* The old territory wasn't even there anymore. The Twolegs had destroyed it to make more Thunderpaths and Twoleg dens. At least they couldn't destroy his memories.

Silverstream . . . my beautiful Silverstream, he thought with a sigh. The RiverClan warrior had been his first love . . . something that, at the time, had made him question his loyalty to ThunderClan. When he'd lost her, he'd regained his devotion to ThunderClan. *I hope she and Millie have had the chance to meet in StarClan, and that they're both happy.*

Thinking of Silverstream drew Graystripe's memories back to Stormfur, his only surviving kit with the RiverClan queen.

At least, I hope he's still alive, but I suppose I can't be sure.

When Silverstream had died, Graystripe had briefly gone to RiverClan to raise their kits, Stormkit and Featherkit. He remembered how he had played with them in the RiverClan camp, always terrified when they ventured too near the water. *They were so brave, and I was so proud of them!*

Now Stormfur had abandoned RiverClan to stay in the mountains with his mate, Brook Where Small Fish Swim, and the Tribe of Rushing Water. Graystripe hoped that Stormfur was far enough away from the Clans' current crisis to be safe, but the more he thought about him, the more certain he became that he *did* know where he had to go next.

I'll make my way to the Tribe and see my son.

A rush of energy flooded through Graystripe, as if the idea had lit him up. He was sure that seeing his son again would help him decide where he wanted to be, and where he might belong. He would tell the others when Snaptooth and Flywhisker returned.

Rustling in the undergrowth distracted Graystripe from his thoughts, and he looked up to see the two young warriors emerging from a clump of ferns. Snaptooth was carrying a thrush, and Flywhisker a blackbird.

"What a feast!" Thornclaw meowed appreciatively. "Who caught that rabbit? It's enormous!"

Graystripe licked one forepaw and drew it over his ear. "That's mine, actually." He glanced at Flywhisker as he spoke; the young she-cat wouldn't meet his gaze, ducking her head to give her chest fur a couple of embarrassed licks.

Thornclaw and Flipclaw finished their washing and padded over, and the group sat down to eat. With so few of them, there was more than enough prey. Watching his younger Clanmates gulping down their share, Graystripe felt a strange sense of protectiveness. Would they want to visit the Tribe with him? Graystripe wasn't sure, but he knew he would feel better if he could keep an eye on them—especially the younger warriors.

I'm older, and StarClan knows I'm more sensible. I need to make sure they're okay.

"It's easier now that we're only hunting for ourselves," Flywhisker commented, finishing her blackbird and swiping at a feather that was sticking to her nose. "In the Clan, we have to hunt for all the cats who can't hunt for themselves, the queens and the elders and . . ." She trailed off, flashing an awkward look at Graystripe, as if she had remembered once again that he had been one of those elders. "Well, this way is more manageable," she finished.

"Only because you're young cats, and fit, and prey is plentiful," Graystripe pointed out. "But what if one of you were about to have kits, or injured? What about when *you're* too old to hunt, one day? Or what about during leaf-bare? That's one thing no cat can argue with—there's strength in ThunderClan's numbers."

Flipclaw cast a sidelong glance at Flywhisker. "If you were expecting kits," he murmured, "I'd make sure you were well fed."

Oh, so it's like that. Graystripe felt a sinking in his belly as he saw Flywhisker's hackles begin to rise. *I never knew Flipclaw was padding after Flywhisker!*

Snaptooth prodded Flywhisker in the side. "Would you ever want to have kits with *Flipclaw*?" he asked his littermate. "Be honest with him. He's looking at you like a fox looks at a rabbit!"

Flipclaw hunched his shoulders, clearly uncomfortable. "I was just speaking generally," he mumbled. "I'd help any queen who was expecting kits."

Flywhisker flicked an ear at her brother. "I don't want kits at all right now—not with everything ThunderClan is going through. But even if I did, I'm not interested in you that way, Flipclaw. You're not my type." She aimed an apologetic glance at Flipclaw, then looked away.

Flipclaw looked utterly crushed. Graystripe caught Thornclaw's eye and could tell that the senior warrior was as unpleasantly surprised as he felt. *Just what we need on this trip—a thwarted romance.* Graystripe could imagine how Flipclaw must be stinging at the rejection, but worse, he was thinking ahead to how these young warriors would get along for the remainder of their journey. Would Flipclaw accept Flywhisker's rejection gracefully? Or would he dissolve into a puddle of misery? *The last thing I want is to end up looking after a lovesick young tom!*

"Now that we can go anywhere," Flipclaw began after a moment's silence, "we should find a new territory all of our own. That would be wonderful—we'd be much safer than we are now, in ThunderClan, and you'd be so comfortable there, Flywhisker. Maybe one day you'd . . . feel differently about things?"

Not gracefully accepting it, then, Graystripe thought, feeling sorry for the young warrior. *Go on, keep trying to push this boulder. She's going to crush you like a bug!*

Flywhisker twitched her whiskers dismissively. "That sounds great, Flipclaw, but unfortunately, we can't all live inside your imagination. Only you can live there."

Graystripe ducked his head against the fur of his chest, stifling a chuckle. *Oof.* Snaptooth let out a snort of laughter; turning on him with an irritable twitch of his tail, Flipclaw meowed, "Well, tell us what *you* think we should do."

Clearly at a loss for words, Snaptooth ducked his head awkwardly. "We're traveling, aren't we?" he muttered at last.

Graystripe bit back a sharp comment. Snaptooth might have laughed at Flipclaw, but clearly the golden tabby tom had no better idea about where they should go. He was about to suggest they travel to visit the Tribe when Flywhisker made an announcement. "I've often wondered what it would be like to be a kittypet."

Both young toms turned shocked gazes on her. Graystripe felt mildly surprised that the young she-cat would ever think about living with Twolegs, but he had known several cats who had made the same decision, and he had lived as a kittypet for a time himself. It had been something of an accident— he'd gotten captured by Twolegs while trying to rescue other cats—and while that kind of life hadn't been for him, it had introduced him to his beloved mate Millie. *I can understand why some cats prefer the soft life of a kittypet.* It certainly was an easier life than a Clan cat's, at times.

"Really?" Snaptooth asked. "You'd give up your freedom?"

"Maybe not," Flywhisker responded, giving her paw a lick and drawing it slowly over her ear. "Not yet, anyway. But kittypets always know where their food is coming from, and they have somewhere warm to sleep every night. It doesn't sound that bad!"

"Of course it's bad!" Snaptooth gave his tail an irritated lash. "And only a mouse-brain would think it wasn't."

"Mouse-brain yourself!" Flywhisker retorted.

As she finished speaking, Thornclaw let out an irritated snort. "I didn't leave the camp to listen to *more* petty squabbles," he meowed. "I left to think about what I want to do next. I left the Clan so that I could be alone." Rising to his paws, he added, "Maybe I'll see you all again if I decide to return to the Clan. Or maybe we'll meet in Flipclaw's imaginary territory. But I'm not going to stay here and waste my time arguing. I'm off."

"Right now?" Graystripe asked, surprised. He admitted to himself that he had taken it for granted that Thornclaw would help him deal with the younger, less experienced warriors. He didn't want to be left with the sole responsibility for them, negotiating their arguments and insults. *That's not what I had in mind for my wander!* It certainly wouldn't leave him much time to think. "Thornclaw, I—" he began, reluctant to let his Clanmate to leave without a proper good-bye.

"Yes, right now," Thornclaw interrupted. With a swish of his tail he stalked off across the clearing and vanished into the undergrowth.

Well, then.

Graystripe watched him go, anxiety rising in his belly. He was happy to guide the younger cats for the first couple of days of their wandering, but he didn't want to be left in charge, as if he were the leader of some new, tiny Clan. The young warriors all seemed disconcerted by Thornclaw's abrupt departure, and they were casting hopeful glances at Graystripe.

"I never thought Thornclaw would leave, just like that," Flywhisker complained, blinking in bewilderment as she stared at the spot where the golden-brown tabby had disappeared.

Me neither, thought Graystripe. *But here we are.*

"What should we do next?" Flipclaw asked. He was staring directly at Graystripe.

Graystripe found it hard to reply. Their trust and reliance were familiar to Graystripe, but they weren't what he needed now. *Even if I tried to lead them, it wouldn't work out for any of us. I already came close to losing the Clan once; I don't want to risk that again.*

They had only one moon to decide whether they wanted to come back. And he could so easily get stuck here close to the lake, hovering just outside the ThunderClan border and mediating the younger cats' fights, while his paws were tugging at him to travel farther away. And he wanted to see Stormfur again.

"Thornclaw made the right decision," he told the others. "For himself, at least. He didn't leave ThunderClan to start a new Clan of his own."

"Then why did he leave?" Snaptooth asked. "And why did you?"

"I can't answer for Thornclaw," Graystripe replied, lapsing into a moment's thoughtful silence. "But I think what I need is to revisit my past," he continued eventually, "so that I can make the right decision about my future. I'm going to travel into the mountains, to visit the Tribe of Rushing Water and see my son Stormfur."

"What?" Flipclaw asked, his eyes widening in shock.

Snaptooth and Flywhisker exchanged a look of confusion. "You want to go all that way?" Flywhisker meowed.

While the younger cats were speaking, Graystripe's anxiety

was driven out by a sense of cool, clear certainty. "I do," he murmured. And he knew it was right.

This is what I'm supposed to do. Revisiting my past will help me understand where I need to spend my future.

CHAPTER 5
❧
— *Then* —

Graystripe pushed his way through the branches of the warriors'
den and out into the clearing. Night had fallen; the spirits of
StarClan glittered in an indigo sky. A warm breeze was wafting across the camp, but Graystripe felt chilled from ears to
tail-tip at the agonized shrieks that were coming from the
nursery.

That's Brightheart! he thought, struggling to suppress panic.
She must be kitting.

He bounded across the camp, but when he reached the
entrance to the nursery he halted, as though frost had suddenly clamped his paws to the ground. Brightheart's cries of
distress were more than he could bear. It was utterly beyond
him to make himself move closer and see her in pain and fear.

She's going to die—just like Silverstream. . . .

Graystripe couldn't stop his mind flashing back to that terrible day when he'd lost his mate. He could see Silverstream
lying beside the river, fighting to give birth. The reek of blood
was in his throat, and her cries, like Brightheart's, still pierced
his ears.

And there was nothing I could do to help her. . . .

The sight of Cinderpelt's head, popping out of the nursery entrance, dragged Graystripe back to the present. Cloudtail, Brightheart's mate, squeezed past her into the open.

"You want juniper berries, right?" he asked the medicine cat. "And chervil?"

"Yes, chervil root, not the leaves," Cinderpelt told him. "You remember what it looks like?"

"Sure I do." Cloudtail tossed the words over his shoulder, already racing across the camp toward the medicine cat's den.

"Graystripe," Cinderpelt meowed, seeming to notice him for the first time. "Are you okay? You're shaking like an aspen leaf."

Graystripe couldn't control his trembling, and fear was gripping him so tightly that at first he couldn't speak. *Stop this, you stupid furball,* he told himself. *This is Brightheart, not Silverstream. And Brightheart is in the nursery, with the whole Clan ready to help her—not giving birth in a hollow beside the river.* He tried to convince himself that the same thing wouldn't happen, that he needed to step up like a leader, just as Firestar would for the cats in his Clan. *I need to be calm. . . .*

"I'm fine," he managed to choke out at last. "Is she all right?"

"She will be," Cinderpelt assured him. "She's making good progress with her kitting."

"Will it take much longer?" Graystripe didn't know how long any she-cat could go on suffering agony and stress like Brightheart's. *How can they stand it? Brightheart, Silverstream . . . all the mother cats. They're all so brave!*

"I've no idea," Cinderpelt replied crisply. "It takes as long as it takes. And I'd better get back to her, not stand here gossiping with you. You can come in if you like."

Graystripe hesitated, trying to summon up courage, until Cloudtail raced back from Cinderpelt's den with the herbs she had asked for. As he slipped inside the nursery, Graystripe braced himself and dared to poke his head in through the entrance.

In the dim light from chinks in the nursery roof he could make out Brightheart lying on a bed of moss and bracken. Ferncloud was sitting beside her head, gently licking her ears. Ferncloud's kits, Spiderkit and Shrewkit, were huddled together in a deep nest of moss, watching everything with wide, scared eyes.

Cloudtail dropped the herbs in front of Cinderpelt, his white pelt glimmering in the shadows. "What's happening?" he demanded. "Why aren't the kits coming yet?"

Whatever Cinderpelt replied was lost as Brightheart let out another earsplitting screech. Her body convulsed; all four of her legs stretched out stiffly. Graystripe shut his eyes, the smell of blood threatening to overwhelm him. His heart was pounding as if he had run all the way to Fourtrees and back; he wanted to hide himself somewhere far away from the wailing of the laboring queen.

Then silence fell, and in the silence Graystripe could hear the soft mewling of a kit. It was followed by Cloudtail's quivering meow, so different from the usual loud voice of the wayward warrior.

"Oh, Brightheart, look! She's so beautiful. . . ."

Brightheart murmured something Graystripe couldn't make out.

Daring to open his eyes, Graystripe saw a tiny white kit nuzzling into Brightheart's belly. There was some blood staining the moss, but not nearly as much as when Silverstream had died. And Brightheart looked nothing like Silverstream: Her face showed her pain and exhaustion, but her one good eye was glowing with happiness.

"Well done, Brightheart." Cinderpelt's voice was full of satisfaction. "You did it! There's only one kit, so it's all over, and you're going to be okay."

Brightheart curled herself around to lick her kit's head, while Cloudtail looked so proud that he might burst.

What should I say? Graystripe wondered. He'd been so busy panicking that Brightheart would end up like Silverstream, he hadn't planned any sort of "welcome to the Clan" speech for the newest ThunderClan member. Firestar always seemed to know what to say at these moments. *Okay, what would Firestar say? Keep it simple!* At last Graystripe felt his heart settle down to a normal speed. "Welcome to ThunderClan, little kit," he mewed. "And as for you, Brightheart, congratulations! Good job!"

Brightheart dipped her head toward him wearily, then went back to licking her kit; Cloudtail settled down beside her, stretching his tail protectively over her shoulders. *Nice job, Graystripe,* Graystripe praised himself, withdrawing from the nursery to give the little family some space. *New ThunderClan kit welcomed!*

Shrewkit's voice, raised in excitement, followed him into the open. "Can we play with her?"

"No, she's too little," Ferncloud told him gently. "Wait a few days, and then you can all play together."

"Aw, that's like forever!" Spiderkit exclaimed.

Stifling a *mrrow* of laughter, Graystripe straightened up and turned around, to see that most of the Clan was standing in a loose semicircle a few tail-lengths away. He realized that he wasn't the only cat to have been roused by Brightheart's caterwauling.

Graystripe stepped forward. "Brightheart has a kit," he announced. "A new member of ThunderClan. And she and the kit are doing well."

Purrs and murmurs of delight greeted his news, as his Clanmates restrained their usual yowls of acclamation so as not to disturb the new mother and her kit. A wave of Clan pride washed over Graystripe at the thought that, even if nothing else happened while he was temporary leader, ThunderClan had already gained a future warrior and not lost a queen.

But his pride was immediately followed by a wave of self-doubt. *Firestar was always ready to help a queen with her kitting. But I didn't do anything—I was too lost in my own fears to help.* Graystripe could only wish that he were as capable and competent as Firestar. *Or at least as competent as he believes I am. Surely he wouldn't have put me in charge if he knew I would become so anxious about each decision a leader makes.* But this thought didn't make Graystripe feel any better. *I get anxious because this doesn't come as easily to me as it does to Firestar. Firestar wouldn't have panicked.*

Graystripe thought of Silverstream again, and his heart ached as if it would crack in two. Gazing up at the glittering stars, he hoped that one of them was Silverstream, looking down on him from StarClan.

I hope she can see Brightheart with her new kit, and I hope it makes her happy.

"Ashfur, I would like you to lead a patrol out toward Snakerocks," Graystripe meowed. "No cat has hunted there for a few days."

It was the morning after Brightheart's kitting, and Graystripe thought he could feel a new sense of optimism in the camp. Most of the warriors had already paid a visit to the nursery to greet the new arrival, and Cloudtail was looking as proud as if he had sprouted an extra tail.

"Sure, Graystripe," Ashfur agreed. "Who should I take with me?"

Before Graystripe could reply, movement at the end of the gorse tunnel caught his attention. Thornclaw appeared, with his apprentice, Sootpaw, following hard on his paws, and Brambleclaw a little way behind. Graystripe let his gaze travel from Thornclaw to Sootpaw, and then to Brambleclaw, noticing that no cat was carrying any prey.

Uneasiness pricked at Graystripe's pelt. Theirs was the first hunting patrol he had sent out that morning, not long before; why had they come back before they had caught anything?

"What happened?" he asked as the three cats bounded across the camp to where Graystripe and Ashfur were standing outside the warriors' den.

"WindClan happened," Thornclaw replied grimly. *"Again."*

Graystripe felt the fur on his shoulders begin to rise. *Great— so I'm going to have to deal with this after all.* "Tell me," he meowed.

"We headed up toward Fourtrees, and we were still way inside our own territory when we picked up WindClan's scent," Thornclaw told him.

"We came across a place where the undergrowth was torn up and there was blood spattered all around," Brambleclaw added. The young warrior's amber eyes were worried. "It looked like the work of at least two different cats, maybe three. And there was a strong scent of squirrel, and some tufts of squirrel fur."

Ashfur lashed his tail. *"Now* will you do something?" he challenged Graystripe.

Pushing down his irritation, Graystripe raced across the camp and sprang onto the top of the Highrock. "Let all cats old enough to catch their own prey join here beneath the Highrock for a Clan meeting!" he yowled.

He stood waiting while Cinderpelt emerged from the medicine cats' den and padded over to sit beside the High-rock. Speckletail and the other elders slipped out of their den by the fallen tree and sat just outside it in a cluster. Cloudtail appeared, too, to sit at the entrance to the nursery, though Brightheart remained inside with her new kit. A moment later Ferncloud came to join him, with her two kits, Shrewkit and Spiderkit, peering out curiously from behind her. Rain-paw and Sorrelpaw, the other two apprentices, scrambled out of their den and scurried across to their littermate, Sootpaw, to begin questioning him eagerly about what had happened. Dustpelt drew up behind Sorrelpaw, who was temporarily his apprentice while Sandstorm was gone, and lashed his tail. "Quiet, you three, or we won't be able to hear what Graystripe tells us."

The apprentices quieted, Sorrelpaw pouting a bit. *She must miss Sandstorm,* Graystripe thought.

As the Clan assembled, Graystripe realized that the dawn patrol hadn't yet returned, but he decided this was too important to delay. "Thornclaw, tell the Clan what you just saw," he meowed.

Thornclaw stood at the base of the Highrock and faced the Clan. "WindClan has been stealing prey again," he announced. He went on to repeat his description of what he and his patrol had found. "There's no excuse this time," he finished. "They were too far inside our territory for the prey to have crossed the border from WindClan."

Brambleclaw nodded agreement. "Squirrels don't live on WindClan territory. It was ThunderClan prey," he confirmed. "And it clearly wasn't an accident. It was a WindClan raid."

But as Graystripe listened to the story for the second time, he still couldn't shake his suspicion that it wasn't as simple as the evidence might suggest. The weather was still good, and prey was running well; WindClan should have had no need to steal prey from another Clan. Why instigate a conflict when they didn't have to?

There has to be some other reason, he thought. *If it were ShadowClan,*

I could believe Blackstar was deliberately trying to start trouble, but Tallstar has never been that kind of cat.

"So what are we going to do?" Ashfur asked when Thornclaw and Brambleclaw had finished speaking.

"You *have* to confront Tallstar," Cloudtail called from across the camp. "Once might have been a mistake, but there's no excuse now."

"Everything would be easier if Dustpelt were deputy," Ashfur added.

Oh, don't start that again! Graystripe thought in annoyance. *I thought Cinderpelt settled it the other day.* Then he began to wonder. *Will Ashfur still be pushing for Dustpelt to take over as deputy, even after Firestar's return?*

Glancing around, he couldn't see the brown tabby warrior in camp, then remembered that he was leading the border patrol with Mousefur and Brackenfur. He had taken no part in the previous argument, either, because he had been on watch.

Does he even know *what Ashfur is saying?* Graystripe asked himself. *I don't particularly like Dustpelt, but I never expected him to undermine me like this. Though he and Ashfur have always been close.* Dustpelt had been Ashfur's mentor.

"Hmm . . . ," he muttered to himself. "Dustpelt and I will have to have a talk."

But this was not the time, Graystripe realized, as Thornclaw began to speak again. Shaking his pelt irritably to get rid of the unwelcome thoughts, he tried to concentrate on what his Clanmate was saying.

"Come on, Graystripe! Don't stand there like a frozen rabbit—you have to do something!"

Yowls of agreement came from the assembled cats. Graystripe gazed down at the blazing eyes and lashing tails of his Clanmates, their bristling fur and claws ready to sink into WindClan pelts. He felt uneasy at the prospect of confronting Tallstar, who was a far more experienced and capable leader. He would have preferred to go away somewhere quiet and think things out, perhaps to discuss the problem with Cinderpelt. But there was no time for that now: His Clan was clearly hungry for him to take action.

"Keep your fur on," he meowed when the yowling had died away and he could make himself heard. "I can't just go stomping into WindClan's camp and tell Tallstar his Clan is a bunch of thieves."

"Why not?" One-eye snapped from where she sat with the other elders. "It's what they are."

"Because that's a job for a Clan leader," Graystripe retorted. "If I do it, Tallstar is going to start wondering where Firestar is. It's hard enough pretending that he's still here without putting myself in a position where Tallstar would expect to see Firestar."

"But if you *don't* go," Brambleclaw mewed hesitantly, as if he was nervous about voicing his thoughts in a discussion with senior warriors, "they'll still wonder where Firestar is. Because Firestar wouldn't let this go."

Graystripe felt a flicker of frustration at the realization that he couldn't get out of the conflict as easily as that.

"You're right, he wouldn't." He gave the young warrior a nod of respect. *That's a bright young cat. He'll go far in the Clan.*

But Graystripe still didn't know what he should do. Something about WindClan's "theft" still didn't feel right to him. And even if he accepted that the other Clan had stolen prey, how *could* he warn WindClan to stay off ThunderClan territory without risking giving away that Firestar had gone on a journey?

"Have you thought that maybe WindClan is trying this because somehow they've *already* guessed that Firestar isn't here?" Thornclaw asked.

"Yeah, they think they can get away with it," Ashfur growled in agreement. "And it's starting to look like they're right."

Graystripe ignored the insult. He felt it was quite likely that if WindClan had discovered Firestar's absence, they might try to take advantage, but it still didn't help him decide what to do. He glanced down at Cinderpelt, who was looking up at him, her blue eyes bright. "Has StarClan shown you anything about this?" he asked her, hoping that she might be able to show him a way forward.

The medicine cat shook her head. "Nothing. Although . . ." Her eyes clouded a little with anxiety. "The signs are hard to read. When I try to look ahead, I see only shadows."

Thanks, that's a big help, Graystripe thought. *I should know better than to expect clear answers from StarClan.*

His Clanmates were muttering among themselves now, casting unfriendly glances up at him. Graystripe knew that within moments he would have to commit himself to some course of action, or he would lose their respect and their cooperation for good.

And I can't say I blame them. A Clan leader ought to be decisive.

He was gathering himself to speak, still not sure what words would come out of his mouth, when a sharp yowl came from the direction of the gorse tunnel. Mousefur, who had been part of the border patrol, appeared and raced across the camp to the Highrock. The Clan's grumbling died into silence as every cat turned to stare at her.

"What's the matter?" Graystripe asked, his pelt prickling once more with apprehension. "Is it WindClan?"

Mousefur paused for a moment, her chest heaving. "No, it's ShadowClan. Russetfur and Rowanclaw came up to us while we were patrolling the border," she explained at last. "They want to speak to Firestar."

What, now? Graystripe scraped his claws on the hard surface of the Highrock as tension rushed through him from ears to tail-tip. *Is there anything else that can go wrong?*

CHAPTER 6

☙

— Now —

The little group of wandering cats drew close to the ThunderClan border and the unclaimed forest that lay beyond. The dawn chill was still in the air, and the rising sun had not yet burned the dew from the grass. The younger cats still hadn't decided yet if they would go with Graystripe to visit the Tribe in the mountains. He was already thoroughly tired of this aimless wandering around the forest.

"We should hunt again before we leave ThunderClan territory," Flywhisker suggested.

She sounded nervous, and the two younger toms seemed to share her misgivings, casting glances back in the direction of the ThunderClan camp. On the day before, full of excitement at the step they had taken by announcing that they would leave the Clan, they had been eager to cross the border. Now, Graystripe guessed, reality was beginning to sink in.

Graystripe bristled a little. He felt that he had wasted enough time taking care of these inexperienced cats. *I have only a moon to make my decision. If I'm leaving, I want to be gone.*

But then, looking at his companions' wide eyes and twitching whiskers, his heart softened. He didn't think that any of the others had ever been outside Clan territory before. They had all been born beside the lake, and they didn't know that the woods beyond ThunderClan's border markers ran just as richly with prey as the familiar land inside their territory.

Graystripe reflected that when he was Flywhisker and Snaptooth's age, he rarely left ThunderClan's territory back in the old forest. Perhaps he'd make the occasional trip to the Twolegplace or to Ravenpaw and Barley's farm. But he wouldn't have wandered farther if he hadn't been forced to. Certainly not when he was as young as Flipclaw. Even though leaving the Clan had been their decision, maybe the younger cats needed a little longer before they crossed the border into the unknown.

"Good idea, Flywhisker," he meowed. "Let's hunt."

The young she-cat visibly relaxed at his agreement, and Graystripe felt satisfied that he had made the right decision.

All four cats spread out into the surrounding undergrowth. Graystripe's spirits lifted as he caught the scent of vole. Before he left the camp, he hadn't hunted in quite some time; becoming an elder meant that the apprentices brought him his food. Graystripe appreciated that, but it felt better to catch his own. Since he had caught the rabbit the previous day, the familiar actions had come back to him as if he still spent every day stalking prey.

He spotted the vole slipping through the stems of long grass and dropped into the hunter's crouch. Paw step by paw step, he crept up on his prey, but just as he was about to pounce, a startled yowl came from one of the other cats.

"Dogs!"

The vole vanished.

"Fox dung!" Graystripe hissed, turning to see Snaptooth and the others peering through the branches of a nearby hazel bush. Hurrying to their side, he picked up the strong scent of the nearby dogs. He could hear them snuffling around on the other side of the bush. He thrust Snaptooth aside to peer through the hazel leaves; his heart lurched as he saw the dogs, one wiry and brown, the other bigger, with a shaggy white pelt. They were pushing their noses into every hole and under every root, but they clearly hadn't scented the cats yet.

"Back away, really quietly," he murmured to the others.

But before they had managed to retreat more than a few paw steps, the smaller dog seemed to scent them. Its head tilted back, its muzzle twitching and nostrils flaring. With a flurry of high-pitched barks, it launched itself at the cats, its companion lolloping behind it.

"Scatter!" Graystripe screeched. "Run!"

Instantly the younger cats raced off in different directions. Graystripe hung back for a moment, letting out a defiant yowl to draw the dogs' attention. When the lead dog veered toward him, he spun around and sprinted for the nearest tree, hurling himself up the trunk until he could scramble onto a branch.

"Great StarClan!" he gasped. "I'm too old for this!"

Looking down, he saw the two dogs whining and sniffing at the bottom of his tree. The white dog reared up on its hind paws, scrabbling with its forepaws at the tree trunk, but for all its efforts it couldn't climb any higher.

"Get lost, flea-pelts!" Graystripe snarled.

Anxiously, he looked around to see what had happened to his Clanmates. Flywhisker had climbed, too, and was balancing precariously on the lowest branch of an elder sapling. Flipclaw was clinging to the ivy growing up a nearby oak tree, but his weight was gradually tearing the tendrils away from the trunk, so that the ivy slowly sagged closer and closer to the ground. At first Graystripe couldn't see Snaptooth at all, until he spotted his head poking out of a bramble thicket a few tail-lengths away. None of the young cats were in a secure enough position to be safe if the dogs spotted them, and all three of them looked frozen with terror.

The dogs didn't seem likely to go away anytime soon, either. Graystripe watched as the white dog sat down and started scratching at its pelt, while its brown companion stood staring up at Graystripe, its tongue lolling and its jaws open to show a mouthful of gleaming teeth.

How do we get out of this mess? Graystripe wondered.

Looking around him, through the trees, he couldn't see any obvious way of escape. He wondered if he could leap down and lead the dogs farther into the forest, away from his Clanmates, but he knew he wouldn't have much of a head start. And he worried that he'd tire before he could climb another tree to safety.

Then they'd catch me, he added to himself, imagining the dogs leaping on him, bringing him down. He shuddered at the thought of those teeth slicing through his flesh.

"Graystripe, what can we do?" Flywhisker called to him. She looked as if she was about to lose her balance. The thin branch where she crouched was bouncing under her weight, and Graystripe worried she would pitch down into the bracken at any moment.

"Just hang on!" he called out to her.

He would have to run for it. He was bracing himself to jump when he heard paw steps approaching through the trees: the heavy, clumping noise of Twolegs. Pricking his ears, he made out two different voices, and a moment later a pair of Twolegs, a male and a female, appeared from behind the bramble thicket.

As soon as he spotted the dogs, the male Twoleg called out; Graystripe thought he sounded annoyed. The dogs hesitated, then padded toward the Twolegs with obvious reluctance, casting glances back at Graystripe as they went.

The Twolegs took out vines and fastened them to the dogs' collars, then led the dogs away. The dogs were still whining and tugging, but eventually the whole group vanished and their scents began to fade. Graystripe huffed out a long breath of relief.

He jumped down and beckoned to his Clanmates with a swish of his tail. Flywhisker and Flipclaw let themselves drop to the ground and joined him, while Snaptooth dragged himself out of the bramble thicket, hissing in annoyance as the thorns caught in his fur.

"Are you all okay?" Graystripe asked. Part of him took in

the young warriors' wide eyes and quivering limbs and felt that they'd better toughen up if they were going to make it as loners. But another part—the part that had mentored countless apprentices—wanted to soothe their fears, help them learn to be smarter next time. That was how Clanmates looked out for one another.

When all three nodded, he continued, "Good. Then we'd better finish our hunt."

Sunhigh was just past by the time the cats had hunted and filled their bellies with prey. All three younger warriors seemed inclined to curl up and go to sleep on a warm stretch of moss, but every hair on Graystripe's pelt was telling him that the time had come to go.

But can I really leave my Clanmates? he asked himself, the terrifying encounter with the dogs still vivid in his mind. The young cats seemed to have forgotten that he had announced his intention to visit the Tribe. He took a deep breath, bracing himself.

"This is where I leave you," he announced, rising to his paws. "I'm sorry, but if I go now, I can make a good start toward the mountains before it gets dark."

Flywhisker and Snaptooth exchanged an uncertain glance. "But—" Flywhisker began, and broke off. Flipclaw was looking doubtful, too. He glanced from Flywhisker and Snaptooth back to Graystripe.

For a moment, Graystripe wavered. *Will they be okay? Should I leave them like this, when Thornclaw is already gone?*

But Flipclaw, Graystripe considered, had been the first cat to announce that he was leaving ThunderClan. He had been prepared to go out on his own before any cat had offered to accompany him. *These cats may be young,* Graystripe told himself, *but they're old enough to make their own decisions and live with the consequences.*

And that was a good thing, because Graystripe's yearning to visit the Tribe, and see his son again, was too strong to ignore any longer.

"I told you where I was going," he reminded the others gently. "This is important to me. As I've said, you're welcome to come with me if you want to," he added, when no cat responded. "It would be a chance to have an adventure. See the mountains. Experience a different way of living than we have in the Clans."

His suggestion was met with silence. Graystripe wasn't sure what answer he'd expected, but he was disappointed when none of his young Clanmates seemed excited by his offer.

"It's good of you to suggest it," Snaptooth mewed finally, with a polite dip of his head. "But I'm not sure Flywhisker and I want to go so far."

Flywhisker nodded in agreement. "We haven't even left Clan territory yet and we've already almost been killed by dogs! And the Tribe is such a long way away. . . ."

"But we'll—" Graystripe began.

"I'm sure there'll be more dogs and Twolegs on the way there," Snaptooth continued, ignoring him. "And probably other things we don't even know about, maybe even scarier, or harder to fight off. No, Flywhisker and I are going to stick close to Clan territory while we decide what to do. It's just safer here."

All this while, Flipclaw hadn't spoken; he just looked worried, and uncertain about what he would decide. Graystripe thought back to how Flywhisker had rejected him the night before, and wondered if the poor lovesick tom was going to keep following her, getting his heart broken over and over. *It's his decision, but that will never make him happy.*

Graystripe let his glance flick from one cat to the next. He couldn't help remembering how thrilled Hollyleaf, Lionblaze, and Jayfeather had been to travel to the mountains when the Tribe cats had come to ask for help. And they had only been apprentices at the time.

I don't know what's come over young cats these days. . . . Then Graystripe stifled a snort of amusement. *I sound like a grouchy old elder!*

But as he watched Flipclaw think it over, his amusement was replaced by sadness. *Compared to these young cats, I am a grouchy old elder.* He had lost his mate; he'd been exhausted by all the Clan troubles of the last few moons. *All I can think about is how much I miss the old days—when things felt simpler.*

Then Graystripe remembered: He wasn't the leader of these cats, and it was a long time since he had been Clan deputy. It was a relief to realize that it didn't matter whether these warriors listened to him or not. It wasn't his place to tell the younger cats what to do; they had the right to make up their own minds. And it wasn't his job to protect them. They'd chosen to leave the safety of the Clan, the same as he had. What happened now was up to them. Besides, if they didn't like it out on their own, they could always return to the Clan.

"Okay," he meowed. "It was only an idea. I hope I'll see you again, back in ThunderClan—if we all decide to return. If not, be safe, and take care of one another."

The three young cats dipped their heads awkwardly, as if they were feeling guilty about refusing to travel with him. "Good-bye," Flywhisker responded. "May StarClan light your path, Graystripe."

At the mention of StarClan, Graystripe started, and he glanced back at the younger warriors to see whether the familiar parting words had struck them in the same awkward way. But it seemed that the reminder of StarClan's absence hadn't occurred to them. *Just as well,* he thought sadly.

"And stay away from dogs!" Snaptooth was adding.

"I'll try my best. You too." Graystripe swept his tail around in a gesture of farewell. "And good luck to all of you."

He turned away and padded off through the trees, heading toward the lake and the border with WindClan. While he had a bittersweet feeling at the thought of leaving Thunder-Clan territory, not knowing whether he would return, it was a relief to feel that at last he was really setting out on his wander. *I'll go and think about what I really want, and when I do return—if I do return—I'll have more to offer my Clan.* Though he was looking forward to seeing Stormfur again, it felt strange to be traveling alone. Even when he'd journeyed to find the Clans in their new home beside the lake, he and Millie had been together.

I hope all four cats I started out with will be okay on their own, he thought with a sigh. Even if they weren't his responsibility, they were his Clanmates . . . or they had been. He couldn't help caring about them.

But as he approached the stream that formed the border with WindClan, Graystripe heard the patter of paws behind him. Turning, he saw Flipclaw racing to catch up to him.

"I want to come with you!" he panted. "I want to travel to the mountains and meet the Tribe. Besides," he added, managing to catch his breath, "you could use some company. It's dangerous outside Clan territory."

"It sure is," Graystripe agreed, although he recoiled a bit at the suggestion that he was old or feeble enough to need protection. Still, he couldn't help feeling a curl of affection for the younger warrior. He imagined that Flipclaw himself could use some company and kind words after Flywhisker had been so clear about how she felt about him—and how she *didn't* feel. Graystripe could remember what heartbreak felt like. He wouldn't have wanted to stay with Flywhisker and her littermate, either.

I can't cope with a whole Clan's problems, he thought. *One Clanmate is as much as I want right now.*

Splashing through the border stream, leaving Thunder-Clan's territory behind them, he and Flipclaw padded on side by side.

CHAPTER 7

❧

— Then —

Graystripe stood frozen on the Highrock, his glance flicking to the end of the tunnel. He was prepared for the two Shadow-Clan cats to appear immediately, to find ThunderClan in the middle of a turbulent meeting and himself in the position of leader, with Firestar nowhere to be seen.

"Did you bring them with you?" he asked. *What will I tell them? How will I explain Firestar's absence?*

Mousefur shook her head. "I ran on ahead to warn you. Dustpelt and Brackenfur are escorting them to the camp."

Thank StarClan! Graystripe felt himself sag with relief. *I have a few moments to think. . . .*

The Clan was silent now, still looking up at Graystripe and waiting for his decision. Graystripe tried to put the whole WindClan problem out of his mind and concentrate on how he should deal with the ShadowClan cats.

"So what do we do?" Mousefur asked, shaking her brown pelt impatiently.

Graystripe couldn't see any alternative. He braced himself

for yet more trouble. "Let them come into camp," he replied.

He waited until Mousefur had dived back into the gorse tunnel before turning back to his Clan. "Continue with your duties as usual," he began. "Ashfur, gather your hunting patrol, but don't leave yet. Apprentices, start cleaning out the elders' den."

"About time," Speckletail put in.

Graystripe ignored her. "While they're doing that, some of you elders might like to pay a visit to Brightheart. Or sit in the sun and share tongues. Cinderpelt, sort some herbs or something. This is a happy, busy camp, with nothing on our minds except our next piece of fresh-kill. And for StarClan's sake," he finished, "no cat mention any trouble with WindClan."

As his Clan hurried to obey his orders, Graystripe leaped down from the Highrock and padded forward into the center of the camp to wait for the ShadowClan cats. It wasn't long before Mousefur reemerged from the tunnel followed by Russetfur, the dark ginger she-cat who was ShadowClan's deputy, and Rowanclaw, a muscular ginger tom. Brackenfur and Dustpelt brought up the rear; both of them stayed close to the ShadowClan warriors as they headed across the camp to meet Graystripe.

Russetfur gave Graystripe a brief nod as she halted in front of him. "Greetings," she mewed. "We'd like to speak to Firestar."

For a heartbeat, Graystripe wasn't sure what to say. When Firestar had left, he had intended to tell the other Clans the truth: that StarClan had called Firestar away on a mission.

But then at the next Gathering, when he'd taken Firestar's place for the first time, it had seemed too dangerous to let them know that the ThunderClan leader had left the forest completely, like an invitation for them to invade. So Graystripe had told them that his leader was sick. He regretted that decision now; how long could a strong cat stay sick? *And what if they ask to visit Firestar in his den?*

"Well?" Russetfur tapped one paw impatiently.

"I'm sorry," Graystripe improvised swiftly, doing his best to seem cool and unconcerned. "Firestar is out of camp right now."

"We'll wait." Rowanclaw sat down and wrapped his tail around his paws. "This is important."

Graystripe hesitated for a couple of heartbeats. He noticed that Cinderpelt had emerged from her den and had angled her ears toward the conversation, while pretending to be intent on laying out sprigs of marigold in a patch of sunlight. Ferncloud still sat at the entrance to the nursery, watching Shrewkit and Spiderkit playing with a ball of moss. Goldenflower and Frostfur ambled across from the elders' den and paused to admire the kits. Ashfur slipped out of the warriors' den with Brambleclaw and Thornclaw, but crossed the camp to stand close to Graystripe instead of leading his patrol out.

Confident that his Clan was backing him up, Graystripe took a breath. "I'm ThunderClan's deputy," he pointed out. "You can tell me anything you want Firestar to know."

Russetfur and Rowanclaw exchanged an angry glance, their shoulder fur beginning to rise. A silent communication seemed to pass between them; then Russetfur gave a tiny nod. "Very well," she meowed, giving her tail an irritated twitch. "I guess we can't sit around the ThunderClan camp all day. We thought Firestar might like to know," she continued, "that we've scented BloodClan at the edge of the Thunderpath not far from the Twolegplace, just opposite your territory."

Graystripe heard gasps of alarm from the ThunderClan warriors behind him. He felt his belly lurch, though he kept his gaze fixed steadily on Russetfur. There had been no sign of BloodClan for moons, not since Firestar had led the Clans to drive them out of the forest. *Even so, it feels like we've only just stopped checking over our shoulders. And now the vicious rogues have come sneaking back?*

"Of course you ShadowClan cats would be the first to scent BloodClan," Cloudtail muttered, padding forward from the nursery. "Are you sure you're not sheltering them on your own territory?"

"I wouldn't be at all surprised," Dustpelt agreed, with a hostile stare at Russetfur and Rowanclaw.

"Yeah, why should we trust you? It was Tigerstar who brought BloodClan to the forest," Mousefur added, her claws flexing as if she was ready to rake them across Shadow-Clan fur.

Russetfur drew her lips back and let out a furious hiss, while Rowanclaw sprang to his paws, his shoulder fur bristling, and began to look around as if he was deciding which ThunderClan cat to attack first.

"Why should we put up with this?" Russetfur asked. "We

came to do you mange-pelts a *favor!*"

"I know, and I'm sorry," Graystripe responded with a polite dip of his head. "Our warriors are naturally worried at the thought of BloodClan returning, and perhaps that makes them too ready with their claws. Of course we're grateful for the warning—aren't we?" he added, with a stern look at his assembled Clanmates.

A murmur of agreement followed his words, though some of the cats didn't manage to look grateful at all, their eyes still wary and their muscles braced to respond if the ShadowClan cats showed any signs of attacking.

"I'll be sure to pass on your message to Firestar when he returns," Graystripe continued, trying to copy the easy way Firestar used during awkward encounters with other Clans. "And I'm sure I speak for him when I say that you have ThunderClan's thanks. Mousefur, Brackenfur, please escort our guests back to the border."

"And may StarClan light your path," Cinderpelt added, stepping up to Graystripe's side.

Russetfur's only response was a grunt. Then she turned and headed out of the camp with Rowanclaw, closely flanked by the two ThunderClan cats.

"I thought BloodClan was gone for good!" Cloudtail exclaimed as soon as the ShadowClan cats' scent trail had begun to fade.

"I knew something like this would happen with Firestar away," Ashfur growled. "He's left ThunderClan vulnerable, and what for? That's what I'd like to know."

"Clan leaders didn't go wandering off in my day," Speckle-tail snapped. "They stayed on their Clan's territory."

"I wish Firestar had stayed," Brambleclaw added, his amber eyes blinking anxiously. "If BloodClan has come back, we'll need him."

Graystripe exchanged a glance with Cinderpelt. Only he and the medicine cat knew that Firestar and Sandstorm were searching for the lost SkyClan. They and Firestar had decided that the other cats should not be told that once there had been a fifth Clan that had been driven out of the forest.

They're resentful about Firestar's mysterious absence, Graystripe thought. *And I can't really blame them.* But how could he handle that?

"Keep your fur on," he meowed to the rest of the Clan. "This is only a rumor. We have no proof that BloodClan is anywhere near our territory."

But his Clanmates were muttering among themselves, their ears laid flat and their whiskers twitching with apprehension. Graystripe could tell that they weren't listening to him. And for once, he wasn't too worried. Thoughts were flickering through his brain so fast that he thought his head might burst; it was as if Firestar had somehow been able to lend him his own quick wits.

"I'll tell you something," he began at last, as one particular thought took shape in his mind, rising above the others. "We don't have a WindClan problem. We have a *BloodClan* problem! Wouldn't it be just like them to roll in WindClan scent, disguise themselves, and then take prey on our territory?

Trouble with WindClan would keep us nicely occupied along that border while BloodClan moved in on us from the Two-legplace. And because our two Clans would be fighting each other, we'd both be weakened—easy pickings for those filthy mange-pelts!"

For a moment, none of his Clanmates responded, only exchanging worried glances. *I'm right,* Graystripe thought. *I know it. But that doesn't make things easier for us.*

"You could be right," Dustpelt meowed at last, and several other cats murmured agreement.

"They even left us a sign," Cinderpelt pointed out. "Blood—blood on our territory!"

Graystripe drew a breath of relief. At least he seemed to have most of his Clan on his side again. The news about BloodClan had given him a good reason not to stir up trouble with WindClan; his instincts had been right. He'd known that Tallstar wouldn't encourage his cats to steal prey in this plentiful season.

Now he just had to decide what action to take next. "For the moment we'll leave WindClan alone—until we can get proof, one way or another. If any of you see WindClan patrols on the border, greet them respectfully, like always. Ashfur," he continued, "you have a hunting patrol to lead. Take Thorn-claw and Cloudtail. Head for Fourtrees, then work your way back along the Thunderpath, and check for BloodClan scent there while you're at it. Dustpelt and Brambleclaw, you can come with me."

"Where are we going?" Brambleclaw asked, an eager light

driving out the anxiety in his eyes.

"To the Thunderpath near the Twolegplace," Graystripe replied, "close to where ShadowClan said they picked up BloodClan's scent. We need to figure out whether they were telling the truth."

"Cool!" the young warrior exclaimed, his tail straight up in the air.

Dustpelt rolled his eyes.

As Graystripe had hoped, the promise of action pulled the Clan back together. Ashfur's patrol bounded across the camp and through the tunnel, and Graystripe followed with Dustpelt and Brambleclaw.

Heading for the Thunderpath, Graystripe noticed how alert Brambleclaw was, padding along as quietly as if he were stalking a mouse, his ears pricked for any unusual sounds, and his jaws open to taste the air. Graystripe could see that the young warrior was trying to prove himself to his older Clanmates.

He's not just worried about an attack from BloodClan, Graystripe guessed, remembering Brambleclaw's anxiety when Tigerstar was mentioned. *He must think that if BloodClan returns, every cat will remember that he's Tigerstar's son.*

"Can you scent anything, Brambleclaw?" he asked.

The young warrior shook his head. "I think a fox has been through here—maybe yesterday," he meowed. "But I can't pick up any trace of BloodClan."

Graystripe nodded. "Well scented," he mewed. "Keep it up, and let us know if you scent anything else."

Brambleclaw's eyes glowed and he puffed his chest out with pride. "I will, Graystripe!"

As the patrol drew closer to the Thunderpath, Graystripe noticed clouds massing to cover the sun. A chilly breeze rustled his pelt, and soon a thin drizzle began to fall.

"Mouse dung," Graystripe muttered, knowing the rain would dampen all the scents and make it harder to track BloodClan. It might erase entirely whatever traces Shadow-Clan had noticed. "That's all we need!"

Gradually the acrid scent of the Thunderpath began to penetrate the rain, and Graystripe could make out the growls of monsters as they rushed along the hard, black surface. In front of the cats lay a stretch of open ground; on one side was a fence around the first of the Twoleg dens, and straight ahead a line of thick bushes marked the edge of the Thunderpath.

"Stay on this side of the bushes," Graystripe murmured to his companions. "We'll work our way along, and maybe meet up with Ashfur's patrol."

But Graystripe had barely taken another paw step before an eerie yowl sounded above the hissing of the rain. He froze with horror as cat after cat poured out of the bushes and sprang toward the three ThunderClan warriors.

BloodClan really has returned! Graystripe realized that until this moment he had been hoping that ShadowClan had somehow made a mistake. *Am I up to dealing with them?* he asked himself. *BloodClan's return would test any leader—and I'm not even a real leader! I wonder, did ShadowClan have anything to do with setting up this ambush, to weaken ThunderClan?*.

The BloodClan cats were all muscular, formidable-looking creatures, their eyes glaring a challenge. Their rank scent was easy to pick up now as they formed a circle around Graystripe and his Clanmates. Graystripe's stomach turned at the sight of them and at the stench that he had hoped never to smell again.

Eight of them, Graystripe thought. *Great StarClan, help us, or we'll be crow-food!*

For a few moments, the BloodClan cats stood still, their shoulder fur bristling and their lips drawn back in identical snarls. All of them looked like tough, experienced fighters, though Graystripe noticed that one of them, a she-cat with patchy black, white, and tortoiseshell fur, was heavily pregnant. Even though she was an enemy, he felt sick at the thought of fighting a queen so close to kitting. He knew it would never happen in ThunderClan; by now she would have been safely curled up in the nursery, with the medicine cat to take care of her and her unborn kits.

But maybe that means she won't fight as fiercely as the others. . . .

Dustpelt was sniffing deeply as he faced the BloodClan cats. "I think I can make out a trace of WindClan," he muttered to Graystripe.

Tasting the air more carefully, Graystripe too could pick up a trace of the other Clan, probably from the WindClan border markers.

"So I was right," he responded. "Thank StarClan I never went to confront Tallstar!"

Then one of the cats, a long-furred tabby she-cat with one

eye, and scars across her muzzle and her shoulders, stepped forward to confront Graystripe. "WindClan, you say?" she meowed. "Do you *really* think any of us would roll ourselves in their stink? How disgusting is that!"

"Yes, I *do* think that," Graystripe retorted. "I expect you enjoyed seeing us dashing to and fro, wondering if we were being invaded. But it didn't work, did it? As soon as we heard about your scent on our borders, we knew exactly what was happening. So you won't weaken us by setting up a battle with WindClan."

"Pity." Still not admitting BloodClan's ruse, the long-furred tabby examined her claws. "Your territory is so nice," she purred, her one eye narrowed menacingly. "And the prey is running so well." Her voice grew harsher as she added, "Promises were made to us before Scourge was killed, and just because he's dead doesn't mean we've given up wanting your territory."

Graystripe suppressed a shudder at the thought of being so outnumbered, but he made himself speak out boldly, just as he knew Firestar would have. "We ran you off before," he pointed out, "when there were far more of you, and Scourge was your leader. You might be acting tough, but none of you can measure up to that scrawny little tom. And he's been dead for moons, at the claws of *our* leader."

While he was speaking, he maneuvered to keep Bramble-claw at his back, and saw that Dustpelt was trying to protect the young cat from the other direction. Brambleclaw was a full warrior now, but he had been an apprentice not much more than a moon ago; he'd be no match for these hard-bitten rogues. He was flexing his claws, eager to play his part in the fight, but Graystripe vowed silently to keep him out of danger if he possibly could.

"Your leader, Firestar, may have killed Scourge," the tabby she-cat went on. "But we've been watching, and we've seen that Firestar is gone. Your precious leader has abandoned you."

Graystripe and Dustpelt exchanged a look of alarm. *That's supposed to be a secret!* Graystripe thought, every hair on his pelt tingling with dread.

"There are still far more cats in ThunderClan than there are in BloodClan," he asserted, letting his fur bush out in the hope of intimidating their enemies. "I count eight of you. How do you think you could possibly fight us?"

Another of the BloodClan cats—a gray tabby tom—let out a purr of laughter. "You stupid flea-brain!" he exclaimed. "Why would you think this is all of us?"

Without further warning, the BloodClan cats leaped into an attack. Wherever he looked, Graystripe could see extended claws and jaws parted to show gleaming teeth. The tabby leader slammed into him and bore him to the ground, slashing with both forepaws at Graystripe's throat. Graystripe jerked his head back just in time for the blow to swipe harmlessly through his fur. He pounded the she-cat with his powerful hind paws until she rolled away with a snarl of frustration, a look of fury on her scarred face.

Graystripe scrambled to his paws. By now the rain was

pelting in a torrent that soaked his pelt and ran down his fore-head into his eyes. Shaking his head to get rid of the droplets, he spotted Dustpelt battling two ginger she-cats, whirling from side to side to land blows on their necks and shoulders while they tried to strike at his exposed underbelly. Bramble-claw was bravely fighting the tom with the patchy pelt, but as Graystripe sprang toward him, the tom raked his claws down Brambleclaw's side. Blood welled up where the claws had passed, and Brambleclaw staggered from the force of the blow.

Graystripe reached Brambleclaw and ducked to support him with one shoulder. "Get out of this!" he hissed into Bram-bleclaw's ear.

"No! I can fight!" the young cat protested.

"I said, get out!" Graystripe repeated. "Go back to camp and fetch help. That's an order!"

Though still obviously reluctant, Brambleclaw dived into a gap between two BloodClan warriors and raced off into the trees. One of the BloodClan cats tried to pursue, but Gray-stripe leaped at him and landed on his back; the BloodClan cat thumped hard onto the ground and was slow to get up again.

Taking a moment to catch his breath, Graystripe looked around for Dustpelt, only to see that a third rogue, a black-and-white tom with a torn ear and a collar studded with dogs' teeth, had joined the two she-cats attacking him. Before he could leap to Dustpelt's aid, the BloodClan leader and her three remaining cats crowded around him in a tight circle, herding him away from his Clanmate. Graystripe noticed that one of them was the pregnant she-cat; her torn fur and the blood trickling from her forehead showed that she had indeed been fighting as fiercely as any of the others.

I was wrong to think we could discount her. . . .

The four cats were driving Graystripe toward the Twolegplace. Once the tom Graystripe had knocked to the ground managed to totter to his paws, he joined them. Graystripe looked around uneasily, wondering if he could shoulder through the line of rogues without inviting another attack. Making a split-second decision, he darted forward, but he was just a moment too slow, and the tom he'd knocked down earlier swiveled to block him. The other cats closed in, and blows rained down on Graystripe from all sides. Even the pregnant queen was pummeling him, though she was clumsy because of the weight of her belly.

He fought back, striking out with claws and teeth, but he was hopelessly outnumbered, and he didn't have enough space to use the best of his ThunderClan battle techniques. His sodden pelt weighed him down, and his paws slipped on the wet grass as he tried to maneuver.

"Don't hold back!" the long-furred leader snarled, her glittering gaze fixed on the pregnant she-cat. "Don't think you can take it easy, just because you're about to have kits!"

That's BloodClan for you, Graystripe thought hazily. *In real Clans, we work to protect one another. In BloodClan, it's every cat for herself.*

He knew that he was weakening, his strength drained by pain and loss of blood. A hard blow to the side of his head knocked him off his paws, and when he tried to get up, his legs wouldn't obey him. He lay where he had fallen, his senses swimming, every muscle in his body throbbing with agony.

Is this where it ends for me? he wondered. *What will Firestar think of me, when he finds out that not only did I fail to keep the Clan safe, but I was defeated so easily?*

"Is he dead?" some cat asked, his voice echoing eerily in Graystripe's ears.

"Let's throw him to the dog in the Twolegplace," the Blood-Clan leader growled. "If he's not dead now, he soon will be."

"Great idea!" another cat sniggered.

Graystripe felt a paw prodding him in the side. "He might have thought he could take over as that Clan's leader," the one-eyed tabby meowed, "but with him gone too, these cats will fall apart."

Even through his daze, Graystripe realized that the Blood-Clan cats must have been observing ThunderClan closely to notice not only that Firestar was missing, but also that he himself was in charge. *Why did we never notice them? Have they been watching us all along, disguising their scent?*

He felt an extra stab of pain as claws dug into him and then a lurch as he started moving sideways; he realized that several of the cats were dragging him toward a hole in the bottom of the fence around the Twoleg den. His fur scraped along the bottom of the fence, and then he was inside; he heard the rogues groaning as they struggled to block the hole with what looked like a rock. There was no way out, and the stink of dog was all around him.

Now what? he asked himself. *I can't fight a dog in this state. . . .*

At first, Graystripe lay still, partly because his fall had driven his breath out of him, and partly because he wanted the BloodClan cats to think that he was dead. In spite of his pain, he didn't think he was badly hurt; none of his limbs were broken, and his senses were beginning to return. Perhaps he hadn't lost too much blood.

At last Graystripe realized that the BloodClan cats must be leaving. Gradually their voices died away into the distance, and their scent too began to fade. When all was quiet, Graystripe rose cautiously to his paws. Blinking to clear his vision, he saw that he was standing at the edge of a Twoleg garden, with grass stretching up to the walls of a Twoleg den. The rain had stopped; Graystripe licked some hanging drops from the leaves of a nearby bush and felt himself beginning to revive.

A moment later, he stiffened as fierce barking broke out from the direction of the Twoleg den. But when he looked around, there was no sign of the dog, and he realized that the noise was coming from behind the walls of the den.

In spite of his wounds, Graystripe let out a short *mrrow* of laughter. "Ha! If those stupid rogues wanted the dog to finish me off, they should have made sure it could get to me."

Every muscle in his body ached, and he shivered with cold, his fur plastered to his body from the rain and the blood he had lost. Knowing that he had to get out of the garden and back to camp, he scrambled up a tree that grew close to the fence, digging in his claws and hauling himself painfully upward.

Once he'd cleared the top of the fence, he crossed into the branches of another tree growing on the other side. Panting with the effort, he took a moment to rest, and scanned the open ground for any sign of Dustpelt. He was terrified at the thought of spotting the brown tabby warrior stretched out in a pool of his own blood, and drew a sigh of relief as he saw that Dustpelt wasn't there.

He must have escaped, back to camp.

But Graystripe's relief was short-lived. As he swept his gaze around the battleground for one last time, he spotted the pregnant she-cat, crouched under one of the bushes that lined the Thunderpath. Panic sparked beneath his pelt as his gaze locked with hers.

It's over!

Graystripe froze, waiting for the she-cat to call out to her friends. *I can't outrun them. I can't fight so many of them on my own. StarClan, help me!*

But as the moments crept by, the she-cat did nothing. The she-cat *said* nothing. Hesitantly, Graystripe began to climb down the tree, and still she made no sound—just kept her clear gaze fixed on him all the while. She remained silent as he limped off into the trees, heading back to camp. Just before he plunged into the undergrowth, Graystripe glanced back over his shoulder and found her still watching him.

I'm safe . . . but why did she let me escape?

CHAPTER 8

❧

— Now —

The sun was beginning to dip toward the horizon, throwing long shadows behind Graystripe and Flipclaw as they toiled up the slope that led to the Tribe's mountain. The ground underpaw was harsh and gritty, with rocks poking up between stretches of sparse grass. Ahead, sheer cliffs rose up, bare except for a few cracks here and there where spindly thornbushes had rooted themselves.

A shiver passed through Graystripe as he gazed at what lay ahead. *I hope I'm right,* he thought. *I think this is the Tribe's mountain, but I've never been this way before. Millie and I followed a different path when we traveled to the lake.*

Graystripe had briefly considered going back to the ThunderClan camp to get directions from one of the cats who had been this way before. But then he would have risked being caught up again in the Clan's troubles, and besides, some cat would surely have insisted on coming with him.

I don't want that. And I've heard so many stories about that journey to the Tribe, when Lionblaze and the others went to help them, that I should be able to find my way.

Graystripe's paws tingled with anticipation, and a little anxiety, at the thought of meeting his son Stormfur again. It had been so long since Stormfur and his mate, Brook Where Small Fish Swim, had left the Clans, and Graystripe had never stopped missing him. But now he wondered how Stormfur would react to having his father turn up, unannounced, in his territory, among the cats he'd adopted in the place of his birth Clan.

The slope grew steeper, and at last the way forward dwindled to a narrow ledge leading upward alongside a sheer cliff. On the other side was a precipice falling into a deep gully where shadows were already gathering.

"For StarClan's sake, keep well away from the edge," Graystripe instructed Flipclaw. "If you slip over, you'll be crow-food, unless you can fly."

"I'll be careful, Graystripe," Flipclaw assured him, padding along with his pelt brushing the inner cliff face. "Isn't this great!?" he added excitedly. "I thought the sides of the stone hollow were high, but this is just amazing! Wait till I tell Bristlefrost and Thriftear—they'll be so envious, their whiskers will fall off!"

So Flipclaw is thinking about going home to ThunderClan, Graystripe thought with a twinge of satisfaction. Even though he was unsure about his own future, it pleased him somehow that the young warrior was feeling the pull of his kin.

"Keep your voice down," he warned him. "We're heading into the Tribe's territory, and I've heard there used to be rogues living around here, too. Remember we're intruders."

His pelt was prickling nervously, and he was almost certain

there were eyes watching them from the darkness among the rocks. But all they could do was go on; Graystripe just hoped that no cat would be so flea-brained as to attack them on this precarious path.

As the last of the sunlight faded, Graystripe saw that the ledge came to an abrupt end a couple of fox-lengths ahead. He halted, staggering as Flipclaw bumped into his hindquarters.

"What's the matter?" the young warrior asked, peering around Graystripe. "Why have we stopped?"

Graystripe's belly cramped at the thought of turning around and heading all the way back in what would soon be darkness. Then he noticed that up ahead the ledge began again, after a gap of about three tail-lengths.

"We'll have to jump," he mewed.

A voice came out of the shadows ahead. "Not unless we say you can."

Flipclaw let out a startled squeak and pressed closer to Graystripe, while a chill spread through Graystripe from ears to tail-tip. Two cats had appeared on the path at the far side of the gap. One was a brown tabby tom, the other a pale gray she-cat. Between the shadows and the colors of their pelts, they almost blended into the rocks behind them. Looking closer, he saw that they had streaked their pelts with mud, too, making it even easier to hide. Only their eyes—one pair of glowing amber, the other glittering green—stood out in the twilight.

The she-cat paced forward until she stood at the very edge of the gap. "Who are you, and what do you want?" she demanded brusquely.

Graystripe also stepped forward and gave a respectful nod of his head. "My name is Graystripe," he replied. "I'm looking for my kin."

The gray she-cat exchanged a wary glance with the tabby tom. "You have kin here?" she asked, sounding as if she didn't believe Graystripe at all.

"Yes, my son Stormfur," Graystripe replied.

"Stormfur!" the tabby tom exclaimed, sounding relieved and suddenly much more friendly. "Then you must be one of the Clan cats who live by the lake."

"Stormfur has told us lots of stories about you," the she-cat added, much less grudgingly. "Welcome to the territory of the Tribe of Rushing Water. My name is Moon Shining on Water, and this is Thorn That Grows in Cleft."

"We're cave-guards," Thorn mewed; he puffed out his chest proudly, showing Graystripe how seriously he took his responsibilities.

"And I'm Flipclaw." The young warrior had crowded close to gaze over Graystripe's shoulder, his eyes gleaming with interest at the sight of the strangers. "I'm a ThunderClan cat, like Graystripe."

Thorn and Moon both stepped backward to leave a clear space on the other side of the gap.

"Come over," Moon invited them. "We'll take you to the cave."

Eagerly Flipclaw slipped past Graystripe and took a run up to the gap, bunching his muscles and pushing off into a soaring leap. He landed safely on the other side with a tail-length to spare.

Graystripe, aware of his aching muscles after the long climb up the rocky path, prepared to follow. The gap seemed to yawn wider and wider with every heartbeat that passed. More afraid of making a fool of himself than of plummeting into the shadowy depths, he sized up the gap with a careful gaze, then gathered his hindquarters under him and thrust himself forward. To his relief, all four of his paws slammed down on the edge of the rock, and he straightened up, twitching his whiskers to show the others how unconcerned he was.

"Lead on," he meowed.

Moon took the lead as they continued along the ledge, with Graystripe and Flipclaw following, and Thorn bringing up the rear. Soon the path veered away into a narrow cleft with rock walls and huge boulders rising up on either side. At one point a shallow stream gurgled across the gully; Graystripe was grateful for the touch of cool water on his tired paws as he splashed through it.

By this time, the light had almost entirely faded, and Graystripe was glad that they had an escort. He was following Moon more by scent than by sight, and he was sure he would never have found the way in the dark.

At last they rounded a jutting outcrop, and the landscape opened out before them. Graystripe halted, staring. In front of them was a sheer wall of rock; a waterfall cascaded from the top, thundering down into a pool below. Starshine touched the falling water with silver and turned the spray above the pool into a shimmering cloud.

"It's beautiful!" Flipclaw breathed, staring at it in awe.

Graystripe shared his wonder. He had heard his Clanmates

describe the home of the Tribe of Rushing Water, but he could never have imagined it was as spectacular as this. He stood drinking in the sight, hardly aware of the spray that was soaking his pelt.

"This way," Thorn meowed briskly.

He took the lead as the four cats scrambled up the rocks beside the waterfall and headed along a path behind the crashing water.

"Watch where you're putting your paws," Graystripe warned Flipclaw; his pelt began to rise with nervousness. The rock had grown slippery beneath his pads, and that water could easily grab a careless cat and drag him into the depths below.

Imagine having to do this every day, he thought, *before you can get into your camp!*

"I'm fine," Flipclaw assured him, though there was a quiver in his voice. "But these mountain cats must be *really* good at climbing!"

Graystripe huffed out a thankful breath once he and Flipclaw reached the cave and he was able to gaze around in the dim light. The walls soared up into the shadows, where long fangs of stone hung downward from the roof. The floor stretched in front of Graystripe for countless fox-lengths.

The scents of many cats flowed over Graystripe, but at first he couldn't see where they were coming from. Then, as his eyes adjusted to the darkness, he saw that the cave was full of cats, perched on ledges or resting in dips on the cave floor, or beginning to approach him and Flipclaw, their eyes full of curiosity.

And in the middle of the cave was one cat in particular, a

muscular gray tom who halted, staring, for a moment, then bounded toward Graystripe and skidded to a halt in front of him.

"Graystripe?" he exclaimed, disbelief and joy warring in his eyes. "Is it really you?"

"Stormfur . . ." Graystripe let out a long purr. Stormfur looked very different from the last time he'd seen him, and yet he was entirely the kit Graystripe remembered. His heart flooded with warmth. *My son!* All the hazards of the journey had been worth it for this moment as he touched noses with Stormfur and breathed in his scent.

"I can hardly believe you're here!" Stormfur continued, stepping back a pace. "Brook—come and see. It's my father, Graystripe."

He gestured with his tail toward a pretty tabby she-cat, who padded forward with a welcoming gaze and dipped her head respectfully to Graystripe. "It's good to see you again," she mewed.

Graystripe nodded back. "It's very good to be here," he replied.

Four younger cats crowded up beside Brook, staring at Graystripe with unconcealed curiosity. "These are our kits," Brook introduced them proudly. "Lark That Sings at Dawn, Pine That Clings to Rock—"

"And we're Feather of Flying Hawk and Breeze That Rustles the Leaves," a young gray tom interrupted cheerfully. "It's great to meet you, Graystripe. Stormfur has told us lots about you."

Graystripe stood gazing at the group of cats in front of

him, bewildered at meeting so many of them. These cats were young and healthy, their eyes shining with excitement at meeting their long-lost kin. *And they're my kin, too; all these young cats are my kin.*

It was wonderful.

It had been a long time since he had seen Stormfur and Brook; his son wasn't a young cat anymore. His lithe figure had thickened out, and there was a hint of silver around his muzzle, but he still looked strong and vigorous, and there was wisdom in his eyes.

A prodding at Graystripe's side reminded him that Flipclaw was standing there, waiting quietly while Graystripe was united with his kin.

"I'm sorry, Flipclaw," Graystripe meowed. "Stormfur, Brook, this is Flipclaw, another ThunderClan warrior."

"Welcome, Flipclaw," Brook murmured, while Stormfur asked, "Is he your kin, Graystripe?"

For a moment, Graystripe was startled by the question, realizing how little Stormfur knew of the present Thunder-Clan, and of the kits he'd had with Millie. He wondered briefly what his life would have been like if he had gone back to RiverClan with Stormfur and Feathertail when they first returned there after the battle against BloodClan, or if he had been able to convince them to stay in ThunderClan. Or he might have left ThunderClan and accompanied Stormfur and Brook when they had returned to the Tribe after their time living by the lake. His life could have been different in so many ways, if he hadn't chosen loyalty to ThunderClan.

Maybe it was the wrong choice, he thought. *Maybe I should try to stay with the Tribe now, with my oldest surviving kit—my only living link to Silverstream.*

It was hard to imagine what else he could have done, when ThunderClan had been his life for so long. But he had seen it go through so many changes. Things had gotten bad, so bad that this ThunderClan was nothing like the Clan he'd grown up in and devoted his life to. All his memories of the old times had only emphasized the differences.

Still, Graystripe hadn't entirely lost his resolve. *Even though it's changed, I want to be there if my Clan needs me. But . . . do they?* He had no idea how he could help. *I don't know how I can help. I'm not even a warrior anymore.*

Meanwhile, Flipclaw had answered Stormfur's question, not at all intimidated by meeting so many strange cats at once. "No, I'm kin to Lionblaze. I think he traveled here when he was Lionpaw."

"Oh, I remember Lionblaze!" Brook purred. "Come and eat with us, and you can tell us all about him."

Stormfur and Brook, with their kits following, escorted Graystripe and Flipclaw across the cave to the Tribe's fresh-kill pile. As he drew closer to the back of the cave, Graystripe noticed the dark openings of two tunnels and wondered where they led. He was about to ask Stormfur, but his son forestalled him by beginning to speak again.

"It's funny you should turn up now," Stormfur began as he padded at Graystripe's side. "A strange thing happened the other day. Some of our prey-hunters met with a rogue on the other side of the mountain, closer to your old forest. He was asking about you by name."

Graystripe halted, blinking in bewilderment. "Asking about *me*?" Who could possibly be asking for him here, so close to the Tribe?

"Yes. But the prey-hunters didn't know you, so they weren't able to tell the rogue anything."

"That's the weirdest coincidence I've heard in a long time," Graystripe murmured as Stormfur urged him on again with a whisk of his tail. "I've no idea who the cat could be. Maybe one of the barn cats I met when I traveled to the lake with Millie, or a kittypet from the Twolegplace near the forest? I suppose that kittypet friend of Firestar's would still know my name, or one of Firestar's sister Princess's kits. They'd be grown cats by now."

"But why would they come looking for you?" Stormfur asked. "And why here?"

"That's the question," Graystripe responded. "Why would they?"

Stormfur just looked back at him with the same blank expression Graystripe could feel on his own face.

As the group reached the fresh-kill pile, a figure appeared from one of the openings at the back of the cave: a dark gray tom with gleaming amber eyes. The other cats drew aside respectfully as he approached, halting in front of Graystripe and Flipclaw.

Stormfur stepped forward and dipped his head to the newcomer. "Stoneteller, this is my father, Graystripe," he meowed.

"And this is Flipclaw, another ThunderClan cat. Graystripe, this is our Tribe's Healer, the Teller of the Pointed Stones."

Stoneteller stretched out a paw in a polite gesture of greeting. "Cats of ThunderClan." His voice rumbled in his chest. "You're very welcome here."

Graystripe bowed his head, remembering from his Clanmates' stories how powerful this cat was—not only the Tribe's leader, but its medicine cat as well. "I am honored to meet you," he responded.

Stoneteller fixed him with an amber stare, and Graystripe felt an uneasy prickling in his fur, as if this cat could see far more of him than he wanted to reveal.

Then Stoneteller gave him a tiny nod. "Eat, and rest," he meowed. "But perhaps later we will talk together, Graystripe." With that, he withdrew into the tunnel again.

Graystripe found himself relaxing as the Healer disappeared. The Tribe cats were friendly, and while their way of life was strange to him, they were not that different from the Clan cats he knew so well. But Stoneteller was another matter.

Maybe it's because he has all that power gathered into one cat, Graystripe thought. *I'm not sure I'm looking forward to talking to him again.*

Graystripe pushed his apprehension away as Stormfur padded up to him, carrying two pieces of fresh-kill. "Will you share prey with me?" he asked.

"Of course. Thank you," Graystripe replied, not sure what his son meant. His belly cramped with nervousness at the thought of getting something wrong and embarrassing his son in front of all these cats.

Then he spotted two of the Tribe cats a couple of tail-lengths away; each one took the first bite from a piece of prey, then pushed it over to the other to finish off. Relieved that now he knew what to do, Graystripe tore off a mouthful from the prey Stormfur set down in front of him, then passed the rest across to his son, receiving Stormfur's second piece in exchange.

"This is eagle," Stormfur told him. "Do you have eagles by the lake?"

Graystripe shook his head. "This is good, though," he meowed with his mouth full. "Very tasty."

Glancing around, he saw that Flipclaw was sharing fresh-kill with Stormfur's son Feather of Flying Hawk. Reassured that his young Clanmate was okay, he settled down to enjoy his meal and his son's company.

Stars were shining through the cave entrance, turning the waterfall to flickering silver. Graystripe noticed that his son was staring up at them, his eyes dark with memory. For a few moments Graystripe respected his silence, until the sound of kits playfully squealing shook Stormfur out of his contempla-tion.

"I sometimes wonder if Feathertail is up there, watching over the Tribe," he mused. "I'm not sure whether she would be in StarClan, or in the Tribe of Endless Hunting, where the Tribe's ancestors go. That seems more likely, since she sacri-ficed her life for them."

The realization struck Graystripe with the force of a blow:

this was where his daughter had died, far from her Clan. He remembered the stories of her courage, bringing down one of the stone fangs from the roof to kill the marauding lion-cat Sharptooth.

"Leafpool once told me that she'd been spotted in StarClan. But perhaps she visits both, somehow? If she is in the Tribe of Endless Hunting," he responded to Stormfur, "then she might be watching over us as we speak."

Stormfur let out a sigh. "She was so bright and fierce and openhearted," he murmured.

"Yes, she always reminded me of Silverstream," Graystripe agreed. "The mother you never knew. The first cat I loved. I had another mate later—Millie," he continued. "But she got sick and died too."

"I'm sorry." Stormfur reached out with his tail and drew it down Graystripe's side. "I can't imagine being without Brook, let alone losing two mates."

When the two cats had finished eating, Stormfur took Graystripe to drink from a pool near the back of the cave, fed by a stream that trickled out from among the rocks. Flipclaw was there drinking, too, while Feather watched with a friendly gleam in his eyes.

"I think the Tribe is great!" Flipclaw told Graystripe enthusiastically, shaking his head so that glittering water drops spun away from his whiskers. "They're just like a Clan, except they don't have to worry about the warrior code all the time. And there are no other Tribes to cause trouble."

"Well, we have a sort of code of our own," Feather pointed

out. "And the rogues who live farther down the mountain can be a problem sometimes."

"Oh, it's not the same," Flipclaw insisted with a sweep of his tail. "And you have this great place to live," he continued, gazing around admiringly at the vast cavern. "Plenty of room for all of you, and you're sheltered from the wind and rain. You don't even have to go out to find water."

Graystripe remembered how Flipclaw had been talking about his Clanmates just recently, on the way up the mountain. Now he wondered if the young warrior had changed his mind about going back. It was clear that he had fallen in love with the Tribe's way of life. *Suppose he decided to stay,* he thought. *It wouldn't be a bad choice, though it must be a hard life, up here among the rocks.*

"Feather has invited me to go hunting with him tomorrow," Flipclaw went on. "He says he can show me some new techniques."

"Yes, I'm a prey-hunter now," Feather announced. "I'd love to take Flipclaw out, if that's okay with you, Graystripe."

"Flipclaw is a warrior," Graystripe responded, proud that the lively and yet respectful Feather was his kin. "He doesn't need my permission."

"And it won't hold you up on your journey?" Feather asked.

Graystripe shook his head. "I guess we'll stay for a day or two at least."

"Great!" Flipclaw gave an excited little bounce, like the apprentice he had been not so long before. "I'm so glad I decided to come with you."

"Good." Graystripe touched his nose to the young warrior's ear.

"I've prepared sleeping hollows for you," Brook meowed, padding up to them. "Come this way."

She led the ThunderClan cats to a spot near the cave wall, where two dips in the stone floor had been lined with moss and feathers. Graystripe suddenly realized how very tired he was, and how inviting the nests were with their soft bedding.

"Thanks, that looks really comfortable," Flipclaw mewed, with a massive yawn. "Good night, Graystripe. Good night, Feather."

He immediately curled up in one of the hollows and was soon asleep, snoring gently with his tail wrapped over his nose.

Graystripe settled down in the hollow next to him, and slipped easily into sleep, too, exhausted by the day's long trek and the emotion of seeing his son again. But his sleep was restless; he seemed to be wandering down dark tunnels, now and again catching glimpses of a cat who was sometimes Silverstream, sometimes Feathertail, sometimes Millie, but however hard he tried, he could never catch up with her.

At last he jerked awake, sitting up with every hair on his pelt quivering, as if he had heard some yowl warning him of danger. It was still night; the flickering starlight still lit up the cave. Everything seemed peaceful: Graystripe could see the furry backs of cats curled up in their nests and hear the sound of their soft breath.

Then he spotted movement beside the silver screen of falling water, and recognized the outline of Stoneteller. His first instinct was to lie down again and pretend to he was still sleeping, but he knew that, sooner or later, he would have to confront the Tribe's Healer.

Okay, he thought with a sigh. *It might as well be now.*

CHAPTER 9

❧

— *Now* —

Graystripe hauled himself out of the nest and padded across the cave floor to stand in front of Stoneteller. "You said we might talk," he mewed, dipping his head in the deepest respect.

Stoneteller gave a nod of assent and settled himself on the ground with his paws stretched out in front of him. "I can see how troubled you are," he told Graystripe. "Why have you come to the Tribe? Can I help you find the path your paws are destined to tread?"

"You're right. I am troubled," Graystripe replied, sitting beside the Healer. His pelt prickled with apprehension that this stranger somehow knew him so well. Yet he wondered, too, whether Stoneteller could possibly understand his worries. *The Clans are so different from the Tribe. And would it be a betrayal to speak openly of our troubles to a Tribe cat?* "I came to see my son," he continued. "But that's not why I left my Clan. . . ."

Suddenly, gazing into those patient, receptive amber eyes, Graystripe felt a lump in his throat. All the words he wanted to say were choked up behind it. He realized that he wished he could pour out everything, from the first hints that something was wrong with Bramblestar, to the disastrous battle when so many Clan cats had died. For a moment he hesitated, then nodded to himself. "It all started last leaf-bare . . . ," he began.

Stoneteller listened without speaking until Graystripe had finished. "I have sensed a shadow in the direction of the Clans when I have consulted the pointed stones to direct my own Tribe," he mewed at last.

Graystripe didn't understand exactly what the Healer meant, but a shiver passed through his pads at the thought that Stoneteller had seen that. *Our troubles must be really bad, to reach so far.*

"The worst thing," he confessed, "is that the Clans still can't communicate with StarClan anymore. They've been silent for so long, even to our medicine cats. Have you been receiving messages from the Tribe of Endless Hunting?"

"Of course," Stoneteller replied. Hesitating for a moment, he continued, "Let me try to help you. Come with me."

He rose to his paws and led Graystripe across the cave and into the tunnel from which he had emerged earlier. The passage was dark, and Graystripe could feel his pelt brushing the walls on either side. Then he realized that moonlight was seeping in from somewhere ahead.

A moment later he padded forward into an open space, and he gasped in wonder at the sight in front of him. This was a smaller cave than the one he had left. A jagged hole in the roof let in the radiance of moon and stars; the light was reflected in pools of water that dappled the floor of the cave. It made him think of Mothermouth and the Moonstone near the old forest territory; Cinderpelt had described a similar shining in the darkness.

Most awe-inspiring of all were the pointed stones that projected from the roof, far more thickly than in the outer cavern. More stones grew up from the floor, some of them tall enough to join with the ones that hung downward, so that Graystripe felt as though he were standing at the edge of a stone forest.

"Come," Stoneteller invited him, weaving his way among the stone trees until he stood in the center of the cave.

Graystripe followed, and stood beside Stoneteller as he settled beside one of the glimmering pools, tucking his paws underneath him and stretching out his neck until his nose almost touched the surface. The sound of softly dripping water soothed Graystripe, and he waited patiently while Stoneteller gazed into the depths of the pool.

At last the Tribe's Healer raised his head to face Graystripe. "There is indeed a shadow lying in the direction where your Clans live," he reported. "Perhaps that is what stops you from communicating with StarClan."

"But what does that mean?" Graystripe asked. "Is there anything I can do to help my Clan?" *Or am I just a useless elder?* he added silently to himself.

"Wait," Stoneteller responded. "I will look again."

Graystripe watched as the Healer bowed his head once more over the pool. His own thoughts were whirling. Stoneteller was still able to see a shadow that lay over the lake, even though StarClan couldn't communicate with the Clans. And he could still reach the Tribe of Endless Hunting.

He watched Stoneteller, whose eyes were closed as he seemed to listen for any message from the Tribe. It was exactly as he'd always imagined medicine cats looking as they touched their noses to the Moonpool. *But what's different here, that lets the Tribe still contact their ancestors? Why is it that StarClan can't—or won't—reach out to us?* He wished he could find an answer, but what hope did he have, when even the medicine cats didn't know?

Anticipation tingled in Graystripe's pads as he wondered whether Stoneteller might be able to give him an answer to that vital question.

He lost count of time as he stood in the eerie stone forest, listening to the whisper of water drops and watching the shifting light on the surface of the pools. He was almost startled when the Healer straightened up once more and faced him.

"Does the Tribe of Endless Hunting have any message for me?" he asked hoarsely. The Clan hadn't heard from StarClan for so many moons; it made Graystripe hungry now for any guidance the Tribe's Healer could offer.

Stoneteller inclined his head. "They tell me that you still have a part to play," he replied. "You must leave the Tribe and continue your journey. So sleep now. When you leave here, you will need all your strength."

As Graystripe settled into his sleeping hollow again, he was more confused than ever. He felt a massive relief that he still had a part to play in the life of his Clan, but he couldn't imagine what that part could be. That knowledge was something that the Tribe's ancestors hadn't seen fit to share.

The Tribe of Endless Hunting sounds just like StarClan, he thought. *Neither of them can give a cat a straight answer.*

Stoneteller seemed to be suggesting that he should return to ThunderClan. But cold dread soaked through Graystripe from ears to tail-tip, as if he had stepped into the icy waters of a leaf-bare lake, when he thought of returning without any kind of guidance for himself or his Clan. In the days since he had left the ThunderClan camp, he had felt himself growing again: hunting, traveling, making decisions, just as he had when he was younger.

If I go back now, I'll dwindle into an elder again, he thought. *And maybe that really is all I am. But I have to find out what I'm meant to do, before I set one paw on the path that leads back to ThunderClan.*

"StarClan, can you hear me?" he murmured, muffling his voice with his own tail so as not to disturb any of the cats curled up around him. "Or maybe the Tribe of Endless Hunting is listening to me. If you are, please send me a sign. Show me what I'm supposed to do."

The cavern was silent, except for the gentle snores of sleeping cats and the endless rush of the waterfall. Nothing disturbed the shimmering light that that flooded into the cave, showing him that outside, the moon was shining through the waterfall.

"I guess that's a no, then," Graystripe muttered to himself.

But a voice inside his head seemed to say, *Not yet.*

Heaving a massive sigh, Graystripe closed his eyes. Sleep

flooded over him as gently as a mother curling herself around her kits.

When Graystripe first woke, he couldn't remember where he was. He opened his eyes expecting to see the interlacing branches of the elders' den, but instead he was surrounded by walls of stone, with jagged spikes pointed down toward him. A rushing sound filled his ears.

Blinking, he sat up. A stone floor stretched in front of him as far as the glimmering cascade of the waterfall that covered the cave opening. At the sight of it all, Graystripe's memories came flooding back: the journey to the mountains, his reunion with his son Stormfur, and the unsettling encounter with Stoneteller. He sprang to his paws, shaking his pelt to dislodge the scraps of moss and feathers that clung to it.

Now I have to find some answers!

Graystripe stepped out of his sleeping hollow and sat down to give himself a quick grooming. Here and there he could see Tribe cats padding purposefully to and fro; some kits were batting a pebble across the floor, while an older cat was demonstrating a hunting move to a group of apprentices—to-bes, they were called in the Tribe, he remembered. Graystripe's pelt prickled with embarrassment as he realized that he had slept late, and the day was well advanced.

Before he had finished his grooming, he spotted Brook Where Small Fish Swim trotting across the cave floor toward him. Graystripe rose to his paws and dipped his head politely to her as she halted beside him.

"Greetings, Graystripe," she meowed. "You slept well?"

"Too well, I think," Graystripe responded ruefully. "I'm sorry."

"No need to apologize," Brook told him. "You must have been exhausted after your journey. Are you hungry?" she continued briskly. "The hunting patrols aren't back yet, but I can probably find you something."

Graystripe's belly had produced a small warning growl at the thought of food, but he shook his head. "I'm fine, thanks. I can wait."

Brook sat down beside him, licked one forepaw, and began to wash her ears. "Stormfur is leading a border patrol," she mewed. "And Feather took Flipclaw out with Pine and some of the other prey-hunters. I hope that's okay."

"I told Feather last night, Flipclaw doesn't need to ask for my permission," Graystripe replied. *But all the same, I'll be glad when he's back. We need to discuss what we're going to do next.*

"I think I'll go out for a breath of air," he went on, rising to his paws. "And to stretch my legs."

"Be careful on the path behind the falls," Brook warned him. "It's easy to slip."

"Thanks, I will."

Graystripe dipped his head once more to Brook, then bounded across the cavern and headed along the ledge until he emerged on the mountainside. An easy scramble took him up onto a flat rock from where he could look around. The air was cold and clear, and he drew it deep into his lungs.

In every direction, as far as he could see, peaks stretched

away, row upon row of them, until the most distant were lost in a misty blur. Close by he could see the gray rock walls seamed with cracks, where scrawny thornbushes had rooted themselves. Here and there were taller trees, dark pines like the ones that grew on ShadowClan territory.

The only other vegetation he could see was around the edges of the pool at the foot of the waterfall.

How can cats possibly live here? he asked himself. *Always to feel hard rock underpaw, never to taste the green scents of the forest . . .*

Movement down below alerted Graystripe, and he spotted four cats emerging from a deep gully and skirting the pool as they headed for the end of the path. Three of them were carrying the body of an enormous bird: Its brown wings dangled limply, almost tripping the cats who carried it, while its cruel talons stuck out at odd angles.

I suppose that's an eagle, Graystripe thought. *Great StarClan, it must have taken some catching!*

The fourth cat—Graystripe recognized him as Thorn, one of the cave-guards who had escorted him and Flipclaw the night before—brought up the rear, scanning his surroundings carefully and keeping watch on the sky. Graystripe had a vision of another vast bird swooping down on the patrol and carrying off a cat in its massive claws.

The prey-hunters climbed up to the path and disappeared behind the waterfall. Thorn paused for a moment, with a nod of greeting for Graystripe.

"You had a good hunt," Graystripe remarked.

"The best!" Thorn responded cheerfully. "The Tribe

should eat well tonight." He went on and vanished after the rest of the patrol.

A chilly breeze had arisen, ruffling Graystripe's fur. The sun was already beginning to dip down behind the mountain peaks, casting long shadows into the clefts and gullies lower down. He realized that he had slept almost the whole day away.

Graystripe rose, preparing to leap down from his rock and return to the cave, when once again he spotted movement on the mountainside. This time it was a single she-cat, racing along a ledge so narrow that Graystripe thought she would lose her balance at any moment and plummet into the depths.

The cat slipped and scrambled down the last rocky slope to the edge of the pool, then began to climb up to the end of the path. Now that she was close to him, Graystripe could see her staring eyes and bristling fur; something had obviously terrified her.

"What's the matter?" he called.

The she-cat ignored him; Graystripe guessed that she hadn't even realized that he was there. She disappeared up the path; Graystripe jumped down from his rock and followed her, his heart beginning to thump with foreboding.

By the time he reached the cavern, the she-cat was the center of an anxious huddle, every cat demanding to know what had happened.

"Fetch Stoneteller!" the she-cat gasped. "There's been an accident."

A horrible premonition gathered in Graystripe's chest, and he felt his shoulder fur beginning to rise. *Flipclaw . . .* He pressed forward, weaving his way through the group of cats until he reached the she-cat's side.

Brook was standing close to her, resting her tail on the younger cat's shoulder to calm her. "Take it easy, Crest," she mewed. "Tell us what happened."

The she-cat, Crest, took a couple of breaths, her chest heaving, before she replied. "We were hunting. . . . There was a rockslide. Feather and that ThunderClan cat were buried!"

"No!" Brook let out the single word as an anguished wail, then clamped her jaws shut, clearly fighting for self-control.

Graystripe took a pace that brought him to her side. "We have to rescue them."

Brook nodded. "We will. Of course we will. But Stone-teller—"

She broke off as the crowd of cats parted, and Graystripe realized that some cat had alerted the Tribe's Healer; he emerged from his tunnel and paced forward to join them.

"Crest of Snowy Mountain," he meowed, dipping his head. "Report."

Crest began her story again, more calmly this time and with more detail. Pine had been scrambling up a slope in pursuit of a rabbit when his weight had dislodged a rock and brought down an avalanche of soil, grit, and pebbles. Feather had seen it coming, and had yowled a warning to Flipclaw, who was standing directly underneath the cascading stones.

"Feather leaped toward him to thrust him out of the way.

But it was too late," Crest finished, her voice shaking. "They were both buried."

Stoneteller's response was swift. "Then we'll go and get them out."

Graystripe remembered that some cat had told him the Tribe's Healer never left the cave, but obviously, for an emergency like this, he was prepared to break the Tribe's custom. "I'm coming with you," he announced.

For a moment Stoneteller looked as if he might argue, then gave Graystripe a curt nod. "You too, Brook," he meowed, and beckoned with his tail to Thorn and another sturdy, muscular tom. "Crest, lead the way."

Resolute now that the rescue mission was underway, Crest led Graystripe and the others out onto the mountainside. At the bottom of the rocks beside the pool Graystripe spotted more cats: Stormfur, returning at the head of his patrol. In a few tense words, Brook told him what had happened.

"I'll come," Stormfur responded, ordering his cats back to the cave, then bringing up the rear of the rescue patrol as it headed deeper into the mountains.

As the last sunlight disappeared and the shadows gathered more thickly, Graystripe was afraid that one careless paw step would send him crashing into the depths. But he forced himself to continue, grimly determined to keep up with the experienced Tribe cats, and do what he could to help his Clanmate.

If Flipclaw is even alive, he thought, with cold claws gripping his heart. *Oh, StarClan, please don't let him be dead!*

Finally Crest led the way onto a small grass-covered plateau. At the far side, a steep, rocky slope stretched upward for many fox-lengths. Graystripe could see a raw scar where earth and stones had fallen away to form a massive heap at the foot of the slope. Two cats were digging frantically at the debris.

"Feather!" Brook sprang forward. "Crest said you were buried!"

"I was." The young gray tom was shaking, and his eyes were distraught as he turned toward his mother and the rest of the cats. Graystripe could see that his pelt was clotted with soil and grit, and blood trickled from a cut on his forehead. "But only at the edge. Flipclaw is still under there."

"Stay back now, and rest." Stoneteller took over, authority in his voice. "You too, Pine," he added to Feather's brother, who was still clawing at the heap of debris. "Stay with Feather, and keep watch for hawks. Give the rest of us space to work."

Reluctantly Feather and Pine withdrew to the edge of the plateau, while Stoneteller and the rest of the cats attacked the heap. Graystripe found a place between the Healer and Stormfur and began scooping at the dirt with his forepaws, kicking it out of the way with his powerful back legs.

The task seemed to go on forever. Graystripe's muscles ached with effort; grit stung his eyes and earth clotted his claws, yet he still went on digging. He knew he would never forgive himself if he gave up before they had uncovered Flipclaw—or Flipclaw's body.

How long can a cat survive underneath all this?

At first the twilight deepened until Graystripe couldn't

even see his own working paws. But gradually he became aware of the darkness lifting and a silvery light washing over the rocks. He knew that the moon must have risen, but he was too intent on his task to look up and see it.

Eventually Stormfur let out a hoarse cry. "Here!"

Glancing aside, Graystripe blinked the grit from his eyes and spotted what looked like a tabby snake emerging from the debris. He realized that it was Flipclaw's tail. He plunged forward, poised to dig deeper and uncover the rest of his Clanmate, but Stoneteller stopped him with a paw on his shoulder.

"Careful," he meowed. "Don't bring down any more on top of him."

Graystripe nodded understanding. Together he and Stormfur scraped cautiously at the dirt, freeing Flipclaw bit by bit: his hindquarters and the length of his body, and at last his head and his outstretched forepaws. Finally they were able to lift him clear and lay him on the grass well away from the landslide.

Flipclaw didn't move. His pelt was covered with soil and grit; his jaws gaped open, clogged with earth, and his eyes were closed. Not even his whiskers twitched.

"He's dead!" Graystripe choked out. He felt a clutching in his chest as panic gripped him.

This is my fault. I brought him here. If I hadn't, he would still be alive, maybe back in ThunderClan, or exploring with Flywhisker and Snaptooth.

"Let me look." Stoneteller shouldered Graystripe aside and crouched beside the motionless tom. "We won't give up yet."

Gently he began to paw at the dirt in Flipclaw's mouth,

freeing his airway so that he could breathe. Graystripe couldn't bear to watch. Instead he raised his head to gaze at the sky.

The moon floated above the peaks, seeming almost close enough to touch. The mountains looked beautiful under the flood of silver light, but Graystripe's heart ached at the thought of the deadly hazards beneath the beauty.

His gaze was drawn to one rock in particular, a narrow pinnacle stretching upward like a cat's raised paw. Under the moonlight it seemed to glow, dazzling and ice-cold.

That must be what the Moonstone looks like, Graystripe thought, blinking against the blaze.

A cough distracted him, along with a quivering cry from Brook. "He's alive!"

Looking down again, Graystripe saw Flipclaw's body convulsing as he coughed up mouthfuls of grit and earth. His eyes fluttered open and gazed up in blank confusion.

"What happened?" he rasped.

"There was a landslide, and you were buried," Stormfur explained, resting a calming paw on Flipclaw's shoulder. "Just take it easy, and you'll be fine."

"Can you stand up?" Stoneteller asked.

Flipclaw tried to scramble to his paws, only to let out a gasp of pain and collapse again as one of his hind legs refused to support him. "My leg . . . I think it's broken."

Stoneteller bent over the hind leg that had given way and felt along its length, his gaze fixed in concentration. Graystripe watched him, sick with anxiety. *What will happen to Flipclaw now? Will his leg heal properly? How will he ever get home to ThunderClan?*

Finally Stoneteller sat up. "The leg isn't broken," he announced. "Just dislocated. I can put it back into its socket." Glancing around, he continued, "Stormfur, hold his shoulders down. Graystripe, keep his other hind leg still."

"Will it hurt?" Flipclaw asked nervously.

"Yes, but it will be over quickly," the Healer replied. Placing one forepaw on Flipclaw's hindquarter, he grasped his leg with his other forepaw and gave a swift, firm thrust. Flipclaw let out an earsplitting screech, but Graystripe, bending close, could still hear the soft click as the leg slid back into place.

Stoneteller gave a satisfied nod. "Now try to get up."

Trembling with the reaction, Flipclaw struggled to his paws and tentatively put weight on the injured leg. "Hey, that's much better!" he exclaimed. He took a few paw steps to and fro, and though he was limping, he obviously wasn't in much pain. "Thanks, Stoneteller!"

"My pleasure," the Healer murmured. More briskly, he added, "Even so, you'd better not try walking back to the cave. Climb up on my back." As Flipclaw hung back, clearly reluctant, Stoneteller gave an impatient flick of his tail. "Come on. We haven't got all night."

Flipclaw scrambled up onto Stoneteller's back, digging his claws deep into the older cat's fur. Stormfur steadied him as the Healer moved off, and the rest of the cats followed.

Graystripe was preparing to bring up the rear when he thought he heard a distant voice calling his name from somewhere behind him. Glancing over his shoulder, he gazed once more at the tall, shining rock. This time a cat was poised at the very top; though she was far away, he could make out every hair on her pelt and her soft, plumy tail, and see the glow of love in her blue eyes.

"Feathertail!" he gasped.

He wanted to spring up, to twine tails with his lost, beloved daughter and drink in her sweet scent. But the rock was too far away; trying to climb up there would be too hazardous. It was as inaccessible as the distant Moonstone. . . .

Feathertail stared at him for a long moment, her silver pelt shimmering brightly. Then her unblinking blue gaze fell to the rock beneath her paws. She looked up at Graystripe again, narrowing her eyes and pushing her head forward.

As if she's trying to make me understand something, he thought. *But what?*

He opened his mouth to call out a question, but hesitated. A sudden image of Firestar flickered through his mind. As Feathertail again stared pointedly down at the rock on which she stood, Graystripe felt like whatever she *was* trying to tell him was a piece of prey in his mind, one he was so close to catching.

Stoneteller's cave reminded me of the Moonstone, and now Feathertail has appeared on this rock, which looks just the way Firestar described it to me. . . . Were the ancestral spirits trying to make him remember the Moonstone? Why?

Graystripe's paws tingled with excitement as he began to realize what was happening. When he looked back to Feathertail, he saw a teasing light in her eyes, her muzzle pursed in amusement.

He nodded at her. "I'm a stupid furball," he muttered to himself. "I asked for a sign, and when it came, I almost ignored it!"

Thoughts were flickering through his mind like minnows in a pool. *Is it possible that the reason we can't communicate with StarClan is the Moonpool, not StarClan itself? After all, the Tribe can still contact their ancestors. And our medicine cats never had trouble contacting our ancestors at the Moonstone.*

But that was back in the old territories. Graystripe's excitement grew as he wondered whether he was being guided back there—or back to whatever was left of it—to find the Moonstone. *Could I find StarClan for the Clans?* Certainty began to swell inside him as he realized that there might be a purpose to his leaving his Clan, beyond what was happening in his own head. Perhaps he could carry out an important service for ThunderClan! *Then I wouldn't have to feel guilty about leaving Squirrelflight. Maybe I'll return to her with vital news!*

"Graystripe!" That was Brook's voice, close by and with an edge of impatience. "Don't get left behind. You'll never find your way back by yourself."

Turning, Graystripe saw that the tabby she-cat was waiting for him at the edge of the plateau. Stoneteller and the other cats had already vanished.

"Sorry. I'm coming," he meowed.

As he followed Brook, he cast a final glance back at the rock. Feathertail had disappeared, and the unnatural glow had faded, its work done. "Good-bye, Feathertail," he whispered. Glimpsing her again had reopened the wound of her loss, and yet, as he quickened his pace to catch up with the others, he felt grateful for the reassurance that she still lived on among the stars.

She's shown me a way that I can solve the Clans' problems, he thought. *I know now what I have to do—I must see if StarClan will send me a message through the Moonstone. Tomorrow I will set out for our old territory.*

CHAPTER 10

❧

— Then —

As Graystripe limped painfully back to camp following BloodClan's attack, he heard rustling in the undergrowth ahead of him. Stiffening, still afraid that BloodClan might still be lurking around, he crouched down behind a gnarled oak root and tasted the air, only to relax as strong ThunderClan scent wafted over him. A moment later, Ashfur, Thornclaw, and Cloudtail emerged from a clump of ferns.

Graystripe rose to meet them. "Thank StarClan it's you!" he exclaimed. "Have you seen Brambleclaw and Dustpelt?"

"Yes, they're both back in camp," Thornclaw replied, "and they sent us to find you. Dustpelt was afraid that you were dead."

"Not yet," Graystripe responded grimly. "But that might change if we don't do something about BloodClan. We have to drive them off before they get any more of a claw into our territory."

Escorted by his Clanmates, Graystripe returned to the camp and headed toward the medicine cat's den. As he approached, Dustpelt appeared from the fern tunnel; he was moving stiffly, and he had a poultice plastered to one shoulder with cobwebs to keep it in place.

"Are you okay?" Graystripe asked.

"I'll live," Dustpelt replied sourly. "But right now I'm going back to my nest, to sleep for a moon!"

"Before you do," Graystripe began, thinking this was as good a time as any to confront his Clanmate, "what's this I hear about Ashfur pushing for you to be deputy?"

Dustpelt, who had started to move away, whipped around and stared at him, blank astonishment in his amber eyes, That look was all the evidence Graystripe needed that his Clanmate had known nothing about Ashfur's demands.

"*What?*" he choked out.

"Ashfur tells me that I ought to appoint you deputy while Firestar is away," Graystripe explained, his tone even. "And maybe after Firestar comes back, too, if I read him right."

Dustpelt looked appalled. He wasn't a cat who was easily confused, but for a moment he scuffled his claws in the earth of the camp floor, seeming as bewildered as a kit out of the nursery for the first time.

"Graystripe, I promise you, I knew nothing about this," he mewed hoarsely. "Or, no—I heard one or two rumors, but there are always rumors, especially now that the Clan is unsettled, with our leader away. I paid no attention, and Ashfur has never spoken to me directly. Is any other cat in on this?"

Graystripe tilted his head, thinking. "Cloudtail . . . maybe Mousefur. But it's Ashfur who is at the bottom of it."

Dustpelt was rapidly recovering his composure. "Of course

I'd like to be deputy—what cat wouldn't?" he admitted. His mouth twisted with sardonic amusement. "But I know that with Firestar as leader, it's never going to happen. I'm not his favorite cat—or yours, either. But what I *am* is a loyal ThunderClan warrior. If I think you're—or Firestar is about to do something particularly mouse-brained, you can bet your tails I'll tell you about it. But when it comes to claws, with BloodClan or any other enemy, I'll back you all the way." He paused, then added in a curiously humble tone, "Do you believe me, Graystripe?"

Graystripe remembered how he and Dustpelt had fought back to back against the overwhelming numbers of the Blood-Clan patrol. "Every word, Dustpelt," he replied.

"Thank you. As for Ashfur," Dustpelt continued, "you can leave him to me. I'll soon give him a flea in his ear. And if I hear one more word of this, I'll make him wish he'd never been kitted. He would always argue, you know," he went on, "even when he was an apprentice. If I wanted to hunt near Snakerocks, he would complain that Fourtrees was better. Well," he finished, "it's about time he learned he can't always have his own way."

With a nod to the tabby warrior, Graystripe headed into the medicine cat's den. Thankfulness flooded over him to think that on top of all his other problems he didn't have to worry about a rebellion in his own camp, or cats undermining him when they ought to be giving him their support.

At the end of the fern tunnel, he found Cinderpelt dabbing herb pulp onto Longtail's eyes.

"That should help," she mewed briskly, before turning to

Graystripe. "Thank StarClan you're back," she continued. "Dustpelt told me what happened. Where does it hurt?"

"Everywhere!" Graystripe responded.

He flopped down and began to clean his fur, while Cinderpelt fetched herbs from the cleft in the rock at the far side of her den. Then she gave Graystripe a good sniff from ears to tail.

"That doesn't look too bad," she meowed. "Mostly just scratches, and I guess you'll have bruises later. There are a few bites, and we'll need to keep an eye on those. I think you should stay here in my den for a couple of days. For now, let's get you started with marigold."

While Graystripe relaxed and let the medicine cat treat his wounds, he began to hear voices coming from outside the den.

"It worries me, the way the BloodClan cats thrashed Graystripe and an entire patrol just now." Graystripe recognized Ashfur's voice. "Firestar would have weathered the attack better. Maybe Graystripe just isn't up to leading us."

So Dustpelt hasn't spoken to him yet, Graystripe thought. *I hope he gets a move on.*

"But there were *eight* of them!" That was Brambleclaw's voice, raised in protest. "What were three cats supposed to do?"

"Where is Firestar, anyway?" Cloudtail grumbled. Clearly, he and the older warriors weren't taking much notice of Brambleclaw. "His Clan is in danger, and he should be *here*. A leader belongs with his Clan."

"Maybe Firestar hasn't gone on a journey for StarClan

at all," Mousefur suggested. "I said it earlier and I'll say it again— maybe he's gone back to his kittypet life."

Graystripe let out a tiny growl of irritation.

"Did I hurt you?" Cinderpelt asked, pausing in her application of cobwebs to a particularly bloody scratch.

"No, not at all," Graystripe replied. He glanced outside, and Cinderpelt followed his gaze, then gave him a knowing look.

"Perhaps," she said, returning her attention to the cobwebs, "you just need to refocus your attention."

Graystripe twitched his whiskers in amusement. *I suppose she's right—I can't let every little thing I overhear get to me.* He glanced around the den and saw Longtail shifting around in his nest. "I wish I could see," he complained, his whiskers twitching in frustration. "Then I might be more help."

"It's not your fault, Longtail," Graystripe reassured him. "Rest up, and you'll feel better soon." But as the other tom settled down, Graystripe leaned close to Cinderpelt.

"I can't stay here for long," he said softly. "Whatever the warriors believe about him, Firestar left me in charge. I'll have to lead ThunderClan against our enemies."

The next morning, Graystripe awoke to the sound of rain drumming on the roof of interlaced ferns that covered the medicine cat's den. Some drops were getting through, trickling into his fur. Shivering with the chill, he rose to his paws. Longtail was still curled up asleep in his nest, but Cinderpelt raised her head and gave Graystripe a doubtful look.

"Are you sure you're fit for this?" she asked.

"I feel absolutely fine," Graystripe lied. In fact, he felt as if every fox in the forest had been tearing at him with claws and fangs. "We need to get moving."

He dragged himself out into the open, cringing under the onslaught of the rain, and splashed his way across the camp until he could slip between the branches of the warriors' den. Most of the cats were still asleep; under ordinary circumstances, no patrols would go out until the worst of the rain eased off.

"Wake up!" he yowled. "We have to deal with BloodClan."

The warriors began to stir, letting out groans at the thought of leaving their cozy nests. When Cloudtail stuck his head up, scraps of moss clung to his white fur. "You're joking, right?"

Graystripe didn't bother to reply. He waited, rain streaming from his fur, until the Clan woke fully.

"You all know that BloodClan is back," Graystripe meowed when he confirmed that every cat was listening. "Today we need to survey our entire territory and search for any sign of them. I want two groups to patrol the border in opposite directions. Dustpelt, Brambleclaw, you're not fit to go out after yesterday's battle, but you can stay here to guard the camp."

"BloodClan won't get in here!" Brambleclaw promised him.

"Good." Graystripe gave his Clanmates a brisk nod. He was trying to seem strong and decisive, but he was chilled by more than the rain when he thought about what might happen if they did find the BloodClan cats today. *Still, I have to stay strong for ThunderClan.* "Sort yourselves out," he finished. "I'll lead one patrol; Ashfur, you can lead the other."

Maybe giving him some responsibility will stop him complaining.

Thick clouds had covered the sky all day, and the gradual fading of the light was the only sign that the sun was going down. Graystripe shook rain from his fur and peered into the forest, scenting the air near the site of the previous day's battle. Throughout the day, his patrols had been searching for the BloodClan cats, crossing the forest from end to end after the border patrol had been completed, and they hadn't found so much as a whisker. But the rain—stopping and starting again ever since the cloudburst of the morning—made it hard to pick up scent. It was unsettling, how thoroughly the rain had washed away any sign of yesterday's bloodshed. Graystripe felt a worm of uneasiness in his belly at the thought of what they might have missed.

Beside him, Mousefur gave her pelt a shake. "Let's head back to camp," she suggested.

"That's the best idea I've heard all day," Thornclaw agreed. "We're all tired and hungry."

Graystripe was surprised that Thornclaw would admit to being tired, but then he spotted the tabby warrior glancing at his apprentice, Sootpaw. The small gray tom was shivering, and looked utterly worn out and miserable.

"Come on, Graystripe," Mousefur urged him. "We're doing no good out here."

"Yes, we can't search the forest forever," Cloudtail meowed. "I know that we need to keep a watch for BloodClan, but we have to take care of *our* Clan first. We need time to hunt and rest, as well as patrol."

"Okay." Graystripe knew that his Clanmates were right. "Let's go."

But as he led the way back to camp, he couldn't stop glancing over his shoulder, his pelt prickling nervously. Because there was no way to track BloodClan's scent in the rain, he was acutely aware that the rogue cats could be anywhere. He expected at any moment to see eyes in the gathering dark, looking back at him.

You can lurk and spy on us all you want, he thought grimly. *But I won't let you take ThunderClan. . . .*

CHAPTER 11

❧

— *Now* —

"I have to leave," Graystripe meowed. "This morning. Now."

He and Stormfur were standing by the screen of perpetually falling water, where morning light dappled the floor. Most of the Tribe cats had gone out on patrol, and the cave was almost empty.

"But why?" There was hurt and a trace of anger in Stormfur's eyes as he gazed at his father. "I thought you were going to stay for a good long time—maybe forever." He pressed his nose into his father's shoulder. "You're our kin. You'd be welcome in the Tribe."

For a heartbeat, Graystripe ached to accept his offer, longed to stay here where he had kin and friends, far away from the troubles of ThunderClan. He knew how impossible that was, how he would never forgive himself if he didn't do all he could for his Clan. Yet he still wondered what would have happened if he had stayed in RiverClan with Stormfur and Feathertail, had been more of a presence in their lives. Seeing all his kin here was a sweet but painful reminder of a part of his life he rarely thought about now . . . and how easily it might all have gone in another direction.

What would have happened if Silverstream had lived, and we could have been a real family? Graystripe's heart ached with the question. *Everything would have been so different!*

"Thank you, but no," he mewed regretfully to Stormfur. "I can't stay. I need to travel to our old territory and see if I can help the Clans by visiting the Moonstone."

Stormfur blinked at him in surprise. "Why on earth would you want to do that?" he asked.

"I had a . . . a kind of a sign, last night," Graystripe explained. "I saw a rock out there shining in the moonlight, and it looked just the way the Moonstone must look."

"Rocks shine in the moonlight all the time," Stormfur pointed out, clearly unconvinced.

"I know, but this was . . . different." Graystripe knew that he could never convey to Stormfur or any cat how the sight of the glowing rock had made him feel. But there was one thing that Stormfur especially wouldn't be able to ignore. "I saw Feathertail," he added.

Stormfur's eyes widened, and he let out a gasp of astonishment. "Feathertail? Really? How was she?"

"Beautiful as always." Graystripe had known that Stormfur wouldn't be able to dismiss a sign that had come from his sister. "It was like she was showing me the rock, and telling me to go to the Moonstone."

"I see." For a moment Stormfur blinked thoughtfully. "But I still don't understand what good you think it will do."

"Stoneteller can still contact the Tribe of Endless Hunting," Graystripe replied, "so what if what's keeping StarClan from contacting us isn't StarClan itself, but the Moonpool? Maybe something is blocking the contact there, or it's just not the right place anymore."

To Graystripe's disappointment, Stormfur just looked confused, eyeing him doubtfully.

Graystripe tried to explain. "You know that the Moonstone is how the medicine cats used to speak with StarClan back in the old forest territory. If I travel back there and visit the Moonstone, I can try to contact StarClan, and maybe even Firestar, that way! And maybe they can tell me how to make the connection again by the lake."

At last he saw understanding begin to dawn in Stormfur's eyes. "Well, I wish you luck with that," he murmured. "I have to admit I would like to see our territory again. If it weren't for Brook and my kin here in the Tribe, I might come with you. Fish from the pool below the waterfall just doesn't taste the same. And I miss the sound of the river, gurgling through the reeds at the edge of the RiverClan camp."

"It won't be like that now," Graystripe reminded him. "I have to keep telling myself that, so I'm prepared. The Twolegs did so much damage before we left, so who knows what they've done to the territories by now? I may not even recognize our old hunting grounds. It's possible the Moonstone won't even be there anymore."

His son gave his pelt a shake. "True. Maybe it's better not to know. But, Graystripe," he went on hesitantly, "no matter what happens, you'll always have a place here. . . . Maybe *after* you try to contact StarClan, you'll reconsider settling down with us?"

"I'll think about it," Graystripe promised, though he wasn't ready to predict whether he'd be looking for a new place to settle, or returning to ThunderClan. *If my journey is successful, the answer will be clear.* "I'll certainly come back for another visit on my way home."

"And what about Flipclaw?" Stormfur continued. "Will he want to come with you? I don't think he'll be fit to travel for a day or two at least."

"I don't think he'll want to come," Graystripe responded after a moment's thought. His paws were itching to be on his way; he certainly didn't want to waste time here in the Tribe's territory until Flipclaw's leg was properly healed. "In fact, I think he might like to stay here. He's really enthusiastic about your way of life, and he's getting along very well with Feather."

Stormfur nodded agreement. "Yes, I'd noticed that. Well, he'd have to get permission from our Healer, but I can't see Stoneteller turning down a trained warrior."

"We'd better go and ask Flipclaw," Graystripe meowed.

Stormfur led the way across the cavern to where Flipclaw was sitting in his sleeping hollow, vigorously grooming his fur. He looked up as the two older toms approached. "Hi, Graystripe, Stormfur," he greeted them.

"How are you feeling, Flipclaw?" Graystripe asked.

"Fine," Flipclaw replied. "Except I don't think I'll ever get all this grit out of my fur. Stoneteller came to see me earlier," he went on. "He says my leg is going to be okay, but I need to rest it for a few days."

"Good," Graystripe purred. "And that's partly what I want to talk to you about. I had a sign last night, and I need to go back to the old territories, to see if I can speak to StarClan through the Moonstone. Maybe even see Firestar again."

Flipclaw blinked in bewilderment. "The Moonstone?"

"Where our medicine cats used to make contact with the spirits of our warrior ancestors, when we lived in the old forest," Graystripe explained. "Didn't the elders tell you any of those stories when you were a kit?"

"Oh, sure, now I remember. And you actually want to go back there?" Flipclaw asked, sounding as if he felt the whole idea was seriously weird, but he was too polite to say so.

Graystripe couldn't bear to repeat all the reasons he had come to his decision. "The thing is," he continued, "I feel I have to leave right away. It can't wait until you're fit to travel."

"Oh, that's okay, Graystripe. Actually . . ." Flipclaw hesitated for a moment, looking slightly ashamed of himself. "I've decided to go back to ThunderClan," he admitted at last.

Graystripe felt as surprised as if one of the pointed stones had broken off the roof and landed on his head. "I thought you would want to stay here."

"Here?" Flipclaw shuddered. "Where the territory falls on top of you and buries you? No thanks—it's far too dangerous." He glanced guiltily at Stormfur, who stood at Graystripe's shoulder. "I think the Tribe is *great*, especially Feather," he added, "and I've *loved* visiting you here in the mountains, but living here just isn't for me. Sorry."

"No need to apologize," Stormfur assured him. "I quite understand."

"The Moonstone sounds really cool, and I hope going there works," Flipclaw went on, "but . . . well, I miss my kin, and seeing the Tribe together has made me realize that I don't need to travel any farther to know where I belong."

"If you're sure . . ." Graystripe began.

Flipclaw gave his chest fur a couple of embarrassed licks. "If I'm being honest, I had the idea it would be exciting to leave the Clan, and it *has* been, traveling here, but . . . well, ThunderClan is my home."

Graystripe knew he would miss his traveling companion, but he was already reconciled to losing him, and he understood that Flipclaw was feeling the pull of his own Clan. And once Flipclaw had realized he had no chance with Flywhisker, Graystripe imagined that his whole adventure had fallen apart. Besides, Flipclaw had never lived in the old forest. The Moonstone was just a word to him, not a memory or a place. He had no reason to want to go there.

"Firestar" is just a word, too, Graystripe thought sadly. *Flipclaw never knew ThunderClan's great leader . . . my friend.*

"Are you sure you can find your way home?" he asked.

By this time the hunting patrols were returning to the cavern, and Brook padded over, carrying a piece of fresh-kill, in time to hear the last part of the conversation.

"When you're ready to leave, you can have an escort down the mountain, Flipclaw," she meowed. "Feather and Pine will go with you."

"Thank you!" Flipclaw's eyes shone happily. "And after that, I can follow our scent trail back," he assured Graystripe. "Even after a few days, there should be traces left, provided there's no heavy rain."

"Just be careful, that's all," Graystripe warned him. "And go easy on that leg."

"Sure I will." Flipclaw's gleaming gaze was fixed on the fresh-kill Brook had set down beside his sleeping hollow. "Is that for me?" he asked. "Oh, Brook, thank you. I'm *starving!*"

Golden light poured through the screen of falling water as Graystripe prepared to set out from the Tribe's cavern.

"It's been great to see you again," he told Stormfur and the rest of his kin; they had gathered to say good-bye near the entrance to the path leading behind the waterfall and out onto the mountainside. Gazing at the younger cats, he was almost overwhelmed by the thought of the legacy he was leaving, here in the Tribe, so far away from his home. "Thank you for looking after us, especially Flipclaw," he continued. He dipped his head to Stoneteller, who stood a little apart. "And thank you for your guidance," he added.

Stoneteller nodded. "I was happy to give it."

"Lark and Breeze will escort you down the mountain," Stormfur meowed, beckoning the two young cats forward. "It's dangerous when you don't know the way. They can take you to where the prey-hunters met the rogue who was asking about you. Maybe he'll still be somewhere in that area."

Flipclaw's accident, and the sign he had received from Feathertail, had driven the memory of the rogue out of

Graystripe's mind. Now he remembered what Stormfur had told him; his pelt prickled uneasily as he wondered who this mysterious cat could be. *I hope he won't cause trouble, especially now that I have a mission to carry out.*

Graystripe thanked his son and looked around for Flipclaw, who had limped across the cavern to touch his nose to Graystripe's.

"Good-bye, then." Graystripe mewed, touching his nose to the young warrior's. "May StarClan light your path."

"And yours, Graystripe. Good-bye! I'll see you soon, back in ThunderClan's camp."

I hope so, Graystripe thought. He still didn't know whether his plan to visit the Moonstone would work, or where it would lead him. But he truly hoped it would set his paws on the path back to ThunderClan.

Suppressing a sigh, he let his gaze travel once more over his kin. Then he turned with his escort in the direction that would take him, eventually, to the old forest.

As Graystripe padded away, he glanced back over his shoulder and saw that Stormfur had emerged from the end of the path and was standing beside the thundering water. He raised his tail in farewell. Graystripe was aware of his son watching him until he followed his guides around a large boulder and his paw steps carried him out of Stormfur's sight.

This is weird. I've never traveled alone before.

Several sunrises had passed since Graystripe had left the Tribe's mountain, and he was picking his way carefully through a patch of thin woodland. He liked the feeling of walking under trees again, but he couldn't get used to being on his own. In the past, he had always been with his Clan, or with Firestar, and the one time he'd been separated from them he had journeyed to find them with Millie by his side.

Thinking of Millie sent a stab of pain through Graystripe, but it soothed him somehow to remember her companionship on their travels, when they were young and in love. She had been so brave while they were wandering in unfamiliar territory, so determined never to give up. He wouldn't even have found his way out of the Twolegplace where he had been a kittypet if Millie hadn't discovered him, starving and in despair, and set his paws on the right path.

Since he had said good-bye to Lark and Breeze at the edge of the mountains, Graystripe had kept alert for any traces of the rogue who had been asking about him, but there had been nothing: no scent, no signs of captured prey, not even a paw mark. Graystripe guessed that the cat had given up his search and gone home.

Ahead of him, Graystripe could see the edge of the wood, and he paused for a moment, pricking his ears and opening his jaws to taste the air. There was more chance of coming across prey here amid the undergrowth than in the open country beyond.

After a few heartbeats, he was rewarded with the scent of mouse, and he managed to pinpoint the tiny creature scuffling about in the debris beneath an ash tree. Graystripe dropped into a hunter's crouch and edged his way forward, setting each paw down as lightly as he could and hardly daring to breathe.

Just before he came within pouncing distance, a whisper of breeze sprang up, carrying his scent toward the mouse. It raised its head in alarm, whiskers quivering. Graystripe lunged toward it as it began to scuttle off, and slammed both forepaws down on the tiny body.

Still got it, he thought with satisfaction. As he straightened up, he glanced at the sky, questioning. *Oh, why not.* "Thank you, StarClan, for this prey."

When he had gulped down his fresh-kill, relishing every warm, juicy bite, Graystripe made for the edge of the wood, his belly feeling comfortably full. As he padded out of the trees, the view ahead of him opened up, and he could see a long way into the distance. He caught his breath as his gaze snagged on a familiar sight. Three jagged peaks surrounded a dark, square opening, impossibly small from this distance. There, outlined against the sky, so far away and yet so familiar, was Highstones.

"Almost home!" Even though the old territory wasn't home anymore, Graystripe's heart lifted with excitement. No matter how things had changed, it would be good to see the old forest again. Surely some of the places he remembered would have survived the marauding Twolegs. Filled with new energy, he raced across a broad stretch of grass toward a line of bushes beyond.

Pushing his way through the bushes, Graystripe realized that he was on the edge of a wide Thunderpath. Full of enthusiasm to reach his old home, he had completely ignored the acrid scent that should have alerted him. He paused briefly to listen for monsters, but the sight of Highstones in the distance pulled him eagerly forward.

He was halfway across the hard, black surface when a sudden growl filled the air and a Twoleg monster came whipping around a bend in the Thunderpath. Its acrid stench rolled over Graystripe, and for a heartbeat he froze, unable to go on or go back. The monster veered, letting out a fearsome screech, and at the last moment Graystripe dashed out from underneath its round, black paws and flung himself into the bushes on the far side.

Crouching there, his heart pounding as if it might break out of his chest, Graystripe tried to catch his breath and stop himself from shaking.

You idiot furball! he scolded himself. *Any cat would take you for an apprentice out of camp for the first time!*

The monster jerked to a halt, and three Twolegs emerged from its belly. Graystripe peered out from his shelter, watching them as they rushed around, calling to one another and looking around in all directions.

They're looking for me, Graystripe realized, too terrified to do more than hunch his shoulders and try to shrink himself smaller than a mouse. *What if they find me? I can't get taken by Twolegs, not* again, *especially not now that I'm on such an important journey.*

Facing the danger of capture reminded him of Millie once more, of his time with her in the Twolegplace, and of their escape together. He had found it hard to believe that a kitty-pet could learn how to survive in the forest as quickly as Millie had. Remembering her determination helped him shake away his fear of recapture. Millie had given him hope when they first came upon the old ThunderClan camp, wrecked and deserted. She had told him that even though his home was gone, his Clan, and the warrior code, still survived. *No matter what happens,* he resolved, *I'll find my way back to ThunderClan, just as we did before.*

The Twolegs had turned away, beginning to search among the bushes on the other side of the Thunderpath. Graystripe waited until they were all looking in the opposite direction, then slid silently out of his hiding place and fled.

CHAPTER 12

❧

— *Then* —

Graystripe slipped out of the warriors' den, sat down, fluffed out his pelt, and looked around the ThunderClan camp. After the torrential rain of the previous day, the sun was shining, and wisps of mist were rising from the puddles on the camp floor. Warriors had been patrolling for BloodClan, but no signs of the rogues had been found, and prey was running well, leaving the fresh-kill pile well stocked. Graystripe could feel some of his Clanmates beginning to relax.

High-pitched squeals caught Graystripe's attention, and he blinked in amusement as he spotted Ferncloud's kits, Spiderkit and Shrewkit, chasing each other around the High-rock. But his amusement didn't last for long. He was aware that the thorn barrier around the camp wouldn't keep out a determined attacker, and he felt as edgy as if he were stepping into a fox's den. All his senses were alert for the first signs of BloodClan.

Those cats won't give up, he thought. *I know they're watching, biding their time.*

Brackenfur appeared at the entrance to the gorse tunnel, at the head of the returning border patrol. As soon as he spotted him, he bounded across to Graystripe.

"Any sign?" Graystripe asked urgently, rising to his paws.

Brackenfur shook his head. "Not a whisker. I don't know if that's a good thing or a bad thing. It's not like we don't know they're out there. And there was no sign of WindClan, except for their border markers," he added. "I reckon that proves it was BloodClan all along."

"It seems that way," Graystripe agreed, remembering how the BloodClan leader had come close to confessing what her cats had done. "They've shown themselves now, so they don't need a disguise anymore."

As Brackenfur padded off to choose a piece of prey from the fresh-kill pile, Graystripe kept puzzling over the threat of BloodClan. *It was good of ShadowClan to warn us,* he reflected. *I think we ought to warn WindClan and RiverClan, and find out if they've seen any signs on their territories.*

Glancing around, Graystripe spotted Cloudtail heading for the gorse tunnel, his apprentice Rainpaw trailing along behind him. "Cloudtail!" he called, beckoning the white warrior with a flick of his tail. "Are you busy?"

"I was going to take Rainpaw for some battle training in the sandy clearing," Cloudtail replied, padding up to Graystripe. "He needs to get back into a routine, after . . ." He let his voice fade away with an expressive twitch of his whiskers.

After his mother died, Graystripe thought. All three apprentices had been shattered by Willowpelt's death at the claws of a badger, and it hadn't been long since they had returned to their duties.

"I think we can do something more exciting than that," Graystripe meowed. "Rainpaw, how would you like to visit WindClan and RiverClan?"

Rainpaw's ears perked up at the idea. "I'd like that. I've never been to their camps."

Pleased that he was showing an interest, Graystripe explained their mission to Cloudtail and led the way out of camp. As they climbed up the ravine and headed into the forest, he stayed alert for any signs of BloodClan, but he picked up nothing except tempting prey-scents and the smell of lush greenleaf vegetation.

"Maybe you scared the mange-pelts off," Cloudtail growled.

"I don't think so. BloodClan cats have never scared as easily as that," Graystripe responded.

Cloudtail snorted. "If they come near me, I'll rip their pelts off to line my nest. I have a kit to protect!"

Graystripe gave him a nod of approval. Convinced as he was that BloodClan would return, he was glad that his Clan could rely on determined cats like Cloudtail. Even Ashfur, who was turning out to be a real pain in the tail, would be a brave and fierce fighter in defense of ThunderClan.

Leading the way across the hollow of Fourtrees, Graystripe ordered his patrol to wait on the WindClan border. Ahead of them rose a swell of moorland, interrupted here and there by rocks poking out of the thin soil. A stiff breeze flattened the coarse moorland grass.

"I can see why it's called *Wind*Clan," Cloudtail muttered, letting his pelt bush out against the chill.

Eventually a WindClan patrol appeared at the top of the moorland ridge. Spotting the ThunderClan cats, they raced down to meet them; as they drew closer, Graystripe recognized the tabby warrior Onewhisker in the lead, with Runningbrook and Webfoot following him.

"Hi, Graystripe," Onewhisker greeted him, hanging back on the other side of the border. "What can we do for you?"

Hearing his cheerful tone, and seeing the friendly nods from the other WindClan warriors, Graystripe became even more convinced that WindClan hadn't been stealing prey. They would surely have looked guiltier if they had.

"We need to see Tallstar," Graystripe told Onewhisker confidently. It felt good to be performing a familiar task; bringing a message was precisely the sort of thing he did all the time as Firestar's deputy. "We've something important to discuss with him."

Onewhisker looked curious, but he knew better than to question another Clan's deputy. He and the other WindClan cats escorted the ThunderClan patrol up the hill and down the other side, heading for a tangle of gorse at the bottom.

"Where's your camp?" Rainpaw asked, gazing around in confusion.

"You're looking at it," Onewhisker replied, with a sweep of his tail toward the gorse bushes.

"Really?" Rainpaw exclaimed.

"Good, isn't it?" Runningbrook asked with a smug smile.

"You'd never know cats were there until you're right on top of us."

Rainpaw didn't say any more, but his round eyes showed how impressed he was.

Graystripe and his Clanmates followed the WindClan cats through the tough gorse stems; Graystripe suppressed a hiss of annoyance as the thorns raked deep into his fur, while the slender WindClan warriors passed through more easily.

On the other side of the bushes, the ground sloped away into a sandy hollow. Onewhisker raced across it, calling out, "Tallstar!" and disappeared around a large boulder at the far end. Webfoot and Runningbrook stayed with the Thunder-Clan cats.

After a few moments, Onewhisker reappeared, followed by the WindClan leader. Tallstar's age was clear in his slow, deliberate movements and the graying fur around his muzzle, but he was still a formidable warrior. He beckoned with his tail for Graystripe and his patrol to come forward.

"Greetings," he meowed when they stood in front of him. "Why have you come to visit my Clan?"

Graystripe dipped his head respectfully to the Wind-Clan leader. "It's bad news, I'm afraid, Tallstar," he replied. "BloodClan has been scented around ShadowClan and ThunderClan, and—"

"What?" Tallstar interrupted, every hair on his pelt beginning to bristle. "Those crow-food-eating rogues causing trouble *again*? I thought we dealt with them last time."

"Not thoroughly enough, I'm sorry to say," Graystripe

mewed ruefully. "I take it you haven't picked up any traces of them on your territory?"

Tallstar shook his head. "If my warriors had scented a single BloodClan paw step anywhere near our borders, they would have told me," he replied. Eyeing Graystripe more closely, he added, "I take it you've met them recently."

Graystripe was uncomfortably aware that his wounds had scarcely begun to heal. But he didn't want to tell Tallstar how bad the attack had been, because he didn't want the Wind-Clan leader to think that ThunderClan was vulnerable. *I know our Clans are friendly right now, but no cat knows how things might change.*

For the same reason, he said nothing about the way Blood-Clan had used WindClan scent to make ThunderClan believe that WindClan had been stealing prey on their territory. Tallstar could easily take offense at the idea that ThunderClan had suspected them for a single moment.

"Let's say they made it clear that they're still interested in our territory," Graystripe responded. "But I think we showed them that ThunderClan won't give in without a fight."

Tallstar let out a long sigh. "Always fighting!" he complained. "And it's harder for you in ThunderClan," he went on, "with your leader ill. How is Firestar, by the way?"

"Much better, thank you," Graystripe replied, hoping he wouldn't have to go into any more detail. He knew he wasn't much good at lying, but he knew too that he had to keep Firestar's absence a secret, both to conceal the truth about Firestar's mission and to make ThunderClan appear strong. At the last Gathering, he had told the other Clans that the

ThunderClan leader was sick. *But how long can I keep up that pretense?*

To his relief, Tallstar appeared to accept what Graystripe told him. "Please give him my good wishes," he mewed. "As for BloodClan, we'll keep a lookout for them. Thank you for warning us."

"You're welcome," Graystripe responded, dipping his head once more to the WindClan leader. He was very glad that he hadn't taken his Clanmates' advice to strike WindClan when the first stolen prey was found—what a disaster that would have been! *Maybe I do have a leader's instincts.* "And we'll be sure to let you know if we encounter them again."

Leaving the WindClan camp, Graystripe and his patrol headed back toward Fourtrees. Rainpaw was still gazing around him in fascination at the strange territory; Graystripe was pleased to see that he was looking brighter than at any time since his mother's death. *Maybe he's starting to come out of his grief.*

The three cats skirted the Gathering hollow, then headed through the trees and paused before the Twoleg bridge into RiverClan territory. "Go on," Graystripe encouraged them. *Normally we'd wait at the border, but I have kin here,* he reflected. *We can bend the rules a bit.* The border markers were fresh, as if a patrol had recently passed by, but there was no sign of any cats. Graystripe decided to head straight for the RiverClan camp.

"Keep close to me, and be careful what you say," he told his Clanmates as they padded alongside the river. "Leopardstar isn't like Tallstar. If she gets one whiff of weakness in

ThunderClan, she'll use it as a chance to take Sunningrocks."

Cloudtail slid his claws out. "She can try."

"Just do as I've suggested." Graystripe flicked Cloudtail over the ear with the tip of his tail. "Haven't we got enough trouble from BloodClan, without looking for it from River-Clan as well?"

The white warrior rolled his eyes. "If you say so."

Long before they reached the RiverClan camp, Graystripe spotted two RiverClan warriors coming up the river to meet them. His pelt tingled with anticipation as he recognized the leader of the two as his son, Stormfur.

He looks well, Graystripe thought at the sight of his son's thick, glossy fur and confident stride. *I'm so proud of him.*

He had been disappointed when Stormfur and his sister, Feathertail, had decided to return to RiverClan after the battle against BloodClan. Their mother, Silverstream, had been a RiverClan cat, but she was watching them from StarClan now. Graystripe had invited them both to join him in Thunder-Clan, because he wasn't sure that he trusted Leopardstar to accept the two half-Clan cats as full members of her Clan. But his kits had chosen to help rebuild RiverClan after the devastation caused by Scourge and Tigerstar. Graystripe had reluctantly respected their choice.

"Greetings, Graystripe," Stormfur meowed, padding up to touch noses with his father. "We—great StarClan!" he exclaimed, his eyes widening at the sight of Graystripe's wounds. "Have you been fighting a fox?"

"Worse than that, I'm afraid," Graystripe replied grimly.

"But Leopardstar had better be the first to hear it, if we can speak to her."

"Of course," Stormfur mewed, turning to escort Graystripe downriver toward the RiverClan camp.

Cloudtail and Rainpaw followed, while the other River-Clan warrior, a thickset tabby tom Graystripe recognized as Heavystep, brought up the rear.

It was strange to be back in RiverClan's camp. The River-Clan cats lived on an island close to the riverbank. Willow trees grew there, sheltering the Clan with their long, trailing branches, and the whole island was surrounded by reeds that hissed gently in the breeze. It was a cozy spot, but seeing it again only helped convince Graystripe that he belonged in ThunderClan. *This is where my kits live, but it was never home.*

Graystripe paused before he stepped into the water. As long as he'd lived in RiverClan, he'd never gotten used to the sensation of getting his paws wet. He lifted his front leg, trying to convince himself to splash it down into the muck. *Come on, Graystripe, an acting leader has to be brave enough to—*

Splash! Graystripe felt a flood of relief as Heavystep sloshed through the reeds with a wave of his tail. "I'll fetch Leopard-star," he called back over his shoulder.

"Thank you!" Graystripe called after him, wondering whether Heavystep had noticed his hesitation.

A few moments later, the reeds parted to reveal the spotted pelt of the RiverClan leader, who sprang nimbly onto the bank to confront Graystripe. Her deputy, Mistyfoot, followed her, and Graystripe was struck all over again by how much she resembled her mother, Bluestar, with the same thick blue-gray fur and blue eyes.

"Well?" Leopardstar asked. Her voice was sharp, without any of the friendliness Tallstar had shown. "Why are you here?"

Graystripe was aware of Rainpaw easing a little closer to his mentor, as if he was intimidated by the RiverClan leader's brusque tones. Cloudtail gave his apprentice a reassuring touch on the shoulder with the tip of his tail.

"We have bad news," Graystripe told Leopardstar, describing how ShadowClan had scented BloodClan on their border, and how he and two other warriors had fought against them. He said nothing about the trick they'd used to make Thunder-Clan believe that WindClan had been stealing prey.

"We've seen no sign of BloodClan on our territory," Leopardstar responded when Graystripe had finished. "And you can be sure we'll drive them off if we scent so much as a whisker."

Mistyfoot blinked worriedly. "I had hoped we'd chased off BloodClan once and for all," she sighed. "I can't believe they would dare to set paw in our forest after the way we drove them out. And now you tell us we have to do it all again!"

Leopardstar gave her deputy a sharp look. "If we have to fight them again, then that is what we will do," she meowed. "We are warriors!" Turning to Graystripe, she added, "What does Firestar think of all this?"

Graystripe hadn't been prepared for that question. "He . . . er . . . he said more or less what you just said," he replied awkwardly. "We're warriors; we can deal with this."

"Good." Leopardstar's eyes narrowed suspiciously. "We missed Firestar at the last Gathering," she added. "I believe you said that he was sick?"

"That's right." Graystripe twitched his tail awkwardly, desperately wondering how to escape from this conversation. "But he's getting much better now." *And I really have to be going....*

"I'm glad to hear it," the RiverClan leader purred. "I seem to have forgotten. What was the matter with him?"

You haven't forgotten, because no cat told you, Graystripe thought, beginning to feel hot under his pelt. Was Leopardstar trying to catch him in a lie? He knew from his time in RiverClan that it wouldn't be unlike the wily leader. He tried to think fast. "It was . . . er . . . whitecough. But then it turned to greencough. He was very sick. He almost lost a life."

As he spoke, Graystripe caught a glare from Cloudtail's blue eyes, and could almost hear what the white warrior wanted to say. *Stop babbling! You're taking the lie too far!*

"Really? Greencough in greenleaf?" Leopardstar licked one paw and drew it over her ear. "How unfortunate."

Graystripe swallowed hard. It was true—it was rare for a cat to develop greencough during the warmth of greenleaf. Which meant that not only was he lying to another Clan leader, he was lying poorly. He knew how badly he was handling this conversation. He was sure that Leopardstar didn't believe him—either that, or she suspected that Firestar's condition was much worse than Graystripe pretended, and was wondering how to turn that to RiverClan's advantage.

"Well, we really should be going," Graystripe mewed, taking a few steps back. "It's been nice talking to you, Leopardstar. We'll be sure to tell you if we see any more of BloodClan."

The RiverClan leader didn't respond, just stood on the bank watching Graystripe and his Clanmates with slitted eyes.

It was Mistyfoot who spoke. "We'll certainly let Thunder-Clan know if BloodClan turns up over here." Her voice was friendly and her blue eyes were warm. "Meanwhile, Stormfur will escort you down to the stepping-stones. There's no need for you to go all the way back by the Twoleg bridge."

"Thank you." Graystripe dipped his head, pleased at the opportunity to spend a little more time with his son.

Then, to his surprise, Mistyfoot turned back toward the camp and called out, "Feathertail!"

Graystripe felt his heart swell as though it might burst at the sight of his beautiful daughter picking her way through the reeds and springing onto the riverbank. It had been too long since he had seen her!

"Yes, Mistyfoot, what did you—" she began, then broke off as she spotted Graystripe. Her plumy gray tail curled up with joy at the sight of her father, and she bounded forward to touch noses with him. She was purring too hard to speak.

"I want you to escort these ThunderClan cats off our territory," Mistyfoot ordered. Her affectionate tone contradicted the sharp words. "Stormfur will go with you in case they give you any trouble."

"Oh, thank you, Mistyfoot!" Feathertail exclaimed. She flicked a glance at Leopardstar, who still stood silent, only waving her tail to indicate that they should all leave.

With a respectful nod to the RiverClan leader, Graystripe turned away and headed downstream with his Clanmates and their RiverClan escort.

"I remember you when you were in ThunderClan," Rainpaw observed to Feathertail and Stormfur as they padded along. Graystripe was pleased to see that he looked much more cheerful now that they had left the prickly Leopardstar behind. "You were apprentices then."

"And you were a tiny kit," Stormfur mewed, bending his head to touch Rainpaw's ear with his nose. "And now look at you! I hope you always listen to your mentor."

"No chance!" Cloudtail let out a *mrrow* of laughter. "But then . . . he's an apprentice. What can you expect?"

"I do too listen!" Rainpaw exclaimed indignantly.

"I'm sure you do." Feathertail stroked her tail down the apprentice's side. "Cloudtail was only joking."

Rainpaw turned an admiring gaze on her and her brother. "I'll be a warrior soon, like you," he announced.

Graystripe exchanged a glance with Cloudtail, and guessed that the white warrior was sharing his thought. *Rainpaw and his littermates will make excellent warriors—if BloodClan gives them the chance.*

When they arrived at the stepping-stones, Cloudtail drew Rainpaw away from the others. "Let's go on ahead," he suggested. "We'll see if we can pick up some prey on the way back to camp, and you can try out that new hunting move I showed you."

"Great!" Rainpaw agreed enthusiastically. Turning, he waved his tail at the two RiverClan warriors. "Good-bye! I hope I see you at the next Gathering."

"I hope so, too," Feathertail responded, blinking affectionately at the apprentice.

Graystripe watched as Cloudtail sent Rainpaw ahead of him across the stepping-stones. The river was fairly low, and the young cat had no trouble leaping from one flat-topped stone to the next. *And this must be the first time he's crossed them,* Graystripe thought, admiring the young gray tom's fearlessness.

When both his Clanmates were safely on the opposite bank, Graystripe turned back to Feathertail and Stormfur. *That was good of Cloudtail,* he thought. *Giving me a few moments with my kits.*

"I just want to tell you how enormously proud of you I am," he meowed. "You've grown into such capable warriors."

"Thank you," Stormfur purred. "That means a lot to us." Feathertail murmured agreement.

Graystripe felt a lump in his throat as he forced out the next words. "I only wish your mother, Silverstream, could be here to see you. She would have loved you so much."

"I'm sure she's watching us from StarClan," Feathertail comforted him, brushing her muzzle against her father's.

For a moment the three cats stood close together, Graystripe drawing in their mingled scents and thinking that no father had ever had such splendid kits. It was hard not to wish that they would join him in ThunderClan, so that he could enjoy their company every single day. *But that's not what they want, and they're old enough to make their own decisions.* At last, regretfully, he had to draw back.

"I must go," he mewed. "May StarClan light your path."

"And yours," Stormfur responded.

"Always," Feathertail added.

As he leaped across the stepping-stones, Graystripe's paws and legs felt heavy; sadness weighed him down. The thought of being separated from his kits for the rest of his life was almost too much to bear. *Maybe someday . . . ,* he thought, as his paws automatically plotted the way back to the ThunderClan camp.

Maybe someday Feathertail, Stormfur, and I will all be together again.

CHAPTER 13

— Now —

It felt strange to arrive at Highstones without the acrid taste of traveling herbs on his tongue. Graystripe was overcome with a sudden memory—and a longing for Yellowfang and Cinderpelt, the medicine cats of his youth—as he clambered up the final slope to the peak of Highstones. He was wheezing slightly, struggling to catch his breath. *I'm a bit older than I was the last time I made this climb. But at least I haven't seen any more Twolegs,* he thought thankfully. After pausing to breathe, he clawed his way to the highest point to look out across what used to be the Clan territories.

I know it won't be the same, he told himself, trying not to let himself hope too much. *We had to leave because the Twolegs were taking over, so it won't look like I remember.*

However, when he could finally gaze out over the scene and take it in, he felt as stunned as if the Moonstone he was seeking had fallen on top of him. He could see the river, the gorge and the waterfall, and, separated from him by the Thunderpath, tiny at this distance, the rooftops of Barley's farm.

Barley, he mused, his pelt warming at the memory of the kind former BloodClan cat who'd settled at the farm. *I'd love to see him again . . . but I'd better find the Moonstone first.* He remembered with a tiny pain in his chest that Ravenpaw, a former ThunderClan apprentice and Barley's companion at the farm, had died. *Barley must miss him terribly.*

Beyond the farm, there were so many Twoleg nests that he couldn't even tell where ThunderClan's territory used to be. Thunderpaths snaked among them, and monsters were running along them, looking like glittering beetles from this far away. The thick, welcoming woodland was gone, along with most of the moorland slopes where WindClan had lived. A chill ran through Graystripe at the thought of how quickly any trace of the Clans had been wiped out.

And if we can't reach StarClan anymore, how long will it be before no cat remembers our time here? Even the memory of the Clans will be lost, washed away like twigs in a newleaf flood.

At least, Graystripe reflected, he should be close to Mothermouth and the Moonstone. He reminded himself that he hadn't come all this way just for a reunion with his old territory. He needed to visit the Moonstone and discover whether it would help him find a way to contact StarClan.

I'll do that and then hurry home, he told himself firmly. *Clearly, there's nothing else I need to see here.* And if his mission turned out to be successful, he would want to get back to the lake as quickly as he could.

Although he couldn't see Mothermouth from where he stood at the top of the rocks, Graystripe knew that the opening must be somewhere on the hillside below him. Cautiously he began to make his way down. His paws slipped on the steep slope, and sometimes the surface was made up of tiny pebbles that gave way when he stepped on them, carrying him down so fast that he had to dig in his claws hard to keep himself from falling off a cliff. His pads were soon sore, and he kept a lookout for dock leaves, but not much grew among these bleak rocks.

All the while, the scarlet light was fading and boulders cast deep shadows over his path. Unable to see his way ahead clearly, Graystripe had to slow down until he was creeping forward, testing each paw hold before he dared put his weight on it.

He had traveled to Mothermouth before, but only from his own territory in the forest. And he'd only come to escort the medicine cats—he'd never gone inside, or seen the Moonstone for himself. Now, approaching from the opposite direction, he wasn't sure whether he was on the right track. Even worse, as the last of the daylight died, he heard an echoing cry above him and looked up to see an owl, its wings spread wide as it circled over him.

"Fox dung!" he muttered.

Graystripe wasn't sure whether an owl could be dangerous to a full-grown cat like him, but he didn't want to find out the hard way. When the bird seemed to be following him, he began to choose his route so that he could take cover beneath overhanging rocks. Soon he had to admit to himself that he was hopelessly lost.

I've come too far down, he told himself, peering through the darkness. Nothing around him looked familiar; he had lost sight of Barley's farm, and he didn't recognize anything that could tell him where he was. Graystripe couldn't remember the last time he had felt so disoriented, as vulnerable as a kit venturing out of camp alone.

He was still trying to decide which way to go when a sudden growling broke out in front of him, and two enormous, bright eyes pinned him in their dazzling gaze.

"A monster!" Graystripe yowled in utter shock. *What is a monster doing here?*

For a moment, all he could do was flatten himself to the ground, terror freezing his limbs. When the monster made no movement toward him, but simply crouched there growling, he managed to recover himself enough to stagger to his paws and dart underneath a nearby bush.

By the light from the monster's eyes, Graystripe could see that he had blundered into some kind of monster camp. Several of them sat there, apparently asleep, and a few Twolegs were moving around among them.

As he watched, another monster woke up; this one started forward almost at once and headed for Graystripe, where he was still hiding beneath the bush. Terror swept over Graystripe at the thought of being crushed under those huge black paws. He scrambled through the low-growing branches, burst out on the far side, and fled.

A moment later, he felt the ground beneath his paws change to the hard surface of a Thunderpath, but in his panic his only thought was to escape from the monster that was pursuing him. He hurled himself forward, almost colliding with a dark cliff that reared up in front of him. Clawing his way up, Graystripe realized that he was climbing a Twoleg fence, and he half jumped, half fell into the garden beyond.

Light and shadow from the monster swept over Graystripe as he hurtled across a stretch of grass and underneath a bush with large, aromatic flowers that made him sneeze. He crouched there while the lights and the growling died away, until all was dark and silent.

That was close! he thought, panting.

While he lay there, shivering and trying to catch his breath, Graystripe looked up through the branches and spotted the owl, still circling. At least it couldn't get at him while he sheltered under the bush.

"Go and find yourself a nice mouse," he muttered, "and stop bothering me!"

Forcing himself to relax, Graystripe decided to stay put until he could be sure it was safe to move on. An uneasy drowsiness had just begun to set in when he heard a voice close by, curious and friendly all at once. "Hello! I haven't seen you before."

Graystripe opened his eyes to see a plump tabby-and-white kittypet peering at him underneath the branches. Embarrassed at being caught hiding like a scared apprentice, he dragged himself out into the open and gave the newcomer a polite nod.

"Hi," he mewed. "It's okay. I haven't come to take your territory."

The kittypet—a she-cat—gave him a puzzled look, as if she had no idea what he was meowing about. "Are you lost?" she asked him. "Maybe I can help."

Graystripe doubted that this kittypet knew much about anything beyond her own garden, but he was growing so desperate that he felt it had to be worth a try. "I'm just passing through," he explained. "I'm looking for Mothermouth."

His tiny hope vanished as the kittypet stared at him. "Mothermouth?" she murmured, as if the word were a strange piece of prey on her tongue. "Is that a different kind of housefolk den?"

"It's the entrance to a huge cave," he told her. "The Moonstone is at the very bottom."

The tabby-and-white kittypet blinked in bewilderment. "I don't know what that is," she mewed. "I've lived here with my housefolk for many seasons, but I've never heard of this 'moonstone.'"

"Never mind," Graystripe sighed. He'd known that asking a kittypet wouldn't get him anywhere. "Thanks for listening, anyway."

"That's okay," the she-cat told him. "Well, I'd better be going. My housefolk usually feed me around this time." She padded off across the garden and disappeared through a small gap at the bottom of the Twoleg door.

The kittypet's mention of food reminded Graystripe of how hungry he was. He had a sudden impulse to follow her and ask if he could share, then stopped himself, feeling thoroughly ashamed. *You're a warrior!* he scolded himself. *You don't go into Twoleg dens or eat kittypet food.* He turned away, reflecting that he still had his pride, but he had a yawning emptiness in his belly, too.

Graystripe realized that he had to keep going or he was never going to find his way to the Moonstone. Wearily, he climbed back over the Twoleg fence and began padding alongside the Thunderpath. By this time, lights had begun to appear inside the Twoleg dens, and the Thunderpath itself was lit up by tiny orange suns on top of thin stone trees. To his relief, the owl had disappeared, but monsters still snarled their way past him, and Graystripe slunk along in the shadow of the fence to stay away from their glaring eyes.

He managed to work out that he must be somewhere on what used to be WindClan territory, but there was nothing to tell him where to go next. What had been open moorland was now entirely filled with Twoleg dens, Thunderpaths, and sleeping monsters. He paused, trying to scent the air, but the acrid stench of monsters swamped anything else. Gagging on the reek, Graystripe wondered whether he ought to turn back and head in a different direction, only to realize that if he did that, he would risk becoming entirely lost.

Whatever happens, I have to keep going.

Graystripe padded on, aware of gnawing hunger, aching limbs, and sore paws. He wanted nothing more than to hunt, eat, and rest, but there seemed nowhere in this alien place where he could do that. Then, as he passed yet another sleeping monster, he heard it open up; whipping around, he saw a Twoleg emerge from its belly and head straight for him.

Fear, worse than when he'd spotted the owl, gave Graystripe strength. He hurled himself at the nearest fence and leaped up it, his paws scarcely touching the wooden surface. When he reached the top he glanced back to see the Twoleg's pale face upturned toward him; then he let himself drop down into the garden and dived for cover into the gap between the fence and a tree. He crouched there in silence, shivering, until he heard retreating paw steps and realized that the Twoleg must have given up and gone away.

As he gradually calmed down, an idea crept into Graystripe's mind. He closed his eyes, trying to shut out all the distractions of Twoleg scents and sounds, to see if the memory in his senses might guide him back to Mothermouth. But however hard he concentrated, he felt no guidance, no sense of a paw pulling him in the right direction. Disappointed, he opened his eyes.

Even my body has forgotten this place.

Graystripe slipped out of hiding and wriggled through a narrow gap in the Twoleg fence to struggle on again beside the Thunderpath. Now it took a massive effort to put one paw in front of another, and he had lost all idea of where he was. But even if he decided to give up and go home, he didn't know which way to go.

Eventually he came to an open area at the far side of the Thunderpath. The line of Twoleg dens ended beside a stretch of grass surrounded by bushes and a few trees. Faintly encouraged by the sight of a place that—so far—the Twolegs hadn't touched, Graystripe opened his jaws to scent the air for prey.

Soon he picked up a trace of mouse, and tracked it down to a clump of grass beside the roots of a tree.

His jaws watering, Graystripe crept up on his prey and prepared to pounce. But just as he was gathering his haunches under him, a flurry of loud barking burst from the nearest of the Twoleg dens. *A dog!* Graystripe thought irritably. *That's all I need!* The mouse had vanished at the first sound.

Graystripe flopped down, utterly discouraged and miserable. He was too exhausted to start looking for more prey. Instead he dragged himself to a sheltered spot among the tree roots and curled up to sleep, trying to ignore the bawling of his belly. Cold, hungry, and lost, he was still confused about how he had wandered so far from the Moonstone.

Nothing is like it used to be, Graystripe thought. *It's as though the Clans never lived here at all.* Drifting into an uneasy sleep, he asked himself, *Was it a mistake to come back?*

Graystripe lay in his nest in the elders' den; he had curled himself around Millie, with her head resting on his shoulder. He could feel every one of her ribs, and her gray fur, which had once been so sleek and shining, was dull and sparse now. Graystripe couldn't hide from the knowledge that her paws were already set on the path that would lead her to StarClan.

"But you can't leave me yet," he whispered. "I can't bear to lose you. Wait a little while, and it will be my time to come with you."

Already, long ago, he had endured the pain of losing a mate, when Silverstream had died giving birth to their kits. Graystripe didn't think he could go through the same anguish twice. And yet, day by day, he could feel Millie slipping away from him. Jayfeather had given her juniper berries for strength, and sorrel to stimulate her appetite, but in spite of every effort the medicine cat made, poor Millie continued to grow weaker and weaker.

Paw steps sounded outside the den, and Graystripe's daughter Blossomfall ducked under the hazel branches. She was carrying a vole, and the rich scent of fresh-kill spread throughout the den.

"This is her favorite," she murmured, setting it down beside Millie. "Do you think she could eat a bit now?"

"We can try," Graystripe replied. He sat up, gently shaking Millie by the shoulder. "Look what Blossomfall has brought for you."

Millie's blue eyes blinked open and she looked up at Graystripe, then at Blossomfall, who nudged the vole closer with one paw. "Oh, is that for me?" Millie mewed, her nose twitching. "Thank you, Blossomfall. It's a beautiful one. But somehow . . . I don't feel like it right now."

"You have to try!" Blossomfall's voice was tight with anxiety.

"Well, maybe a mouthful . . ." Millie stretched out her neck and tore a scrap from the juicy fresh-kill, then swallowed it with difficulty. "That tastes so good! Maybe I'll finish it later." She laid her head down and closed her eyes again.

"Oh, Millie, don't leave us!" Blossomfall exclaimed. "Surely there must be something Jayfeather can do?"

Graystripe shook his head, unwilling to admit the truth, yet unable to lie to his daughter. "I think it's her time. You should fetch Bumblestripe."

Blossomfall met his gaze, her eyes wide and disbelieving; then she whipped around and shot out of the den.

Graystripe rested his head beside his beloved mate, drinking in her sweet scent for what he knew would be the last time. "I need you here with me," he meowed. "What will I do without you?"

Though Millie's hearing had dulled in the last moons of her life, she seemed to hear him now. Her eyes opened again, fixed on Graystripe and full of love for him. "We've had a marvelous life together," she murmured. "I've never regretted leaving my Twolegs, not for a single moment. But it's over now, my dear. I have to leave you. And you have to find your way forward without me."

"I don't think I can," Graystripe choked out.

"But you must," Millie responded. "You must go on being the same brave, loyal ThunderClan cat you have always been. Your Clan needs you."

"Not anymore. Now I'm just a useless elder." Graystripe's words were forced out past a huge lump in his throat. "I haven't been necessary to my Clan for moons . . . whole seasons."

"You will never be useless." Millie's breath was warm in Graystripe's ear. "You are Graystripe! You're a strong warrior, and a determined one; you are the most important cat in the world to me. You must never give up."

As Millie finished speaking, Blossomfall slipped back into the den with her brother, Bumblestripe, just behind her. And Graystripe's eyes widened in wonder as a third cat followed them beneath the hazel boughs.

"Briarlight!" he breathed out.

His daughter, who had been so badly injured by a falling tree, walked gracefully now on all four paws. Her fur and her eyes shone, and starlight glittered at her paws and around her ears.

Millie looked up and let out a purr of pure happiness. "All my dear kits . . . ," she whispered. She touched her nose to Graystripe's ear and sank back limply into the nest with a sigh. Her eyes closed.

"No!" Blossomfall protested. She crouched beside her mother's body, pushing her nose into Millie's cooling fur. Bumblestripe's legs seemed to give way, and he slid down beside her.

But Briarlight stood still, her head raised, as if she was waiting, and *before Graystripe's astonished gaze Millie seemed to rise from her body, transformed into a vision of the young, vigorous cat she had once been. She looked down at Graystripe, all the love they had shared shining through her brilliant blue gaze.*

"Good-bye, my dear," she mewed. "I shall wait for you in StarClan, but you have far to go before you meet me there. And remember what I told you—you must never give up."

Then she turned and followed their starry daughter out of the den. Darkness folded down over Graystripe like the black wing of an enormous crow.

Graystripe shuddered as he came back to consciousness. He was still curled up among the tree roots beside the Twoleg dens, as cold and hungry as he had been since climbing down from Highstones. Grief gripped him in powerful claws as he remembered Millie's death. It had been hard for him to lose her, and he still dreamed about it often.

But as he struggled against the fuzziness of sleep, his grief was eased by a sense of wonder. Millie hadn't died in exactly the way he had just dreamed. He had certainly never seen Briarlight, or the young, revived spirit of Millie leaving with her to join StarClan. His heart swelled with joy as he remembered how strong and beautiful both his beloved cats had been.

And Millie had never said the last words of advice that she had spoken in his dream, either. "You must never give up." *It was almost as if she could see me here, lost and miserable,* Graystripe thought. Then another idea came to him, striking like a bolt of lightning: *Maybe she can.*

Was it too much to hope that Millie had come to his dream

from StarClan, to deliver a message, that she had spoken those words to encourage him when everything seemed so hopeless? At least, Graystripe thought, he could carry on as if it were true.

"Don't worry, Millie," he mewed aloud. "I won't let you down."

As Graystripe sat up, his nose twitched; a wisp of familiar scent was floating on the breeze. *What is that?* he wondered, his mind still half caught up in the memory of his dream. Then, as he shook off the last shreds of sleep, he realized that he could smell the river in the distance.

Invigorated by hope, Graystripe sprang to his paws and shook out his pelt. Glancing around, he realized that he had been sleeping under the tallest tree in sight. He raced up the trunk and leaped from branch to branch until he could look out over the tops of the Twoleg dens.

He'd spotted the Twolegplace from Highstones, but now that he was in the middle of it, its sheer size overwhelmed him. *Why do the stupid creatures need so many separate dens? They can't possibly be comfortable living like that!*

Then, in the distance, past all the red-topped nests, he saw what he had been seeking.

The river! Graystripe gazed at the rush and sparkle of the surging current, feeling as if he were drinking in great drafts of its cool water. *I can see the waterfall . . . oh, and the old Twoleg bridge is still there!* And far away—so far that in the early morning haze he couldn't be quite sure—Graystripe thought that he could make out Sunningrocks.

His heart lurched as he remembered fighting there alongside

Firestar. He could almost hear the screeches of battling cats and see their lithe forms outlined against the glittering river. More memories followed the first, gushing over Graystripe like a flood: training in the sandy hollow, stalking prey in the depths of hazel thickets, padding up to Fourtrees for Gatherings under the light of the full moon.

This is where I became a warrior. Where I became the cat that I am now, he thought.

But Graystripe couldn't dwell on the joy and pain of the past. He looked around the changed landscape, and suddenly it struck him: *I'm on ThunderClan territory. At least, what used to be ThunderClan territory.*

He felt his heart sink as he looked around at the stinking Thunderpaths and repeating rows of Twoleg dwellings. *It's all gone.* He felt the air go out of him. He'd thought he was prepared for the reality that Twolegs had likely changed everything about the old hunting lands in the forest. But seeing Twoleg dwellings where the ThunderClan that had formed him had lived was more distressing than he could have imagined.

Take a breath. He closed his eyes, trying to calm himself. *You knew it would be gone, Graystripe. The past is the past.*

He opened his eyes. He had to stay focused; he needed to reach the Moonstone. Now he knew roughly how to get to Mothermouth. But he noticed too that the Twoleg nests stopped short of the river, and on the other side, on what used to be RiverClan territory, lay the same reed beds, thickets, and lush grass that he remembered from the Clan's time there. He'd lived there once, among those reed beds and thickets.

He'd played with Featherkit and Stormkit, and had tried to convince himself he could be a RiverClan cat.

At least their territory hasn't changed.

As Graystripe climbed down the tree, he knew that he ought to head straight for Mothermouth. But his whole body was urging him to pay a visit to RiverClan territory, to pretend, just for a short time, that his paws could carry him back into the past.

There's no harm in checking it out, he decided. *Just to see if it really is the same.*

Swiftly, Graystripe threaded his way through the last of the Twoleg dens. It was so early in the morning that all the monsters seemed to be asleep, and none of the Twolegs were stirring. Eventually he emerged onto the stretch of open ground along the riverbank, then headed downstream toward the Twoleg bridge.

On the way, he caught the powerful scent of rabbit and spotted the creature nibbling at a clump of dandelions at the very edge of the river. His belly aching with hunger, Graystripe crept up on it. At the last moment before he pounced, something alerted the rabbit; it sat up, ears quivering, and began to bound away, only to be faced by the swift-flowing current. Scrabbling to keep its balance, the rabbit turned around and charged forward almost into Graystripe's paws; he killed it with a swift blow to the throat.

"Thank you, StarClan, for this prey," he mumbled automatically, but then cheered up. His dream about Millie had left him feeling a bit more hopeful about StarClan and the possibility of making contact with them at the Moonstone. Encouraged, he tore into the warm flesh.

A little while later, Graystripe sat back, swiping his tongue around his jaws. Nothing was left of the rabbit except for fur and bones. Normally, a whole rabbit would have been too much for him, but Graystripe had been starving from the night before. Now his belly felt full to bursting, and energy was flooding back into his muscles.

Prey tastes different here from how it does beside the lake, he reflected as he rose and padded on. *It tastes like home.*

Heading once more for the Twoleg bridge, Graystripe kept all his senses alert in case any RiverClan cats happened to be patrolling. Then he huffed out his breath, half laughing at himself. *What am I thinking? There are no cats here anymore—only Twolegs.*

Graystripe bounded across the bridge, eager to see River-Clan's territory once again. For almost the first time on his journey, he felt relaxed, unsuspicious of any danger. *For once I can explore without any hostile cats or Twolegs.*

But as he stepped off the bridge, the morning air was split by a terrifying yowl. Gaping in shock, Graystripe glanced around to see a young she-cat, the size of an apprentice, leap out of a nearby bush. Before he could raise a paw to defend himself, the cat barreled into his side and knocked him off his paws. He landed with a thud, the breath driven out of him, and looked up to see his attacker sprawled on top of him with a gleam of triumph in her green eyes.

"Do you surrender?" she asked.

CHAPTER 14

— Then —

Graystripe gazed doubtfully up at the full moon riding high in the sky as he led his Clan toward Fourtrees. He would really have preferred it if Firestar had returned before this Gathering, but there had been no sign of the ThunderClan leader, and once again Graystripe would have to take his place.

Cinderpelt was padding along at Graystripe's shoulder, while behind them followed ThunderClan's strongest warriors: Dustpelt, Cloudtail, Mousefur, Brackenfur, and Thornclaw. Brambleclaw was with them, too; though he was still inexperienced, Graystripe admired his dedication and knew he would be an asset if they should run into trouble.

But even though his Clanmates were padding along with heads and tails held high, determination in their eyes, Graystripe could detect tension among them, as if they were worried about having to keep up the pretense that Firestar was still in the forest, somehow ill or indisposed, for another Gathering.

And I can't blame them. I'm tense myself.

The night was quiet, with only the faintest breeze stirring the branches and the long grass as the cats brushed their way through it. The air was warm with the scent of prey, but every cat knew this wasn't the time for hunting. Instead Graystripe kept all his senses alert for possible traces of BloodClan; though he couldn't hear or scent anything, he could imagine eyes staring out at him from the dark moon shadows of the undergrowth. His pelt itched uneasily, and he kept wanting to glance over his shoulder, though he knew that all he would see was his own Clan, following in his paw steps.

"They're out there somewhere," he muttered to Cinderpelt.

The medicine cat twitched her whiskers. "Maybe," she responded. "But there's nothing we can do about them right now."

"I'd like to tear the pelts off the lot of them!" Graystripe growled.

Cinderpelt rested her tail briefly on his shoulder, a calming gesture. "Maybe you scared them off when you fought," she meowed. "No other warriors have seen any signs of the rogues since then."

Graystripe snorted. "They almost made crow-food of us. No way were they scared!"

"But you were outnumbered," Cinderpelt pointed out. "They may think that if three cats can fight as fiercely as that, what chance would BloodClan have against all of us?"

"I'd like to believe that," Graystripe sighed. *But I can't. There's trouble coming; I can scent it!*

He leaped across the stream and led the way up the final

slope toward Fourtrees. The mingled scents of many cats flowed down to meet him. When he reached the top of the hollow, he saw that RiverClan and ShadowClan were already there, and WindClan was just arriving, streaming down the opposite slope from the direction of the moor.

The group of ThunderClan cats began to split up as they made their way through the ferns that lined the hollow, heading to greet friends in other Clans, while Graystripe headed straight for the Great Rock and leaped up to take his place beside Leopardstar and Blackstar on the top. He sensed murmurs of surprise from some of the warriors gathered in front of them. *They weren't expecting to see me here—they were expecting to see Firestar.*

"Firestar's still sick, is he?" Leopardstar asked, eyeing Graystripe from a few tail-lengths away. He couldn't tell what she was thinking from her even gaze.

Graystripe remembered that on his visit to RiverClan he had told their leader that Firestar had been suffering from greencough. *A foolish lie,* he mused, *but now I'm committed to it.* "Yes," Graystripe replied. *Keep it simple and they'll ask fewer questions,* he thought. "He's still sick, but improving."

Leopardstar kept her eyes on him, and Graystripe sensed that she wanted to ask another question, but they were all distracted when Tallstar sprang up to join them a few heartbeats later.

Graystripe heard Leopardstar greet him, and turned away. Everything about playing "leader" at this Gathering felt strange and wrong. His paws felt unsteady on the hard surface of the rock, and though this was his second Gathering as acting leader, he still wasn't used to seeing Fourtrees from this angle. For a moment he was distracted by the view between the massive oaks, opening up into the distance, until he spotted Feathertail and Stormfur below him, sitting a little apart from the other RiverClan cats.

A pang of sadness pierced Graystripe's heart to see his kits so close to him and yet so far away. *At least they're happy in River-Clan . . . I suppose.*

While Graystripe was still watching Stormfur and Feathertail, Blackstar rose to his paws and let out a yowl, signaling for the Gathering to begin. The chatter in the hollow died away into silence, and every cat turned to gaze up at the leaders. Graystripe suppressed a shiver at the sight of the mass of eyes, glimmering with reflected moonlight.

"ShadowClan is growing stronger every day," Blackstar began his report. "Our scars from the time Tigerstar brought BloodClan to the forest went very deep. But at last I can say that we have rebuilt our Clan."

Yowls of support came from the cats all across the hollow: from Blackstar's own Clan, but from the others too. *We're all stronger when every Clan is strong,* Graystripe thought. In many ways, he admired Blackstar, whose paws had been set on a very difficult path when he became Clan leader, after the damage caused by the previous leader, Tigerstar. But he still wasn't convinced that he could trust ShadowClan.

Will they become less secretive? Can the rest of us depend on them? Graystripe asked himself. *Or will they still be troublemakers, like before?*

Blackstar stepped back, and Tallstar rose to speak. "All is

well in WindClan," he reported. "We have plenty of prey, and our warriors are stronger than ever." He sat down again.

Leopardstar was next to rise and step forward to address the cats in the hollow, the moonlight gleaming on her spotted pelt. "Prey is running well in RiverClan too," she announced.

"Or swimming," Blackstar muttered with a flick of his ears.

Graystripe stifled a *mrrow* of laughter; clearly, Blackstar didn't understand RiverClan's preference for fish any more than Graystripe himself.

"A fox passed through our territory two days ago," Leopardstar continued, "and Mistyfoot led a patrol to chase it off. For the time being we have stepped up our border patrols—on both sides of the river," she finished, with a glance at Graystripe.

Does that mean she's going to have another try at taking Sunningrocks? Graystripe wondered. *I wouldn't put it past her.* He resolved that ThunderClan too would step up their patrols. *I definitely can't lose any territory while Firestar is gone!*

His belly cramped as he realized that Leopardstar was stepping back, indicating with a swish of her tail that it was his turn to speak. Swallowing, he took a deep breath and rose to his paws.

"Life is good in ThunderClan," he began, trying to make his voice ring out across the hollow. "Prey is running well in our territory. We had a brief bout of greencough, but our medicine cat Cinderpelt was able to cure all the cats who suffered from it, and no cat has died."

He was aware of some murmuring from the cats in the

hollow below, and spotted a few of them exchanging skeptical looks.

"And Firestar's health is improving?" Leopardstar put in smoothly. "Even though he's not here tonight?"

"Yes," he responded. "He's . . . much better."

"Then where is he, exactly?" Blackstar asked. "Russetfur told me that he was out of camp when she visited you."

Graystripe's head spun briefly as he tried to remember which lies he had told to which cats. He wished once again that he had stuck to his first intention of telling every cat that Firestar had gone on a mission. It would certainly have been simpler.

But it's too late now, he thought. *And who knows what the other leaders might have done, if they knew that Firestar wasn't even here?*

"That's right," he told Blackstar. "Firestar went out to hunt, despite Cinderpelt's warning him that it was not a good idea. And it appears he overtaxed his strength. Cinderpelt thinks it will now be several more days before he is fully recovered." He looked out into the crowd, hoping to find Cinderpelt, so that she could somehow confirm this. *Help me!* But all the pelts seemed to blend together in the darkness.

The other three leaders looked unimpressed by Graystripe's explanation; it was all too clear that they knew he was hiding something.

"So is he seriously ill?" Tallstar asked. "He must be, if he sent you to this Gathering."

"He needs rest, that's all," Graystripe retorted. "Don't worry; he'll answer all your questions when he's back on his paws."

"So you're sure he will be back . . . on his paws?" Blackstar probed.

Graystripe fought to push down panic. *Will he be back? Does Blackstar know that Firestar isn't even in the forest right now?* Rapidly pulling himself together, he replied, "Of course. Why wouldn't he?"

"Firestar was once a kittypet," Blackstar reminded the others with a flick of his tail. "Who knows where he truly is, or where his loyalties lie?"

I'm not getting into this with you, Graystripe thought, glaring at the ShadowClan leader from narrowed eyes. "Firestar's loyalty is to ThunderClan," he growled. "I have no doubt of that. And he is a fine, dedicated leader." *I need a change of subject!* "Have I mentioned?" he added suddenly, lightening his tone. "We have more good news in ThunderClan. Our warrior Brightheart has given birth to a kit, and named her Whitekit. Cloudtail is her father."

"Brightheart! Whitekit!" The cats in the clearing responded joyfully to Graystripe's news.

Glancing down, Graystripe saw Cloudtail gazing proudly around him, as if he were ready to take all the credit for having brought new life into the Clan. And he had reason to be proud, Graystripe reflected; it was mostly due to Cloudtail that Brightheart had overcome her terrible injuries and become once more a full member of her Clan. *I'm more than happy to share the attention with any cat right now!*

"Congratulations to the new family," Tallstar interrupted, with an irritated twitch of his ears toward Blackstar. "But we have one more important matter to discuss. Graystripe, what more can you tell us about BloodClan?"

Graystripe had hoped that he wouldn't have to discuss BloodClan, but now he felt almost relieved. *I'll talk about anything, if it distracts the other Clans from wondering where Firestar is!*

"I've no more news," he reported. "Except to tell Shadow-Clan, if they don't know already, that I and some of my warriors had a skirmish with some BloodClan cats near the Twolegplace. Since then, we have not seen nor smelled any of them. We searched the whole territory."

"We haven't seen them, either," Tallstar meowed. "Perhaps you scared them off, Graystripe."

"Perhaps," Graystripe agreed, though, as he had said to Cinderpelt earlier, he didn't believe it. "Leopardstar, have you seen anything?" he asked. "Blackstar?"

Both Clan leaders shook their heads.

"We should all agree to pass on the news immediately if we spot signs of BloodClan on our territories," Tallstar suggested. "It's too important to wait until the next Gathering."

No cat objected, and with that, Blackstar drew the Gathering to an end. As he leaped off the Great Rock, Graystripe felt as uneasy and apprehensive as he had on the day when Firestar had first told him he had to leave the Clan.

He was afraid he had made ThunderClan seem vulnerable by discussing the trouble with BloodClan, when the marauding rogues hadn't targeted any of the other Clans. He wondered what the others would do if BloodClan succeeded in taking ThunderClan's territory. Graystripe worried that they might see it as a good thing, and begin fighting to take the rest of his Clan's territory for themselves.

I wonder if I can ever really trust the other Clans. Oh, Firestar, you always seemed so much better at getting along with the others!

Graystripe was looking around for the rest of his Clan when Stormfur and Feathertail bounded up to him.

"Don't go yet," Feathertail mewed, touching noses with him. "We haven't had time to say hello to you."

"Yes, you were stuck on top of the Great Rock," Stormfur added. "How long will it be before Firestar is back and we're able to talk to you again?"

Graystripe wondered why Stormfur should ask him that. *Does my own son mistrust me now? I suppose I am lying to him, like I'm lying to every cat—though I wouldn't have to lie to him if he would just join me in ThunderClan!*

"You'd have to ask our medicine cat that," he responded. "But I'm sure he'll be back by the next Gathering."

Stormfur nodded, seeming satisfied by that answer. "I'm going to catch up with some of your Clanmates," he announced, and slipped off into the crowd.

Graystripe was left with Feathertail, regretful that their meeting would have to be so short. He thought that he could detect sadness in her beautiful blue eyes, and remembered how, during the Gathering, she and her brother had been sitting slightly apart from the rest of their Clan.

"Are you happy in RiverClan?" he asked.

"Yes—yes, of course," Feathertail answered, her ears flicking up in surprise. "Why do you ask?"

Graystripe wasn't completely convinced by her answer. "No reason," he meowed. "Just that you and Stormfur are my kits, and you have the right to become warriors in Thunder-Clan if you want to do that." He hesitated, and then softened his voice as he added, "It would make me very happy to have you in ThunderClan."

Feathertail hesitated, and for one wild moment, Graystripe thought she would take him up on his offer. "I appreciate that," she responded at last. "But while Stormfur is part of RiverClan, I feel I should try to find my place there, too."

"I understand." Graystripe touched his nose to her ear, drinking in her scent. "Just remember that the offer is open. You'll always be welcome in my Clan."

Feathertail ducked her head awkwardly, then vanished into the crowd of cats, following Stormfur. Graystripe turned away, a pit of regret in his belly, and headed up the fern-covered slope and out of the hollow.

But as he padded through the forest, toward the Thunder-Clan camp, a new feeling came over him. He sensed once more a nervous prickling in his pelt, and wondered about hostile eyes staring at him from the darkness.

Are you out there, BloodClan? Are you watching me?

CHAPTER 15

❧

— *Now* —

"*Great StarClan, what are you meowing* about?" Graystripe demanded testily. He swiped at the young she-cat with one paw, his claws sheathed, easily shoving her off him. Rising to his paws, he shook debris off his pelt and looked around.

Graystripe stood in the center of a circle of young cats: six, he realized, counting them. For one wild moment, he wondered if somehow a fragment of RiverClan could have survived here. *No, that's impossible,* he thought. Besides, these cats didn't smell like RiverClan; they smelled like kittypets.

The she-cat who had attacked him—a tortoiseshell with white chest and paws—stepped forward until she stood nose to nose with Graystripe. He had to stifle a *mrrow* of laughter; she was trying so hard to look threatening.

"You're trespassing on our territory," she accused him. "And as we're fierce warrior cats, we don't take too kindly to that."

Graystripe stared at her. "Wait . . . warrior cats?" Glancing around at this collection of fluffy furballs, it was obvious that they were pampered kittypets and not warriors at all.

Even though they were all snarling and showing him their claws.

"Yes, we're WarriorClan," the tortoiseshell kittypet continued. "Clan cats have lived on this territory for seasons. You must either submit to our authority—or face our wrath!"

"Or join us," a very fluffy orange kittypet added. "That's an option, too, if you're tough enough."

They've got a whole swarm of bees in their brain, Graystripe thought, bemused. "So, you're . . . 'warriors,'" he murmured. "What do you do?"

"We fight!" a black-and-white tom yowled.

"We hang out here on this territory," the orange kittypet explained. "Because it's *ours*, and we work together to hunt and to fight our enemies. During the day, anyway," he admitted after a pause. "At night we have to go home to our housefolk."

"I'm Monkeystar," the tortoiseshell announced. "I'm Clan leader, so I mostly decide what we do each day."

Monkeystar? What sort of a name is that? "What's a monkey?" Graystripe asked.

Monkeystar looked faintly embarrassed. "I don't know," she confessed. "But it's the name that my housefolk gave me, so it must be something fierce, like me."

"And what are the rest of you called?"

"I'm Bugeater," a tabby she-cat told him.

"And I'm Fireface." That was a ginger tom with unusually red fur around his face and ears.

"I'm Bigteeth," the black-and-white tom mewed. There was

no need, Graystripe thought with amusement, to ask where he got his name.

"And I'm Clawwhistle," the fluffy orange tom declared. Graystripe gave him a puzzled look, and the kittypet went on to explain, "You know, like the whistle a claw makes when it flies through the air as you're about to tear into some cat." He demonstrated by swiping one paw a mouse-length from Graystripe's nose.

"Er . . . yeah, I see," Graystripe responded, managing not to duck backward. "Good name."

"And I'm Chester," the sixth cat, a gray tom, announced.

Chester? Graystripe was puzzled. Monkeystar had at least made her kittypet name into a Clan leader's name by adding "star" to the end of it, and the others had all made an effort to give themselves fierce warrior names. *So what's with . . . Chester?*

The gray tom seemed to understand what was confusing Graystripe. "It seemed too much to keep track of, to have one name at home and a different one in WarriorClan," he meowed helpfully. "So I decided to stick with the name my housefolk gave me. But I'm still a dedicated warrior," he finished, puffing out his chest proudly.

I suppose that makes as much sense as the rest of it, Graystripe mused. *Actually, aren't there some strange names in SkyClan? I suppose that happens sometimes with their cats who used to be "daylight warriors."*

"So you're all kittypets?" he asked.

"Well, yes . . ." Monkeystar sounded reluctant to admit it. "We're kittypets when we're with our housefolk, but when we get out of our gardens—and that's most of the day—we're fierce warriors. Except that Fireface's housefolk feed him at midday, so he goes home for that."

Graystripe wasn't sure how to react. He didn't know if these fierce warriors would let him go without a fight, and though he was sure he could beat the lot of them with one paw—even at his age—he didn't want to hurt them.

"How did you learn about the warrior way of life?" he asked finally, playing for time.

"There's an old kittypet who lives on the other side of the river, called Smudge," Monkeystar explained. "He told us that the whole forest used to be filled with warriors. They lived in the open, and hunted their own prey, and sometimes they would even fight one another. But they were brave and loyal, and they defended the forest."

"Whatever happened to them?" Graystripe asked, curious to know what stories he and his Clanmates had left behind them.

"It's sad, really," Bugeater replied. "Smudge doesn't know. One day the forest was filled with warriors, and the next it was like they just all left at once."

"Well, you might like to know," Graystripe began, wondering whether he would regret this later, "that *I'm* one of those warriors. The Clans live far away now, many days' journey, but I've come back to check on the old territory."

Surprised squeals came from the WarriorClan cats, who gazed at Graystripe with round eyes and jaws gaping.

"You? Really?" Fireface gasped.

"Really," Graystripe told him.

"You must be *way* old!" Chester exclaimed.

You're right there, Graystripe thought ruefully. "Not as old as all that," he retorted.

Monkeystar was twitching her whiskers frantically, her eyes stretched wide with curiosity. "But why did you leave?"

Graystripe waved his tail at the rows and rows of Twoleg dens across the river. "The Twolegs—housefolk—took our territory."

"That's dreadful!" Bigteeth breathed out. "Couldn't you fight them? If you were as fierce as the stories say?"

Graystripe shook his head. "You can't fight Twolegs."

"Smudge told us stories about an orange cat called Firestar," Bugeater meowed. "You're not orange."

"Well spotted," Graystripe murmured, amused. "True, I'm not Firestar. My name is Graystripe, and when we lived here in the forest, I was Firestar's deputy. He and I were best friends."

The young cats' eyes stretched even wider; clearly, they were massively impressed at meeting a friend of the great Firestar. *It's like I'm one of the heroic warriors out of a nursery tale,* Graystripe thought.

"Is Firestar with you?" Clawwhistle asked, glancing around as if he expected to see this legendary cat stepping out of the bushes.

"No," Graystripe answered with a sudden pang of sadness. "Firestar is dead. He died bravely, saving his Clan."

"You must miss him," Chester mewed, blinking sympathetically.

"I do." Graystripe felt a lump in his throat as he thought of how much he missed his friend, but he didn't want to dampen the young cats' enthusiasm by dwelling on past grief. He lifted his head and spoke bravely. "But we will never forget him, and many of his kin are now noble warriors of ThunderClan."

"So did you become Clan leader, when Firestar died?" Bugeater asked.

Graystripe shook his head. "No, I—"

"Enough questions!" Monkeystar interrupted, her tortoise-shell fur fluffing out. "If you're a true warrior, you'll prove it by fighting me."

Graystripe blinked at her. He was reluctant to fight any of these young kittypets, but he had to admit that at least Monkeystar had courage. "Okay," he meowed. "You—"

He broke off as Monkeystar hurled herself at him, fore-paws flailing. Graystripe dodged aside and aimed a blow at her flank, careful to keep his claws sheathed. Monkeystar staggered, but managed to keep her balance, and leaped at him from behind, scrambling up onto his shoulders and lash-ing at his ears. Graystripe let her get one or two good blows in before letting himself go limp and falling to the ground, then using the unexpected shift in momentum to roll them over. He pinned her down with his forepaws on her shoulders. For a few heartbeats, Monkeystar struggled to free herself, then relaxed with a sigh of resignation.

"Well?" Graystripe's voice was a soft growl. "Am I a true warrior?"

Monkeystar snarled, but then reluctantly agreed, "I guess you are."

Graystripe got up and stepped back to allow the young tortoiseshell to rise to her paws. Meanwhile the other cats of WarriorClan began crowding around him, letting out admiring meows.

"That was *brilliant*!"

"Can you teach us to do that?"

"Please!"

Graystripe had to admit that part of him was enjoying the young cats' hero worship, even though he knew he should be concentrating on his mission. He detached himself and dipped his head respectfully to Monkeystar. He didn't want her to feel ashamed at having been bested by another cat in front of her Clanmates. "You fought well, for a young cat," he told her. "You have courage and determination."

Monkeystar's ears flicked up with pleasure at his praise, and she gave her shoulder a couple of embarrassed licks. "I wish you would train us," she mewed.

"I'm sorry," Graystripe responded. "I don't have a lot of time to hang out. I'm on my way somewhere, to carry out an important warrior task."

"Maybe we can help you!" Monkeystar suggested with an enthusiastic little jump.

"Yeah," Clawwhistle added. "Just tell us what to do."

Graystripe shook his head. "No, it's something I have to do alone." He meant to turn away and head back across the river, but he found he couldn't bear the sight of their disappointed faces. And he couldn't deny that he was enjoying their admiration. "Okay," he meowed. "I'll stay for a little while—just for this morning—and show you some hunting moves."

The WarriorClan cats jumped up and down, letting out eager yowls. *So loud that they'll scare off all the prey between here and Highstones,* Graystripe thought ruefully. "Okay, settle down and watch me," he began. "We call this the hunter's crouch. . . ."

"Suppose there was a mouse under that bush," Graystripe meowed, waving his tail at a low-growing holly a few fox-lengths ahead. "What would you do first?"

Fireface waved his tail. "Creep up on it!"

Graystripe shook his head. "No, not *first*. Clawwhistle, do you know?"

"Check the wind?" the orange kittypet guessed.

"That's right. Very good!" Clawwhistle's orange pelt seemed to glow even brighter in his pride at being praised by Graystripe. "Okay, if we check the wind, what do we hope we'll find?"

Monkeystar was bouncing up and down in her eagerness to answer. "It's blowing toward us, so the mouse can't smell us, so we can catch it!"

"Right!" Graystripe stifled a purr of amusement. "But it's not quite as easy as that. What you have to remember with a mouse is that it's *very* sensitive to vibrations in the ground. It will feel you coming long before it sees you or scents you. So what does that mean? Yes, Bugeater?"

"We have to creep up *really* carefully."

"You're right, we do. So let's see you all practice that. Show me your hunter's crouch, and then creep toward the mouse that we're pretending is under the holly bush over there. And don't forget—tails down!"

Graystripe stood back as the WarriorClan cats began their training exercise. He was surprised at how much he was enjoying himself. The kittypets were working hard; their hunting techniques were coming along nicely. It reminded Graystripe of training apprentices, back when he was still a warrior. He'd loved training Brackenfur—and, briefly, Stormfur—teaching all the skills he'd learned, and making the Clan stronger. It had been so many moons since then. *Elders don't take apprentices,* he told himself with a sigh.

The kittypets were still stalking carefully up to the holly bush, their shadows stretching out beside them on the grass. *Their shadows . . . !* Graystripe looked up at the sun, stunned to see how close it was to setting. The whole day had slipped away in training the young cats. *However did I let that happen?*

"That's very good," he called out to the kittypets. "I'm sorry, but we have to stop now. I really must be going; I have an important task to complete for my Clan." But even while he was speaking, he felt as if a claw had lodged itself in his heart. It felt strange to act as though ThunderClan had sent him on some important mission, when in truth he'd left them without any assurance that he was going to return. He'd been feeling that it was likely that he *would* return, depending on what happened at the Moonstone, but the mention of his Clan brought it all back: the nightmare of Bramblestar's death, the confusion about StarClan's long silence, and the tension in ThunderClan over Squirrelflight's leadership. Everything felt so much more complicated than it had been in the forest, with Firestar leading. *Will I ever feel as connected to ThunderClan as I did when I lived here?*

"Oh, no! You can't go yet!" Chester exclaimed. "We've still got loads more to learn."

All six cats abandoned their imaginary mouse and crowded around Graystripe, adding their protests to the gray tom's.

"Where are you going?" Fireface asked.

"And why is it so important that you can't stay another day or two with us?" Bigteeth added.

Graystripe paused. He knew these cats wouldn't understand the details, but he did feel that they deserved to know a bit more about why he was leaving them so abruptly. "I have to go to the Moonstone," he admitted.

"The Moonstone!" Monkeystar yowled, her green eyes flaring with excitement. "That's where the warrior cats talk to StarClan!"

Graystripe's pelt prickled with surprise that the kittypets had even heard of the Moonstone. *I suppose Firestar must have told Smudge about it, but it's hardly the sort of thing a kittypet would understand. The kittypet I spoke to last night certainly didn't!* "What do you know about the Moonstone?" he asked.

"It's a big stone underground," Clawwhistle replied. "And the cats of StarClan make it light up!"

"They appear in the stone and tell the Clan cats what to do," Monkeystar added.

Well . . . sort of, Graystripe thought, admitting to himself that he wasn't entirely sure how medicine cats and Clan leaders communicated with StarClan at the Moonstone. "Do you know where it is?" he asked.

All six kittypets shook their heads. "Do you?" Monkeystar asked in her turn.

"I think I do," Graystripe replied. "Everything looks so different with all these Twoleg dens, but I've a pretty good idea of the way."

"We could come with you." Monkeystar's green eyes sparkled. "We could help; we're good at traveling among housefolk dens."

Every drop of blood inside Graystripe turned to ice at the thought of leading six kittypets up Highstones to Mothermouth. "Absolutely not," he responded, making his tone as stern as he could. "Besides," he continued, "it must be getting close to the time when you're fed. Surely your Twolegs will be worried?"

The kittypets exchanged disappointed glances. "Okay," Monkeystar mewed at last. "I guess I am getting hungry. Thanks for all the training, anyway."

"Yeah, it was great!" Clawwhistle agreed. "I never thought we'd ever meet a *real* warrior cat."

Bugeater flexed her claws in and out. "It's been so exciting!"

"Will you be come back this way?" Bigteeth asked.

"I'm not sure," Graystripe replied. "That depends on what happens when I reach the Moonstone. But if I do pass this way again, I'll surely look out for you."

"And we'll look out for you," Monkeystar responded, dipping her head respectfully. "And meanwhile, may StarClan . . . watch your paws?"

"Nearly right." Graystripe made a massive effort to hide his amusement. "Warriors say, 'May StarClan light your path.' And may they light yours also, cats of WarriorClan."

The six kittypets chorused a farewell, then turned and vanished into the bushes, heading for the Twoleg bridge and their Twoleg nests on the far side of the river.

Graystripe stood watching them go, feeling cheered by having spent time with them. Then, when he thought he had allowed them long enough to disperse to their dens, he padded across the bridge in what he hoped was the direction of Mothermouth.

The sun was going down in a blaze of scarlet light, though clouds were massing over the hills ahead, and Graystripe guessed that the night might bring a storm. *That's all I need—to be stuck out on Highstones in the pouring rain!* He began to regret even more the day he had spent training the kittypets.

The path Graystripe had chosen skirted the Twolegplace, and he hoped he might be able to find his way around without actually venturing back into the maze of dens and Thunderpaths. But still, he didn't feel that he was on familiar territory. There was evidence of Twolegs everywhere: debris lying half hidden in the grass, the acrid scent of monsters, damaged undergrowth where Twolegs had shoved their clumsy way through.

It's not the way it was when I traveled this way with Firestar, Graystripe thought. *Everything looked different then . . . bigger, somehow. . . .*

Then Graystripe halted at the edge of a wide, circular path. It was made of some hard, grayish stuff, and it surrounded the top of a hollow lined with smooth grass. A mass of broken stone lay at the bottom. Graystripe's belly lurched as he recognized where he was.

It looked very different now, with the oak trees cut down and the Great Rock crushed into rubble. Graystripe had been told what had happened, but it knocked all the breath out of him to see it in real life.

This was Fourtrees.

CHAPTER 16

❧

— Then —

The rabbit was streaking through the trees, heading for the Shadow-Clan border. In a few more heartbeats it would cross, and escape the ThunderClan fresh-kill pile. Graystripe put on an extra burst of speed and leaped on top of it with less than a fox-length to spare. Its squeal of terror was cut off as he bit down on its throat.

"Thank you, StarClan, for this prey," Graystripe panted, flopping down for a few moments to catch his breath. It was a good, plump rabbit and would fill the bellies of several cats. *Maybe the elders would like it....*

Once he had recovered from the chase, Graystripe rose to his paws, ready to return to camp with the rabbit. "Brackenfur?" he called, gazing around for his Clanmate, who had been hunting with him.

But there was no reply, and no sign of the golden-brown tabby warrior. Graystripe realized that in his frantic chase after the rabbit, he had strayed a long way from their original hunting ground.

I'll probably find him on the way back, he thought, picking up his prey and heading in the direction of the camp.

But before Graystripe had gone more than a few fox-lengths, he heard a rustling in a clump of elder bushes just ahead of him. "Brackenfur?" he mumbled around his mouth-ful of rabbit fur.

There was no response; clearly, whatever was in the bush, it wasn't his Clanmate. Instantly alert, Graystripe dropped the rabbit and slid out his claws, bracing himself for an attack. He thought once more of the eyes he had been imagining in the darkness. It had been only a quarter moon since the last attack—long enough to begin to relax, but certainly not long enough for the threat to be gone. Now that he wasn't carrying the rabbit and his jaws weren't filled with the over-whelming tang of fresh-kill, he could pick up BloodClan scent coming from the bush. His heart began to pound as he fought to wrestle down his panic.

Have some of the BloodClan cats caught me alone?

"Come out, whoever you are!" he commanded. A moment later, a single cat emerged into the open. Graystripe rec-ognized the pregnant queen with the patchy-colored fur. She was the one who had allowed him to escape after the ambush, when her Clanmates had left him for dead in the Twoleg garden; he didn't imagine that she would attack him now.

"What do you want?" he asked.

"I'm not looking for trouble," the she-cat assured him, giv-ing him a respectful dip of her head. "In fact, from what I've seen, I think we could be helpful to each other. My name is Gremlin."

"That's an odd name," Graystripe muttered.

Gremlin flicked her ears dismissively. "No odder than Graystripe."

Graystripe flinched, offended. But the she-cat went on: "It's the name my housefolk gave me, back when my brother and I had housefolk."

"You were a kittypet?" Graystripe asked, surprised; she did not look, or smell, like any kittypet he had ever met.

"Once," Gremlin replied. "A while ago now. But then my housefolk had a kit, and as soon as it could move about, it started pulling our tails and ears, so my brother and I decided to leave. And then we found BloodClan."

"I think I would rather have put up with the Twoleg kit!" Graystripe meowed. *Even being a kittypet would be better than joining those crow-food-eating rogues!*

Gremlin snorted. "BloodClan was there for me when I needed some cat," she told him. "For a long time, I trusted them with my life. But now I'm expecting kits . . . and I'm worried about them."

"Why?" Graystripe asked. Tired of standing nose to nose with this BloodClan cat, he gestured with his tail for her to sit on a patch of moss underneath a nearby ash tree, and settled himself beside her.

"BloodClan separates parents from kits as soon as the kits are old enough to feed themselves," Gremlin explained. "Families are not allowed to live together, and the kits must kill BloodClan's enemies or be killed themselves. I've seen this happen to many queens, and the fathers, too. They can't protect their own kits, and often lose track of them entirely. Now that I'm about to have kits myself, I understand how they feel." Her voice quivered. "These kits are a part of me . . . I love them already, more than I've ever loved any cat, except maybe my brother. But I know I'll have to say good-bye to them, and it breaks my heart. I can't bear the thought of it. What if something bad happens to them? They'll be too young to defend themselves."

As she was speaking, Graystripe found himself becoming more sympathetic toward her, but he was still confused about why she was telling him this. What could she possibly want from him, or from ThunderClan? "I have kits myself, so I understand how you feel," he told her. "But what can *I* do to help? You're my enemy, and I'm yours."

"We are now, but . . ." Gremlin leaned closer toward him. "I've been watching the Clans for some time," she confessed in a low voice. "I've seen how Clan cats treat their queens and kits. The queens get to stay with their kits while they nurse, and they get all the help they need from the medicine cat and the rest of the Clan. Queens don't even have to hunt for themselves! It's so different from BloodClan, where the queens are really on their own."

Now Graystripe was more deeply shocked than ever, hardly able to believe what he thought Gremlin was saying. "Wait—are you saying you want to *join* ThunderClan? A BloodClan cat?"

Gremlin nodded. Graystripe could see desperation in her green eyes. "I know it's unusual, but I hope you'll consider letting me in, along with my brother, Scraps. No—don't refuse yet!" she added as Graystripe opened his jaws to do just that. "I mean, I'll prove my worthiness first, of course. I can contribute a lot to your Clan!"

Suspicion prickled all along Graystripe's spine, raising the fur there. "How do you plan to do that?" he asked.

"I can help you keep your Clan safe!" Gremlin declared. "Isn't that the most important thing a leader does? And I know that you're acting as leader right now. I know that Blood-Clan has threatened you. And I have to tell you, Scourge was fierce, but our new leader, Fury—she's more bloodthirsty than Scourge ever was! And she's dead set on getting revenge on the Clans. Right now, she thinks ThunderClan is vulnerable because your leader is gone. But I can find out all the details about when they plan to attack, and where and how they'll do it. I can share those with you, so you can easily overcome them—*if* you promise to take me into the Clan when the battle is over, so I have a safe place to raise my kits."

Graystripe held her gaze for several heartbeats. "Why should I trust you?" he asked eventually. "You are part of BloodClan, after all. Don't you care about those cats? How do I know this isn't all a trick?"

"I can't prove it to you," Gremlin answered with a sigh, "because no cat knows what I've been planning. I haven't even told Scraps, and he's the only BloodClan cat I care about. I know he loves me, but . . ." Gremlin ducked her head. "I'm afraid he's still loyal to BloodClan."

"Why try to bring him with you, then?" Graystripe asked. "How do you know he wants to be a Clan cat?"

"I can't be sure . . . but I've seen BloodClan start to turn my brother into the worst cat he could possibly be." Now Gremlin's eyes were deep green pools of sorrow. "He needs a way out. There was a BloodClan cat who was like a mentor to him . . . no, not a mentor—a *father*. But he was killed in the battle with the Clans. Now Scraps is so angry, and he takes that anger out on other cats, always lashing out at them." She paused, swallowing, and her voice shook as she went on. "Fury rewards that behavior, because she wants us angry, ready to kill our enemies. I know that, deep down, my gentle brother is still inside that cat somewhere. But I'm afraid that if we stay in BloodClan, Scraps will lose that part of himself forever. Or worse—he'll die in some stupid fight before he ever comes to his senses."

Graystripe could understand that. Scraps wouldn't be the first to lose his way through grief for a cat he loved. But he was still dubious that joining ThunderClan would solve Scraps's problems. "What about your kits' father?" he asked. "Can't you go to him for help?"

Gremlin shook her head. "The father of my kits was never a BloodClan cat. He's a kittypet. He did offer to let me join him in his housefolk's den. But . . . well. I've tasted freedom, and I don't want to go back to the kittypet life. Besides, I know Scraps would never agree to that, and I won't leave him."

"But you think he would agree to living in a Clan?"

Gremlin let out a small purr, half-amused, half-affection-ate. "Yes. It might take some getting used to, but I think Clan life is just about wild enough for Scraps, and just safe enough for me."

Graystripe tucked his paws underneath him and sat gazing at Gremlin, blinking in deep thought. His first instinct was to try to help her, but natural caution was holding him back. She was a BloodClan cat, after all, one of the Clan of rogues who'd tried to kill Graystripe. Not to mention, they had brought devastation to the forest not all that many seasons ago. *And I know my Clanmates won't exactly be thrilled if I let two of their cats join ThunderClan—especially as even she admits that one of them doesn't know when to keep his claws sheathed.*

Taking a deep breath, Graystripe began, "I'll think about—"

He was interrupted by an indignant yowl, rising from behind the elder bushes where Gremlin had been hiding. Brackenfur stormed out into the open and stood in front of Graystripe with his shoulder fur bristling.

"What is there to think about?" he demanded. "We can't trust this cat!"

"Have you been eavesdropping?" Graystripe retorted, springing to his paws. "How much did you hear?"

"Enough," Brackenfur meowed grimly. "And it's a good thing I did. We searched for BloodClan all over the terri-tory and couldn't find so much as a whisker. I'd bet this cat is lying about this supposed BloodClan attack, just to get into our Clan, and there isn't any threat at all. That or her pack of rogues is still lurking around and this is another of their tricks. What if she wants to lead us into a trap, where Blood-Clan is waiting to tear our pelts off?"

Well, it can't be both, Graystripe reflected, his head beginning to spin. *Either there's no BloodClan attack planned, or there is, but this deal is part of the trap.* "If you'd been involved in that fight the other day, you wouldn't doubt that BloodClan is still strong enough to hurt us," he mewed grimly.

"I'm not lying, I promise!" Gremlin protested. "It's up to you to decide whether to trust me or not. But remember, if you choose wrong, I won't be the cat who dies. I've fought in many battles and seen many deaths. And with Fury leading us, and your leader gone . . . I know that BloodClan is strong enough to take ThunderClan's territory."

She rose to her paws, then headed off in the direction of the Twolegplace, raking Brackenfur with a scorching green glare as she passed him. When she reached the elder bushes, she stopped and turned back.

"Graystripe, if you want to discuss this, you can ask for me at the red den in the Twolegplace," she told him. "It's right next to the one where Fury and the others tried to feed you to the dog. Smudge, the kittypet who lives there, knows where to find me."

"Oh, Smudge!" Graystripe exclaimed, recollecting the den Gremlin meant. "I know him. He's a good friend to the Clans." It heartened Graystripe to know that Smudge was on good terms with Gremlin. Perhaps she could be trusted after all. "I'll think about what you've said, and then get him to send you a message."

"Don't think too long," Gremlin warned him.

She turned again and stalked off with a lash of her tail.

Graystripe and Brackenfur were left gazing at each other; for a moment, neither cat spoke. "Let's get back to camp," Graystripe mewed at last, padding across to where he had left his rabbit.

"Just like that?" Brackenfur responded, his shoulder fur beginning to rise with indignation. "You're considering making a deal with a cat from BloodClan—the cats who almost destroyed the whole forest—and you want us to stroll back to camp as if nothing has happened?"

"Nothing *has* happened, not yet," Graystripe pointed out. "And I only told Gremlin I would think about her offer. I haven't promised her anything."

Brackenfur let out an angry snort. "You shouldn't even have done that! If I were you, I would have sent her back to the Twolegplace with a few scratches to remember me by."

Graystripe could feel his own anger beginning to swell at the way his Clanmate was questioning his decision. *No cat ever argued with Firestar like this.* But he forced his fur to remain flat and his voice even as he replied. "You weren't there when the BloodClan cats attacked me and Dustpelt and Brambleclaw, Fury *is* bloodthirsty, and I don't like knowing that she's confident she could take our territory. Can we afford to ignore something that might give us an edge?"

"*If* that cat is telling the truth." Brackenfur gave his pelt a furious shake. "But she's a BloodClan cat. How can you even think about trusting her?"

There was something about her . . ., Graystripe thought. But he had more sense than to say that aloud to Brackenfur. "What she said about her kits made sense," he replied. "If you were a BloodClan queen, wouldn't you be worried?"

"We only have her word for it that BloodClan would take her kits away," Brackenfur retorted. Puffing out his breath, he continued, "Graystripe, you were my mentor. I've always trusted you. I thought Firestar made the right decision when he left you in charge of the Clan. But now . . . I think you must have bees in your brain!"

Pain clawed at Graystripe's heart as he saw how close he was to losing the younger cat's respect. *But I can't make decisions for the whole Clan based on what one cat thinks about me.* All the same, his confidence had taken a hard knock. *What if I'm wrong, and Brackenfur is right when he tells me not to make a deal with Gremlin?*

"I promise I'll think really carefully about this," he told his Clanmate. "But meanwhile, will you give me your word not to spread this around the Clan? I don't want unnecessary trouble."

"*Unnecessary* . . ." Brackenfur spoke the word under his breath, but loud enough for Graystripe to hear. "Okay," he added ungraciously. "But you'll have to tell them, sooner or later."

"I will," Graystripe responded. "When I'm ready."

Brackenfur let out an irritated snort. "So let's get back to camp," he snapped.

He whipped around, headed behind the elder bushes, and returned with a couple of mice dangling from his jaws. "I still think it's a terrible idea to make a deal with that cat," he muttered around the mouse tails.

"It would be an even worse one to sit and wait for Blood-Clan to attack us with no idea of when or how the attack will come." Graystripe still hadn't given up hope of persuading the younger tom. "Suppose some cat offered you a nice, juicy rabbit. Wouldn't you take it?"

Brackenfur shook his head, setting his two mice swinging. He was obviously still unhappy. "If it was a BloodClan cat, I wouldn't touch it with a single claw. But you're acting leader," he growled, "so I guess it's your decision."

It is, unfortunately. "Let's get back," Graystripe meowed, picking up his rabbit.

As they headed toward the camp, Graystripe let his Clanmate walk a few paces ahead, aware of his still-bristling fur and the irritated twitching of his tail. *I guess he's showing me how the rest of the Clan will react if I make a deal with Gremlin.* He could almost hear the furious yowls that would erupt from his Clanmates, and see their glaring eyes. *I'm not looking forward to that, not one bit. But I might have to put up with it, for the sake of the Clan.* He let out a long, despairing sigh. *Oh, Firestar, when are you coming home?*

Then he realized that he wasn't entirely alone. There was one cat whose wisdom he could trust, who would give him her advice without blaming him or growing angry. *Thank StarClan I have Cinderpelt to rely on!*

Back in the camp, Graystripe took his rabbit to the elders, then pushed his way through the fern tunnel into the medicine cat's den. Cinderpelt was there, pulling out a thorn from

Sorrelpaw's pad. As he waited, Graystripe pondered the conversation he'd just had with Brackenfur. *Would Firestar agree with him that a deal with Gremlin is too risky? What would Firestar do?* It was hard to imagine.

"There, give it a good lick," Cinderpelt meowed as a few drops of blood trickled out from where she'd removed the thorn. "Go back to your den and rest, then come and see me again first thing tomorrow. No more duties until then, and if Dustpelt complains, send him to me."

"Thank you, Cinderpelt!" Sorrelpaw responded between vigorous licks.

"And stay off that paw," Cinderpelt added as the young apprentice rose to leave.

"I will!" Sorrelpaw tottered out of the den on three legs, dipping her head in a respectful nod to Graystripe as she passed him.

Watching her go, Cinderpelt let out a sigh and carefully moved the thorn aside. "When will cats start to watch where they're putting their paws?" Turning to Graystripe, she continued, "Hi, Graystripe. What can I do for you?"

"I need your advice," Graystripe replied. Settling himself beside the medicine cat, he told her about his encounter with Gremlin in the forest, the deal she had offered him, and Brackenfur's outraged reaction. "What do you think I should do?"

Cinderpelt had listened to his story without interrupting, her expression calm but serious. When he had finished speaking, she turned her head away, deep thought darkening her blue eyes. Graystripe felt his belly churning as he waited for her reaction.

Eventually, the medicine cat turned back to Graystripe. "This is a big decision," she murmured. "I don't feel comfortable making it alone. I want to go to the Moonstone and seek advice from StarClan there."

CHAPTER 17

— Now —

Still skirting the outside of the Twolegplace, Graystripe headed back toward Highstones and the Moonstone. Now he was sure he was on what had once been WindClan territory, where the trees and thick undergrowth of the remaining forest gave way to moorland with patches of gorse and jutting rocks breaking up the sweep of rough grass.

As he padded up the long slope toward the ridge, his gaze firmly fixed on his destination, he couldn't shake off the weird feeling that he was being watched. The sensation had followed him all the way from Fourtrees; it felt as if ants were crawling through his pelt.

Am I imagining things?

Graystripe couldn't imagine who—or what—might have been watching him for so long. The only cats around there were kittypets, and any predator would have attacked long before.

He paused to taste the air, but he couldn't distinguish anything useful from beneath the mingled scents wafting from the Twolegplace. But once he had stopped, he realized that he could hear faint sounds coming from behind him: the snap of a twig, the stirring of a branch in the gorse bushes.

His suspicions rising, he whirled around. "Who's there?" he demanded. "I'm a ThunderClan warrior, and I'll tear the pelt off any cat who tries to mess with me!"

For a long moment, nothing happened. Then Graystripe spotted movement among a clump of gorse bushes several fox-lengths farther down the hillside. He saw the flash of a tortoiseshell pelt, and then Monkeystar slid out into the open, followed by Clawwhistle, Bigteeth, Bugeater, Chester and Fireface. They stood looking up at him, shuffling their paws in embarrassment.

At first, Graystripe was torn between annoyance and grudging respect. *I've taught them too well,* he realized. *They've been able to stalk me all the way from the river!*

"We're sorry," Monkeystar mewed, though after her initial awkwardness her eyes began to sparkle and she didn't look a bit sorry. "We just really, really want to know where the Moonstone is. And our housefolk are used to us disappearing for a night or two to have adventures. They won't worry too much."

"Staying away for a night or two is the best way to get extra treats!" Bugeater added excitedly. "Our housefolk always spoil us whenever we've been missing for a while."

Annoyance finally won. "There's no reason for you to follow me," Graystripe snapped, "because you *can't* go inside Mothermouth to see the Moonstone. *I* shouldn't even be going inside—it's for medicine cats and Clan leaders only—but this is an emergency."

"What emergency?" Clawwhistle asked. "Maybe we could help."

"Never mind what emergency," Graystripe retorted.

He couldn't face trying to explain to these kittypets what had been happening among the Clans. It was just too depressing. And he had no idea what WarriorClan would make of the news that an evil spirit cat had possessed a Clan leader's body. He wasn't even sure he understood it himself.

Let them believe that being a warrior is all about hunting and being fierce.

"Please let us come with you," Monkeystar begged, blinking appealingly at Graystripe. "I promise none of us will go in, if you'll just show us where it is."

Graystripe hesitated. They had stalked him this far, and he was pretty certain that if he refused to take them, they would just carry on following him in secret. The only way he could stop them would be to claw them up and chase them off the hard way, and he really didn't want to do that. *I like the stupid furballs far too much!* Reluctantly, he realized that whatever he decided, he would slow himself down. Letting the kittypets come with him might be the most practical choice.

"Okay," he meowed eventually. "But you have to remember, you can't go inside, and you have to do exactly as I tell you."

"Oh, we will!" Monkeystar gave an excited little bounce. "We promise!"

The kittypets swarmed around Graystripe as he set off

again up the hill. They seemed to be full of energy, in spite of the long way they had already traveled, bounding off to stick their noses into every hole or patch of reeds, like overeager kits. Their squeals of excitement rose into the air, and Graystripe reflected how lucky they were that there were no more WindClan warriors patrolling the territory. He wasn't sure how they would cope once they grew tired, but he doubted they would give up on their long journey now.

As they reached the outskirts of WindClan's old territory, the sun had gone down and twilight was gathering. Graystripe began to pick up the harsh scent of the Thunderpath, and spotted the glaring eyes of monsters as they cut through the darkness.

"Come here!" he called to the WarriorClan cats.

He was startled at how quickly they obeyed, clustering around him so that he could lead them up to the edge of the Thunderpath. "Stop right there," he ordered, raising his tail to halt them before they could venture out onto the hard surface.

"Oh, we know about this," Bigteeth meowed. "Monsters aren't dangerous if you're careful."

A chill ran through Graystripe's pelt. The little Thunderpaths that divided Twoleg dens were much less perilous than this wide expanse, where the monsters growled up and down at terrifying speeds.

"That may be true," he responded to Bigteeth, "but now I'm going to show you how *warriors* cross a Thunderpath. Line up along the edge, and don't move until I tell you that it's safe."

The kittypets did as they were told; they jostled for position at first, then settled down and gazed seriously at Graystripe as they waited for his instructions.

"Right," Graystripe continued. "Now we wait until we can't hear or see any sign of a monster. Then when I say 'run,' I mean *run*. Straight across, and no stopping to chase moths. Got it?"

"Got it!" the kittypets echoed.

Graystripe waited for a monster to sweep by, his fur buffeted by the wind of its passing. When its noise and glare had retreated into the distance, and the stench had started to fade, he looked up and down the Thunderpath and couldn't see any more monsters approaching. Even so, he was determined not to give the order until he was certain the crossing would be absolutely safe. "Now! Run!" he yowled at last.

The kittypets all took off for the opposite side in a blur of churning paws; Graystripe hesitated for a couple of heartbeats to make sure they were all on their way, then followed. But he didn't relax until all six of them were safely across, rolling around in the grass and letting out *mrrows* of laughter.

"That was *fun!*" Fireface exclaimed, sitting up and swiping at a grass stem stuck on his nose.

"Can we do it again?" Chester asked.

StarClan, give me strength! Graystripe thought, rolling his eyes. "You'll be able to do it again on the way back," he pointed out. "Now we have to get to Highstones."

As he led the way onward, the last of the daylight had almost faded away, leaving a thick darkness; clouds were covering almost the whole of the sky, cutting off the light of moon and stars. Graystripe wondered how the kittypets would deal with a night on the inhospitable hillside, especially if the threatening storm finally broke.

"It's good we're with you," Monkeystar meowed, padding along at Graystripe's side. "Now we can help you deal with any threats that you face on your quest."

I hadn't been thinking of it as a quest, Graystripe thought with amusement, *but I guess Monkeystar is right. Let's hope there are no threats needing to be faced, though!*

Aloud he pointed out, "Remember, you all promised to do what I tell you."

Monkeystar had opened her jaws to reply when a dark figure appeared just ahead of them, from out behind the shelter of a large boulder. Instantly Graystripe took a stride forward, placing himself between the newcomer and Monkeystar and making her draw up short. He let his fur bush out defensively, flattening his ears and letting out a hiss. "Who's there?"

In answer, he received another hiss, and he realized that the newcomer was a cat. He wondered what sort of cat it might be. The WarriorClan cats had already surprised him; who else would want to mess with him? *Is this some sort of dangerous rogue?*

Around him, the WarriorClan kittypets were taking up what they thought were fierce stances, with their claws extended.

"Awesome!" Monkeystar whispered. "A fight!" But Graystripe could hear the quiver in her voice.

"We don't want any trouble," Graystripe mewed, making his voice calm. "We're just passing through."

To Graystripe's surprise, the strange cat responded in a similarly gentle tone. "I don't want trouble, either. In fact...," he added, moving closer and scrutinizing Graystripe carefully, "I think I might be looking for you. Is your name Graystripe? You look like the way he was described to me."

Stunned, Graystripe let his jaws gape open. *Who would be looking for me on the old forest territory, after so many seasons?*

At that moment, the moon appeared from behind a cloud, so that Graystripe could see the cat clearly for the first time. He was a skinny gray tom, with darker patches on his fur and vivid green eyes. One of his forelegs had a patch of torn fur, close to his paw, as if he had been in a fight or attacked by a predator. Staring, Graystripe felt there was something familiar about him, but he couldn't recall ever having met him before.

"Do I know you?" he asked.

The cat shook his head. "No, but you knew my mother... Gremlin."

For a moment, Graystripe almost staggered under the impact of shock after shock. Suddenly a rush of memories came flooding back to him: That was a name he had not thought about in more moons than he could have hoped to count. *Gremlin,* the BloodClan queen, heavy with kits, who had let him escape after her Clan's first attack on a Thunder-Clan patrol.

"My mother told me," the newcomer went on, "you once made a vow to her, that you would do anything to help her, no matter what."

Graystripe felt a stirring in his heart as he remembered that vow. And he remembered what Gremlin had done for him, and for all of ThunderClan.

"Does that vow extend to Gremlin's kits?" the strange cat asked. "Because I could do with a warrior's help right now. . . ."

CHAPTER 18

— *Then* —

Graystripe followed Cinderpelt across the WindClan border, and the two ThunderClan cats began the long trek up the moorland slope. He could still taste the bitter tang of traveling herbs on his tongue.

Night had fallen, and only fugitive gleams of moonlight shone through gaps in the clouds. Graystripe couldn't help looking around him at every heartbeat, alert for the glitter of eyes in the darkness. His ears were pricked for the sound of stealthy paw steps that might betray the presence of Blood-Clan, following them. But everything was silent.

Mouse-brain! Why would BloodClan bother following you here? he asked himself. *It's ThunderClan territory that they want. To begin with, at least,* he added. He knew that if BloodClan succeeded in overcoming ThunderClan, they would want to spread out into the other territories too. *We're protecting the other Clans, if they only knew it.*

Graystripe wondered what message StarClan would give to Cinderpelt. He tried to remember a time when he'd seen

Firestar accompany Cinderpelt to the Moonstone for advice, but he couldn't. *Maybe he doesn't need to. Maybe Firestar always knows exactly what he wants to do.* Graystripe missed his Clan leader all over again, but more than that, he wished once more that he had his friend by his side.

His legs were aching and his paws sore by the time he and Cinderpelt hauled themselves up the last steep, rocky slope to where Mothermouth gaped open, darker than the night.

Cinderpelt, who was a couple of paw steps ahead, halted outside the cave and turned back to face Graystripe. "You're not expecting to go inside, right?" she asked him.

Graystripe shook his head, indignation in his tone as he replied. "I know not to!"

Cinderpelt gave him a brisk nod. "Then wait here. Try to get some rest. I don't know how long this will take." Not waiting for a response, she slipped inside the cave, her gray pelt swallowed up by the darkness.

When she was gone, Graystripe paused for several heartbeats, gazing into the black maw of the tunnel. Even here, on the outside, he felt overwhelmed by the importance of this place, by the weight of meaning it had held for the Clans, for season upon season. He shivered from his ears to his tail-tip at the thought of going inside. *Thank StarClan there's no question of that!*

Instead he backed away a pace or two and tried to make himself comfortable on a flat stone beside the path. He couldn't help worrying that he would be an easy target for BloodClan right now, all alone in this desolate place, but he knew that no cat had followed them, and that BloodClan had no way of knowing they were here.

Thinking back to his meeting with Gremlin, he reminded himself that she had told a plausible story, and he couldn't help but feel sympathy for her plight. But he wondered once again whether he could trust her.

Quickly, Graystripe pushed the thought away. If Blood-Clan truly did have enough cats to take on ThunderClan, they wouldn't need to resort to subterfuge; it would be easier for them to attack ThunderClan with claws and teeth. Besides, there was something about Gremlin that made him believe, deep down, that she was sincere.

The night dragged on as Graystripe waited for Cinderpelt to return. His anxiety mounted with every passing heartbeat, as he thought about his dilemma: Should he accept Gremlin's offer, or should he refuse it? He imagined how bad he would feel if everything fell apart while he was in charge, and Firestar returned to find a shattered Clan.

How would I ever explain it to him? Graystripe wanted nothing more than to keep the Clan safe for his friend and leader. *We've been through so much together!*

Graystripe closed his eyes, though he expected that his worries would keep him awake. But moments later, he felt sun warm on his pelt, and found himself basking on a flat stone at the top of Sunningrocks, with light dazzling the surface of the river as the current slid by.

Firestar was stretched out beside him. "I'm proud of you," he purred. "You handled everything so well!"

"Er . . . I don't know about that," Graystripe began, giving his chest fur an embarrassed lick.

"Daft furball!" Firestar gave his friend an affectionate prod with his nose. "I just want you to know how pleased I am, and how confident I feel that you'll be an excellent leader when I'm gone."

Graystripe felt a surge of terror at the thought. *Me? Leader? Without Firestar to guide me?* He reflected that he had done it before, and obviously it had turned out okay, but . . . *How did things work out with Gremlin and the BloodClan cats? I can't remember. . . .*

When Graystripe turned back to face Firestar, he saw with a shock of horror that his friend had turned into a one-eyed she-cat with scars and long tabby fur. *Fury!*

The BloodClan leader hurtled toward him, her claws reaching for him. "Wake up!" she yowled.

"Graystripe! Wake up!"

Forcing his eyes open, Graystripe saw Cinderpelt standing over him. He realized that he had fallen asleep outside Mothermouth, and the medicine cat had returned from the cave. Her blue eyes were still unfocused, as if her paws had only just carried her out of StarClan's territory.

Graystripe struggled to his paws. "What did you see?" he asked eagerly. "What did StarClan tell you?"

He noticed that Cinderpelt seemed to be struggling to appear calm, as if something had disturbed her deeply.

"There are far more cats in StarClan these days," she murmured. "And I don't think I'll ever get used to seeing

Yellowfang there. She used to be my mentor, and now . . ."

Remembering the cranky old medicine cat, Graystripe could understand how much Cinderpelt must be missing her. She had died after breathing too much smoke in the fire that had roared through the camp a few seasons before.

"She was a fine medicine cat," he mewed. "We all grieve for her. The Clan feels different without her."

Cinderpelt gave her head an impatient shake. "I suppose this is just the way it is. Things change, and you lose Clanmates. I'll just have to get used to it."

When she said no more, Graystripe rested his tail-tip gently on her shoulder. "Did StarClan provide any guidance about Gremlin, and what we should do about BloodClan?"

"I'm not sure," Cinderpelt replied. "I sent out the question to StarClan, but what I got back wasn't a direct answer."

"Why am I not surprised?" Graystripe muttered under his breath; he was aware by now that StarClan never seemed to offer a straight answer to a straight question. Turning back to Cinderpelt, he asked, "Well, what *did* they say?"

"They told me . . . 'Like a three-headed snake, many paths split off into the forest. Graystripe must walk his own path . . . but he must beware the snake's bite.'"

Graystripe's pelt bushed with alarm. "And what does *that* mean?"

"StarClan wants you to make your own decision," Cinderpelt responded. Graystripe detected a tiny sliver of doubt in her tone, and guessed that she was trying hard to sound certain. "I promise I'll support you, whatever you choose."

Graystripe shook out his fur, then dipped his head to the ThunderClan medicine cat. "Thank you." But though he felt real gratitude, he couldn't help being disappointed at the same time. He had hoped that StarClan would help him in some way, or at least show him the path his paws should follow. Instead they had laid the burden of deciding squarely on his own shoulders.

If only Firestar were here . . .

CHAPTER 19

❧

— Now —

"*I don't think I believe this* cat!" Monkeystar declared, glaring at the newcomer from where she stood at Graystripe's shoulder.

"I certainly don't," Clawwhistle agreed. "What kind of name is Gremlin for a cat?"

"Would you like us to drive him away for you?" Bugeater asked. She flashed her claws, but Graystripe could see from the way her paws were trembling that she didn't really want to use them.

The other cats of WarriorClan had arrayed themselves in a loose line facing the strange tom, their fur bristling and their teeth bared, but none of them seemed as though they were looking forward to leaping into battle.

"Don't make a move," Graystripe warned them. "We can sort this out without claws."

He hoped he was right. Here on the dark hillside, with ominous clouds massing overhead, it seemed as if almost anything could happen. And yet it would be an incredibly stupid cat who would attack a group of seven others, even if six of them were young kittypets.

Taking a pace forward, Graystripe let his gaze travel slowly over the stranger and drank in his scent. He didn't smell like any cat or Clan that Graystripe had ever known, and yet the tom said he was Gremlin's kit.

Then Graystripe remembered what his son Stormfur had told him when he was visiting the Tribe of Rushing Water. *There was a rogue cat asking about me, on this side of the mountains. This must be him!*

"Thank you for your protection," he continued to the kittypets, "but Gremlin was a friend to me, and I did promise to help her in any way I could." Glancing back at the newcomer, he added, "Yes, that includes helping her kits. So what can I do for you?"

The tom ducked his head respectfully to Graystripe, relief and gratitude shining in his eyes. "My name is Fang," he began. "I escaped a moon or so ago from a Twoleg den, and I've been looking for help ever since. I—"

Suspecting that the rogue was about to ask him to take him back to ThunderClan's camp so that he could join them, just as his mother had done so long ago, Graystripe held up a paw to stop him. "I'd have to consult with the Clan before I can bring in another kittypet," he stated.

"No, you don't understand," Fang responded. "I don't want to leave. I want to go back to the Twoleg den. I have to."

"Why?" Graystripe asked. He was relieved that Fang didn't expect to be offered a place in ThunderClan, but completely confused by what the gray tom had said he meant to do. *I've never heard of a cat who escaped Twolegs wanting to go back!*

Fang hesitated, digging his claws into the ground as if he was remembering something really painful. Then he took a deep breath and continued. "Things are very bad there. I was only able to escape because the Twoleg left a hole in the door just big enough for me to slip through. Once I was outside, I wanted to save every other cat, but I couldn't work out how to do it. But there are still cats I care about in there." His voice shook as he added, "My mate, Daffodil, is there, and she's ill. She smells strange, and she's having trouble breathing. So that's why I need your help, Graystripe. Please—I'm desperate."

Graystripe could see that Fang was telling the truth; his distress was too deep for him to be faking it. *And he must be really out of options if he thought he could solve his problems by looking for me—a cat he's never met, who lives so far away!*

"I wish I could help," he replied, "but I don't see what I can do. I'm sorry, but if you couldn't find a way back into a den where you've lived for so long, what makes you think that a stranger would be able to?"

"I don't know," Fang meowed. "But you're a warrior! Gremlin always said that warriors were clever and honorable. The least you can do is try." When Graystripe hesitated, he went on more urgently, "Just follow me to the den and see what you think."

"Where is it?" Graystripe asked, determined not to delay his own mission with any more traveling. "Far from here?"

"Not very," Fang replied. "Just on the other side of what

used to be RiverClan territory. Please, Graystripe . . ."

"Well . . . ," Graystripe mewed hesitantly. *Crossing RiverClan wouldn't be too bad. I wanted to pass through there, anyway—before I got sidetracked by WarriorClan. It's not as if he's asking me to trek all the way to the sun-drown-place.*

"You've never seen anything like it," Fang told him. "It's terrible. I've already been out for more than a moon, searching for you or any cat who might help. But I haven't been able to travel far—I try to check on the other prisoners as often as I can, and with every sunrise it seems to be getting worse in there."

"It sounds dangerous . . . ," Graystripe murmured. "And I'm sorry, but I already have somewhere else I need to be."

And yet Fang's resemblance to his mother was so strong . . . Graystripe's thoughts were flooded with memories of Gremlin. He couldn't forget how she had once put herself at risk for him and the rest of ThunderClan when she'd had so many reasons not to. *If I can repay her by helping her kit, I want to do it. It's no more than she deserves.*

"I'll help you if I can," he promised Fang. "But I have to go to the Moonstone first."

Fang blinked in confusion. "What's the Moonstone?"

"Something I hope will help me get some answers from the spirits of my warrior ancestors," Graystripe replied. "The Clans are in need of guidance. In other words, Fang, I need help . . . just like you do."

Fang couldn't restrain an impatient twitch of his whiskers, clearly anxious to get on with his own mission. Then he nodded. "Thank you. I accept your help, and I'll come with you to this Moonstone, if that's okay."

"You can't come inside," Graystripe explained, "because it's a place that is sacred to the Clans. But you can accompany me to the Mothermouth—the cave it rests inside. These cats are traveling with me, as well—despite my best efforts." He cast a wry glance toward the WarriorClan cats, who puffed out their fluffy chests.

"We're on a *quest*," Clawwhistle said excitedly. "It's very important."

Fang looked them over and nodded. "Let's go, then."

Graystripe and Fang set off side by side, with the Warrior-Clan kittypets following at a respectful distance. Graystripe couldn't help stealing glances at the tom as they started up the hill. *He looks so much like her.*

The slope was becoming steeper now, the rough grass more sparse as the moorland began to give way to the towering rocks of Highstones. *But at least,* Graystripe thought with sincere relief, *we've left the Twolegplace behind.*

At first they traveled in silence, until Graystripe heard a hollow growl coming from Fang's belly. "Are you hungry?" he asked. "Have you eaten? Do you know how to hunt?"

Fang shook his head. "I'll be fine," he mewed, sounding embarrassed.

Graystripe halted. "No, you will *not* be fine. If you need to eat, we'll eat. I don't want a collapsing cat on my paws while we're all the way up here."

"Okay, I'm really starving." Fang gave in with a sigh. "My

belly thinks my throat's torn out. I told you," he continued, "I've been searching for you, or some other cat to help, for more than a moon now. Finding prey hasn't always been easy, and I didn't want to waste too much time hunting. It's a while since I've eaten, and longer still since I've felt really full. . . ."

No wonder he's skinny, Graystripe thought, shaking his head. *He's lucky he came across me when he did.* "We'll look for some prey, then," he meowed.

"But I don't see anything up here," Fang objected. "It's too bleak. And we would waste so much time if we went back down."

"Just because we can't see the prey doesn't mean it isn't there," Graystripe grunted.

He padded a little way ahead, raising his head and opening his mouth to taste the air. A trace of rabbit drifted on his indrawn breath. His pads prickled and his jaws began to water with anticipation. *It's a while since I've eaten, too.*

Gathering WarriorClan together with a sweep of his tail, he bent his head and spoke in a low voice. "Stay here, and keep perfectly still. And quiet," he added as Monkeystar opened her jaws—to protest, he assumed. "You too, Fang."

The clouds had grown thicker still, but there was just enough light for Graystripe to see what he was doing. He crept across the moor, following the tantalizing scent trail, until he spotted a hole in a shallow bank, almost hidden by two jutting stones. Careful to keep downwind, he crouched just above the hole and batted a loose pebble into it.

A moment later, he heard faint scrabbling from inside the

hole, and a rabbit poked its head out to investigate. Graystripe looked down on its smooth brown head and two furry ears, then launched himself onto its shoulders and sank his teeth deep into its neck.

Well, that was easy, Graystripe thought with satisfaction as he picked up his prey and carried it back to the others.

Fang let out an impressed hiss as Graystripe dropped the rabbit at his paws. "You caught that rabbit so quickly!" he exclaimed. "How did you do that?"

Graystripe felt faintly embarrassed, though he told himself privately that it *had* been a pretty outstanding bit of stalking. "So much of effective hunting is about patience, scent, and putting yourself in the right position," he told Fang. "We might not always be faster than our prey, so we have to be smarter."

"Can we eat, *please?*" Monkeystar asked. "We're all *so* hungry!"

"Of course," Graystripe replied, though he made sure to push the rabbit directly in front of Fang. "There's plenty for every cat."

As they all crouched down to share the rabbit, Graystripe was aware of Fang eyeing him, curiosity and awe in his green eyes. *I hope I don't disappoint him,* he thought.

When there was nothing left of the rabbit except some bones and scraps of fur, Bigteeth and Bugeater both started yawning, as if they wanted to curl up and go to sleep. As Graystripe rose to his paws, ready to go on, the two kittypets exchanged an awkward glance. Graystripe could tell that the idea of traveling even farther from their Twoleg nest didn't seem so appealing, now that they were faced with the reality of it.

"Actually, now that it's getting darker, I think we should go home," Bigteeth began. "Some cat has to defend our territory."

"Yeah, who knows what might be happening back there?" Bugeater added. "Sometimes the human kits get scared in the dark, so I have to snuggle with them."

"That sounds like a good idea," Graystripe meowed, hiding his amusement. "I'm glad they have such brave warriors willing to guard their dens."

While they were talking, the first drops of rain began to fall, and within heartbeats a thin drizzle swept across the moor. Graystripe shivered as the chill penetrated his pelt.

"You know, I think I'll come with you," Fireface mewed to his friends. "You might need help finding your way back."

"Me too," Chester added.

Monkeystar sighed and rolled her eyes. "Well, okay, if you must," she responded. "But I'm sticking with Graystripe. What about you, Clawwhistle?"

"I'm staying, too," the fluffy orange tom replied. "I want to see where the Moonstone is."

"See you tomorrow, then," Monkeystar meowed as her four Clan members turned to go.

"And be careful crossing back over the Thunderpath!" Graystripe called after them. "Remember how we did it, and wait until you're *sure* it's safe!"

Chester acknowledged his warning with a wave of his tail.

Graystripe was slightly anxious about letting the four kittypets head off alone in this bleak landscape, but there was no way of stopping them. He had no time, and he couldn't delay his own mission to go back now. He only hoped that if the four of them stayed together, they would be okay.

The four remaining cats toiled on up the hill. The last of the moorland grass gave way to bare stone, slick with rain that made their claws slip. The drizzle had grown heavier until the cats' pelts were drenched and they could hardly see a fox-length in front of them. It felt like forever that they were scrabbling up the wet, slippery rocks.

Finally, the dark hole of Mothermouth loomed up ahead.

"At last!" Monkeystar let out a grateful squeal. "We can get in out of the rain!"

As she began to bound forward, Graystripe barred her way with his tail. "Stop! Remember what I told you. You can't go in."

"You're joking," Fang meowed, gaping in disbelief. "I know we can't go *all the way* inside. But you mean we can't even take shelter? We have to stand out here in this deluge to wait for you?"

Graystripe nodded. "I'm sorry. But this is something I have to do alone."

"But we came all this way," Monkeystar protested. "We have to go in to protect you!"

"And to get dry," Clawwhistle added. His fluffy pelt was plastered to his sides, and he made a futile attempt to shake it out.

"I'm sorry," Graystripe repeated. "But I can't let you enter under any circumstances. It's for your own safety. Honestly, I'm not sure *I'm* supposed to go in, either. The Moonstone cave is only to be entered by leaders or medicine cats. I just hope I'm reading StarClan's wishes correctly. I need to make contact with them—some cat must, for the future of all of the Clans—so I'll have to risk StarClan's disapproval."

While Graystripe was speaking, Fang had padded closer to the entrance of the cave, sniffing the air curiously. "This all seems a little strange to me," he admitted. "Who's StarClan? It's so dark inside there, and I'm not sure I recognize the scent."

Because it smells like our ancestors, Graystripe thought. He saw deep unease in the faces of his companions, but he felt safe at Mothermouth, even if he knew that warriors usually weren't allowed inside. *These cats were my kin, my mentors, the cats who shaped me. Of course I belong here. I only hope that I can speak with them again.*

For a moment, Graystripe's mind was invaded by the memory of all the cats he had loved and lost. *Silverstream, Feathertail, Millie, Briarlight . . . and Firestar. Always Firestar.*

So many cats had died more recently, in the troubles Bramblestar's impostor had brought to the Clans, but suddenly it was grief for his long-lost friends and kin that threatened to overwhelm him. Strangely, his grief also filled him with purpose. His legs felt stronger and his paws seemed eager to carry him into the dark. For a moment, he forgot about the rain and the cold. "StarClan is what we call our ancestors," he told Fang, his voice strong. "They're the cats we loved deeply while they were alive, and now they guide us by giving their advice. But to get it, I *must* go in alone."

If I have any chance of connecting with Firestar, he thought, *or any of our ancestors, surely it will happen here!*

"Fang," he went on, "I noticed an overhanging rock a few tail-lengths farther down the path, if you turn past the cave. You can take Monkeystar and Clawwhistle and shelter there. Wait for me until I come back."

"Okay," Monkeystar meowed. "Just yowl if you need us."

Fang dipped his head to Graystripe. "We'll be ready," he promised, and led the WarriorClan kittypets down the path.

Graystripe watched them pad away through the driving rain, then turned back to Mothermouth. As he slowly stepped inside, he heard the first rumble of thunder muttering across the mountainside.

He was thankful to get out of the downpour himself, and shake raindrops from his pelt so that at least he could stop dripping. But he found it unnerving that as soon as he took his first tentative paw steps into the cave, he was engulfed in pitch-black darkness.

If this is what the medicine cats had to contend with every time, I'm glad they never invited me inside.

But then, he reflected, it would be far less terrifying to walk into the tunnel behind a medicine cat than to do it alone, as he had to now.

"Come on," he muttered to himself. "Are you a warrior or a mouse?"

Determinedly, Graystripe set off into the darkness. The

cave floor was smooth underneath his pads, and it sloped gradually downward; the tunnel was so narrow that his pelt brushed the walls on either side. Now and again he felt a current of air from the other passages that opened up on either side, but there was never any doubt about which was the main pathway he needed to follow.

As he ventured farther, Graystripe became conscious of the massive weight of earth and rock above his head. His chest began to heave as he imagined the mountain sinking down upon him, cutting off his breath, or the tunnel roof collapsing behind him, trapping him underground. He began to fear that the passage had no end, and he would go on like this, padding through the stone tunnel, forever and ever.

He was wrestling with his terror when he realized that the blackness ahead of him was beginning to grow lighter. The pale radiance grew until he could see the end of the tunnel in front of him, and a few paw steps later he stepped out into an enormous cavern.

Its walls soared up on every side, and in the roof a ragged hole showed roiling clouds illuminated by a sudden flash of lightning. Thunder rolled out again, even louder now.

But Graystripe gave the cavern's jagged ceiling no more than a passing glance. All his attention was focused on the center of the cave, where a large translucent rock reared up more than three tail-lengths toward the roof. It glowed faintly in the dim light from the stormy sky above.

"The Moonstone," Graystripe whispered, his eyes wide with wonder. Awe filled him, so that it took all his courage to move his paws. He padded forward hesitantly, paused, then forced himself to cross the rest of the space between himself and the mystic, faintly shining stone.

His heart was beating hard as he approached and sank into a crouch a tail-length away. Bowing his head in deepest respect, he spoke hesitantly into the void, picturing in his mind the face that always floated first into his memory.

"Firestar," he began, "my fearless friend, I miss you. Every cat in ThunderClan misses you. And even though you're not with us in life anymore, we need you more than ever. I hope that you can help us—help *me*—now."

Graystripe stopped speaking, hoping to hear Firestar's bold voice fill the silence. But nothing happened, nothing but another flash of lightning somewhere above and another rumble of thunder as the storm thrashed the mountaintop.

Have I angered StarClan? he wondered. *Maybe I should have spoken to all of them, not just to Firestar.*

"StarClan, I hope I'm not offending you by being here," Graystripe continued when he had waited several moments for an answer. "I would never have come unless I really needed your help. To tell you truly, all five of the Clans need help, and I am not sure how much longer we can go on without the spirits of our ancestors to guide us. So please," he finished, trying to put all his heart into his words, "if you have any wisdom for me, I would be grateful if you shared it now."

The echoes of his voice died away into silence. Graystripe began to feel as if all he was doing was talking to himself. He could hardly bear the aching of his heart.

Maybe I was foolish to think that StarClan would speak to me, even here, where our leaders and medicine cats sought guidance for seasons upon seasons. Maybe there truly is something the Clans have done to offend StarClan, just like the false spirit cat told us . . . or maybe the intruder has done something to cut us off.

Maybe I don't know any more than those goofy kittypets who followed me here.

Weary and disillusioned, Graystripe rose to his paws. He wasn't only angry with StarClan; he was angry with himself, too, for wasting so much time when there were other, more practical demands upon him.

He was turning to leave when . . .

CRASH!

Without warning, a sound louder than anything he had heard before shook the cavern walls. He let out a yowl of pain as the noise filled his ears, and just a breath later he worried that he might be blinded, as the whole world seemed to disappear in a flash of dazzling white light. *What's happening?* The light blinked out but Graystripe was still seeing spots as he stumbled backward and fell to the cave floor, wrapping his forepaws around his head.

I've made StarClan angry! Is this the end? Firestar, where are you?

CHAPTER 20

❖

– Then –

Graystripe crouched at the edge of the trees and stared across the stretch of open ground that separated him from the outlying dens of the Twolegplace. Every hair on his pelt was prickling with the sense of danger looming ahead.

"This certainly could be a trap." Cinderpelt, crouching beside him, gave him a long look from steady blue eyes. "Are you sure you want to go ahead?"

For a moment, Graystripe wasn't sure how to answer his medicine cat. Earlier that day he had sent a message, via the kittypet Smudge, for Gremlin to meet him here, but he was well aware that the BloodClan queen might bring a patrol of her vicious Clanmates with her, all of them ready with teeth and claws.

"I trust Gremlin," he responded at last. "But if I'm wrong, and there's trouble—Cinderpelt, your job is to get out and head for camp as fast as you can. Bring help, but keep yourself safe. ThunderClan can't do without its medicine cat."

Cinderpelt simply nodded. Graystripe knew that she

understood her duty even better than he did.

He tasted the air, picking up the fading scents of the last ThunderClan patrol that had passed through, and mingled kittypet scents from the Twoleg dens ahead of him. There was dog-scent, too, but none of it nearby, or fresh. With a last wary glance around, he rose to his paws.

"Let's do this!"

He streaked across the patch of open ground, raced up the fence, and leaped down into Smudge's garden. Cinderpelt, hampered by her lame leg, followed more slowly.

A stretch of grass, bordered by bright Twoleg flowers, separated the fence from the walls of the den. Smudge was lying on his side in a sunny spot, lazily batting with one paw at a butterfly that fluttered just out of reach, as if it was teasing the plump kittypet.

Smudge sprang to his paws, startled, as Graystripe appeared. "Wow! It's you again. You scared me out of my fur!"

"Sorry." Padding up to Smudge, Graystripe nodded toward his Clanmate. "This is Cinderpelt, ThunderClan's medicine cat."

"Hi, Cinderpelt," Smudge meowed as the gray she-cat padded up to join Graystripe. "Would you like to come inside my den?" he added politely. "There's plenty of food, and a bowl of milk."

"No, thanks all the same," Graystripe replied. "We're here to meet Gremlin. Is she—"

"She's here," a voice interrupted from the top of the fence that separated Smudge's garden from the next one.

Graystripe looked up to see the BloodClan queen drop down into the garden, clumsy because of her pregnant belly. He noticed that Cinderpelt was observing her with narrowed eyes, though the medicine cat said nothing.

"Okay, Graystripe," Gremlin began, trotting up with a brief nod to Smudge. "What's your decision? Will you let me and Scraps join your Clan?"

"I'm still thinking about it," Graystripe told her. He felt terribly awkward knowing that he and Cinderpelt were still hiding this deal from the rest of the Clan, but he needed to know more. "First I need to know what you have to offer us."

"I won't fight for you," Gremlin began.

"No cat would expect you to," Cinderpelt interrupted. "Not with your kits to think about."

Gremlin's mouth twisted wryly. "*Fury* expects it. I'll have to be there at the battle, but I won't be fighting for BloodClan, either."

That sounds familiar, Graystripe thought. It reminded him of the reason he'd left RiverClan.

"I'll get you away to a safe place," Cinderpelt promised. "But first, Gremlin—I don't want to scare you, but I do not like the look of how you're carrying your kits."

Gremlin's eyes widened in apprehension. "Why? What's the matter?"

"I'd guess that one of your kits is going to come out paws first," the medicine cat continued. "You should sleep on your back, and chew on chervil root—do you know what chervil looks like?"

Gremlin nodded, her eyes wide and her muzzle tight with tension.

"Then, if you come to ThunderClan, I'll help you with your kitting. It will be fine—but if you want a healthy litter, you absolutely *can't* get involved in any battles."

Graystripe had a sudden memory of Silverstream, and the scent of her blood when she'd birthed Stormkit and Featherkit. His stomach clenched, and he flexed his claws impatiently, eager to change the subject. "Enough about what she *can't* do, Cinderpelt. Let's concentrate on what she can. Gremlin, can you really tell us what BloodClan is plotting?"

"I told you, I can," Gremlin mewed with an irritated twitch of her tail. "I don't know all the details yet, but I will find them out. Fury and the rest still think I'm loyal. But I'm not going to stick my neck out for ThunderClan unless I have a promise from you that Scraps and I will be safe after the battle."

"That's reasonable," Graystripe agreed, with a glance at Cinderpelt, who nodded approval. "So when—"

Cinderpelt, who had been sitting on the grass with her paws tucked under her, suddenly shot upright. "I scent Blood-Clan!" she hissed.

Obviously, she didn't mean Gremlin. Graystripe took a gulp of air and picked up a reek that brought back the ambush that had left him in the dog's garden. *Fury!* "Hide!" he gasped.

Cinderpelt swung around and dived into a clump of the strong-smelling Twoleg flowers, clearly hoping their scent would disguise hers. Graystripe dashed across the garden and into the shelter of a pile of cut grass.

Peering out, he saw that Gremlin had not moved. She sat on the grass beside Smudge, licked one paw, and used it to wash her ear. "So, Smudge, have you thought any more about joining BloodClan?" she meowed clearly.

Fury appeared through a gap in the fence leading to the next garden. Her lone eye glared at Gremlin as she crossed the grass toward her. "What are you doing with this kittypet?" she asked.

"Oh, I thought you'd have heard." Gremlin turned an innocent green gaze on the BloodClan leader. "I'm trying to persuade him to join us."

Fury transferred the glare to Smudge. "And will he?"

"I . . . er . . . I'm making up my mind, still," Smudge replied.

He was clearly terrified, his ears flattened and his eyes stretched wide, but he was facing up to Fury, and he hadn't fled for the safety of his den. Graystripe was reluctantly impressed. *Maybe he's not the coward I thought he was.*

"You do that," Fury growled. Sniffing the air suspiciously, she added, "I smell ThunderClan!"

"Oh, ThunderClan cats visit me all the time," Smudge responded. He gave his shoulder fur a couple of complacent licks. "Firestar is my friend!"

"Huh!" Fury clearly wasn't convinced. Her glance raked over the garden; then she gave an irritated shrug and muttered something Graystripe couldn't catch.

Leaning closer in an attempt to overhear, he got a noseful of the grass cuttings; their pungent scent gave him an overpowering need to sneeze. Desperate, he clamped a paw over his nose. *If I give myself away, we're all crow-food, and so is my plan!*

To his relief, Fury began heading back to the gap in the fence where she had appeared. But when she was halfway there, she glanced back over her shoulder. "Clan meeting at sunset," she told Gremlin. "Be there." With that, she disappeared through the fence.

Graystripe had the sense not to move out of hiding too quickly. Staring at the clump of flowers that concealed Cinderpelt, he willed her to stay where she was. *I wouldn't put it past Fury to come back. She knows something's going on, if only she could catch us at it.*

A few heartbeats later, he was proved right when Fury's head appeared in the gap, her suspicious gaze roving around the garden once more. After a moment, finding nothing, she disappeared again, but Graystripe still waited a good while before he dared to venture out from his hiding place, shaking bits of grass from his pelt and at last allowing himself his longed-for sneeze.

"That's one terrifying cat!" Smudge exclaimed as Graystripe and Cinderpelt joined him and Gremlin in the middle of the garden.

"She's certainly not my favorite," Graystripe replied, padding carefully to the edge of the fence and opening his mouth to taste the air. The reek was gone—which meant Fury hadn't lingered to eavesdrop. He strolled back to Smudge and Gremlin with a relieved sigh.

"You dealt with her very well," Cinderpelt mewed, with a kind glance at the trembling kittypet.

"Thanks." Smudge ducked his head in embarrassment. "But I think what I need now is a drink of milk and some strokes from my housefolk. Excuse me." He waved his tail in farewell and bounded across the garden to disappear through a small opening in the Twoleg door.

It is strange that Fury believed Smudge might consider joining Blood-Clan, Graystripe mused. *He is brave—for a kittypet. But he's not meant for the Clans, much less battle-thirsty BloodClan!*

"So . . . Fury has called a Clan meeting." Gremlin passed her tongue around her jaws as if anticipating a tasty morsel of fresh-kill. "That will be where she sets out her plans to the rest of us. So, what about it, ThunderClan cat?"

"I have to put it to my Clanmates," Graystripe replied. "I'm only our acting leader, and if they won't accept you, there's nothing I can do about it."

Gremlin snorted. "That's not any good to me."

"I will do my best," Graystripe promised. "Suppose we meet here again at sunhigh tomorrow. I should have an answer for you by then."

"Okay," Gremlin agreed. "But I can tell you this, Gray-stripe: If you and your Clan don't trust me, ThunderClan will be *shredded.*"

Graystripe stood on the top of the Highrock and gazed down at his Clanmates gathered beneath him. Throughout the night he had lain awake, worrying about how to present Gremlin's offer to ThunderClan, and he still wasn't sure if he had spoken the right words.

"And so . . . ," he finished, suddenly aware of just how silent his Clanmates were, "I agreed to the deal Gremlin offered."

Thornclaw was the first to speak. "You can't be serious!" he yowled. "You've made a 'deal' with some strange Blood-Clan cat? StarClan help us! And now we have to let her *join our Clan*?"

Graystripe tried to interrupt. "Only after she's proven—"

"Of course, only if she proves herself," One-Eye meowed with a scoff. "But how much will we really know about her, even then? This BloodClan rogue will already be living among us—with her *brother*? What do we know about him, besides that he likes to fight?"

Stay calm. Graystripe fluffed his pelt, trying not to let his Clanmates see how their reaction rattled him. "I believe that I can trust Gremlin," he said. "And as I told you, I think she can provide us important information—"

"You've got bees in your brain if you think she's telling the truth!" Ashfur told him, his face twisted into an expression of mockery as he turned his shoulder away from Graystripe.

"You would really risk the safety of your entire Clan for those BloodClan mange-pelts?" Thornclaw hissed, his ears flattened in fury.

Graystripe could see a few of the younger warriors, like Cloudtail and Brambleclaw, watching him thoughtfully. *At least not every cat thinks it's a terrible idea,* he thought as he addressed Thornclaw. "The Clan is at risk whether we like it or not," Graystripe tried to explain. "This plan will—"

"This plan will end with us all turned into crow-food!"

The speaker was Brackenfur; the golden-brown tabby tom, usually so calm and reasonable, was standing stiff-legged at the base of the Highrock, eyes blazing in rage as he glared up at Graystripe. "I'm sorry, Graystripe—I always trusted you as a mentor. But you wouldn't have asked me to keep it a secret if you thought it was really the right thing to do! I heard what Gremlin told you, and I can't *believe* that you would trust her as far as I could throw a fox. You just want to take another stray into the Clan, and in doing that, you'll end up destroying us all!"

"Yes, why should we care what happens to her, or to the brother she herself admits is a danger to every cat around him?" Brightheart demanded. She was sitting with Cloudtail and Ferncloud at the entrance to the nursery, and her one good eye was narrowed with fury. "Do we have to risk our Clan's safety every time you fall in love?"

Graystripe bristled, knowing that Brightheart was talking about the time he had brought his kits to live with him in ThunderClan. The dispute over the kits had almost led to war between ThunderClan and RiverClan.

His eyes wide in frustration, Graystripe glanced down at Cinderpelt, who was sitting at the base of the Highrock. He had hoped for support from the medicine cat, but she just shook her head sadly, as if asking him, *You didn't really expect this to be easy, did you?*

Of course not, he thought in response, *but that's why I need your help!*

"This is different," Graystripe retorted to Brightheart.

"Gremlin and I are not mates. And we have no intention of ever being mates. She's just a cat who really cares about her brother, and she is trying to do what she thinks is best for him. And that means bringing him to stay in ThunderClan after we've dealt with the BloodClan threat—together." Letting his gaze travel across the rest of the Clan, he added, "If any of our kin were at risk, each one of us would do the same. And Gremlin has even more to lose, since she's expecting kits at any moment."

No cat responded directly to that, and Graystripe began to hope that at least some of his Clanmates were starting to take Gremlin's offer more seriously. When Thornclaw rose to his paws, looking thoughtful rather than hostile, he felt more hopeful still, but when the tabby warrior spoke, his words were completely unexpected.

"Actually, Mousefur and I and some of the others were discussing this," Thornclaw began, "before we ever heard about this Gremlin plan. And we have another idea."

Graystripe felt a flutter of uneasiness in his belly. *I'm sure I'm not going to like this.* "Okay, let's hear it," he meowed.

"We think that we ought to ask the other three Clans for their help against BloodClan," Thornclaw declared.

"Yes." Mousefur rose and came to stand beside Thornclaw. "If BloodClan destroys us, then the way is open for them to attack any of the others. It's in the other Clans' best interests to help us. Why should ThunderClan face the danger alone?"

A murmur of agreement rose from the cats around the

Highrock. Gazing down at them, Graystripe saw their eyes bright with interest, and relief on many faces. *They're pleased that there's another way, instead of taking the risk of trusting Gremlin. But that's not what I wanted—I wanted them to back my plan!*

Graystripe himself had realized, when he was on his way to the Moonstone with Cinderpelt, that ThunderClan was blocking the way for BloodClan to attack the other Clans, just as Thornclaw had declared. Yet he could see there were problems with the tabby warrior's suggestion that his Clanmates maybe hadn't considered. *And they won't like it when I point them out.*

"How would that work?" he asked. "Assuming the other Clans agree, what do we want them to do? We don't know when BloodClan will attack, and we can't have warriors from the other Clans living in our camp while we wait for the battle."

"Are you mouse-brained?" Ashfur asked, with a lash of his tail. "We set a watch, and once we see BloodClan approaching, we send three cats—the fastest runners—to the other three camps to bring back warriors to help."

Graystripe took a deep breath. He would have liked to leap down from the Highrock and give the gray warrior a good clawing around the ears, but he knew how stupid it would be to antagonize him further.

"I don't think that's a good idea," he responded in a mild tone. "We'd be deprived of three useful warriors at the beginning of the battle, and by the time they came back with reinforcements, it could all be over."

Ashfur hunched his shoulders, letting out an annoyed grunt; he wouldn't admit that Graystripe was right, but he said nothing more.

"Even if that wouldn't work," Thornclaw continued, "there must be some way to organize it . . . some kind of signal, maybe."

Once again Graystripe was aware of his Clan's approval of the plan. Cats were glancing at one another, bright-eyed, nodding their agreement. One or two let out encouraging yowls.

"I'm sure we could work something out," he began, and went on swiftly before his Clanmates began to believe he would accept Thornclaw's suggestion. "But there are two problems that you haven't thought of. First, if we go to the other Clans for help, they'll think ThunderClan is weak. That's the last thing we want."

"No," Mousefur objected, with a sharp edge to her tone. "The last thing we want is to be ripped apart by BloodClan."

True enough, Graystripe thought, but he ignored Mousefur's interruption as he continued. "The second problem is that we can't ask for help, or fight side by side with warriors from other Clans, without letting them know that Firestar isn't here."

There was a moment's silence, as the Clan cats considered that. Finally, Cloudtail spoke. "Would that be so bad?"

"If he has gone to be a kittypet," Ashfur meowed, "then he's not coming back. How much longer can we go on keeping it a secret?"

"Firestar has *not* gone to be a kittypet," Graystripe retorted, feeling his pelt begin to bristle with a mixture of anger and frustration. "I wish you could get that idea out of your heads once and for all."

"But how can we?" It was Dustpelt who spoke, rising to his paws from where he sat beside Ferncloud, outside the nursery. "No cat will tell us where Firestar *has* gone, except that he's on a mission for StarClan. What are we supposed to think?"

"You're supposed to think that he's on a mission for StarClan," Graystripe pointed out. "Because he is. And that's the one thing that Firestar made clear to me and Cinderpelt before he left. No cat must know where his mission is taking him, and I decided it would be easier if the other Clans didn't even know that he's gone." He puffed out a gusty sigh. "We've been through all this before. I know it's frustrating, but that's the way it is."

Dustpelt didn't go on arguing, simply shook his head and sat down again beside his mate.

"So you won't consider our plan?" Thornclaw asked; he sounded more disappointed than angry.

"I wish I could," Graystripe responded. "It's not a bad plan, if we could work out the details. But it would mean telling the other Clans that we've been lying to them, and do you think they would want to help us after that?"

"Then maybe you shouldn't have lied to them," Mousefur pointed out sharply.

"Maybe I shouldn't have," Graystripe admitted. "But that prey is eaten now. And I still believe that we need to show the other Clans that ThunderClan is strong, and that means dealing with BloodClan without their help."

He was aware of grumbling among the Clan, of twitching tails and flattened ears, but this time no cat spoke up to challenge him. He glanced down at Cinderpelt beside the Highrock; she gave him a vigorous nod. "Go on. Get back to Gremlin."

"As I see it," Graystripe meowed, "we have two choices. Continue as we are, keeping watch for BloodClan and dealing with them when they finally attack. Or trusting Gremlin and using the information she'll give us." He paused, then added, "Talk about it among yourselves. See what you think."

He waited as the crowd of cats broke up into smaller groups, beginning to argue about what they had just heard. From the top of the rock, he caught scraps of their discussion.

". . . maybe Graystripe has a point," Ferncloud was saying. Brambleclaw nodded in agreement.

"But you can't ever trust a BloodClan cat!" Dustpelt insisted. "That's just inviting trouble!"

"What's going to happen to our kits?" Brightheart asked.

Eventually, Dustpelt broke away from the rest of his group and strode up to the Highrock. "Graystripe, tell us, what exactly is your plan? If we decide to trust Gremlin, what will happen?"

Graystripe gazed down at the brown tabby tom, faintly surprised that he should be the first cat to ask a reasonable question. He raised his tail for silence, and waited until the rest of the muttered conversations in the clearing died down.

"After Brackenfur overheard me speaking with Gremlin in the forest, I sent a message to Gremlin in the Twolegplace," he replied, "and I took Cinderpelt to meet her, not far from where you and I and Brambleclaw fought the BloodClan cats. We decided that Gremlin would go on pretending that she's loyal to BloodClan, so she can pass information to us. And in fact, Fury showed up during this very conversation, and told us that there would be a BloodClan meeting tonight." He looked from cat to cat. "Gremlin believed that Fury would lay out her plans at that meeting. She's meant to report back to us, so we can plan our attack."

"And she'll fight on our side?" Brambleclaw asked.

Graystripe shook his head. "No, she—"

"Why does that not surprise me?" Brackenfur growled.

"Gremlin has to think of the safety of her kits," Graystripe continued, with a glare at the golden-brown tabby tom, "so she will be staying out of the way once the battle starts."

"And I'll go to be with her," Cinderpelt added, scrambling onto the Highrock beside Graystripe so she could survey the Clan and make herself heard more easily. "I could tell as soon as I set eyes on her that her kitting won't be easy. From the way her belly is sticking out, I think at least one of her kits will come paws first."

For the first time, Graystripe heard some murmurs of sympathy arising from his Clanmates. He saw Ferncloud and Brightheart exchange a glance; the worst of Brightheart's hostility seemed to fade. Graystripe hoped that some cats in his Clan were shifting from the idea of Gremlin as an evil Blood-Clan spy and instead seeing her as a queen in trouble.

"I told her to sleep on her back and chew chervil root,"

Cinderpelt went on. "That might help move her kits into a more natural position for the birth."

Graystripe gave Cinderpelt a warm glance. "Thank you for helping her," he mewed, "and for being so accepting."

"Hey, not so fast," Cinderpelt responded, alarm in her blue eyes. "It's not my place to decide if she can become a member of ThunderClan. But if she can't, I'm going to suggest that she should find a Twoleg to live with."

"A *Twoleg?*" Speckletail, sitting with the other elders beside their fallen tree, sounded shocked down to the tips of her claws. "You'd send her off to be a *kittypet?*"

Cinderpelt shrugged. "I wouldn't suggest that to any of *our* cats," she explained. "But it might be Gremlin's best option, if she can't come here. She's going to need all the help she can get with her kitting, and BloodClan cats don't believe in helping one another. If Gremlin stays with BloodClan and goes into labor, she will die, and so will her kits. And even if her kits survive, she won't be there to raise them in a way that a parent should. . . ."

The medicine cat's plain speaking seemed to have influenced her Clanmates. He saw Speckletail shoot Frostfur a thoughtful look, and they drew close and begin speaking quietly.

"I would hate to think . . . ," he heard Speckletail murmur.

Meanwhile, Mousefur and Goldenflower drew closer to the Highrock, mewing in questioning tones.

"Do you really believe . . . ?" Mousefur began.

He knew that there was some convincing still to be done,

but they were actually *listening* now. They were really considering his plan.

This is the time for me to press home my advantage, he thought, opening his jaws to continue. *I'm sure I can convince them now!*

Cinderpelt shifted her paws and glanced over at Graystripe. "Maybe StarClan was right," she suggested wryly. "You *can* work this out on your own."

Graystripe flicked his ear in amusement. "Well, I didn't have much choice. Maybe now's my chance to make my final plea?"

Cinderpelt shook her head gently, resting her tail on his shoulder. "Don't say anything more," she murmured into his ear. "You've done all you can. Now let them work it out for themselves."

Finally, it was Dustpelt who addressed Graystripe again. "We've had an idea," he began, angling his ears toward Brambleclaw, Ferncloud, and Brightheart, who stood around him. "A compromise."

"Okay, what is it?" Graystripe meowed.

"Once the battle with BloodClan is over," Dustpelt continued, "we think we should allow Gremlin and her brother to come live with us, but only—"

"Only until what?" Ashfur yowled. "Until they claw us up in our sleep and take us over from the—"

A low growl grew in Dustpelt's throat until finally it was loud enough for Ashfur to notice. He stopped abruptly.

"As I was saying," Dustpelt went on, "only until Firestar comes back. He'll have the final decision about whether they're allowed to stay or not."

Approving murmurs rose from the crowd of cats; even Brackenfur, who had been so hostile toward Graystripe's plan from the very beginning, was looking thoughtful. Only Ashfur still scowled.

"She'll probably have her kits while Firestar is still away," Cinderpelt pointed out approvingly. "So whatever he decides, she'll still have the protection of the Clan when she needs it most."

"We'd better keep a sharp eye on that brother of hers," Ashfur called out. "If he sets one claw out of line, I'll chase him off our territory myself."

Graystripe let out a snort of amusement. "Don't worry; once he's here, he'll be an apprentice, and he'll have so many duties to keep him busy, he won't have time to start anything. Would you like to be his mentor, Ashfur?"

The gray warrior looked down at his paws; obviously, Graystripe's suggestion was not a welcome one.

"Okay," Graystripe went on, satisfied that there would be no further interruptions. "This is the plan. Provided Gremlin does what she has promised to do, and helps us in the battle with BloodClan, we allow her and her brother to live in the Clan until Firestar returns. Does any Clanmate object?"

No cat spoke.

Cinderpelt leaned closer to Graystripe and mewed softly into his ear. "Off you go—it's almost sunhigh, so run to the Twolegplace and tell Gremlin what we've decided, before the Clan changes its mind."

Graystripe could see the wisdom of that; he gave the medicine cat a brisk nod. "I'm on it."

He leaped down from the Highrock, slid through the crowd of his Clanmates, and plunged into the gorse tunnel. His belly fur brushed the grass and his tail flowed out behind him as he raced through the forest. After the struggle of the Clan meeting, his optimism was rising like the sun in newleaf.

This just might work out for every cat.

CHAPTER 21

— Now —

Graystripe lay with his eyes squeezed tight shut, his heart hammering in his chest as he waited for StarClan to unleash more of its wrath. At last, when nothing more happened, he dared to open his eyes again, but all he could see were mingled colors floating in front of him. He couldn't hear anything, either; he felt as though his ears were stuffed full of thistle-fluff.

Have I gone deaf and blind? he wondered, fighting back panic.

Gradually his vision cleared, the walls of the cavern took shape around him, and the sounds of the storm seeped back into his ears. Graystripe looked back toward the Moonstone and saw . . . nothing.

Horror clutched at his chest as he blinked, drawing closer, only to confirm . . . the Moonstone had disappeared. A heap of shattered fragments, giving off a faint, eerie glow, lay where it had been.

Lightning must have struck it! Graystripe stared disbelievingly at the broken shards. His mouth was dry, and every hair on his pelt was bristling. *Not only did I not succeed in reaching StarClan—I destroyed the Moonstone! Was that StarClan's answer . . . or just a coincidence?*

Graystripe realized that it didn't matter; he only knew that he had to get out of this place. StarClan obviously wasn't going to speak to him now. He stumbled to his paws, his legs shaking with terror, and flung himself across the cavern and up the tunnel as fast as he could. Only after he burst into the open, still trembling and panting, did he turn back and look down the passage toward the cave of the shattered Moonstone.

Was that a sign? he asked himself again. *Did it mean that Firestar is angry with me?* He found it hard to believe that his old friend would unleash such fury on him, even for daring to enter a sacred place when he'd never been a leader or a medicine cat. *Perhaps I'm just imagining things—imagining that the lightning and thunder is something more meaningful than an ordinary storm.* But the more he thought about that option, the worse he felt. *Which is worse, that StarClan still exists but is angry at me . . . or that StarClan is gone, or no longer cares at all?* His throat grew tight as he considered the possibilities. *What if the young ThunderClan warriors were right? What if the message is that I'm an old fool who needs to accept that StarClan is gone?*

Graystripe stood, panting, for a few moments, letting the thought sink in. As his heart slowed back to normal, Graystripe realized that the thunder was growling farther off in the distance, and the rain had almost stopped. The storm was passing. Above his head, the clouds were clearing away, leaving ragged gaps where the moon and stars could shine through, and on the horizon the outline of the hills told him that dawn was already beginning to break. His beating heart had slowed, too, and he could breathe normally. Giving his pelt a shake, he set off down the path to find Fang and the others.

His limbs felt heavy, as if he were trying to wade through deep water. He had fastened all his hopes on receiving an answer from StarClan at the Moonstone, and now that hope was gone. *What now?* He knew he'd promised to help Fang, and he would fulfill that promise. But what about ThunderClan? What about his journey?

He'd been so sure that Firestar would help him figure everything out.

When he reached the overhanging rock, he saw Monkey-star and Clawwhistle curled up together asleep, pressed as close as they could to the inner wall. Fang was sitting upright, his tail wrapped around his paws and his ears pricked for the first sign of trouble. He sprang up as soon as he saw Gray-stripe.

"What happened?" he asked.

Graystripe didn't know how to reply. How could he even describe to Fang what he had seen in the depths of the earth? Where would he begin? His spirit felt broken. He had failed in his quest to get answers from Firestar, or the Moonstone. He asked himself if Stoneteller had been wrong; perhaps Graystripe had no more to offer his Clan.

I'm no kind of savior. No leader. Not even a deputy, not anymore.

"It was . . . terrifying," he began, describing how he had ventured down the tunnel and asked his question, only for the

Moonstone to explode in a flash of dazzling light. Monkeystar and Clawwhistle woke up at the sound of his voice and listened with wide, astonished eyes.

"It sounds like you made contact with *something*," Fang meowed when Graystripe had finished telling his story.

"I'm not sure," Graystripe said evenly, not wanting to share his internal doubts with this kittypet. "Anyway, now I've no idea what to do next. I haven't forgotten that I promised to help you," he added with a nod to Fang. "But when I'm done, I . . . I don't know how I'm going to help my Clan."

Monkeystar spoke up, her claws flexing with excitement. "I've got an idea!"

"What?" Graystripe asked, doubtful that a kittypet could have anything to offer him in his confusion.

"We know a wise cat who might have some answers," the tortoiseshell replied. "He lives on a farm not far from here, and he loves to tell long stories."

"Yeah," Clawwhistle added. "He knows about the warriors, too."

Graystripe felt a warmth spreading beneath his pelt. *A wise cat who loves to tell long stories and knows the warriors . . . ?* "Are you talking about Barley?" he asked.

Monkeystar and Clawwhistle exchanged a glance. "Yes, that's his name," Monkeystar mewed. "How did you know?"

"He's is an old friend of mine—a very old friend, in fact." Graystripe felt hope returning with every heartbeat. What a comfort it would be to see his old friend Barley, especially now. Even if Barley couldn't help him with his present difficulties, it would be good to catch up with him, after so many seasons.

"Take me to him right away," he ordered.

Monkeystar took the lead, with Clawwhistle beside her, heading away from Mothermouth. Graystripe felt a renewed stirring of amusement at the sight of the young cats padding importantly down the path; now and again Monkeystar gave a little leap of excitement, as if, after the struggles of the night and the storm, she had recovered her sense of adventure.

At first, Fang brought up the rear, then quickened his pace to walk beside Graystripe. "There's something I have to know," he whispered, looking up at Graystripe with hope sparkling in his eyes.

"Okay," Graystripe meowed, mystified. "Spit it out."

Fang still hesitated, as if he was afraid to speak. Finally he asked, "Graystripe, are you . . . are you my father?"

Graystripe halted, stumbling over his own paws in his astonishment. "What?"

"My mother didn't talk much about my father," Fang explained. "When I asked questions, she usually changed the subject. I think she hoped I wouldn't notice."

"As if you can stop a kit from being curious!" Graystripe murmured.

"But she always spoke so fondly of you," Fang continued. "I think she respected you more than any cat. It made me wonder if you had been more than a friend to her. And then, when she told me to seek you out if I ever needed help, I thought maybe . . ."

Graystripe felt a pang of regret biting into his chest. He had grown to like Fang in the short time he had known him, and he hated to put out the spark of hope he could see growing in the gray tom's eyes.

"Fang, I'd be proud to call you my son," he began, "but your mother and I were never mates. I'm not your father."

Fang bowed his head, his tail drooping. Graystripe was truly sorry for the skinny tom; he could see disappointment washing over him like a surge of brown water in the leaf-fall floods. The loner seemed so heartbroken that, for a moment, Graystripe wondered if he should have lied. *What harm would it have done if I'd said yes? At least one of us would have found the answer that we were searching for.*

But Graystripe knew in his heart that it was always better to tell the truth. *Somehow, somewhere, we would both have paid the price for that lie.*

"Thank you for being honest with me," Fang meowed. "After we visit Barley, will you come with me to the den to help my friends?"

"Of course." Graystripe nodded. "Anything for Gremlin's son."

He set off again, following the WarriorClan cats, who by now had drawn a long way ahead. Fang's ears were pricked and alert, but his paw steps were slow, dragging on the rough stone of the path.

Graystripe padded beside him, feeling the younger cat's despondency as if it were his own. *I wish I were his father, but I can't be. All I can do is hope that one day he will find his real father, just as he found me.*

* * *

The storm was over, the clouds had cleared away, and the sky was flooded by the pale light of dawn by the time Graystripe and the others reached Barley's barn. Graystripe paused outside, glancing around and parting his jaws to taste the air. The scents were familiar, especially mice and the dried grass that was stored there—and, more distant, the Twolegs and a dog. But the only scent that Graystripe cared about just then was that of his old friend Barley.

The weather-beaten barn doors looked just the same as when Graystripe had first visited as an apprentice. There was still a gap at the bottom, where the two WarriorClan kitty-pets were already vanishing inside.

Graystripe followed, with Fang hard on his paws. It took a moment for his eyes to adjust to the dim light seeping through the holes in the roof and a few small windows high up in the walls. When he could see clearly, he spotted Barley curled up in a corner between the barn doors and a heap of dried grass; he was deeply asleep, his breath riffling a stalk of hay that was clinging to his muzzle.

Monkeystar and Clawwhistle were crouching beside him, their eyes shining with glee, their tail-tips twitching impatiently. Monkeystar beckoned to Graystripe with her tail. "Come on!" she whispered. "Seeing you is going to be such a great surprise for him."

Graystripe didn't need telling twice. Excitement surged up inside him as he bounded across the barn and stooped over Barley, gently touching his nose to the old tom's ear.

"Wake up, Barley," he whispered. "It's Graystripe. I've come to visit you."

Barley blinked awake and raised his head, fixing bleary blue eyes on Graystripe. At first his stare was blank; then, gradually, a puzzled expression crept over his face. "You look like Graystripe." His voice was a hoarse whisper. "But you can't be."

"I *am* Graystripe," the gray warrior responded, licking Barley's ear and giving his neck an affectionate nuzzle. "It's so good to see you," he added, wondering why his old friend didn't get up to greet him.

Barley's expression cleared. "It *is* you, Graystripe!"

"He's *super* old," Clawwhistle announced, answering Graystripe's thought. "That's why we come around to check on him. He tells us stories, and we keep him entertained by telling him all about our fierce warrior adventures, and make sure he's safe. Isn't that right, Barley?"

The entire time he was speaking, Clawwhistle was hopping around with excitement, and now he gave a massive leap into the middle of one of the piles of dried grass that covered the floor of the barn.

Barley exchanged an amused glance with Graystripe, who guessed that the old tom could probably do without quite so many visits from the energetic young cats.

"Oh, yes," Barley mewed politely. "What would I do without the members of WarriorClan watching over me?"

Monkeystar solemnly nodded her head. "You'll never have to find out," she promised. Then she turned away with an exasperated sigh. "Clawwhistle, get out of there!"

She padded over to help Clawwhistle extract himself from the pile of grass. The orange tom emerged, spitting out grass seed, with his fluffy pelt almost completely covered in stray stems.

"Barley, this is Fang." Graystripe introduced the gray tom, who had stood quietly waiting until now.

While the two toms greeted each other, he took a hard look at his longtime friend. Though most cats probably looked "super old" to Clawwhistle, the young kittypet wasn't wrong about Barley. The loner's once-sharp blue eyes seemed clouded, and his black-and-white pelt was run through with gray. But his broad shoulders and large paws still hinted at the tough cat Graystripe remembered.

"It's not as bad as it looks," Barley meowed, clearly aware of Graystripe's scrutiny. He rose to his paws and winced as he arched his back in a long stretch. "My joints don't work as well as they used to, and my ear hurts sometimes. My sight has weakened, too, so I hardly ever leave the barn. But I can still get around, with a bit of help." He settled himself back into the hay with a contented sigh.

Graystripe tried to hide how sad Barley's words made him feel. "Is that why you're still here, so long after the last time I saw you?" he asked.

"Well, it is my home," Barley replied. "And I'm lucky. The Twolegs who live here are kind and take care of me. In fact, that'll be them now."

A scraping sound made Graystripe whirl to see the barn door beginning to open, pushed from the outside. Warm daylight slanted in, and he realized that the sun had risen while they'd been talking. Beckoning with his tail for Fang to follow him, he ducked quickly into the shadows behind the door, while Monkeystar and Clawwhistle, who had been chasing each other around the piles of grass, flattened themselves into one with an alarmed squeak and peered between the grass stalks with wide, curious eyes.

A female Twoleg entered the barn carrying a bowl; as she put it down beside Barley, Graystripe could see that it was full of water. Then she took out some small object from her pelt, stooped down beside Barley, and tilted his head to one side. Graystripe stiffened at the thought of being so close to a Twoleg, but Barley seemed undismayed and kept still as she dropped some kind of liquid into his ear. Then she ruffled Barley's fur and went out again, closing the door behind her.

"What was that she put in your ear?" Fang asked as he and Graystripe emerged from their hiding place.

"I'm not sure, but I think it's some kind of Twoleg herb," Barley told him. "After she puts those drops in, my ear doesn't hurt so much."

All this while Graystripe had been aware of the overwhelming scent of mice in the barn, and the increasingly hollow place inside him. It seemed a long time since they'd shared that rabbit on the way up to Highstones.

"Barley, may we hunt?" he asked.

"Of course." Barley waved his tail. "Help yourselves. There's plenty. But I warn you, the mice in here seem to be much faster lately. Not so easy to catch."

I wonder why, Graystripe thought, with a sympathetic glance at the old tom. "We'll do our best. Would you like some prey too, Barley?"

His friend swiped his tongue around his jaws. "I won't say no. Twoleg food is okay, but it doesn't fill you up like a good, fat mouse."

Graystripe turned to where the two WarriorClan kittypets were once more chasing each other around the barn. "Hey, you two!" he called. "Stop that! You learned some hunting moves yesterday. Want to put them into practice?"

The two cats skidded to a halt, their eyes gleaming excitedly. "Would a warrior say no? Of course we would!" Monkeystar meowed, bouncing on her paws.

"Then settle down and be quiet. You'll scare all the prey from here to Highstones, racketing around like that."

The two kittypets were immediately still, their faces serious, though their whiskers still quivered eagerly.

"Right," Graystripe began. "Start by showing me your hunter's crouch." He walked around the two of them, carefully examining their position. *It's just like having apprentices. Somehow, it makes me feel young again.* "Very good, Clawwhistle. Monkeystar, draw your hind legs in a bit more. That's right. Now let's find some prey."

"But the barn is full of prey," Clawwhistle pointed out. "We don't even have to search. Just listen!"

It wasn't difficult for Graystripe to hear the continual squeaking and rustling in the piles of dried grass, or to pick up the overwhelming smell of mouse. "That's true," he told

Clawwhistle, "but you still have to find *your* mouse. Pinpoint one and stalk it, and ignore all the others until you make your catch."

He stood back and watched the two young cats as they tasted the air and then padded cautiously up to the nearest pile of grass, approaching it from opposite sides. He could see that Monkeystar had focused on a mouse almost at once; she dropped into the hunter's crouch and crept up, paw step by delicate paw step, until at last she pounced.

But as she made her leap, the mouse burrowed frantically through the grass and popped out on the other side of the pile, right under Clawwhistle's nose. Instinctively he slammed a paw down on it.

"Hey! I got one!" he yowled triumphantly.

Monkeystar's fur bristled with indignation. "That was *mine!*"

"It's okay," Graystripe meowed, stepping forward before the two kittypets could start clawing at each other. "Hunting as a team is a very advanced technique. Warriors do it all the time. You *both* caught that mouse. Why don't you take it to Barley," he suggested. "He'll enjoy it all the more if he knows you caught it especially for him."

Monkeystar and Clawwhistle glanced at each other. "Okay," Monkeystar agreed. "But *I* get to carry it."

As she grabbed up the mouse, Graystripe meowed, "Wait! You should th—"

He stopped himself.

"What?" Monkeystar asked, dropping the mouse in confusion.

You should thank StarClan, Graystripe thought. The habit was so ingrained in him, he'd meant to teach it to the WarriorClan "leader." But now the thought of StarClan brought him back to that terrifying moment when lightning had struck the Moonstone, and the hopeless feeling he'd had leaving Mothermouth. *Either StarClan was angry enough to destroy the Moonstone,* he mused now, *or it was only lightning, and StarClan didn't answer my call at all. Either way, thanking StarClan for prey isn't going to change anything.*

"Never mind," he told Monkeystar. "Now take it to Barley."

Without hesitating, she picked up the mouse and darted over to Barley.

A deep melancholy settled over Graystripe as he thought about what he'd just done. *WarriorClan wants me to teach them the ways of true warriors, and I'm not teaching them to honor StarClan?* But what made his chest ache was that he knew it was the right decision. Perhaps Flipclaw had been right when he'd argued with the other warriors—maybe StarClan would never return. And maybe the Clans had to find a way to survive without them.

But Graystripe found it very hard to picture a place for himself inside such a Clan.

The two young cats skittering off across the barn floor shook him from his somber thoughts. "Hey, Barley, look what we've got for you!" Monkeystar yowled.

Graystripe watched, amused and suddenly more hopeful to see their enthusiasm. Then he turned to look for Fang. The gray tom had been hunting quietly while Graystripe had been training his "apprentices," and by now he had three or four mice piled up at his paws.

"That's great!" Graystripe meowed. "You're a good hunter."

Fang puffed out his chest with pride at the older cat's praise. "It's easy in here," he murmured. "I still need more practice hunting outside."

Graystripe felt that he couldn't eat until he had made some contribution. "One more and we're done," he decided, and stalked among the heaps of grass until he spotted a mouse and caught it with a massive leap.

The five cats settled down to feast on their prey, Monkeystar and Clawwhistle exclaiming about how good mouse tasted.

"The others will be so sorry they didn't come with us," Clawwhistle declared between gulps. "Just think what they're missing!"

"This is almost like old times," Graystripe meowed to Barley, "when we used to visit you on our journeys to the Moonstone."

Barley nodded, though his eyes were sorrowful. "Yes—but there's one other cat who should be here."

Graystripe didn't need to ask him what he meant. "The SkyClan cats told me Ravenpaw visited them when they were still in their gorge, and he died there," he murmured, thinking sadly of the nervous young apprentice who had found refuge with Barley from the murderous intentions of the first Tigerstar. He had never become a warrior, but he had grown into a cat that any Clan would have been proud to claim. "You must miss him."

"Every day, every heartbeat," Barley responded. "But it's

easier now. I know my time is near, and whatever path Raven-paw's spirit walks, soon I will walk beside him."

Graystripe took in a quick breath. *I hope you will, Barley. I hope you will,* he thought. He stretched out his tail to touch Barley on the shoulder. For a moment, he could not speak. Finally, it was Barley who broke the silence between them.

"Graystripe, you haven't told me what brings you here, on such a long journey, and without any Clanmates," he meowed. "Are you on some sort of scouting mission? Surely Thunder-Clan can't be thinking of moving back here."

At first, Graystripe hardly knew how to reply. It would take the rest of the day to describe to Barley the chaos the intruder had brought to the Clans, and how no cat knew how to bring back their connection to StarClan.

"Things are bad beside the lake," he began at last. "It seems as though StarClan has abandoned us. I thought I might help my Clan by traveling to the Moonstone to see if I could make contact there."

"And did you?" Barley asked.

"I tried, but . . . Barley, it was terrifying! Lightning struck the Moonstone, and it shattered into pieces. StarClan never spoke to me in words, but I wonder if that was a sign from them."

Barley looked puzzled. "I've never pretended to understand StarClan," he meowed. "If it was a sign, do you know what it might mean?"

Graystripe shook his head. "That they're angry. That they're not interested in helping. Or worse, it *was* only light-ning, and they're not listening at all. When I think of the future, I'm just bewildered. You're so wise, Barley—do you know what I should do?"

"Wise? Me?" Barley gave a snort of amusement. "I'm about as wise as a kit before its eyes open. But I suppose I do know one thing. From what I've heard, signs from StarClan make more sense after you've had time to sleep on them. You'll likely know what to do once you've had a good rest."

"You're right." Graystripe realized that every cat was exhausted after the long trek to Highstones and the night spent out in the storm. He glanced across the barn at the two kittypets and saw they were struggling to stay awake, their jaws extended in massive yawns. "Come on, you two," he continued. "Time to sleep. More adventures later."

Monkeystar and Clawwhistle were too weary even to protest. They made nests for themselves in the dried grass and were asleep as soon as they curled up, their pelts brushing and their tails wrapped over their noses.

Graystripe was finding it hard to keep his eyes open, and Fang was also drooping. But before they too made nests amid the grass, Fang turned to Barley.

"Did you know my mother, Gremlin?" he asked.

Barley's eyes widened, and he regarded the gray tom with new respect. "You're Gremlin's kit?" he asked.

Fang nodded.

"Yes, I knew Gremlin," Barley mewed softly. "She was a wonderful cat. She was part of a harsh, violent Clan, but she had a good heart, and she loved her brother very much. And more than anything else, she loved her kits."

Fang looked briefly more cheerful to hear Barley's praise of his mother. But a heartbeat later, sadness crept over his face again. The sight made Graystripe even more determined to help him, although he wondered what he could possibly do, when StarClan seemed so remote, so distant. So uncaring.

As Graystripe curled up among the piles of grass, the thoughts still buzzed around in his mind like a whole hive of bees. Even with a full belly, and in the warm, sweet-smelling barn, it was a long time before he could sleep.

CHAPTER 22

— Then —

I really hope this isn't a trap.

Graystripe crouched underneath a bush at the edge of Smudge's garden, his nose wrinkling at the mingled scents of strange flowers and Twolegs, and the distant tang of dog. Even though the den was on the outskirts of the Twolegplace, he felt uneasy, every muscle in his body telling him to flee back into the safety of the forest.

But it isn't safe anymore, he told himself. *It's crawling with those BloodClan mange-pelts.*

This time, there was no sign of Smudge in the garden. Graystripe guessed that the black-and-white kittypet would be keeping close to his Twolegs until the whole BloodClan conflict was over. Even his scent had faded.

Digging his claws into the ground, Graystripe forced himself to wait. This was the place where Gremlin had promised to meet him, to hear his decision. Yet sunhigh had come, and so far there was no sign of the BloodClan queen.

Suppose this is a trap? Suppose BloodClan means to kill me here, far away from any help? I know I'm not ThunderClan's real leader, but it would still be weaker without me.

He couldn't believe how hard his choices were, forced upon him by BloodClan's return. And there was now nothing that he could do except forge ahead in the best way he could manage. Being a leader meant making hard choices every day. Graystripe felt more keenly than ever before how complicated Firestar's life must be.

I can't imagine how any cat could want to lead their Clan.

He jumped, startled, at the sound of something banging inside the Twoleg den, and peered out through the leaves. He knew there were Twoleg kits living there, because he had heard their high-pitched caterwauling before, and now he was afraid that they would come running out into the garden and find where he was hidden. But the door of the den stayed closed.

Then Graystripe heard a rustling in the bushes behind him. Turning, he spotted Gremlin pushing her way through the branches. She puffed out her a breath as she flopped down next to him and lay on her side to rest her pregnant belly. Graystripe thought that she must be very near to kitting; she seemed to have grown even since he'd last seen her the day before.

"Well?" Gremlin asked. "Have you made your decision? Will ThunderClan help me?"

"Yes, we will," Graystripe replied. "But on one condition. I'm not the real leader of ThunderClan. Firestar is, and I can't promise you and Scraps a permanent place in the Clan without his knowledge. When he returns, which will be soon"—*I hope that's true,* Graystripe thought—"he will have the final say on whether you and your brother can be ThunderClan cats. But in the meantime, you're free to live among us, and of course Cinderpelt will help with your kitting."

Gremlin blinked thoughtfully as she considered that, and Graystripe waited tensely for her reaction. If his offer wasn't good enough, then he and his Clanmates would have to face BloodClan without whatever help Gremlin could give them.

"I'd really hoped that we would be accepted permanently into the Clan," Gremlin responded at last. "That way, Scraps and I wouldn't have to always be looking over our shoulders. If Firestar kicks us out, after I've betrayed BloodClan, we could be in a lot of danger. Fury wouldn't rest until she'd taken her revenge."

"I know. And I'm sorry—but I can't speak for Firestar," Graystripe pointed out. *Though it certainly feels like everyone wants me to!* "I know what kind of cat Firestar is, though, and I can't imagine him putting any cat who helped ThunderClan in danger." Graystripe was being sincere, but he knew as he said it that while many cats—including Cinderpelt and, yes, Firestar—would feel this way, he knew that others within the Clan might balk at the idea of helping a former Blood-Clan cat. Even Brackenfur couldn't seem to wrap his mind around Gremlin's possible worthiness. *For some cats,* Graystripe mused, *only ThunderClan cats can ever be considered trustworthy.* He only hoped that Firestar would see things his way, and that together they could convince the objectors.

Gremlin paused, deep thought in her eyes. Graystripe

felt his belly cramp as he was forced to wonder, once again, whether his Clan was strong enough to defeat BloodClan without her help.

Finally, to his relief, Gremlin nodded. "That sounds fair," she meowed. "And Scraps and I will do whatever it takes to prove ourselves good ThunderClan cats."

"Warriors," Graystripe corrected. "We call ourselves warriors."

Light kindled in the depths of Gremlin's beautiful green eyes. "I like the sound of that," she purred, "and I think Scraps will, too."

"Okay, then," Graystripe continued. *Now, let's get to the reason we're here.* "What can you tell me about BloodClan's attack?"

Please, StarClan, let it be something we can use, he added silently. Gremlin had promised to give him information, but he worried that advance knowledge could only do so much—Thunder-Clan might still end up being overwhelmed by BloodClan when the time came to face them in battle. And he couldn't banish the suspicion, insidious as a worm gnawing his belly, that Gremlin was a loyal BloodClan cat after all. He'd argued for her in front of his Clanmates, but, he reflected uneasily, they could be right: She could be trying to trick him.

"Listen." Gremlin leaned in closer to him. "BloodClan will attack in two sunrises, when the sun clears the top of the trees. They—"

"Not at night, or at dawn?" Graystripe interrupted. "That's what I would do."

"And you would lose the battle, fur-for-brains!" Gremlin

growled. "No, BloodClan will wait until your patrols have gone out and the camp is mostly empty except for kits and elders. Then they'll be able to take the camp and pick off the rest of your warriors when they're scattered through the forest with nowhere to retreat."

"Okay, then we just won't send any—" Graystripe broke off as he saw the flaw in that plan.

"If you don't send your patrols out, BloodClan will just wait until you do," Gremlin pointed out. "You can't stay penned up in your camp forever. For one thing, you'd all starve. Besides," she added, leaning even closer to Graystripe and speaking urgently, "if you change your routine, Fury will know that some cat has betrayed her. And it won't take her long to realize that it was me."

Graystripe stared at her, all his suspicions returning. *So our only hope is to leave our Clan weakened, and let BloodClan into our camp on purpose?* Yet at the same moment, his mind was already busy with possible strategies: If he sent most of the warriors out of camp, they didn't have to go far. They could entice BloodClan into ThunderClan's camp and be ready to trap them there.

"Trust me or not, Graystripe." Gremlin was clearly aware of his misgivings. "Your choice."

Time seemed to slow as Graystripe faced her. He knew that the choice he was about to make could affect the future of his Clan for seasons upon seasons. Yet even as he accepted the risk he was taking, he had to rely on his instincts. And they had told him that Gremlin was being honest.

Gremlin was clearly tense, digging her claws into the

ground, fearful of her fate if her betrayal was discovered.

Surely if she were lying to me, she couldn't pretend so well.

Graystripe took a deep breath, feeling as if he were leaping off a precipice in darkness so thick, he couldn't see what was at the bottom.

"I do trust you," he declared. "Two sunrises from now. We'll be ready. And I promise you, we won't do anything that will give Fury reason to suspect you."

"Then there's more advice I can give you," Gremlin mewed, huffing out a sigh of relief. "To begin with, you'll want to pay special attention to a ginger cat called Brick. . . ."

Graystripe listened carefully, trying to memorize everything the BloodClan queen was telling him. *Please, StarClan, let this be the thing that drives BloodClan away for good. . . . I don't want to be the cat responsible for the end of ThunderClan.*

CHAPTER 23
🍀
— Now —

Graystripe woke after a while, and the rest of the day slid by as he and Barley talked, telling stories about the Clans, and remembering Fang's mother and her courage.

"I remember how she faced up to a dog, one of the times she came to visit me and Ravenpaw," Barley recounted. "It could have swallowed her in one gulp, but she raked her claws across its muzzle, and the stupid creature ran off yelping to its Twolegs."

Monkeystar and Clawwhistle paused in chasing each other through the grass heaps to listen, round-eyed, while Graystripe let out a small huff of laughter. "That sounds like Gremlin," he commented. "She was brave—and trustworthy."

Finally, as the daylight faded, Barley stretched his jaws in a massive yawn. "It's nice to have a cat visit who remembers these times," he told Graystripe. "I won't have many more chances to share my stories with any cat who was there. But now all these memories have made me sleepy," he continued. "We'll talk again tomorrow, before you go." With that, he curled up in his nest and closed his eyes.

As soon as Barley's snores began echoing through the barn, Fang rose to his paws and began working his claws impatiently in the grass. Clearly, he wasn't at peace.

"What's the matter?" Graystripe asked him. "I thought you would like to hear how your mother risked her life for others. Doesn't it make you proud to know she was such a brave cat?"

"No!" Fang flashed back at him. "It was nice to hear those stories, but all they did was remind me that there are cats that I have to save right now, just like my mother did then. Do you even know how she died?"

Graystripe shook his head, realizing that he had never asked. *Maybe because I didn't want to believe that she's gone.*

"She died in the same Twoleg den that I escaped from," Fang told him, settling down among the dried grass again.

"What?" Graystripe stared at him, devastated to hear that. Fang had told him how terrible the conditions there had become, but he hadn't let himself imagine them leading to any cat's death. Certainly not the death of a cat as brave as Gremlin. "I thought once that she would become a warrior, but I hoped she would be happy wherever she ended up," he meowed, trying to push away the horrific images that invaded his mind.

"She was, at first," Fang sighed. "The female Twoleg was good to her. She had one other kittypet, a she-cat called Petunia, and then Gremlin had her litter—three kits, including me. The Twoleg gave my two littermates to other Twolegs, though I used to see them sometimes in their Twolegs' gardens. After that, the three of us lived with her happily for many seasons."

"So what went wrong?" Graystripe asked.

"I don't know." Fang began working his claws again. "The Twoleg got older, and I think she got sick. She started forgetting to feed us, sometimes for whole days. And instead of letting us go outside, she kept us shut in her den. Then she brought in another cat, and another—toms and she-cats. Some of the she-cats had kits, until the den was full of them."

Weird, Graystripe thought. He had never heard of Twolegs behaving like this. *Was she trying to start her own Clan? And somehow it didn't occur to her that if she didn't feed them, they would have to go outside to hunt?*

It was too easy for Graystripe to imagine what the cats must have suffered, trapped in an overcrowded Twoleg den, hungry and dirty and scared. Pain clawed at his heart to think of Gremlin, so clever and brave and honest, reduced to that, after she had sacrificed her freedom to give her kits a good start in life.

"And what happened to Gremlin?" he asked.

"One day, she began to cough," Fang went on, his eyes narrowing with the pain of remembering. "Of course I knew that was a bad sign. She needed help—herbs, or Twoleg medicine, or something! But by then the old Twoleg was too far gone to see that."

"What did you do?" Graystripe asked.

Fang's eyes closed completely for a moment, and he had to pause before he could manage to force the words out. "I kept yowling at the Twoleg, begging her to get some help, but she didn't understand what I was saying. Even if she could have, by then she wasn't even able to help herself. Her own clothes and bedding were getting dirty, and she was so skinny because she was always forgetting to eat. The den reeked of rotting Twoleg food. And always there were more and more cats—brought in by the Twoleg, or born right there in the den. There was never enough food to go around, the Twoleg stopped cleaning our dirt boxes, and she kept the doors and windows shut, so that you could hardly breathe. You would not believe the stench!"

Graystripe suppressed a shudder. Back in ThunderClan's camp, one of the apprentices' most important duties was to change bedding regularly, and every cat in every Clan took part in keeping their camps clean. And that was in the open air! *What it must be like, stuck in a Twoleg den . . .* The walls would trap the stink and make it even worse. *That just goes to show that it's not right for cats to live behind walls.* "Go on," he mewed, his respect for Fang growing as he understood more of what he had survived.

"Gremlin's cough kept getting worse," Fang continued, his voice quivering. "She got weaker and weaker, and then . . ." He closed his eyes, and Graystripe knew before he continued that what he would say next was going to be painful. "Then she died. But just before she did, she told me that I had to find a way out—that I had to help the others to escape, too. I promised her that I would, and now I have to fulfill that promise, no matter what it takes!" For a heartbeat, his eyes glowed with the fervor of his resolve. But then his head drooped and his shoulders sagged. "But I don't know if I can," he confessed.

"Not without your help. Are you still going to keep the promise that you made to my mother?"

Briefly, Graystripe was offended at the thought that Fang expected him to go back on his word. But then he realized that Fang had no experience of honorable warriors.

"Of course I will!" he replied. "I know it took a long time to go to the Moonstone, and then to visit Barley, but I don't intend to break my promise. You just have to be patient for a little longer. . . ."

Fang raised his head, meeting Graystripe's gaze directly. "I'm not sure you understand how bad it is in there," he meowed. "Every day we delay, there's a greater chance that another cat will die in that Twoleg den."

Graystripe realized that the gray tom was right. He hadn't known how bad it was in the Twoleg den, but also, he had been so busy feeling sorry for himself and disappointed by his experience at the Moonstone that he had forgotten there was a cat right in front of him who needed his help, and needed it urgently.

I failed to reach StarClan at the Moonstone, but surely I can do this one thing without their guidance?

"Suppose we spend one more day here in the barn," he suggested. "We'll need time to plan, and hunt to build our strength up, so—"

Fang interrupted him by rising to his paws. "I'm going *now*," he declared. "With you or without you."

"No." Graystripe rose, too, and stretched out his tail to block the younger cat's path. "It's getting dark out there, and we both need sleep. So let's compromise. At dawn tomorrow, I'll come with you, and I promise I won't leave you until we've freed every cat."

And that word, "promise," means something, he reflected, *between me and Gremlin's son.*

For a moment, Fang hesitated, then settled into the dried grass once more. "Okay," he agreed reluctantly. "But if for some reason you change your mind, I'm leaving at dawn."

Graystripe nodded agreement, admiring the younger cat's resolve. *He's headstrong and heroic, just like his mother.* "Gremlin would be proud of you," he murmured.

He glanced across at the two WarriorClan kittypets, who had spent most of the day chasing each other around the piles of grass, practicing their hunting moves, and pretending to defend the barn against invading foxes. Now they were fast asleep, side by side in a grassy nest, with their noses resting on their forepaws and their tails twined together.

"We'll need to decide what to do with them," he murmured. "But we'll worry about that tomorrow, when we make the rest of our plans."

Graystripe woke to find the first pale light of dawn seeping into the barn through the gaps in the roof. Beside him, Barley was stirring, too.

"You're up early," Graystripe remarked, as the black-and-white tom rose to his paws and shook grass seeds out of his pelt.

Barley shrugged. "Early to sleep, early to rise," he mewed.

"But why are you awake at this time? I thought you'd need your rest, after what you've been through."

"I'm still turning things over in my head," Graystripe admitted. "I traveled so far to get to the Moonstone, but what I found there only made me more confused and upset. I miss ThunderClan," he added with a sigh, "but I'm not sure I have a place there anymore. Especially now that I'm nearing the end of my life. I'm just so weary. . . . Giving up seems more and more like the wisest choice."

To his astonishment, Barley let out a deep-throated *mrrow* of laughter. "If you're old, what does that make me?" he asked. "Ancient!"

"I'm sorry," Graystripe protested. "I didn't mean to insult you. It's just that I'm beginning to feel like my best days are in the past."

Barley dismissed his apology with a wave of his tail. "Graystripe, to me you're still a fairly young cat with a lot of life left in you."

"I guess you're right," Graystripe admitted with a sigh. "But what does it matter how much time I have left, if I don't know where to go or what to do? If every day I grow less sure that I have anything to offer my Clan?"

"I know that the path of a warrior isn't always easy," Barley went on. "You don't always get what you want when you want it, but you keep on going, helping others along the way if you can. You know, Graystripe, you don't need any cat, living or dead, to tell you what feels right in your gut. If you think it over for yourself, the right answer will be clear."

Graystripe glanced over to where Fang was still sleeping peacefully. For a moment he wondered whether he should wake the tom, but then he decided to let him rest. *This will be a long day for him, and he's already suffered so much,* Graystripe thought. It was obvious in the way the cat carried himself, as if he had aged beyond his seasons; a Clan cat who looked like that would be almost ready to join the elders. And yet he refused to give up.

So how can I? Graystripe asked himself. *No, like Millie told me in my dream, I have to go on.*

For the first time since his scare at the Moonpool, he saw at least the next few steps of his path before him, clear as day.

CHAPTER 24

— *Now* —

Warm rays of sunlight were slanting into the barn from the gaps high in the walls when Fang finally awoke. Instantly, he sprang to his paws.

"Why didn't you wake me?" he demanded, glaring at Graystripe. "You agreed we would leave at dawn. I thought I could trust you!"

"Keep your fur on," Graystripe responded. "You needed sleep, and now you need to eat. We've a long way to travel, right to the other side of RiverClan territory, and we'll go much faster if you're strong and prepared."

"But you promised—" Fang began, then broke off with an awkward shrug, as if he was conceding that Graystripe might have a point, even though he obviously wasn't happy about the delay.

Graystripe, who had hunted—with a little help from Barley and the kittypets—after he awoke at dawn, brought Fang a couple of mice and set them down at his paws.

"Thanks," Fang mumbled, rapidly gulping down the prey.

Then he added, with a penitent glance at Graystripe, "I guess you're right. I'm really hungry. I could have easily eaten another couple of mice."

"You can try some kittypet food, if you like," Barley offered; his Twolegs had brought him a massive bowlful not long ago. "Take as much as you can eat. The Twolegs always give me too much—these days, I don't have the appetite that I used to."

"Try some," Monkeystar urged Fang. "We always have a taste when we visit Barley; it's really good!"

"Better than the stuff our housefolk give us," Clawwhistle muttered enviously.

Graystripe suppressed a *mrrow* of amusement, wondering now whether WarriorClan's frequent visits to Barley were entirely out of concern for the old cat.

"Well, maybe, if you insist . . ." Fang eyed the bowl doubtfully and stretched out his neck to taste a single food pellet. A heartbeat later he was munching away with his nose buried deep in the bowl.

While Fang was eating, Graystripe settled down once more beside Barley, trying to lend his old friend some of his strength through the brushing of their pelts.

"Thank you for your advice," he mewed. "It's been so good to see you again."

"For me too," Barley purred in response. "If it's the last time I see a Clan cat before I die, I'm glad it was you, Graystripe."

Graystripe leaned closer to touch Barley's ear with his nose. "That means a lot to me."

Before Barley could say any more, Fang rose from where

he had been crouching over the old tom's food bowl. "That was great," he meowed, swiping his tongue around his jaws. "Thanks, Barley. I couldn't eat another mouthful. And . . . thanks for telling me those stories about my mother."

Barley dipped his head. "Any kit of Gremlin's will always be free to share my food and my home."

"Time to go," Graystripe declared, rising to his paws. "Barley, if I can, I'll drop in to see you again on my way back to the lake"

"I would love that," Barley responded. "But don't take any extra risks for my sake. And whatever happens, good luck on your journey." He dipped his head meaningfully. "May StarClan light your path, my old friend."

Graystripe felt words leave him for a moment. *If only I knew whether StarClan was watching! If only I could be sure Firestar and the others were guiding my paws.* But looking into Barley's cloudy gaze, Graystripe understood that his friend was wishing him more than StarClan's attention.

He was wishing him a future—and the hope to look forward to it.

"And yours, Barley." Graystripe stepped forward to touch noses one last time with his old friend. "Always yours."

"And what about us?" Monkeystar asked, bounding up to Graystripe with Clawwhistle a paw step behind.

"You can come with us," Graystripe replied, adding hastily, as the two kittypets exchanged a delighted glance, "only as far as your home. It's on our way."

"But we're not going home," Monkeystar objected. "We want to come with you to Fang's den. We can help!"

Graystripe let out a sigh. *I should have foreseen this! Now I have to let them down gently,* he added to himself. *It's great that they want to help, but they'd only end up being two more cats I had to watch out for. I'd never forgive myself if anything happened to them.*

"You've been such a big help already," he told them, "helping me get to the Moonstone and then to the farm. But look—the truth is, what Fang and I have to do now is far too dangerous for you to get involved."

"Is not!" Clawwhistle twitched his tail indignantly; both he and Monkeystar stood tall, bushing out their fur to show how big and tough they were. "We're brave!"

"I know you are," Graystripe meowed. "But even though you feel like full warriors, back in the Clans you would still be just apprentices, with a lot to learn. Being a warrior is dangerous even for the most experienced cats."

"We don't care!" Monkeystar insisted. "We still want to come with you."

Graystripe hesitated, wondering what arguments he could use to convince the young cats that where he and Fang were going was no place for them. It didn't make it easier that in one way he admired them for their courage and enthusiasm; if they had been Clanborn, they would have made fine warriors, in time.

"If the recent battles in the Clans have taught me anything," he began, "it's that as much as I love Clan life, it isn't always easy, or safe. I've experienced so many senseless deaths, and I don't want the two of you becoming more cats I need to mourn."

Monkeystar exchanged a glance with Clawwhistle, seeming

more serious now. "I don't think you're being fair to us," she told Graystripe. "We've learned a lot since we met you, and we're not afraid. Let us help!"

"Please!" Clawwhistle added.

Graystripe remembered how all six kittypets had stalked him most of the way to the Moonstone, and knew that shaking these two off wouldn't be as easy as he had hoped. He realized that the only way to handle them would be to give them a task: something that wouldn't get them killed, but would give them a reason not to follow him in secret. After all, that was how he would deal with an overeager apprentice, back in the Clans. He glanced around for inspiration, and his gaze settled on Barley.

"Okay, I know you're brave cats," he admitted, "so I guess I can trust you with the most important part of this mission."

Fang stared at him disbelievingly, while the two kittypets bounced up and down with excitement. "Yes, you can trust us!" Monkeystar promised. "What do we have to do?"

"Stay right here and look after this territory, and watch over Barley," Graystripe explained. Before the young cats had time to look disappointed, he went on quickly, "Fang and I won't be as effective if we have to worry about Barley, because . . . er . . . he's so old, and he seems so . . . vulnerable. What if . . . well, what if a badger should wander onto the farm? Only fierce warriors like you would be able to help."

"I'd be really grateful," Barley put in. "I could never fight a badger on my own."

Clawwhistle puffed out his chest proudly. "I can do that!"

he boasted. "I'm not scared of badgers. Nothing will happen to you on my watch, Barley!"

But Monkeystar was watching Graystripe through narrowed eyes. "A badger, hmm? We don't see many badgers on the farm."

Graystripe held her gaze. *She sees right through me,* he mused. *Good, then: Monkeystar will be a wise leader after all.* "There's always a first time," he mewed gently.

Monkeystar stared at him for a moment, then raised her head proudly. "Good idea. We'll make sure the territory around the barn is safe, as well," Monkeystar added. "In case you and Fang need a safe place to retreat."

"Good idea," Graystripe praised them. Then he added sincerely, "I know I've left this mission in the right paws."

"Good-bye, then," Fang mewed, giving Graystripe an impatient prod.

"Good-bye!" the kittypets chorused. "And may StarClan light your path."

With a final farewell, Graystripe and Fang pushed their way through the gap in the bottom of the barn door and into the open.

"So, you say this Twoleg den is on the far side of River-Clan's old territory?" Graystripe asked Fang as they left the barn behind them. He gave a quick glance over his shoulder to make sure that the WarriorClan cats weren't following them.

"Yes, across the river from the treecutplace," the gray tom replied, angling his ears in that direction.

"Then lead the way."

Fang headed along a narrow path that led away from the farm and alongside a hedge. Graystripe remembered the direction from his previous visits to the barn, though when they reached the former WindClan territory, they had to skirt around the new Twoleg dens, keeping very close to the edge of the river. Some of the Twoleg gardens stretched right down to the water's edge, and the air was filled with the scents of Twolegs, dogs, and kittypets, along with the distant reek of monsters. Graystripe was overtaken once more with longing for the past, mingled with sadness at how everything had changed. He was relieved when he and Fang approached the Twoleg bridge and were able to cross into RiverClan's old territory, which had hardly changed at all from how he remembered it.

"I hope we don't meet the rest of WarriorClan," he murmured to Fang. "I never thought I'd meet kittypets I liked so much, but we don't want to deal with them now."

Though he caught a few traces of familiar scent, the young cats didn't appear. Graystripe allowed himself to relax a little when he was able to plunge into the lush undergrowth on RiverClan's side of the river.

I could almost imagine I was back home, he thought, remembering the day when he had visited Leopardstar to give her the news that BloodClan had reappeared. But there was a bittersweet tang to the memory, as he recalled his unexpected chance to talk to his two kits. Now Feathertail was dead, and Stormfur lived far away in the mountains, far away from the Clans.

You can never go back, however much you might want to.

Although there were no new Twoleg dens here, Graystripe

couldn't pretend that nothing had changed. There were no border markers, there was no scent of cats, and when they passed the island where RiverClan had made its camp, there was no sign of life. Graystripe looked across the stream to what had been his own territory, but could see nothing but rows and rows of Twoleg dens.

The last of the Clans have gone from this place, he thought, struggling with the biting pain of regret. *WarriorClan keeps our memory alive, but even what they know of the Clans is far from the real story.*

Fang led the way alongside the river, past Sunningrocks and the stepping-stones that Graystripe had often crossed in secret to meet his mate Silverstream. Eventually he spotted the dark mass of Tallpines and the fences of the treecutplace. That, at least, had not changed; a shudder passed through Graystripe as he remembered how the dog pack had escaped from there and almost destroyed ThunderClan before Firestar had saved them.

He shook off his brief memory to see that he had fallen behind Fang as the gray tom veered away from the waterside and plunged into a stretch of woodland. "We're almost there," he mewed.

As Graystripe trailed him through the trees, he began to scent something foul in the air. He halted, nose twitching, and opened his jaws to taste, but he couldn't identify what he was smelling. Cat scent was mingled with it; partly it reminded him of his camp's dirtplace, and partly of one time when he'd had an infected wound, before Leafpool had healed him with fresh, tangy herbs. All of it was rolled together into the most eye-watering, throat-gagging stench that he had ever experienced.

"What's *that*?" he demanded.

Fang glanced back over his shoulder. "That's the Twoleg den," he replied.

For the first time, Graystripe began to have a true inkling of what he was walking into. The stink was so bad he just wanted to turn tail and run, and he couldn't even see the walls of the den through the trees yet.

"Coming?" Fang asked, a wry twist to his mouth suggesting that he wouldn't be surprised if Graystripe backed out.

Graystripe was tempted to do just that, but he braced himself to continue, remembering the vow he had made to Gremlin. "Lead on," he growled. "I'm right behind you."

Moments later, as he followed Fang around a clump of elder bushes, he caught sight of the den, still several fox-lengths ahead. The walls had been built from gray stone, and though a stone path edged by plants suggested there had once been a garden, the wooden fence was broken down and the ground had been invaded by brambles and straggling grass. Various bits of Twoleg rubbish were strewn around. A small Thunderpath passed in front of the den, disappearing into the trees on either side.

Graystripe would not have believed that the stink could get any worse, but as he and Fang crossed the Thunderpath and approached the den, it did just that. There was no escaping it; with every breath he took, he wanted to vomit. *If it's this bad out here, what must it be like inside?* he wondered, a shudder running through him.

The small windows of the den were covered by flat pieces of wood; one of them was hanging off, held up by only a single reddish claw. Springing up onto the sill, Graystripe peered through the gap. Inside, he could see cats running in and out of the room, perched on ledges fastened to the walls, or curled up on the soft rocks Twolegs kept in their nests.

It is like there's a whole Clan in there! he thought.

"How many cats are there?" he asked, springing down again to Fang's side.

"I'm not sure." Fang blinked uncertainly. "Ten, or maybe even fifteen. It's hard to keep track, because there are always new kits being born. When I left, a couple of the queens were pregnant, and some of the very old cats may have died while I've been away."

I hadn't thought of that. Graystripe's confidence of succeeding in their mission began to falter. *If there are pregnant or elderly cats in there, that will make an escape even more dangerous.*

Graystripe began to inspect the den more closely. At first, because it seemed to be falling apart, he thought it would be easy to find a way in. But he realized that he was wrong. The door and the windows were all closed, even though the sun was beating down and the air was warm. The only open area Graystripe could see was a space beneath the den, which was propped up on piles of square-cut stones.

"What's under there?" he asked.

Fang shrugged. "Nothing. Just the underside of the den floor."

"Then how are we supposed to get in?" Graystripe wondered aloud, hardly expecting an answer.

Fang shook his head. "The Twoleg always keeps the place shut tight," he replied, "except when she goes in or out, but the door around the back is made of little pieces of clearstone. One of them was broken, and I managed to squeeze through. I tried to make it bigger so the rest of them could escape, but I only managed to cut my paws."

Graystripe had noticed earlier that Fang had torn fur near his paws; now the gray tom stretched out one leg, showing his pads. Graystripe winced to see the scars that cut across them.

"Couldn't any of them have squeezed out like you did?" Graystripe asked.

"Well, I'm skinnier than most." Fang looked down at himself; Graystripe noticed that he was beginning to fill out, after a couple of days eating well. "Or I was. The kits are smaller, but they wouldn't leave without their mother. Besides, the others are scared," Fang continued, "and they wouldn't listen to me. They need a cat with authority to tell them what to do."

Authority? Me? Graystripe thought with wry amusement. "Then let's give the door at the back another try," he meowed. "Together we might be able to make the hole bigger. It's as good a plan as any."

Graystripe and Fang picked their way around the den, avoiding debris spilled on the ground, and broken bowls, made of curved red stone, that held long-dead plants. They jumped over Twoleg things made of sticks and soft pelts splitting open to show something like thistle-fluff stuffed inside.

Looks like this Twoleg doesn't only collect cats, Graystripe thought.

When the two toms reached the back door, Graystripe

spotted the broken glass immediately, only to see that a piece of wood had been fastened across the hole on the inside.

"Oh, no!" Fang exclaimed with a frustrated lash of his tail, his eyes widening in despair.

"Keep your fur on," Graystripe advised. "Maybe we can move it."

But when he thrust at the wood with one paw, it would not give way—and the sharp edges of the broken glass meant it would be no use trying to lever it off by clawing at the side.

"Fox dung!" Graystripe snarled, and gave up the attempt, peering instead through the neighboring piece of glass into the room beyond.

This close to the den, the stench was so overpowering that it was all he could do not to retch. Inside, among piles of rubbish and rotting food, he could make out at least a dozen cats. They were all scrawny and ragged-looking, like rogues who hadn't seen prey in many moons, nor groomed themselves for at least as long. And it was clear that these cats seemed to make dirt wherever they felt like it.

That's no way for a decent cat to behave, Graystripe thought, bile rising into his throat at the very idea. *Even kittypets use those funny little boxes.* Then, as he looked again at the tightly closed door, he realized that with their Twoleg neglecting them like this, the imprisoned cats had no choice.

Beneath the smell of dirt and debris, Graystripe could make out the sickly-sweet scent of infection. At least one cat in there was sick or injured, and without treatment they would only get worse.

That might be Fang's mate, Daffodil, he thought. *Fang said she was sick. And he's right. These cats need to be rescued, and there's no time to spare.*

Graystripe returned to Fang, who was waiting for him a few tail-lengths away. He felt a sudden rush of sympathy for the skinny tom. *Now I understand what he's been through. . . . It would be cruel to send him back in there.* "If I can find another way in," he meowed, "maybe I can open the door from the inside, and you can lead the cats into the woods."

Fang shook his head despondently. "I don't know. . . . Do you really think you can pull that off?"

With Fang trailing behind him, Graystripe began to prowl around the outside of the den, alert for any sign of an opening that he could use. He had almost arrived back at his starting point when he spotted a window standing ajar on the upper floor. The gap was tiny: A mouse might have slipped through it easily, but it was hardly big enough for a full-grown cat to squeeze through.

It's the only chance we have, though . . . so I have to at least try.

"If I can get up there," he told Fang, pointing with his tail, "I might be able to pry it open further and wriggle inside."

Fang surveyed the window doubtfully. "I suppose we could attempt it."

"But you aren't coming with me," Graystripe continued. "There's—"

"What?" Fang interrupted. "No way!"

Graystripe raised his tail to silence the younger cat. "As I was saying, there's no point in both of us getting stuck in there. Besides, I need you out here, to encourage the cats to leave, once I've found a way. They know you, and they'll trust you."

"Okay," Fang agreed reluctantly.

Glancing around, Graystripe spotted a tree growing near the den, with a branch stretching most of the way to the open window. The branch looked uncomfortably spindly, and he would have to jump a couple of tail-lengths from the end, but he thought he should be able to do it.

StarClan! I'm getting too old for this!

Graystripe was aware of Fang's watching him with clear admiration as he clawed his way up the tree; it made him feel unusually self-conscious as he ventured out onto the branch. It bounced under his weight, and for a moment he froze, digging his claws into the bark and squeezing his eyes tight shut. But he knew he couldn't face Fang if he retreated now, without even trying to get into the den.

Forcing his eyes open, Graystripe advanced cautiously along the branch, paw step by paw step, while the branch dipped and swayed beneath him. When he reached the end, he could tell it wasn't solid enough to push off for a really good leap, but he didn't have much of a choice. For a moment, he paused, sizing up the distance between the branch and the windowsill. Then, taking a deep breath, he coiled his hind legs under him and jumped.

At first, he thought he was going to fall short, crashing to the ground and breaking all his legs. Then his forepaws slammed against the sill. He scrabbled frantically with his hind paws and managed to achieve a precarious balance while he tugged with one paw at the edge of the window to enlarge the gap. His paws were slipping, and once again he imagined plummeting down, legs and tail flailing helplessly, before the window creaked open another mouse-length and he was able to slide into the den.

Graystripe stood for a moment, breathing hard, his legs trembling after the struggle to get inside. He had hoped that he would be able to lead the trapped cats to freedom through the open window, but now he realized that if they were sick or weak, they would never be able to manage it. Pregnant she-cats or very young kits would have no hope, either.

I hope I don't have to go back that way, he thought grimly.

Up here, the light was dim, struggling to reach through the filthy window, and the air was musty, but there were few signs of cats. To Graystripe's relief, the door of this room, at least, was open; he padded silently across to it and peered out into a passage.

He was about to venture further when he heard the sound of Twoleg paw steps in the room next to him, and the Twoleg's voice calling out. Graystripe had no idea what she was meowing about, but he waited tensely until he was sure that she was staying put. Then he stepped out into the passage, all his senses alert for signs of danger.

Graystripe could hear cats yowling from somewhere below, and, slinking along the passage, he came to a jagged slope leading downward. He padded down, leaving the Twoleg noises behind him.

As his paws touched the floor at the bottom, he felt something sticky on his pads; looking down, he saw something brown and foul-smelling stretching in all directions.

Yuck! I don't even want to know what that is!

Padding forward, Graystripe found himself weaving his way through a maze of filth. He cringed at setting his paws down on the disgusting surface of the floor, thinking how much trouble a warrior apprentice would be in for leaving even a trace of mess like this in the camp.

Everywhere he looked were weary cats, who raised their heads to give him a blank stare as he passed by, but didn't speak or even seem curious to see a newcomer among them. In a dark corner he spotted a ginger-and-white she-cat lying on a heap of dirty pelts; her eyes were glassy, and her chest heaved with her labored breathing. The smell of infection was even stronger as Graystripe approached her.

That must be Daffodil, he thought, remembering how Fang had described his mate. She looked just as bad as Fang had warned him, but at least she was still alive. He hesitated, wondering whether to speak to her, to tell her that her mate was close by, but then he decided that it was more important to open the gap in the door and let the cats out.

Eventually, Graystripe found his way to the door with the broken pane of glass. Fang was waiting for him on the other side, and glanced up with a look of relief as Graystripe appeared.

Graystripe clawed at the edges of the piece of wood that was blocking the gap, but however hard he tried, he couldn't pry it away from the door frame. All he managed to do was break a claw.

"Fox dung!" he hissed, and rammed himself against the door with outstretched paws in the hope of pushing it open.

Fang leaped up on the outside, trying to grab at the shiny round thing that Twolegs used to open the door. But it didn't work for Fang. All his tugging and Graystripe's pushing were quite useless. The door was shut fast.

As Graystripe stood there panting, trying to think of another way to get out, he heard a creaking sound coming from the upper floor. Fang leaped backward, gazing up; his eyes widened with alarm.

"What is it?" Graystripe called.

"The window!" Fang called back. "The Twoleg has shut the window! Oh, Graystripe, you're trapped in there!"

CHAPTER 25

— Now —

"Don't panic!" Graystripe told Fang, though he was struggling not to panic himself. His heart was beating fast, and a sickly feeling rose in his throat. It reminded him of another time, now long past, when he'd become stuck in a Twoleg's den. It hadn't been nearly as bad as this one, but still, he'd been desperate to escape! "There must be another way out. We both need to calm down and think."

"Did you see that hole near the other door?" Fang meowed after a moment.

"Yes," Graystripe replied, "but it's far too small for a cat to get through."

"That's true," Fang agreed, "but maybe if you claw at it, you can make it bigger and get out that way."

Graystripe had his doubts. If it were that easy to escape, Fang and the other cats would have done so long ago. But anything was better than standing here in the filth and not making any effort to break out.

"I'll try," he declared.

As he padded back through the den, the other cats barely paid him any attention. Graystripe guessed that they must be used to new cats turning up all the time, as Fang had told him. Or maybe they were just too tired, or too sick, to care anymore. But he noticed that one old, weary she-cat was watching him listlessly, and rose to follow him as he approached the door. Graystripe dipped his head to her, but she didn't speak.

Graystripe found the hole without any difficulty: a jagged, three-cornered gap in the wall at about the height of his head. Fang had been right that it was too small for a full-grown cat; even a kit would have difficulty squeezing through. But Graystripe wasn't about to give up. He pawed determinedly at the edges of the gap, and at first he was encouraged as they began to crumble away under his scraping claws.

"Do you think we haven't tried that?" a voice came from behind him.

Graystripe turned to see the old she-cat. She had once been beautiful, he realized: She had fluffy gray fur that she at least made an attempt to groom, and large, lustrous amber eyes, which were fixed on him now with an irritated expression.

"It's no use clawing," she snapped. "You might shift a bit of that crumbly stuff, but there's harder rock underneath that won't budge. The hole will never get any bigger, and there's no way out. Honeysuckle just got lucky."

"Honeysuckle?" Graystripe asked, bewildered.

"That skinny gray tom out there," the she-cat responded, jerking her head toward the back door.

"Oh . . ." Now Graystripe understood. Honeysuckle must

be Fang's kittypet name. When he escaped, he must have given himself a tougher-sounding one. *Maybe to impress me,* Graystripe thought. In spite of his terrible situation, he had to suppress a small *mrrow* of amusement.

From where he was standing, Graystripe could hear Fang— or Honeysuckle—clawing at the other side of the hole from outside the den, but the old she-cat had been right: The hard rock wouldn't budge.

"It's no use, Fang," Graystripe yowled through the hole. "Just sit tight. I'll think of something."

Peering through the opening, he could see Fang, sitting back and waiting with a trusting expression on his face. *What if I let him down?* he thought. However hard he tried to think of another way to escape, his mind was a blank.

"You're new here," the old she-cat remarked. "What's your name?"

"Graystripe. What's yours?"

"I'm Petunia. I've been here longest. I've seen all the new arrivals, and they all try to get out at first. But it can't be done. You'll be a lot happier if you just settle down and accept it."

Graystripe couldn't imagine ever being happy in this disgusting place. "If you've been here longest, you must have known Fang's—I mean Honeysuckle's—mother," he mewed.

"Oh, yes, I knew Gremlin very well," Petunia replied, her eyes filling with sadness. "She was such a kindhearted cat. She did her best to take care of the rest of us when our Twoleg couldn't do it anymore. It was hard on all of us to see her get sick and die."

Yes, that sounds just like what Gremlin would have done, Graystripe thought, remembering the queen's love for her brother and her unborn kits. *Trying to take care of cats who were unable to take care of themselves.*

As Petunia was talking, Graystripe began to hear a shuffling sound, and turned to see a very old Twoleg carrying two bowls. Her skin was wrinkled and her back hunched; her pelts were dirty, hanging off her scrawny body, and her head fur was white and straggly. Graystripe felt a stab of pity; clearly, she wasn't looking after herself any better than she looked after the cats.

Graystripe braced himself, ready for the Twoleg to spot him, but her watery gaze passed over him without any reaction. Obviously, she had so many cats that she just assumed he was one of hers.

But how is that possible? Graystripe asked himself. *I smell so different from them!*

The Twoleg said something as she put the bowls down, her voice kind and gentle. Graystripe didn't understand her words, except that she seemed to be calling all the cats Petunia, but it was clear from the affection in her voice that she loved every one of them.

Instantly cats appeared from every corner of the den, like crows descending on a dead animal. They were yowling with hunger, pushing and squirming to reach the bowls. There wasn't nearly enough food for so many cats; the smaller and weaker ones were thrust to the back of the crowd, where they didn't get so much as a sniff.

When was the last time she fed them enough for all of them? Graystripe wondered as he watched, appalled. *From the looks of them, it's been too long.*

The gray she-cat, Petunia, barreled into the midst of the skirmish and grabbed up a mouthful of scraps. But instead of gulping them down, she fought her way out of the throng and headed to the corner where the orange-and-white she-cat was lying.

Graystripe followed her in time to see her setting down the scraps in front of the sick cat.

"Here you are, Daffodil," Petunia mewed. "Eat up. You need your strength to get better."

Graystripe watched, a purr rising in his throat at the old cat's gentleness. She stroked Daffodil's flank with her tail while the sick she-cat forced down some of the food. Petunia only finished off the leftovers after Daffodil had eaten all she could.

As soon as the Twoleg had retreated and the cats had finished devouring the scanty food, Graystripe sprang up onto a nearby window ledge and let out a commanding yowl, to get the cats' attention before they dispersed again.

The cats turned toward him, some of them blinking in confusion, some of them looking vaguely curious. "Who are you?" a black-and-white tom asked. "You weren't here this morning."

"My name is Graystripe, and I'm a friend of Fang's—I mean, a friend of Honeysuckle's," Graystripe replied. "But that doesn't really matter. The important question is, do you want to get out of here?"

Several cats nodded. One of them, a bright orange tabby with amber eyes, stepped forward until she stood right under the window where Graystripe was perched.

"Hi, I'm Lily," she began. "Of course we want to get out of here. We've wanted to leave ever since we first arrived. But we've *tried*. There's just no way to escape this place."

"There has to be," Graystripe insisted, "and if we all put our heads together, I'm sure that we can find it."

"And *I'm* sure that hedgehogs might fly," some cat muttered from the back of the crowd.

But Graystripe thought that most of the cats were considering what he had said. Their eyes even looked brighter, as if his words had encouraged them.

"I've got an idea," one of the younger cats meowed. He was a lean tom with amber eyes and patches of bare skin where his fur was missing. "Maybe we can all attack the Twoleg the next time she opens the door."

A chorus of agreement greeted his plan, but the old she-cat, Petunia, looked outraged. "Absolutely not!" she snapped. Her fur bristled up, and she slid out her claws as if she might attack the young tom.

"But it might work," Graystripe pointed out to her. "Why are you so against it?"

Petunia turned her amber gaze on him with a look of deep unhappiness. "My Twoleg rescued me from a place where they kill cats who have no home," she replied. "She saved my life. I know what she's become, but in spite of that, I still love her, and I could never do anything to harm her."

The young tom who had suggested the attack let out a snort of contempt.

"Flea-brain!" Petunia narrowed her eyes in a glare of withering scorn. "It's not the Twoleg's fault that she's old and sick now and gets confused. We cats might be the only thing keeping her alive. It will break her heart if we all escape. Especially me, because I was her first cat."

"Is that why she seems to call you all Petunia?" Graystripe asked, impressed by the old she-cat's loyalty.

Petunia nodded. "I think she can only remember one name now."

Graystripe could sympathize with her. When he'd been trapped by the Twolegs, he had ended up living as a kittypet for a while. Though it hadn't been his choice, and he'd longed to get back to his life as a warrior, his Twolegs had taken good care of him, and he knew there were more good Twolegs out there. Clearly this old Twoleg didn't mean to be unkind to her cats.

"I understand," he told Petunia, "but this is no way for a cat to live."

"I've gotten used to it," Petunia argued. "And sooner or later, the others will, too."

"But some of them won't live long enough to get used to it," Graystripe pointed out. "There are sick cats here, some who are starving, some who are expecting kits, and you all need more care than the Twoleg can give you. It isn't fair for them to be treated this way."

A murmur of agreement came from the crowd of cats, while

Petunia fell silent, bowing her head in acknowledgment that Graystripe was right.

After a few long moments, she looked up and spoke again. "I may know of a way to get out," she mewed.

"And you never told us about it?" Lily exclaimed, as if she didn't believe what she had just heard.

Petunia sighed. "I don't know for sure that it will work. But every so often, the Twoleg goes outside to collect something from a box out there, or to do something in the garden. It doesn't happen every day, and we'd have to be ready in case it *does* happen. But I thought we might try finding something to prop the door open the next time. She might not notice, and then we can escape."

"Good idea," Graystripe commented. "Even if it takes some time, it's worth a try."

"But I'm not going anywhere," Petunia mewed defiantly. "This is my home, for better or worse."

"We can't abandon you here!" Lily protested.

"You have to come with us!" another cat meowed from the back of the crowd.

But Graystripe saw how resolute and certain the old cat looked, and he respected her decision, even though he didn't think it was the right one.

"I'll find something to prop open the door." Lily darted away and returned a moment later dragging a small piece of Twoleg pelt. She concealed it behind one of the heaps of debris that lay all around the den. Graystripe went to the broken door again to tell Fang the new plan. He encouraged the tom to rest nearby, and to be ready to help if the Twoleg left the den.

Then all the cats slid away to hide in shadowed corners, or behind more of the Twoleg rubbish. Graystripe stayed where he was, watching; he could see the gleam of eyes from the cats' hiding places, each gaze trained on the closed door.

Time seemed to slow down as Graystripe and the other cats waited. The sun's rays slid up the walls and then disappeared altogether, and the light turned pink, then pale blue. Graystripe was beginning to feel sleepy, but he was determined to stay awake. Finally, when the light from outside was nearly gone, Graystripe heard the Twoleg's shuffling paw steps, and saw her heading for the door. She was carrying a green container with a spout sticking out of one side. Water was sloshing out of the top; Graystripe wondered if she was going to give some water to the long-dead plants in the bowls outside. *Why now, when it's nearly dark?* But he supposed much of what the Twoleg did now wasn't easy to explain.

Graystripe leaped down to fetch the pelt, but by the time he had retrieved it from its hiding place, the Twoleg was already out of the door and closing it behind her. Hissing with frustration, he crouched close by, so that he'd be ready when she returned.

When the Twoleg finally came inside again, the door swung back into position behind her. For just a moment, Graystripe could see the garden outside, and he spotted Fang watching from a nearby overgrown bush, his eyes wide and hopeful. Graystripe moved quickly to shove the pelt into the gap. But the door was too heavy; as it closed, it pushed the pelt aside and shut with a snap.

No!

The room was cloaked in gloom; Graystripe felt it sinking into his pelt like gray fog as he stared despairingly at the barrier. His chest was so tight he could hardly breathe.

What if I never get out of here?

CHAPTER 26

⚜

— Then —

Graystripe burrowed down into his nest and tried to ignore his itching paws and the sensation of ants crawling through his pelt. Though two moons had slipped by since Firestar's departure, he was still sleeping in the warriors' den; it felt wrong to use Firestar's when his leader was still alive.

At least, I hope he's still alive.

He had never regretted that decision until now, when he wanted to pace and shake out some of his nerves, but had to stay curled up and pretend to be asleep so as not to disturb his Clanmates. For the approaching day was when BloodClan would launch their attack.

That is, if Gremlin was telling the truth, he reminded himself. Then he murmured aloud, "I trust her. BloodClan is out there. They're coming. And ThunderClan will be ready."

Finally, dawn light began to show through the chinks in the roof of the den. "Thank StarClan," Graystripe breathed out, rising to his paws and shaking scraps of moss out of his pelt.

Quietly he padded from nest to nest, rousing his warriors and leading them out into the center of camp. Not all of them had been asleep; some were as tense as Graystripe himself, ready to defend the camp at any moment, and rising to follow him with heartfelt huffs of relief.

Then Graystripe bounded from den to den to fetch the elders, the apprentices, and the two queens from the nursery. There would be no yowling today to call a special Clan meeting; if any BloodClan cats were listening—and Graystripe was sure that they were—they must hear nothing but the ordinary sounds of a camp waking for the day's duties.

Last of all, Graystripe slipped into Cinderpelt's den.

"Is it time?" she asked, her blue eyes gleaming in the dawn twilight.

Graystripe nodded. "Come outside. I'm going to address the Clan. You too, Longtail," he added to the pale tabby warrior. "I'll need you."

"I'm ready!" Longtail sprang up and followed Graystripe into the open, with Cinderpelt's tail on his shoulder to guide him.

Graystripe beckoned with his tail for his Clanmates to draw closer until the whole Clan was huddled around him, tense and silent, their gazes fixed on his face. He spoke in a low voice, but every word carried clearly.

"According to Gremlin," he began, "BloodClan will attack when the sun clears the tops of the trees. That gives us a little time. Until then, we must convince BloodClan that we don't suspect anything, and that this is just a normal day in

ThunderClan. We have to carry out our duties just as we usually do."

Graystripe paused, letting his gaze rove around his Clan. When he had made his plan, he'd realized that he didn't have quite enough warriors for everything he would like to do, and his thoughts had turned to Frostfur and Goldenflower. They had retired to the elders' den less than a moon before Firestar had left on his quest, and they still had plenty of life left in them.

"Frostfur," he continued, turning to the white she-cat, "how would you and Goldenflower like to be warriors again, just for today?"

Frostfur sat up straighter, her blue eyes gleaming, while Goldenflower sprang to her paws, flexing her claws eagerly in the earth of the camp floor. "Just try us!" she exclaimed.

Graystripe dipped his head in respect for the older cats' commitment to their Clan. "Then go and do the dawn patrol," he meowed. "If you see or scent BloodClan, just ignore them— and whatever you do, *don't* get into a fight with them unless there's no way to avoid it."

"We can fight," Frostfur mewed, sounding slightly indignant.

"Of course you can," Graystripe told her. "So as soon as you hear the attack start—and believe me, you *will* hear it start— come straight back here and help."

"Right." Frostfur swished her tail. "Come on, Goldenflower."

Graystripe watched the two she-cats head toward the

gorse tunnel, hoping that if BloodClan were watching they wouldn't realize that he wasn't sending out quite as many cats as usual. He wanted this to seem like an ordinary day, and he had planned his battle strategy accordingly, but he couldn't drain the camp of all his experienced warriors.

"Brackenfur," he went on, once the she-cats had left. "You've always excelled at spotting prey. You and Brambleclaw can be a hunting patrol. Stay fairly close to the camp, between the camp and the Twolegplace. I expect BloodClan will come from that direction. If you spot them, come back and report, but in any case, come back as soon as you hear the attack start."

Brackenfur, who by now seemed reconciled to the Clan's agreement with Gremlin, gave him a brisk nod and headed out, with Brambleclaw padding along at his shoulder.

"What about us?" Sootpaw asked, wriggling between his Clanmates to the front of the crowd. "Don't we get to do anything?"

His mentor, Thornclaw, gave him a cuff around the ear, his claws sheathed. "Shut up, you little mouse-brain. This isn't a fun game for apprentices."

"Oh, I have something for the 'paws to do," Graystripe meowed. "Thornclaw, Dustpelt, Cloudtail," he added, naming their three mentors, "you're going to take your apprentices and do some battle training in the sandy hollow. When you hear the attack begin, I want you to get back here as fast as you can and fall on BloodClan from behind."

"Cool!" Rainpaw exclaimed.

"No, not 'cool,'" Graystripe told him, doing his best to look sternly at the younger cats. "As soon as you three hear the fighting, you are to climb the nearest tree, and you're to stay there until it's all over."

"But that's not fair!" Sorrelpaw blurted out. "We want to fight. I just learned a new move." She reared up on her hind paws and batted at the air with her forepaws, as if she were raking her tiny claws across an enemy's pelt.

"Very good," Graystripe mewed drily. "You're *still* staying up in your tree."

"Apprentices fought in the first battle against BloodClan," Rainpaw muttered.

"And those apprentices were experienced, almost warriors," his mentor Cloudtail pointed out. "You three are barely out of the nursery."

"And that's where you'll end up, if I hear any more arguing," Graystripe snapped. "We're wasting time. Go now."

The three mentors bounded off toward the gorse tunnel; their apprentices followed in a cluster, grumbling among themselves.

"Okay, the rest of us will stay here," Graystripe continued, gazing around at his remaining Clanmates. He could see from their bristling fur and twitching tails how nervous they were, but their eyes glittered with determination. "Brightheart, Ferncloud, your job is to guard the nursery."

"Don't worry, Graystripe," Brightheart responded, her one good eye gleaming fiercely. "No BloodClan cat will harm our kits."

Graystripe gave the two queens an approving nod, then turned to the remaining elders. "Go back to your den," he instructed them. "Longtail, you go with them. They'll need a warrior for some extra strength."

Dappletail slid out her claws. "We can still fight."

"Yeah," Speckletail added, raising one hind paw to scratch her neck. "We've forgotten more battle moves than those BloodClan mange-pelts ever knew."

"I don't doubt it," Graystripe agreed. "I still want you to hide in your den, and surprise BloodClan with a second wave of defense if they seem to be winning."

"You got it," One-eye meowed, and led the way back to the fallen tree.

Longtail brought up the rear, his chest puffed out with pride to be counted among the warriors again. Graystripe hoped he had understood his real task: to keep the elders out of harm's way unless things got really desperate.

"And what about us?" Ashfur asked. He was crouched next to Mousefur, the only two warriors left without a specific task. They were both looking annoyed, as if they felt they had been passed over in Graystripe's battle plan.

"Go and hide in the long grass at the edge of the camp," Graystripe instructed. "You're going to give BloodClan the shock of their miserable lives. And once the battle starts," he added, "yowl as loudly as you can, to let our Clanmates outside know."

The two cats' annoyance vanished, and their eyes lit up as they dashed off in different directions to find hiding places.

To Graystripe's relief, Ashfur seemed to be fully committed, his complaints about the leadership forgotten now that the crisis was upon them.

That left Cinderpelt. "Once the battle starts, I will look for Gremlin," she mewed. "I'll get her away if I can, and we'll hide out at Sunningrocks. You can send some cat to fetch us when the fighting is done."

"You're assuming we're going to win," Graystripe responded with a twitch of his whiskers.

Cinderpelt flicked his ear with her tail. "Of course we're going to win."

"Has StarClan told you that?" Graystripe asked hopefully.

The medicine cat shook her head. "They don't need to. We're ThunderClan!"

She headed back to her den; Graystripe knew she had already prepared healing herbs, ready to treat any injured warriors injured after the battle.

With all his Clan in place, Graystripe went to sit at the entrance to the warriors' den so that he could duck inside once BloodClan approached. He wanted them to think they were entering a completely empty camp, or at least a camp whose strongest defenders were busy elsewhere.

Considering the desperate situation, he felt optimistic. No cat had seriously argued with his battle plan; for the first time, he felt like a Clan leader. *But I'm not a Clan leader,* he thought. He had seen the confidence the other warriors had in him, but he couldn't feel the same confidence in himself.

He sat there, immobile, outwardly calm, but inwardly he

was beginning to worry whether his plan would work, and he was especially worried about the warriors he had sent out of camp. He had told them not to attack BloodClan out in the forest, but what if BloodClan attacked them? They'd be able to pick them off one by one. All he had to rely on was Gremlin's assurance that BloodClan meant to take the camp first.

His anxiety had begun to grow unbearable when he saw the first sign of movement at the end of the gorse tunnel. *BloodClan already?* he thought, his belly lurching and his heart beginning to pound. The sun was still casting shadows across the floor of the camp. Had Gremlin lied to him after all? Would ThunderClan be surprised by BloodClan arriving early?

Graystripe realized he just had to trust his instincts. *That's what I did when I made the bargain with Gremlin. Trusting their instincts is sometimes the only thing that a leader can do.*

Then he saw that the cat emerging from the tunnel was Brackenfur, racing across the camp to stand stiff and panting in front of Graystripe, his golden-brown tabby fur bushing out. Brambleclaw followed more slowly.

"They're almost here," Brackenfur gasped when he had got his breath. "Slinking through the trees from the Twolegplace, just like you said they would. StarClan, there are a lot of them!"

"There are a lot of us, too," Graystripe responded calmly. "And even if we are outnumbered, we're better trained than they are."

Dismissing the two cats to hide in the long grass, Graystripe slipped inside the warriors' den and crouched just beside the entrance, peering out through a chink between the interlacing brambles.

If this doesn't work, he thought, *I'll have proven to the rest of the Clan that I was never fit to fill in for Firestar. . . . Where does that leave me as deputy?* A pang of longing for his leader passed through Graystripe from ears to tail-tip. *Firestar . . .* He wished so much that his friend were here to talk over the plan with—and to make the final decision.

But the decision is already made, he reminded himself. *I made it—and now I have to deal with the consequences.*

The tree shadows were growing shorter, and at the moment they vanished, as the sun cleared the treetops, the cats of BloodClan poured into the camp. With Fury at their head, they spread out across the clearing, snarling and hissing, with teeth bared and backs arched and claws extended.

"Come out, come out, ThunderClan!" Fury yowled. "Or are you all hiding like scaredy-mice?"

Graystripe sprang out of the warriors' den, letting his fur bristle up to look twice his size—and, he hoped, twice as threatening. "Now!" he screeched.

Ashfur and Mousefur rose up out of the long grass, letting out fearsome caterwauls. On the opposite side of the camp, Brackenfur and Brambleclaw leaped out of hiding, their yowls too giving the signal to the cats still outside.

Massively relieved that the waiting was over, Graystripe hurled himself into the battle, his Clanmates only a paw step behind him. He wanted to get to Fury, hoping that if he could defeat their leader, the BloodClan attack would fall apart. He could see her only a few tail-lengths away; even though she had only one eye, she was battling with a skill and determination that sent a chill right through Graystripe.

Do I have what it takes to beat her? he wondered. *Well, there's only one way to find out.*

A younger cat with patchy fur like Gremlin's was fighting at his leader's side. *That must be Scraps,* Graystripe thought, noting how swiftly the tom could dart in, slash an opponent with his sharp claws, and then hop away to safety. *Not too swift for me, though. Don't get in my way,* he added silently. *I'd rather not have to kill you.*

By now the center of the camp had become a mass of heaving, clawing cats, spitting defiance at each other. The ThunderClan warriors were overwhelmed. Graystripe saw Ashfur pinned down under Scraps, while two other Blood-Clan cats were driving Mousefur and Brambleclaw paw step by paw step back toward the nursery.

Oh, StarClan! Graystripe's belly cramped with tension. *We're going to lose!*

Then he spotted Cloudtail, Thornclaw, and Dustpelt barreling out of the gorse tunnel, flinging themselves on the BloodClan cats from behind.

Thank StarClan! But— Graystripe gave up his struggle to get to Fury through the crowd as he spotted the three apprentices dashing in after their mentors. *Fox dung! I should have expected that!*

Forgetting Fury, Graystripe fought his way through the grappling cats toward the apprentices, but by the time he reached the end of the tunnel, Rainpaw and Sootpaw had disappeared. The only apprentice he could spot was Sorrel-paw, who was facing up to a hulking tabby tom three times her size.

She's going to get shredded!

Grabbing Sorrelpaw by the scruff, Graystripe pulled her away and hissed at the tabby tom until he turned and vanished into the crowd.

Graystripe looked down at Sorrelpaw and gave her a not-so-gentle shake. "Nursery! Now!" he snarled.

The little tortoiseshell glared up at him defiantly. "I want to fight! I want to protect my Clan!"

I haven't got time for this! "You can protect your Clan by guarding the kits," Graystripe ordered.

Sorrelpaw's eyes widened. "Yes! I can do that."

Graystripe released her, giving her a shove in the right direction, and she scurried off, skirting the edge of the battle.

By now Graystripe had lost sight of Fury entirely. Looking for her, he spotted a flash of ginger fur racing past him, and recognized Brick, one of the cats Gremlin had described to him. Graystripe focused on the bare patch on Brick's back; Gremlin had told him it came from an old injury, not properly healed. *That's his weak spot.*

Graystripe pelted after Brick and sprang up onto his back, digging his claws into the bare patch. The BloodClan tom let out an earsplitting screech and collapsed to the ground; Graystripe landed on top of him and started slashing at his spine with his claws.

Brick yowled in pain, kicking and thrashing in a desperate

attempt to wriggle free. At last he managed to throw Graystripe off, though Graystripe was pleased to see that the patch on his back was much bigger now, and blood was trickling from the claw marks.

Brick faced up to him with another cat by his side, a tom whose head and neck swung around menacingly in a weird studded collar. *That must be Snipe,* Graystripe thought. *Gremlin said he always goes for the throat.*

With the fight raging around them, Graystripe braced himself nervously, tucking in his chin as the two cats advanced on him side by side.

"Call yourself a leader?" Snipe mocked him.

"Yeah, you're all alone," Brick added. "Not a single warrior here to help you."

"He's *not* alone!" The furious meow came from behind Graystripe as Brambleclaw leaped past him and threw himself at the two BloodClan cats without a trace of fear or hesitation. He began cuffing Snipe around the ears with both forepaws, ducking and thrusting to put his opponent off balance. Graystripe recognized a move that his mentor, Firestar, must have taught him.

He's going to be a great ThunderClan warrior, Graystripe thought. *He'll get better with each passing battle—though I hope we don't have too many more of those!*

But Graystripe took only a couple of heartbeats to admire Brambleclaw's fighting technique before throwing himself back into the conflict. He spotted Frostfur by a flash of her white pelt, and realized that the dawn-patrol cats had returned too. Ashfur was fighting fiercely beside Mousefur, while Goldenflower was chasing a shrieking BloodClan tom across the camp.

Then Graystripe noticed Gremlin slinking around close to the edge of the camp, half concealed by the long grass and undergrowth. Cinderpelt was padding softly behind her. But his relief at seeing the BloodClan she-cat making her escape was short-lived.

Before Gremlin could reach the gorse tunnel and the safety of the forest beyond, a furious screech rang out across the camp. Graystripe spun around to see Fury perched on top of the Highrock, her enraged gaze trained on the fleeing queen. A pulse of anger throbbed through him at seeing the Blood-Clan she-cat there, in the place that belonged to Firestar.

"Traitor!" Fury growled. "Snake! Ice! Stop her!"

Two black-and-white toms broke away from the fight and raced toward Gremlin, who tried to run away from them and beat them to the tunnel. But she was too slow, heavy with her kits. Ice ran ahead of her and blocked her way, while Snake barreled into her side, carrying her off her paws, and held her down. Cinderpelt sprang forward to try to help the Blood-Clan queen, but another BloodClan tom pushed her away and stood in front of her with his teeth bared.

"Bring her to me," Fury ordered.

Snake, Graystripe thought, as he watched the powerful tom with his paws planted on Gremlin's neck and her hind legs. A chill ran through him. *Is that what StarClan meant when they told me to beware the snake's bite?*

Ice joined Snake, and together the BloodClan cats hauled Gremlin to her paws and forced her through the knots of still-battling cats toward the Highrock. For all his foreboding, Graystripe began struggling toward her, but before he could get anywhere near, Scraps leaped up from where he had Dustpelt pinned down, and thrust his way through the crowd to his sister's side.

"Leave her alone!" he snarled, trying to shoulder Snake away.

Both Ice and Snake rounded on him. "Do you really want to do this? Really?" Ice demanded.

"She's not a traitor!" Scraps insisted, gazing up at Fury on the Highrock. "She just doesn't want to fight—she wants to protect her kits."

It was Snake who replied, "She knows the rules. She would have to give up her kits once they were born, anyway. The fact that she cares so much for them that she would betray us in battle proves that she is not one of us . . . she is not a true BloodClan cat."

"And if you're so determined to protect her," Fury sneered at Scraps, "the same could be said of you." She turned her gaze toward Ice and Snake, her meaning clear in her one malignant eye.

At the signal, both Snake and Ice turned on Scraps, lashing out at him with outstretched claws. Gremlin tried to help him, batting with all her strength at Snake's hindquarters, but Snake contemptuously thrust her away with one hind leg.

"No!" Scraps yowled at her, while struggling to fight off

both BloodClan cats at once. "Get out of here!"

Graystripe was still fighting his way through the crowd of tussling cats, trying to reach Scraps's side. But he couldn't get there in time. Just as he broke free and hurled himself at Snake, Scraps's legs gave way and he collapsed. Knocking Snake aside with a blow from each of his forepaws, Graystripe could only watch in horror as blood poured out from a gash in Scraps's neck and the light faded from his eyes. Gremlin let out a high-pitched wail of grief.

Graystripe stooped over Snake, digging his claws into the BloodClan tom's shoulders and baring his teeth to sink them into Snake's throat and end his life. But a yowl from Fury halted him before he struck. "Stop!"

Looking up, Graystripe saw Gremlin in front of him, gripped by two huge BloodClan cats. Her green eyes were full of misery, her gaze fixed on her brother's body. The nearby cats, ThunderClan and BloodClan, realized that something important was happening, and paused in their fighting. A pool of silence spread out from the Highrock where Fury stood, rippling out to the edges of the camp, until every cat was frozen in place, staring up at the BloodClan she-cat.

"Well?" Fury's voice was silky with menace. "Kill Snake and the traitor dies. Is that what you want, ThunderClan *leader*?"

CHAPTER 27

— Then —

"Keep fighting!" Ashfur called out, as Graystripe stood unmoving. "We *have* to drive BloodClan out."

One or two more of the ThunderClan warriors growled their agreement, but Graystripe couldn't bring himself to tear Snake's throat open if, in doing that, he would ensure Gremlin's death. Ignoring the angry, muttering yowls from his own Clan, he sheathed his claws and stepped back, allowing Snake to scramble to his paws.

"Fury," he began, gazing up at the BloodClan leader on the Highrock, "there's no way that BloodClan can win this fight. We have too many warriors, and all of us are trained. If you continue, you're condemning your Clanmates—if that's what you call them—to death. Is that what you really want? Don't you have any sympathy for the cats who followed you here and suffered wounds for it? Don't you care about their safety?"

Fury's expression was as hard as stone. "I'm doing my best for their safety by taking this territory for BloodClan," she replied.

Graystripe huffed out his breath in frustration. "What good is having territory if most, or even all, of your Clanmates have died in the taking of it?" he asked.

"It'll be worth it to make sure *I* survive," Fury snarled. "I'll fight on until I have no cats left to back me up."

In StarClan's name, how can I ever reason with a cat like this? Graystripe wondered. *And how could any cat follow her?*

Then, in the frozen silence that followed Fury's words, he heard the sound of dripping blood. Glancing around, tasting the air, he saw that Fury had taken a severe wound in the fight: A deep gash ran along her side. Blood was still oozing from it, falling onto the Highrock.

Graystripe glanced across at Cinderpelt, who had picked her way through the crowd of cats to stand beside Gremlin, and angled his ears toward the BloodClan leader. Cinderpelt took a look, then turned back to Graystripe with such a concerned expression that he was sure the wound was as dangerous as it seemed.

I've never been so happy to see a cat injured! Graystripe thought. *That might give me a way of reasoning with her.*

Graystripe padded closer to the Highrock, looking up at Fury. "That's a bad wound you have there," he remarked.

Fury glanced down at herself with a look of surprise, as if she had only just noticed the wound. Graystripe saw her wince, as the pain hit her for the first time.

"I can tell it's serious," Graystripe continued. "And you've been in enough fights to know what happens to cats who bleed as much as that. If the wound goes untreated, they usually die."

"The bleeding will stop soon, mange-pelt!" Fury snarled, though Graystripe thought she didn't sound convinced.

"Even if it does," he told her, "the wound is likely to get infected. And if that happens, you'll be in serious pain."

Now the BloodClan leader looked even more doubtful. "I'm tougher than any scratch," she insisted.

"Graystripe is right," Cinderpelt put in, coming to stand by his side. "I'm the ThunderClan medicine cat, and I know what I'm talking about. Infection isn't the same as just being cut. If that wound gets infected, it will bring pain inside your body that you can't lick away or sleep off. But we can stop the bleeding, and give you some herbs to fight off infection."

Graystripe nodded in agreement. "Our medicine cat is right. ThunderClan can treat you and help you to get better. You don't have to die from this wound."

Their words had clearly given Fury something to think about. She looked away for a moment, her gaze thoughtful. She pawed at the Highrock beneath her feet, seeming conflicted, and Graystripe's heart sped up in anticipation. But just as he began to believe she might accept their offer, she met his gaze again, shaking her head. "You're just trying to scare me," she declared. "I'm a BloodClan cat, and BloodClan is the toughest Clan in the forest. A little scratch won't stop—" Fury's speech cut off as a wave of pain seemed to wash over her.

Standing beside Graystripe, Cinderpelt glanced toward him, a questioning look in her eyes. He knew she was silently asking him if she should act as a medicine cat to their enemy.

For a moment, Graystripe didn't reply; he was wrestling

with his conscience, his kindness facing off against his caution. The most ruthless part of his brain was telling him that he should wait out this moment. The worst that could happen was that an enemy—a vicious, pitiless enemy—of Thunder-Clan would die. *And it would be a just death,* he told himself. Fury had brought such chaos and grief to ThunderClan that he knew StarClan would not punish him, nor his Clanmates, if she were to perish today.

But he had to give her a chance.

"You can say anything you want," he meowed to Fury, doing his best to keep his voice level. "But that won't change the fact that you will soon die. ThunderClan is willing to help you, but you will have to swear that BloodClan will leave us alone for good."

"I'll never do that!" Fury snarled. "I never back down in the face of any cat's threats. I'm a strong and powerful leader! I take what I want, when I want, and if you ThunderClan cats think you're just going to—"

Fury couldn't continue as another wave of pain washed over her, fiercer than the last. Her legs shook, and she almost lost her balance on top of the Highrock. A look of fear spread across her face, and her gaze flicked to the other BloodClan cats. Graystripe could see that not one of them made a move to go to their leader's side. None of them seemed at all concerned by her wounded state.

After all, she's made clear that she's not concerned about them.

As she took this in, Fury's shoulders sagged as if she was overcome by weariness. She had to be well aware that even if she survived her injury, her followers were no longer united behind her. The battle was over.

ThunderClan had won.

Fury half slipped, half scrambled down from the Highrock and collapsed to the ground, not even trying to hide her injury any longer. Cinderpelt took a pace forward, but Graystripe stretched out his tail to block her.

"No," he growled. "She has to *ask* for our help. And she has to promise in front of all these cats that she will take Blood-Clan far away from here and never attack ThunderClan again."

Fury raised her head and glared up at Graystripe, hatred in her eyes. "All right, you flea-ridden excuse for a cat," she snarled. "Have it your own way."

"Do you promise?"

"Yes," Fury replied. "I promise."

Later, as the last rays of sunlight dipped below the tree line, Graystripe headed across the camp toward the medicine cat's den. He had spoken to Cinderpelt earlier, while she had been patching up the wounds of the ThunderClan warriors; she'd told him that she had applied a poultice of marigold and cob-web to Fury's wound, and had given her poppy seeds so that she could sleep.

After Fury had agreed to Graystripe's demands, the rest of BloodClan had deserted their leader, scattering in all directions. Graystripe had sent out the least injured warriors to make sure that they left the territory. He couldn't be entirely sure that they would never come back, but he hoped that they had been humiliated enough by their defeat to leave Thunder-Clan alone in the future. In any case, with their leader gone, they weren't an organized fighting force any longer.

Now, when Graystripe thrust his way through the ferns, he found Fury sitting up, gulping down the last few mouthfuls of a vole. "How do you feel?" he asked her.

"I'm fine," Fury replied, still with a hostile glare. "I'm just about to leave, so you do not have to go to the bother of kicking me out."

"We don't kick out any cat in need," Graystripe responded mildly. "Cinderpelt, is she fit to go?"

The medicine cat turned away from the heap of herbs she was sorting. "Yes, just about," she meowed. "But, Fury, if the wound opens up again, or if it starts to look red and angry, you should come back to see me again."

At first, Fury's only reply was a grunt. She rose to her paws and padded out of the den, tossing a terse "Thanks" over her shoulder at Cinderpelt as she went.

"Don't forget what you promised," Graystripe reminded her, following her out into the camp. He halted in front of Fury, forcing her to stop. "You'll leave ThunderClan alone from now on."

"Don't worry." Fury was clearly making an effort to sound confident. "I won't be coming back to this flea-ridden terri-tory. In fact, I'll probably leave the forest altogether."

I hope you do just that, Graystripe thought as he watched the BloodClan cat pad painfully across the camp and disappear into the gorse tunnel. Several cats beside the fresh-kill pile turned their heads to follow her progress; Ferncloud and Brightheart narrowed their eyes into a baleful glare as she went. No cat moved or taunted her, but the force of their hostility was so strong Graystripe could almost taste it.

Good riddance! he thought, thankful to see his Clan united. *If I never see you again, Fury, it'll be too soon.*

Taking a deep breath, Graystripe finally let go of all the nervous tension he had been tamping down from before the battle until now. It flowed through his body in a rush, so fierce and powerful that he felt as if he could throw up.

All at once, Graystripe realized how easily he could have lost ThunderClan. Firestar might have come home to an empty camp—or, worse, walked right into BloodClan's new territory, without any idea that he was now the intruder. BloodClan would have killed him, and he would never have understood what had happened. *But we avoided that,* Graystripe thought thankfully. *Everything's okay.*

As the wave of emotions ebbed, Graystripe felt so exhausted that his legs began to tremble, and he thought they might collapse beneath him as he headed for his den.

Before he reached it, he spotted Dustpelt, Cloudtail, and Thornclaw clustered together near the fresh-kill pile, with their three apprentices huddled in front of them, looking up with wide, scared eyes at their mentors.

Ah, yes, the apprentices . . . , Graystripe thought, veering in their direction.

As he approached, he heard Cloudtail meow, "I think a

moon of tick duty would be about right, don't you?"

"At least," Thornclaw agreed. "For a start."

"And no more hunting patrols until every scrap of soiled bedding in this camp has been taken out and replaced with fresh," Dustpelt added.

To Graystripe's relief, none of the apprentices looked badly injured. Rainpaw was licking one paw as if it had been hurt, and Sootpaw had a cobweb patch on his shoulder, but they were otherwise unscathed.

"Okay, off to your nests," Thornclaw ordered.

"But we haven't eaten!"

"We're *hungry!*"

"We won't be able to sleep now."

"Then you can lie awake and think about what happens to apprentices who disobey orders," Dustpelt retorted unsympathetically.

The three apprentices scurried off. As they passed Graystripe on their way to their den, he heard Rainpaw mutter, "It was worth it."

Sorrelpaw gave an excited little skip. "It was *awesome!*"

Graystripe shook his head, stifling amusement. The young cats were being rightly punished, but he had to admire their courage and their dedication to their Clan. It reminded him of his apprentice days, alongside Firestar. *Was there anything we wouldn't have done to impress the older warriors?*

Heading for the warriors' den, Graystripe noticed that a group of his Clanmates was waiting outside, quickly joined by the three mentors. Graystripe braced himself, fully expecting that they would blame him for letting the rogue leader go, for trusting her to keep her promise that she was no longer a threat.

As he halted in front of the group, Graystripe was faced with a long, awkward silence. *If you're going to yowl at me, let's get it over with.*

Finally, it was Mousefur who spoke. "Well done, Graystripe," she meowed loudly. "You did a great job."

As Graystripe stood still in utter astonishment, the rest of his Clanmates began to crowd around him.

"Yes, you had us worried for a while there," Thornclaw declared. "But you made the right choice."

"As long as Fury doesn't round those mange-pelts up again and come back," Dustpelt put in. "But even if she does, we'll be ready."

Brackenfur pressed forward until he stood face-to-face with Graystripe, and dipped his head respectfully. "I'm sorry I got angry with you, Graystripe, when you decided to trust Gremlin," he meowed. "You were right and I was wrong."

The golden-brown tom looked so miserable that any last traces of resentment Graystripe might have felt were swept away. He leaned forward to touch noses with Brackenfur. "That's okay. I know what I did was risky. You were right to tell me what you felt."

Relief flooded into Brackenfur's amber eyes. "Thanks, Graystripe."

Standing beside him, Ashfur scuffled his forepaws in the earth of the camp floor. "I guess that goes for me, too."

Well, it's not exactly an apology, Graystripe thought. *But I suppose it will have to do.* "It's okay, Ashfur," he meowed.

Speckletail padded up and touched her nose to Graystripe's ear. "You've proven yourself a worthy deputy," she told him. "And I think I speak for every cat when I say that when Firestar joins StarClan—and let's hope that day is far off—ThunderClan will be in safe paws with you as its new leader."

A chorus of agreement met the elder's words. Graystripe blinked happily, half embarrassed by his Clanmates' praise, half terrified by the prospect Speckletail had opened up for him. In dealing with BloodClan, he thought, he had understood for the first time what Clan leaders had to go through.

He had devised the battle plan. He should have foreseen that the apprentices would come back, and if they had been killed, it would have been his fault. He had needed to find the best way to ensure the safety of the elders, and the kits in the nursery.

And this was just one incident, Graystripe thought. *If I were leader, I would have to make these important decisions all the time.*

It was clear to him, he didn't *want* all that responsibility.

The next morning, as Graystripe padded across the clearing, he saw with satisfaction that his Clanmates were busy going about their duties: Ashfur leading a hunting patrol back into camp, all four warriors laden with prey; Brackenfur and Dustpelt repairing the warriors' den where bramble tendrils had been torn out in the battle; the three apprentices staggering away from the elders' den under the weight of massive balls of soiled moss.

Outside the nursery, Ferncloud and Brightheart were

basking in a patch of sunlight, watching Shrewkit and Spiderkit play fighting in front of them.

"Get out, BloodClan mange-pelt!" Shrewkit squealed.

"No!" Spiderkit unsheathed tiny claws. "This territory is mine!"

Whitekit, whose eyes were only just open, was watching them wonderingly, while Brightheart kept her tail curled protectively around her, in case she decided to join the bigger kits in their rough play.

Graystripe nodded a greeting to the two queens and was about to slip inside the nursery when he saw Cinderpelt trotting toward him, grasping a bit of chervil root in her jaws. "On your way to see Gremlin?" he asked.

Cinderpelt nodded. "She's not far off from kitting," she mumbled around the root.

"Before you do, there's something I want to discuss with you," Graystripe meowed.

The medicine cat's blue eyes narrowed a little in irritation as she set the root down on the ground. "Okay, but make it quick," she responded. "Gremlin needs me."

"It's just . . . Cinderpelt, I keep thinking about what StarClan told you at the Moonstone. 'Like a three-headed snake, many paths split off into the forest.' They said I must walk my own path, but 'beware the snake's bite.' Now that it's all over, what do you think they meant? Were they telling me to make the deal with Gremlin, or warning against it?"

Cinderpelt thought for a moment, turning her head to give her shoulder a few long, slow licks. "I told you at the time that

I don't think they were *telling* you anything," she replied eventually. "Except that it was up to you to decide what to do."

"*So* helpful!" Graystripe muttered.

"But that's how StarClan works," Cinderpelt explained. "If they told every Clan leader, or even every medicine cat, what to do in a crisis, then the warrior Clans wouldn't be independent anymore. We'd be like StarClan's apprentices, and they'd be our mentors. Would you or any cat really want that?"

Graystripe heaved a massive sigh. "I guess not," he admitted. "But it would surely be easier! And what about the second part of what they told you?" he went on rapidly, as Cinderpelt bent her head to pick up her chervil root again. "'Beware the snake's bite.' That has to refer to Snake the BloodClan warrior, right?"

"I should think so," Cinderpelt agreed. "It sounds like they were telling you to avoid Snake. Maybe he was the BloodClan warrior destined to kill you, if the battle had gone differently."

Graystripe nodded, though he wasn't entirely satisfied. "I didn't know which cat was Snake," he murmured, half to himself. "So how could I have avoided him? I only noticed him when Fury told him to grab Gremlin. And after that . . . Cinderpelt!" he exclaimed suddenly. "Remember the end of the battle, when I was crouching over Snake, ready to tear his throat out? What if StarClan was warning *me* to beware biting *Snake*?"

Cinderpelt's blue eyes widened in sudden understanding. "Graystripe, I think you might be right," she meowed. "If you had killed Snake, then the BloodClan cats would have killed

Gremlin, and the battle would have continued. And who knows what the result might have been?"

A shiver passed through Graystripe from the tips of his ears to the ends of his claws. "I came so close . . . ," he whispered. "I *wanted* to kill him."

"But you *didn't* kill him," Cinderpelt reminded him. "You chose mercy, for Snake and for Gremlin. And, in the end, for Fury. It was the right choice. BloodClan is gone, and the forest is peaceful again." She let out a little *mrrow* of laughter. "Graystripe, you're becoming wise enough to be a Clan leader!"

"I hope not!" Graystripe meowed fervently. "Firestar can't get home soon enough for me."

"And think of the story you'll have to tell him!" Cinderpelt flicked his ear with her tail. "Come on, let's go and see Gremlin."

Inside the nursery, the pregnant she-cat was lying stretched out on the thick, mossy bedding. Cinderpelt gave her the chervil root to chew, then examined her, sniffing her carefully from head to tail and feeling her distended belly gently with her paws. Graystripe felt a stab of uneasiness as he saw his medicine cat's eyes widen in concern, and she moved her paws back to check part of Gremlin's belly for a second time.

"How are you feeling, Gremlin?" Graystripe asked.

The she-cat let out a long sigh. "I'm fine," she replied listlessly.

Graystripe could see that she was not fine. At dawn she had led the Clan in burying her brother, and now she seemed to be filled with a deep sadness. Graystripe wished he could do something to help her, but all he could do was renew his promise.

"You're safe here in ThunderClan. And after a few days, you'll be feeling stronger again."

Gremlin blinked uncertainly. "I'm grateful to you for keeping your part of the bargain," she began. "You're an honorable cat, Graystripe."

"You deserve your place here," Graystripe murmured, in between embarrassed licks of his chest fur.

"But now that Scraps is gone," Gremlin continued with a sigh, "everything seems different to me. I know that being in a Clan is a good thing for a pregnant cat, but I'm feeling really tense at the thought of fighting all the time. That seems to be your way of life, out here in the wild. ThunderClan is safer than BloodClan—but how safe?"

"We don't fight *all* the time," Graystripe protested.

"Throughout this war between ThunderClan and Blood-Clan," Gremlin went on, her green eyes wide with distress, "all I've been able to think about is my unborn kits. That's not the BloodClan way, but it's been *my* way, ever since I found out I was pregnant. I'm terrified at the thought of my kits' lives being threatened. Their safety is the only thing that matters to me now—and I don't know if ThunderClan is safe enough for a new family."

"So what are you going to do?" Cinderpelt asked gently.

Gremlin hesitated, taking a deep breath before she replied. "I never thought I'd say this, but . . . I think I'm going to try my luck with some Twolegs."

Graystripe gaped in shock. "You want to be a *kittypet*?"

"I'll be sorry to give up my freedom," Gremlin admitted. "But I'll welcome the security and help with my kitting, and Scraps isn't here anymore to refuse."

"But *we'll* help with your kitting," Cinderpelt promised. "And what if the Twolegs take your kits away after they're born?"

"That would hurt," Gremlin admitted. "But if they were given to other Twolegs, I would at least be certain that they were safe, that they were going to be looked after. Besides, it's more complicated than that," she continued. "I know that Fury backed down at the end of the battle, and she probably will honor her promise to leave ThunderClan alone, but she knows I helped you. I'm afraid that if my path should cross with hers in the future, she'll just kill me for betraying BloodClan. She's that sort of hateful, vengeful cat. And if she finds me"—her voice shook a little—"she'll go after my kits too. And I can't bear to think about that. They're the only kin I have left."

Her words saddened Graystripe, but he could see her point. For a moment he wondered whether he had been right to let Cinderpelt treat Fury and save her life. But then he pushed the thought away. *What sort of leader would just stand by and watch as another cat died—even a cat like Fury?*

"We'll be sorry to lose you," he meowed, "and we'll always be grateful to you for what you did for us."

"I did the right thing," Gremlin responded. "I don't need gratitude for that."

Cinderpelt was looking more and more unhappy as

Gremlin explained her plans. Now she stroked her paw over the she-cat's pregnant belly again.

"I wish you would rethink this," she mewed. "Or at least stay here until the kits come. I've examined you, and as I told you before, I'm pretty sure one of the kits is coming paws first. It'll be better for you to stay close to my den. If you still want to leave, you can do it when the kits are weaned."

Gremlin shook her head. "No, this is the right thing for me. And I hear that Twolegs have the best herbs, so I'm sure I'll be fine."

Cinderpelt looked only slightly reassured. "You'd better hope you find some Twolegs quickly," she warned Gremlin. "And remember, you'll need to find chervil root. I know you know what it looks like. You have to get some and keep chewing it."

Gremlin rose to her paws. "I'll remember," she meowed. "And thank you for everything you've done for me, Cinderpelt. For us." With a respectful dip of her head to the medicine cat, she headed out of the nursery.

Graystripe followed her and padded by her side toward the gorse tunnel. He was sad to see her go; if she did become a kittypet in the Twolegplace, who knew where she would end up? The Twolegplace was huge, and it was unlikely that he would ever see her again. He noticed Brackenfur and Dustpelt watching curiously as they passed, and thought he could detect a trace of regret in their eyes.

Now that they know Gremlin kept her promise, maybe they were just starting to come around to the thought of having her as a Clanmate.

At the entrance to the tunnel, Gremlin paused and let her gaze travel around the camp. Then she turned back to Graystripe. "I'm sorry to leave," she told him, "but I really do think it's best."

"ThunderClan will always be in your debt," Graystripe responded. "I wish you and your kits the long, happy life you deserve. And if you ever need help with anything, please come back. I promise—all you have to do is ask."

CHAPTER 28

— *Now* —

Graystripe roamed through the Twoleg den, searching for any possible way out that he might have missed the first or second or third times he'd made the same circuit. But he couldn't find any gaps big enough to let a cat through. Night had fallen, and he was no nearer escaping from his prison.

The fetid air seemed to soak into his pelt, until he felt he would never be clean again. His belly was bawling with hunger, for although the Twoleg had given her cats more food, Graystripe hadn't been able to bring himself to fight the other trapped cats for a share of the miserable scraps they were offered.

Pacing back and forth, frustrated, he spotted Daffodil curled up in her corner, with Petunia sitting beside her, gently grooming the sick cat's fur. Graystripe padded up to them.

"How are you feeling?" he asked Daffodil.

The orange-and-white she-cat heaved a little sigh. "I'll be fine," she mewed in a flat, hopeless voice.

That was so obviously untrue that it made Graystripe want

to find a way to cheer her up. "I've seen your mate, Fang—I mean, Honeysuckle," he told her. "He came back for you."

Daffodil raised her head, gazing at him. Her eyes were beautiful, a vibrant blue, her look now a mixture of disbelief and hope. "Really?" she whispered. "Where is he?"

Graystripe wasn't sure. He hadn't seen Fang since his failed attempt to prop open the door, though he'd peered out the broken panel a few times. He couldn't believe that the gray tom had given up and gone away, when he had been so determined to find an escape route. *I suppose he might have gone to hunt,* Graystripe thought anxiously. *I hope nothing has happened to him.*

"He's not far away," he assured Daffodil. "We're trying to find a way of getting you out of here—all of you."

He caught a dubious look from Petunia, as if she wanted to say, *Good luck with that,* but she remained silent, only bending her head to give Daffodil an affectionate lick around the ears.

"Why don't you get some sleep?" she mewed after a moment. "Then you'll be strong and ready when Honeysuckle returns."

"Maybe I will," Daffodil responded. Laying her head down on her paws, she closed her eyes and folded her tail over her nose.

Graystripe gave Petunia a nod of respect and softly padded away. He was impressed by the old she-cat, who was managing to care so well for Daffodil, even though she was suffering as much as all the other denmates.

Springing up onto a windowsill, Graystripe leaned all his weight against the clearstone in a desperate effort to force it open. But however hard he pushed, the window wouldn't budge, even though he could feel a faint trickle of air from the outside. He laid his muzzle close to it, sniffing up the cool, fresh flow, with a faint tang of the growing things in the forest.

On the other side of the window, he could see the overgrown garden, the Thunderpath, and the woodland beyond, quiet under the moonlight. His paws ached for the touch of grass, and he longed to feel the wind blowing through his fur.

How can any cat stand to live as a kittypet? he asked himself, flexing his claws in frustration as he remembered his own stay in a Twoleg den. *Getting to see the outside like this, but not to be out there? It's the worst torture.*

Graystripe scanned the garden carefully, but he still couldn't see any sign of Fang, and stuck here in the stench of the den, there was no hope of picking up his scent. His worries for the gray tom's safety increased; he refused to believe that Fang would deliberately abandon his denmates, especially Daffodil.

Giving up on opening the window, he turned back to scan the room yet another time. He was almost convinced it would be futile, when he spotted something that made the fur on his shoulders begin to rise. The floor here was made of flat wooden branches, unlike the rest of the house, where the floors were covered with pelts. And in the middle, there was one place where the surface looked uneven, as if a single branch was off balance, poking up above the rest.

Hope was pulsing inside Graystripe as he sprang down from the windowsill and raced over to the uneven spot. When he thrust his forepaws down on the branch, he felt slight movement in it: He could rock it back and forth. Only by a claw's breadth, but it was a start.

Crouching, Graystripe slid his claws down the side of the branch and tugged at it. If he could only pull it up, it would leave a hole big enough for the trapped cats to escape. But though he managed to raise it a little, it was too heavy and awkward for him to lift it all the way out.

"Honestly!" he hissed. "You would think some of these useless cats could come and help."

"Hey, not so much with the 'useless.'" An indignant voice spoke behind Graystripe, and he turned to see Lily, the bright orange tabby. "Do you think we haven't tried that, too?" she continued. "You don't even know how long it's been since we gave up trying to escape."

Looking more closely at the branch, Graystripe could make out the marks of claws along its edge, and he realized that Lily was right. "I'm sorry," he meowed. "But we *can't* give up, or we'll all die in here."

Lily simply shrugged and padded off into a corner of the room.

Looking around at the rest of the trapped cats, Graystripe saw once again their sickness, hunger, and despair. Even if they did have the desire to escape, they were all so beaten down by what they had suffered as kittypets, shut away in this Twoleg den, that it wasn't surprising they had given up.

Sinking back on his hindquarters, Graystripe tried to focus his thoughts on StarClan. If they were still out there, surely now was a desperate enough time for them to send their guidance? *Please help us,* he prayed. *Firestar, if you can see me now, please . . .* His entreaty trailed off as he remembered the terrifying moment in the cavern of the Moonstone when StarClan had either remained silent and absent, or had sent the lightning bolt to show him just how angry they were.

If Firestar had been there, I know he would have helped me. He's truly gone, he thought, struggling with the savage pain of loss. *I'm on my own.*

Then Graystripe forced himself to thrust the despairing thoughts away. He tried his hardest to hope that he had not been abandoned by StarClan, that somehow they would come through for him, and for all the Clans.

Please, StarClan, if you can still hear me . . . we need your help.

But no answer came to his prayer. Not even a bolt of lightning to strike the Twoleg den and open up a way. Graystripe flopped down with his nose on his paws and closed his eyes, wondering if he should never have left ThunderClan in the first place.

I was a warrior, a deputy—I was even Clan leader for a little while. Am I really going to end up like this?

Then Graystripe heard a faint scratching sound. Looking up, he realized it was coming from the window; he could see vague shapes moving behind the glass. A muffled voice was calling from the outside. "Graystripe! Graystripe!"

It's Fang! Thank StarClan he's okay!

Graystripe jumped back onto the windowsill and saw Fang pressing himself against the glass from the other side. Dawn was already breaking, and in the pale light, Graystripe caught sight of Monkeystar and the rest of WarriorClan in the garden.

"I brought help!" Fang called, while the WarriorClan kittypets jumped up and down with excitement.

"It's no use," Graystripe yowled in response. "Even with more cats, we can never break through the glass and reach each other." He let out a frustrated growl. "Believe me, I've tried, and there's no way out."

Then, as he turned away from the window, Graystripe's gaze fell on the loose branch that he had tried to pry up earlier. He remembered how the den was raised up on square rocks, leaving a narrow space underneath.

"Fang!" he exclaimed, raising his voice to be heard through the window. "There's a place here where the floor is loose. If you crawl under the den, you might be able to shift it."

"I know about that," Fang responded, his expression doubtful. "We never managed to lift it."

"Not from inside, no—but no cat has tried pushing it from underneath," Graystripe told him. "It's worth a try."

Fang's eyes suddenly lit with optimism. He spun around eagerly and vanished under the den. The WarriorClan kittypets scurried after him.

Graystripe leaped down from the windowsill and crossed the floor to the loose branch, setting his paws down as heavily as he could so that Fang could follow him from the outside.

"Are you there, Fang?" he called.

"Right here," the gray tom's voice came back. "I think we can work the branch loose, but you'll need to lift it from inside at the same time."

"Okay."

A few moments later Graystripe saw the branch lift slightly. He tried to thrust his paw underneath it, but the gap was too narrow, and he had to draw back sharply to avoid being crushed as the branch settled into place again.

"Push harder!" he meowed.

This time the branch lifted a little higher, and Graystripe managed to fit his forepaws underneath it, clawing vigorously at the edge in his efforts to pull it up. "Keep pushing!" he panted.

As he struggled with the branch, he could hear enthusiastic mews from WarriorClan, who were helping Fang to push from below.

"Clawwhistle, take your tail out of my ear!"

"Bugeater, we need you down at this end!"

"When I say 'three,' heave!"

Graystripe winced as he drove one of his claws too hard into the branch, and wrenched it out as he tried to free himself. His pads were scratched, too, and he thought regretfully that the nearest medicine cat was the Tribe's Healer, in the mountains. But he was so excited to be almost free that he barely felt the pain.

Some of the trapped cats padded over to see what Graystripe was doing.

"Have you found a way out?" a black-and-white she-cat asked, then turned and raised her voice to the rest of her denmates. "Hey, he's found a way out!"

More cats crowded around, purring with excitement as they realized Graystripe really had found an escape route.

"Can we help?"

"Tell us what to do!"

Graystripe looked around at the trapped kittypets. It thrilled him to see something that had been missing from their eyes this whole time: *hope.*

"Spread out along the branch," Graystripe instructed them. "Fit your paws into the crack and pull!"

The trapped cats got into position, jostling one another and letting out mews of determination. Graystripe thought that it was like watching cats wake up after a long, disorienting nap. *They believe we have a chance now!*

Daffodil tottered up, leaning on Petunia's shoulder, and stood close to the branch, her head tilted as she listened to Fang and the kittypets below.

"Honeysuckle, is that you?" she called in a quavering voice.

"Yes, I'm here!" Fang yowled. "You'll be free soon!"

But at first the combined strength of all the cats could only lift the branch a couple of mouse-lengths out of its hole. "Fox dung!" Graystripe snarled, his renewed energy beginning to turn sharply to panic. "We're never going to shift it."

"Yes, we are," Lily meowed resolutely. She was standing next to him beside the branch, her paws dug deep into the gap. "We all have to pull together. Are you listening down there? When I say 'now,' give it all you've got!" She paused, taking a deep breath, then yowled, *"Now!"*

Grunts and gasping breaths came from the cats as they put all their strength into raising the branch. As they strained at it, Graystripe felt his despair and despondency draining away from him like rain sinking into dry ground. It wasn't just the chance of escape that invigorated him; it was being one cat in a group, all working together to achieve something.

This is how cats are supposed to live.

Finally, with a deep groan, the branch lifted free of the hole; Graystripe and the others thrust it to one side. Cool air flowed in from the outside, and Graystripe took deep breaths of it, reveling in the taste of freedom. He looked down into the hole to see Fang and the WarriorClan kittypets staring up at him.

"We did it!" Monkeystar squealed.

"We did, and you did great," Graystripe responded, "but stand back now and let these cats come out."

One by one, the trapped cats began to slide through the hole and onto the ground underneath the den. Some of them leaped down eagerly, while others hesitated, gazing around into the dim space as if they were uncertain about leaving the only home they knew.

Graystripe turned to Lily, who was standing beside him. "Go and find the others," he directed her. "You know where they might be hiding. Make sure we don't leave any cat behind."

Lily dashed off, while Graystripe stayed beside the hole, making sure the trapped cats got out safely. Fang and the kittypets retraced their paw steps and led the rest of the cats out into the open. Petunia disappeared for a moment and returned with a she-cat and three kits; the queen jumped down, while Petunia took each kit gently by the scruff and lowered them through the gap to where their mother was waiting for them.

Graystripe helped Daffodil into the hole, and Fang met her and supported her as she fell more than jumped to the ground. The two cats twined their tails together, purring too hard to speak.

Glancing around, Graystripe saw that only Lily and Petunia remained. "That's every cat," Lily told him.

"Good," Graystripe meowed with a nod of approval. "Then you're next, Lily." The orange tabby she-cat slid down through the hole and vanished. "Now you, Petunia."

Taking a pace back, Petunia shook her head. "I told you, I'm not going. I want to stay with my Twoleg."

Graystripe remembered how the old she-cat had been determined to stay when he first suggested escaping, but he hadn't realized that she would stick to her decision once the way of escape was finally open. Sadness threatened to overwhelm him at the thought that the rush of fresh air, and the freedom it promised, hadn't affected her at all.

"You can't really mean that," he argued; he knew he would blame himself forever if he didn't give her the chance to change her mind. "Life will be much better on the outside, believe me."

Petunia shrugged. "I'm too old to go on adventures," she responded, "and I *did* mean every word when I said I couldn't break my Twoleg's heart. She doesn't keep cats in her den because she wants to torture them. Her cats are her only friends, and she loves them. If I leave, she'll be all alone, and I don't want that."

Graystripe couldn't understand the old she-cat's loyalty to a Twoleg who had put her and her denmates through such suffering, but he realized he had to accept it. "Good-bye, then," he mewed. "I hope it all goes well for you. May StarClan light your path."

Petunia gave him a curious look, as if she didn't understand his last words. *Well, why should she?* Graystripe asked himself. *She's not a Clan cat.* Perhaps she was right, and she would have a hard time adjusting to life in the wild. Realizing that made him feel just a little better about leaving her in the den.

With a last nod of farewell, he slid through the hole and down onto the ground beneath the den. The simple feeling of earth underneath his paws was bliss, even though he had spent such a short time trapped inside. For a couple of heartbeats, Graystripe did nothing but stand there, flexing his claws with sheer enjoyment. Then he slithered out into the open to join Fang, the cats of WarriorClan, and the escaping kittypets in the overgrown garden.

The escape had taken so long that by now the sun was up. Some of the kittypets were basking in it, beginning to groom themselves, while others seemed freaked out by the open spaces, and huddled in the long grass, or under the shelter of bushes. For the first time Graystripe started to wonder what was going to happen to them now that they were out of the den. Where could they go? Some cat would have to teach them to fend for themselves.

He padded over to Fang and WarriorClan, dipping his head in gratitude as he approached. "Well done, Fang," he

meowed. "That was a great idea, going to fetch WarriorClan."
To the kittypets he added, "We couldn't have done it without
you."

The WarriorClan cats puffed their chests out proudly. "It
was a real warrior mission," Monkeystar declared.

Maybe it had been, Graystripe thought, amused.

He glanced at Daffodil, who was curled up nearby in the
shade of a holly bush. "Fang, we need to decide—" he began,
only to break off at a shrill sound, almost like birdsong, coming
from farther along the Thunderpath. *What now?* he wondered,
crouching ready to spring.

The shrill sound rapidly grew louder until a Twoleg
appeared, striding along purposefully. The sound was coming
from his pursed lips. He had a lumpy pelt, hanging at his side,
and as he approached the Twoleg den, he fished inside it and
took out something like a bunch of white leaves.

Graystripe followed him with his gaze, expecting him to
pass by the den. But to his surprise the Twoleg turned in
through the gap in the fence. He was heading for the den
when he halted, the shrill sound dying into silence as he stared
around at all the cats.

"Touch one of us," Graystripe hissed, "and you'll feel my
claws."

But the Twoleg made no attempt to grab any of the cats.
Instead, he seemed to become aware of the stench, his nose
wrinkling as he gazed from the cats to the den and back again.

Eventually the Twoleg hurried up to the den, pulled open
a narrow slat in the door, and thrust the white leaves through

it. Then he stepped aside to look in through the window. He stayed there for a long time.

"What is he doing?" Fang whispered to Graystripe.

"I've no idea. I wish he'd just go."

A moment later, Graystripe had his wish as the Twoleg turned away from the den and retreated through the garden, giving the cats another long stare as he went. He pulled out a small Twoleg object from inside his pelts, clapped it to his ear, and started squawking into it as he disappeared along the Thunderpath in the direction he had come, almost at a run.

Graystripe shrugged. "I don't know what all that was about," he meowed, "but it means that there's a Twoleg who knows we're out here. It's time we made a move." Raising his voice, he called all the cats to gather close to him.

Glancing around as the escaping cats obeyed, Graystripe could see that many of them were hesitant; their ears were flattened and their fur bristling, their eyes wide with fear. They had spent most of their lives in that Twoleg den. The open spaces must be terrifying to them.

"Listen, every cat," he began when they were clustered around him. "The first thing we need to do is get away from here. Then we'll hunt, and feed, and rest, and decide what—"

"I'm not sure about this," an elderly black tom interrupted. "I don't much like it out here. What happens if it rains?"

We get wet, Graystripe thought, though he stopped himself from saying something so unsympathetic out loud.

"Yeah, and what's all this talk about hunting? We don't know how to do that," an older tabby she-cat mewed. "Maybe we should go back inside."

"At least we know we can survive in the Twoleg's den," the black tom agreed. "We did it for so long."

Murmurs of agreement came from several of the other cats around Graystripe. He stifled a hiss of exasperation, knowing he couldn't be unkind to cats who had suffered so much.

Fang, however, wasn't so gentle with them. "Some of us *didn't* survive," he pointed out, a hard edge to his tone. "My mother, for one."

His words shamed the other cats into silence. "Sorry, Honeysuckle," the old black tom meowed. "We all remember Gremlin."

"Of course, you can do what you want." Graystripe spoke briskly, needing to move on. "You can go where you're comfortable. But for what it's worth, *I* believe a cat's place is out in the wild. Don't you want to breathe the fresh air, and eat fresh-kill whenever you're hungry, and feel soft grass underneath your paws?"

"We'll teach you what you need to know," Fang added.

"Maybe it will be okay, then," the tabby she-cat admitted. "If we can live out here, we'd be better off than trapped in there, treated as we were."

"And I wouldn't be sick like this if we'd found a way out sooner." It was Daffodil who spoke up, surprising Graystripe with her courageous tone. "Do you want to end up like me?"

Awkwardly the cats glanced at one another; though none of them gave Daffodil a straight answer, it was clear that none of them did.

To Graystripe's relief, he, Daffodil, and Fang seemed to

have convinced the escaping cats that they were doing the right thing. "So what do we do?" Lily asked.

Graystripe found it hard to answer that question. He didn't know where all these cats would eventually end up. There were no Clans nearby, so some of them might become rogues or loners, or even go back to being kittypets someplace else. Only one thing was very clear. "First we have to get away from this den," he announced.

He led the way out of the garden and—after checking carefully for approaching monsters—across the Thunderpath into the forest beyond. Fang helped Daffodil, and the Warrior-Clan kittypets padded beside a few of the older cats, guiding them along. Graystripe kept an eye on the three kits, who seemed to be enjoying the new experience of being outside, and trotted along after their mother, gazing around them with bright, curious eyes.

But before they had ventured far into the undergrowth, Daffodil sank to the ground, and one or two of the older cats halted, too.

"We can't go on at this pace," the black tom meowed.

Graystripe looked them over, watching their flanks heave as they took deep, gasping breaths. "Okay, we'll take a rest," he responded. "Maybe some prey will get your strength up."

But when he cast a glance back over his shoulder, he realized he could still see the gray walls of the Twoleg den through the outlying trees. His pelt prickled with panic; they hadn't traveled nearly far enough to be safe if Twolegs came searching for them.

"Take cover in the long grass," he directed the escaping

cats. "And don't move until Fang and I come back with some fresh-kill."

At least, Graystripe reflected, there seemed to be plenty of prey in this part of the forest. Obviously, no cat had hunted there for a long time, and he guessed there were no foxes or badgers, either. Before long, he and Fang had collected a good haul of mice and voles and carried them back to the escaping cats.

They shared out the prey between the older kittypets and the sick ones; Graystripe watched them sniff it suspiciously, hesitate a moment, then begin gulping it down enthusiastically.

"This isn't bad at all," the old black tom mumbled around a mouthful of vole. "Very tasty."

Graystripe noticed that some of the younger cats were looking on wistfully as their older denmates devoured the prey. "Don't worry," he told them. "As soon as we find somewhere safe, we'll hunt for you, too. And you'll be hunting for yourselves before you know it."

Eventually, when all the prey was eaten, the older cats rose to their paws. "We're ready to go on now," the tabby she-cat declared.

But as the cats gathered around him, ready to continue, Graystripe heard the sound of an approaching monster. It was followed a moment later by a warning hiss from Fang, who had been keeping watch by the Thunderpath.

"Stop! Get down!"

Graystripe dropped to the ground and crept forward with his belly fur brushing the grass, as cautiously as if he were stalking a mouse. When he reached Fang's side, he saw a monster halted outside the Twoleg den; two Twolegs in black-and-white pelts were emerging from it. They stared around and began brushing aside the straggling branches of the bushes in the garden.

Every hair on Graystripe's pelt rose in horror. He recognized these Twolegs: They were like the ones who had captured him from ThunderClan's territory and taken him away to be a kittypet. Those Twolegs had appeared in a monster just like this one; it had been lined with cages inside, and Graystripe wondered if there were cats trapped in there now.

But even if there are, they're not my problem, he decided.

A few of the escaped cats slid through the long grass to join Graystripe and Fang. Their eyes widened as they spotted the newcomers.

"Keep back!" Graystripe snapped. "Do you want the Twolegs to see you?"

"I know who they are," Lily whispered. "They round up cats when their Twolegs can't take care of them properly."

And wild cats minding their own business, Graystripe thought. "Do Twolegs still take cats to the cutter?" he asked with a shudder.

Lily nodded. "They do," she replied. "I've heard that new Twolegs—usually young ones—come after a while and take them to their den."

"That doesn't sound too bad to me," the old black tom commented.

He could be right, Graystripe thought, casting a glance around at the cats, his gaze resting especially on the ones that were old and sick. *That might not be the worst idea for some of these cats, to be rounded up by Twolegs. At least they'd get plenty of food, and the right herbs to make them well again.*

Anxiously, Graystripe turned back toward the black-and-white Twolegs. At the moment they were still searching the garden of the den, but he knew that when they failed to find any cats there, they would start looking in the forest.

Just then he heard a terrible wailing sound approaching rapidly up the Thunderpath. A huge white monster surged into view and halted outside the den. Not waiting to see what it was doing there, Graystripe began urging the rest of the cats farther into the trees.

"We have to go," he meowed urgently. "If we don't pick up the pace, those Twolegs will catch us."

"No, wait," the old black tom put in as the rest of the cats rose to their paws, ready to go. "Suppose I run toward the Twolegs. I can keep them distracted while the rest of you seek your freedom."

"No chance!" Lily protested. "We escaped the den together, and we're going to *stay* together."

She started to shove the black tom in the direction Graystripe had indicated, but the tabby she-cat raised her tail to stop her. "Sunflower is right," she insisted. "We old cats don't want to be a burden on the rest of you. We don't have much time left anyway; let us do this for you younger cats."

Graystripe felt the weariness of age in his own bones as the elderly tabby spoke. He couldn't help but admire the courage of these older cats and their willingness to sacrifice themselves.

"Thank you," he murmured. "Thank you from the bottom of my heart."

But when Graystripe turned to round up the cats he would lead to freedom, he saw Fang standing beside Daffodil, shuffling his paws awkwardly, as if he was reluctant to move.

"Fang, I can't go with you," she mewed mournfully. "I've had weak legs my whole life, and my sickness has gotten worse since you ran for help. Even if you gave me all the fresh-kill you could catch, it wouldn't make me run as fast as I'd need to run to get out of here. I don't want to cost any cat their chance of freedom."

Graystripe didn't want to leave Daffodil behind, but he had to admit that she was right. Though she was younger than some of the others, she looked weak, and the scent of her infection was strong; he remembered how she had tottered across the floor of the den to make her escape through the hole, and how she hadn't been able to control her fall down to the ground.

She needs more help than we can give her, without a medicine cat.

Fang, however, was staring at her, his green eyes full of distress. "You don't know how strong you really are, Daffodil," he told her. "You can make it. I believe in you!"

But Daffodil only shook her head. "You have to go on without me. I know how badly all of you wanted to be free. And if I hold you back, you might be trapped along with me."

"I'm willing to risk that!" Fang meowed. "As long as we're together, I'll be okay."

Graystripe felt pain clawing at his heart as he realized

how much Fang must love this she-cat. He watched as Fang stooped over her and gently licked her ears. "I'll stay with you," Fang murmured.

"No!" Daffodil nuzzled him affectionately, then drew back. "I won't let you do that. You have to leave with the others. Besides, if these Twolegs capture us, do you think that they'll let us stay together?"

"Why wouldn't they?" Fang asked. "Once they see how much we love each other . . ."

Daffodil shook her head. "Twolegs don't think the way we do. Besides, Fang, our other denmates will need you. Some of them have never set paw outside the den walls. You'll have to look after them. Teach them how you've survived out here."

Fang hesitated a heartbeat longer, then bowed his head in acceptance. "If that's what you want, Daffodil. I promise I'll never forget you."

As they said their last good-byes, Graystripe turned back to the den and saw the old Twoleg, wrapped up in a huge pelt, being guided by some other Twolegs into the big wailing monster. "Now what's happening?" he asked.

It was Lily who replied, sounding almost relieved. "I've seen that monster before. It's a special one. It seems to know when a Twoleg is sick or injured, and it takes them away somewhere, to get better."

Oh, then those are medicine Twolegs, Graystripe thought. *That's good. They'll take care of her.*

Then he noticed that Petunia had followed the old Twoleg out of the den and padded along in her paw steps until the medicine Twolegs helped her into the monster. Petunia was wailing almost as loudly as the monster itself had. She tried to follow her Twoleg into the monster, but one of the Twolegs gently pushed her away and closed up the monster, leaving Petunia outside. She stood caterwauling on the Thunderpath as the monster started up and moved off.

The black-and-white Twolegs had disappeared—searching around the back of the den, Graystripe suspected. Though his pelt prickled with fear, he snapped at the others, "Wait here," and darted out onto the Thunderpath to Petunia's side.

Petunia turned to him, her amber eyes bewildered and sorrowful. "They took my Twoleg away, and they wouldn't let me go with her. What should I do now? She needs me!"

"They'll take care of her," Graystripe tried to reassure her. "She's ill, and they'll make her better."

But Petunia refused to be comforted. "She needs me!" she repeated. "And I need her."

"You don't need her anymore," Graystripe asserted. "You can come with us."

"With you?" Petunia sounded outraged. "I'm not going anywhere with you. That's what I keep telling you. I'm staying right here until my Twoleg comes back."

Graystripe could hear the black-and-white Twolegs moving around behind the den. He knew they only had moments before they came back, and he and Petunia would be spotted. Every muscle in his body was telling him to flee back into the woods, but he could not bring himself to leave Petunia; though she was old, she was strong enough to make a new, free life for herself. He thought it was unlikely that her Twoleg would ever return, though he was sure he would never convince Petunia of that.

"Listen," he began. "Back there are more Twolegs searching for cats. If they find you, they'll take you away and give you to other Twolegs."

"They wouldn't!" Petunia exclaimed, shocked.

"They would. But . . . if you come with us, you won't be have to go far away. You can stay nearby and check the den as often as you want to see if your Twoleg comes home."

Petunia blinked, obviously deep in thought. Graystripe waited, his pelt prickling with impatience; he flexed his claws on the hard surface of the Thunderpath, while keeping his gaze fixed on the corner of the den for the first signs of the black-and-white Twolegs returning.

Here we are, out in the open, without even a scrap of cover. . . .

Then Graystripe flattened his ears as he saw the first Twoleg appear around the side of the den. It let out a loud yowl, pointing toward the two cats. The sound seemed to shake Petunia out of her thoughts.

"Okay, I'll come with you," she mewed.

"Then *run!*" Graystripe yowled.

With Petunia at his side, Graystripe pelted across the Thunderpath and into the trees, but as they rejoined the other cats, he realized that he'd made a mistake—he had just shown the Twolegs where they all were hiding. "We have to go *now!*" he gasped.

"Keep your fur on," the old black tom, Sunflower, meowed. "We'll handle this."

With the rest of the older cats behind him, he led the way toward the Thunderpath, yowling loudly to attract the attention of the Twolegs. Graystripe saw Fang staring after them, rigid with misery, as the old tabby she-cat let Daffodil lean on her shoulder, and the two of them brought up the rear.

"Okay, the rest of you, this way!" Graystripe called, signaling with his tail to the remaining cats.

He led them at a brisk pace through the woodland and down to the lush undergrowth beside the river. Eventually, when he felt they were far enough away, he called a halt beside a clump of hawthorn bushes and gestured for the cats to slip into the center, out of sight.

"This is great!" Monkeystar exclaimed, settling down on the thick covering of dead leaves and debris beneath the bushes. "It's the first time we've been a real Clan."

"Yeah, doing real Clan stuff, like escaping from bad Twolegs," Fireface agreed.

Graystripe hid his amusement, purring happily to see them so excited. They deserved to feel proud of themselves. Without their help, pushing the loose branch from underneath, he and the other trapped cats would never have escaped from the den.

"Those Twolegs aren't totally bad," Fang reminded the WarriorClan cats. "They always show up whenever kittypets are in real trouble."

"Fang is right," Graystripe agreed. "Those Twolegs aren't our enemies; they just don't understand that some cats want to live free, that's all."

Leaving the WarriorClan cats on watch, Graystripe and

Fang went off to hunt. They were back on the old RiverClan territory now, and Graystripe still knew where to find ample prey near the waterside. Even so, the sun was sliding down the sky by the time they had amassed enough to feed the whole of WarriorClan and the escaping cats, and Graystripe was exhausted. *Been a long time since I had to catch enough prey to feed a crowd this size!* For a moment, he thought longingly of his relaxing life in the elders' den.

"We might as well camp here for the night," Graystripe meowed when every cat was full-fed. "Tomorrow we'll decide what we're going to do."

"We'll keep watch, if you want," Monkeystar offered. "In case any of those Twolegs come looking for us."

"Yeah, we know that the Clans always have cats to guard the camp," Clawwhistle added. He was hiding a yawn as he spoke.

"That's a very good idea," Graystripe responded, suppressing amusement. "Look, why don't you lie down in this soft grass, just outside the bushes, so any intruders won't realize you have your eye on them."

"Sure!" Monkeystar agreed; she and Clawwhistle settled down side by side in the grass, with a good view of the trees in the direction of the den.

Every cat was exhausted; some of them were already curled up and beginning to snore. It wasn't long before Monkeystar and Clawwhistle were snoring along with them.

Graystripe sat down beside Fang, who was crouching with his paws tucked under him and his gaze fixed on something that no other cat could see.

"I don't think I can go on like this," he murmured. "After my mother died, Daffodil was the only cat who made living in that horrible Twoleg den bearable. I don't know how I'll cope, knowing that I'll never see her again."

Shall I tell him that life is long? Graystripe wondered. *Shall I say that at some point he's likely to fall in love again? I know how that can happen.*

But Graystripe also knew from bitter experience how it felt to be separated from a cat he loved. He had thought that the pain would never heal, and that he would feel that way forever, no matter what any cat might tell him. *Just like now . . . I still miss Millie so much.*

So Graystripe said nothing, simply stayed beside the younger tom, their pelts brushing as they settled down for the night.

CHAPTER 29

❧

– Now –

Graystripe was the first cat to wake the next day; the sunlight trickling through gaps in the hawthorn branches told him that the morning was well advanced. Sitting up, he saw that Fang was stirring too, but the WarriorClan cats and the escaped kittypets were all still fast asleep, the air beneath the hawthorn bushes warm with their breath.

Uneasily, Graystripe wondered how these cats would manage living out in the wild. They didn't know how to hunt, or fight, and they might be too used to their sheltered life inside the Twoleg den. However horrible it had been, at least they hadn't needed to think for themselves.

Then Graystripe let out a purr of amusement as he spotted Bigteeth and Bugeater striking out with their paws, as if they were fighting in their sleep. Clearly, they'd developed a taste for adventure. But when he looked at Fang, he could tell that the tom was still grieving; he was awake, but he hadn't moved from his nest among the dead leaves. Instead he was staring into space with a look of sorrow in his green eyes.

He'll relive yesterday, too, Graystripe thought, *but it won't be out of excitement.* Fang was obviously thinking about the she-cat he had left behind to be taken away by the Twolegs.

"Try not to be too sad," Graystripe murmured, touching Fang's shoulder with his tail-tip. "Daffodil was so sick, and she might not have survived out here. She made a *heroic* decision, to stay behind so that other cats could have their freedom. She's a truly brave cat."

"I know that's true," Fang murmured. "But right now, I almost wish she weren't. What I keep thinking about was the kind of life she and I had planned to have when we were free. We so wanted to have kits together. And now . . . I don't know what I'm going to do without her."

Graystripe let out a sympathetic *mrrow.* A pang of pain swept through him, swift as lightning, as he remembered his own sorrows, but he had to set them aside to give Fang the comfort he needed. "Take it from me: A cat will experience many, many heartbreaks in their lifetime," he meowed. "Heartbreaks and setbacks are like enemies, attacking you out of nowhere. Even when you're strong enough to fight them, the important thing is not to let them follow you. And the way to do that is to keep moving forward, so that you're constantly putting the enemies of grief and loss behind you."

Fang looked up at him, perturbed. "I don't think I'll forget Daffodil in a hurry."

"I know." Graystripe nodded understandingly. "I would never ask you to give up those precious memories. But moving forward will stop them hurting quite so much, so that eventually you'll be able to find comfort in looking back on the time you and Daffodil shared together."

Fang sighed. "Maybe. But it's hard."

Graystripe stayed by his side, hoping that his silent presence was would be a comfort, until the other cats began to wake.

"What are we going to do now?" Monkeystar asked, poking her head out through the branches of the hawthorn clump. "Come on! It's a whole new day!"

Some of the escaped cats groaned at being roused, and Graystripe heard one of them mutter, "Shut up and let me sleep." But soon all of them, yawning or beginning drowsily to groom themselves, had gathered in a ragged circle around Graystripe and Fang. Graystripe realized they were expecting him to speak.

"I know this is new to all of you who escaped from the old Twoleg," he began. "And life out here will be difficult for you at first. But it will be easier if you decide right now what kind of life you want it to be."

"Well, I'm going to stay out here, and live under the stars." The speaker was the tom with patches of missing fur, who had suggested escaping from the den by attacking the Twoleg. "If I never see another Twoleg, it'll be too soon."

Several other cats murmured agreement, but others were looking wary. A black-and-white she-cat hesitantly raised her tail.

"I've had a night to think about it, and what I'd really like is to be taken in by *nicer* Twolegs," she admitted reluctantly.

"Ones with a cleaner den. And not so many cats."

"Good luck with that!" the tom scoffed.

"You keep your jaws shut, Buttercup!" Petunia, who was sitting next to him, batted him over the ear with her tail. "There are good Twolegs, if you take the trouble to look. My Twoleg was wonderful until she got old and sick. You do that," she added to the black-and-white she-cat. "I'm sure you'll have a very nice life."

"What I'd like," Lily, the orange tabby, meowed, "is to join WarriorClan. Will you have me?" she asked Monkeystar.

Two or three other cats echoed Lily's request.

"Of course we will!" Monkeystar purred, and the rest of WarriorClan yowled in eager agreement. "And we know a barn cat who might enjoy some company," Monkeystar continued, "if any of you decide you don't like the warrior life after all."

Graystripe twitched his whiskers in amusement. He wasn't sure Barley was up for the excitement of hosting the WarriorClan cats, much less a group of assorted former kittypets. But he supposed at least life at the farm wouldn't be boring! "Then Fang had better be your deputy," Graystripe suggested. "If that's okay with both of you."

Fang nodded, a light beginning to kindle in his eyes; Graystripe was pleased to see that the discussion was drawing him a little way out of his fog of misery.

Monkeystar pretended to think for a moment, then also nodded. "Okay. That would be fun. I've never had a deputy before."

The WarriorClan cats and their new recruits drew together, beginning to talk over the adventures they might have. The queen with her three kits had stayed with them; the kits were wrestling happily among the dead leaves, as confident as if they had been Clanborn. Even Buttercup had lost his hostile attitude and joined in enthusiastically. *I think he was just scared,* Graystripe reflected. *He'll be fine now that he has a home, and friends to share it with.*

Fang signaled to Graystripe with a twitch of his ears, drawing him a little way out of the group. "We're going to have our work cut out for us, licking these cats into shape," he murmured.

"You mean, *you* will," Graystripe responded.

"What do you mean?" Fang asked, clearly taken by surprise.

Graystripe blinked, his thoughts straying back to Thunder-Clan's camp by the lake. *The elders' den. Squirrelflight. Blossomfall and my other kin.* "Being with all of you has helped me decide something," Graystripe explained. "No matter what they're facing, cats are at their best when they're working together. I'm going back to my Clan."

Fang stared at him, utterly taken aback. "Graystripe, I can't do this alone!" he protested.

"You can and you will," Graystripe meowed evenly. "These cats will be your responsibility. I couldn't tell Monkeystar she's not leader anymore, but you know these cats best. You'll be the cat in charge of them. They'll be your Clan."

"But I don't know anything about leading a Clan. Besides, these cats can't really be a Clan," Fang continued. "It's all a big game to the kittypets—but they can go home to their Twolegs at night. These cats we've just freed can't do that."

"That's why I made you deputy," Graystripe told him. "You have experience living in the wild; you know how to hunt, and you're strong. Without you and your initiative and good sense, we would never have shifted that branch so we could escape from the den. If you can do that, I guess that in a pinch you could fight off a fox or a badger, and teach the others, too."

Fang gulped. "I'm not sure you're right. I don't feel strong."

"Of course I'm right," Graystripe declared, touching the younger cat on his shoulder with the tip of his tail. "The other cats already look up to you. If you hadn't escaped on your own in the first place, none of the others would be free now. You became their leader the moment you broke out of the den and went for help. Now you *must* be a cat worth following."

For a moment Fang looked appalled at the responsibility Graystripe was laying on his shoulders. Then slowly his expression changed, and he raised his head as if he was discovering a new self-respect. "I'll do my best," he promised. "But there's something else. Your Clans all have a connection with StarClan, and we don't have that here."

"I'm not sure that you ever will," Graystripe responded, thinking with a pang of foreboding about the situation in the Clan he had left. *I'm not sure we will, either.* "StarClan might make themselves known to you, or they might not. Cats connect to their ancestors in all sorts of different ways. But even if you never make any connection with them, you can live as a Clan, with every cat caring for the others, especially the sick and the old, and training your kits to be warriors in their turn."

As he spoke, a feeling of comfort came over him. *If WarriorClan can live as a Clan without StarClan,* he mused, *then maybe our lakeside Clans can do that, too. It will be wonderful if StarClan returns, but will it really be such a disaster if they don't?*

For the first time, he felt he could imagine a future without StarClan. It would be difficult, and it would hurt sometimes—he knew how much it had hurt him to call out for Firestar's help and get nothing in return. But he had survived . . . and he was still here to help form this makeshift Clan in the old forest. *I can survive without you, StarClan, and still do good things,* he thought. *I don't want to . . . but I can.*

"Yes, we can do that," Fang mewed resolutely. "But are you really sure that I'm the one cat to lead them?"

"Absolutely positive," Graystripe assured him.

Fang dipped his head. "Thank you, Graystripe. That means a lot." He turned and padded back to the group, taking his new place beside Monkeystar.

Graystripe sat watching them for a moment. His mention of sick cats had given him an idea. Eventually he got up and skirted the group, until he reached Petunia. The old gray she-cat was listening to Fang and the others, but she seemed detached, her eyes still full of grief for her Twoleg.

"Come with me," Graystripe murmured. "I want to ask you something."

Petunia looked puzzled, but she didn't object, and followed Graystripe as he pushed his way through the hawthorn branches and into the open.

"Are you going to stay with WarriorClan?" he asked.

"For a while," Petunia replied. "Until my Twoleg comes home."

Graystripe still couldn't tell her that it was unlikely her Twoleg would ever come home again. He knew it wouldn't help; it was something Petunia would have to come to terms with on her own, in time. Instead he began, "A Clan of warriors always has a medicine cat. She, or he—"

"Oh, I know about medicine cats," Petunia interrupted. "Gremlin told me. She said that they talk to StarClan in dreams, and heal sick and injured cats."

"That's right," Graystripe meowed. "Back in the den, I saw how you were helping Daffodil, and how you helped the queen with her kits. You have a natural instinct to care for those around you—look how you still love your Twoleg! That's so important for a healer."

"Me? A healer?" Petunia scoffed. "If I were, I could have saved Gremlin. I could have cured Daffodil."

"You probably could have, if you'd had the right herbs," Graystripe told her. "And I want you to be WarriorClan's medicine cat. No, I know you can't talk to StarClan," he continued swiftly as Petunia opened her jaws to protest. "But you could be a healer. I noticed that one of those cats we just freed is expecting kits."

"Well, I've delivered kits before, back in the den." Petunia blinked thoughtfully. "I don't know much about herbs, though."

"I'm no medicine cat, but I can teach you some." Graystripe

thought back to all the times he had ended up in the medicine cat's den, being treated for wounds or sickness. *I'm sure I would have died long ago, without a competent medicine cat.* "We use cobweb to stop bleeding, and we put a poultice of marigold on wounds to fight infection. I'm pretty sure you'll find marigold by the river."

He began to pad in that direction, carefully scanning the vegetation on both sides as he went. "Dock leaves for sore pads," he continued, "and poppy seeds to ease pain. Not too many, though," he warned Petunia, "or you might put a cat to sleep and they'd never wake up again."

Reaching the waterside, Graystripe indicated a clump of marigold with a wave of his tail, then pointed to some tall, spiky plants with purple flowers. "Look, you've got watermint here," he mewed. "That's the best of all herbs for bellyache. I can't see any chervil, though," he added, remembering what Cinderpelt had told Gremlin, so many seasons ago. "And that pregnant cat really should be chewing the root."

"Oh, I know chervil," Petunia told him. "My Twoleg used to grow it in her garden. It might still be there. I can fetch some when I next go to check if she's home. She grew catmint, too," she added, closing her eyes as if at a blissful memory. "Is that useful for anything?"

"Yes, it's really good for coughs," Graystripe replied. "You're bound to need some in leaf-bare."

"If I'm still here then," Petunia meowed discouragingly. Then she added, "But I guess I can teach another cat what you've taught me. Lily might be good—she's bright enough."

"That's a great idea," Graystripe purred. "An apprentice."

"I'd better have a word with Fang," Petunia mewed, turning back toward the hawthorn clump. As he followed her, Graystripe could hear her muttering, "Marigold for infection, watermint for bellyache, chervil root in pregnancy . . ."

I made a good choice there, Graystripe thought. Petunia had so much love to give, and without her Twoleg to love, she might have despaired. But with an entire Clan of cats needing her care . . . *By the time she realizes that her Twoleg isn't coming back, she'll have a whole new life.*

When Graystripe and Petunia returned, the other cats had emerged from the hawthorn. The black-and-white she-cat who wanted to be a kittypet, and two others with her, were saying their farewells, and soon they headed off upriver. Graystripe guessed they were making for the Twoleg bridge, and the new Twolegplace on the old WindClan and ThunderClan territories. *I wonder where they'll end up,* he thought as he watched them grow smaller and fade into the distance.

The remaining cats were being taught the hunter's crouch by Monkeystar and the rest of WarriorClan, while the three kits seemed to be everywhere at once, getting underpaw just like Clanborn kits. Because the WarriorClan cats were so young, it almost looked as if apprentices were teaching warriors, but Graystripe could see that they had remembered what he had taught them on that first day.

That seems so long ago now.

Graystripe stood watching, aware of a new sensation creeping over him. So much of what he'd taught the WarriorClan cats had been taught to him by ThunderClan. Even at the beginning of his "wander"—even when he hadn't been sure he belonged in his Clan anymore—the wisdom he'd gained from ThunderClan remained an essential part of him. And ThunderClan carried on, even if it was no longer the ThunderClan of his youth. *It's been good to come back to the old forest,* he thought, *but I realize now that the lake is my home, and where I belong.*

It was time to go home.

He thought of what Stoneteller had told him: *I still have a part to play.* He'd assumed that had meant going to the Moonstone. But suddenly he realized it could mean something entirely different. Maybe his "part" wasn't about what he did on his wander; maybe it had everything to do with the part he'd play upon his return.

All this while, Fang and Petunia had been deep in conversation. Eventually Fang dipped his head to the old she-cat and padded over to join Graystripe.

"So you've found a medicine cat for us," he mewed. "I never dared hope for that. Maybe we *can* be a real Clan, after all."

"Of course you'll be a real Clan," Graystripe told him. "You'll care for one another, and that's the most important thing."

Even while he was speaking, he realized that his words meant more than he had originally intended. *It's true of Thunder-Clan, too.*

"I have to go home now," he announced to Fang.

Fang twitched his whiskers in surprise. "But . . . Are you

sure you don't want to stay with us? I wish you would. We could use your help."

"I can't," Graystripe responded, shaking his head. "I'm sure now where I belong. Besides, if I stay, these cats will just look to me as a leader, not to you and Monkeystar, and that will never do."

Fang bowed his head in reluctant agreement. "Well, I'll miss you, Graystripe. And I'll never forget you. You've been like a father to me."

"And I'd have been proud to have called you my son," Graystripe meowed.

He padded over to the other cats, who all rose and turned to him as he approached. "I have to go now," he declared, ignoring their mews of protest. "I wish you all well, and I know you'll make a success of your Clan. You're more than kittypets and rogues—you will be *warriors*."

The escaped cats and kittypets purred with pride, calling out farewells as Graystripe gave them one last wave of his tail, then turned away to head upriver.

Before Graystripe had traveled many paw steps through the old RiverClan territory, he spotted a small group of WarriorClan cats brushing through the thick vegetation closer to the river, and paused to let them pass.

I've said my good-byes. They're on their own now.

Then the cats emerged into a clearer space beside a small stream that trickled through the grass and fell into the river in a tiny waterfall. Monkeystar was in the lead, followed by the young tom Buttercup and two more of the escaped cats. Graystripe ducked behind a clump of horsetail to listen as Monkeystar addressed her Clanmates.

"Right, we're going to do a border patrol," she announced. "We'll follow the river as far as the Twoleg bridge, then work our way back until we come to your old Twoleg's den. And on our way we'll mark our borders so that every other cat knows that this is our territory."

Who told her about marking borders? Graystripe wondered. *Maybe it was Smudge, with all his other tales of the Clans.*

"What if we meet any other cats?" The speaker was a small tabby-and-white she-cat. "What do we do then?"

Monkeystar tipped her head. "Good question. Any cat?"

Buttercup's whiskers quivered with anticipation. "We rip their throats out?"

"No, Buttercup." Monkeystar rolled her eyes. "There'll be no throat-ripping when I'm in charge. If we do meet any other cats, we'll just tell them that this is WarriorClan territory now and ask them to leave."

"But what if they won't leave?" the she-cat persisted.

Buttercup flexed his claws. "*Then* we rip their throats out!"

Graystripe stifled a *mrrow* of amusement. He didn't think any of these cats would be so excited to face a real fight. But he thought he could rely on Monkeystar to cope with any intruders who might encroach on the new territory, one way or another. Already she sounded more mature than the silly young kittypet he had met a few days before.

"Buttercup, haven't you learned *anything* from Graystripe?"

the tortoiseshell leader asked. "Did he attack the Twolegs who came looking for you? No, he did not."

"Yeah, and he wouldn't let us claw the old Twoleg in the den," the fourth cat, a sandy-colored tom, meowed.

Monkeystar nodded vigorously. "Right. And when we first met Fang on the moor, he didn't attack then, either. He found another way. And that's what we have to do. Graystripe is such a noble cat; we have to try to be exactly like him!"

Me? Graystripe thought. A hot wave of embarrassment flooded through him from ears to tail-tip. He was deeply grateful that the kittypets didn't know he was listening; he would have crept away, except that he was afraid they would spot him as soon as he moved.

"Graystripe is brilliant!" the she-cat mewed admiringly. "Oh, Fang is great, too, but it was Graystripe who really rescued us. He let himself be trapped with us, so that he could help us."

"He gave us hope," the sandy tom agreed. "And he showed us how we could escape."

"I think he's the best cat in all the Clans," Monkeystar declared. " Graystripe traveled so far, and he went into a forbidden place to try to help his Clanmates, and then he helped us, and all of you trapped in that den."

Buttercup gave a reluctant nod. "I guess he is pretty special."

Oh, no, I'm not, Graystripe thought. *I'm just a creaky old elder. I might have been useful to my Clan once—I even led them for a while, and that didn't turn out too badly. But those days are long gone.*

But even as the thought passed through his mind, he felt a weird sensation, as if his old friend Firestar were speaking to him from a long way off: *You daft furball!*

Graystripe's whiskers bristled indignantly, but as Firestar's amusement still echoed around him, he considered again what the kittypets had said. *It's true I did all that. I traveled to the mountains, and then here to the old territories. I did venture down to the Moonstone—and, great StarClan, that frightened my fur off! And I helped these kittypets escape, and set them up in their own Clan.* Blinking incredulously, he added to himself, *But that wasn't being brave or noble. That was just doing what had to be done.*

And again he thought he could hear Firestar's voice—or perhaps he only knew what Firestar would have said. *Mousebrain! That's what being brave and noble means.*

The WarriorClan cats were still halted beside the stream. "What do you mean, he went into a forbidden place?" the she-cat asked.

"Oh, that was a *fantastic* adventure!" Monkeystar replied. "Clawwhistle and I went with him—part of the way, at least," she added honestly. "I'll tell you all about it after sunset, when the Clan is together and we're eating our fresh-kill."

The she-cat gave an excited little wriggle. "I can't wait!"

And so another story is born, Graystripe thought, with another *mrrow* of amusement. *Maybe elders will tell their kits for seasons upon seasons, all about the valiant warrior who ventured into the heart of the mountain. Nothing about how he was shaking so much his whiskers nearly fell off!*

"Okay, come on," Monkeystar ordered. "We can't stand

here gossiping all day. We have a border patrol to finish."

She leaped over the little stream and disappeared into the undergrowth, with the rest of her patrol hard on her paws.

Graystripe waited for their scent to fade a little before he began to follow. As he headed across the old RiverClan territory, he felt a deep satisfaction that the Clans who had lived here for so long would not be entirely forgotten, and that even their way of life would carry on with Monkeystar, Fang, and the rest of the kittypets.

They won't be a Clan like ours, he realized. *But they will care for one another. And that, at heart, is what a Clan is. If that's all I've accomplished on my wander, it's not bad. Not bad at all.*

Then Graystripe remembered what Stoneteller had told him: that he still had a part to play in the troubles that beset his own Clan. When he had first heard those words, he had felt intimidated, as if an old, tired cat like him couldn't possibly be that important.

But who's old and tired now? he asked himself, giving his pelt a shake and lifting his head boldly. *No, I'm the fierce warrior Graystripe, and I can face anything. Bring it on!*

Partly he was mocking himself, knowing that he was far from being the splendid cat that the kittypets believed him to be. But partly, deep inside, he had recovered courage and a sense of purpose. For the first time, he could imagine that Stoneteller might have been right.

Millie had said the same thing, he remembered, in his dream of her dying. She had told him that his life wasn't over, that he was still an important cat. "You said I must never give up," he murmured aloud, half imagining that his mate was padding along beside him. "And I won't. I promise you."

One more night with Barley, he decided. *And then back to the mountains, to spend one more night visiting Stormfur. And after that—home to the lake, and whatever my destiny demands!*

CHAPTER 30

❧

− *Then* −

Graystripe let out a sigh of relief: After so much turmoil, things in ThunderClan were getting back to normal. The kits were frisking outside the nursery, Whitekit joining in now with her older denmates. The elders were lounging beside their fallen tree, deep in some gossip or story. Near the fresh-kill pile, Dustpelt was drilling all three apprentices in the warrior code.

"Remember that you must never kill another warrior, not even in battle, unless it's a matter of their life or yours," he meowed.

"Not even a stinky ShadowClan cat?" Sootpaw asked.

"Not even a ShadowClan cat," Dustpelt replied crushingly. "Not even if they are stinky." He raised one paw and inspected his claws. "Would you like me to show you how stinky a ThunderClan cat can be?"

Sootpaw flattened his ears. "No, Dustpelt. Sorry."

Stifling amusement, Graystripe noticed movement at the mouth of the gorse tunnel; Brambleclaw appeared at the head of the returning dawn patrol, and bounded over toward Graystripe.

"Anything to report?" Graystripe asked.

Brambleclaw dipped his head politely. "Nothing, Graystripe," he replied. "Everything's quiet. We looked especially for traces of those foxes or BloodClan, but there weren't any."

Graystripe had to force himself not to purr with contentment: not just at the news of the absence of any threat, but also in seeing the way that Brambleclaw clearly respected him.

I've doubted myself and my competence so many times, he thought, *but this young warrior obviously thinks I'm doing a good job. The Clan has accepted me now as their temporary leader.*

Graystripe dismissed Brambleclaw with a nod, trying to look confidently unsurprised by his report. Although nearly a moon had passed since the battle with BloodClan, Graystripe knew privately that it would be many moons before he could entirely convince himself that the dangerous cats wouldn't be back, or that Fury wouldn't forget her promise and find another way of causing trouble. But he also knew that the confidence he'd gained from leading the charge to drive BloodClan off had made him a stronger leader. Just days ago, he'd led all four Clans in a battle to force out a family of foxes that had made their den at Fourtrees. He didn't think *they* would be coming back in a hurry.

More movement by the gorse tunnel alerted him: This time it was Ashfur, pelting across the camp and skidding to a halt in front of him.

Graystripe sprang to his paws, his fur bristling and his

heart beginning to thump uncomfortably. "More trouble?" he asked.

"No!" Ashfur was gasping for breath, his chest heaving and his blue eyes blazing with excitement. "I've seen Firestar! He's home!"

The news spread through the camp like ripples from a stone dropped in a pool. Cats poured out of their dens, and by the time Firestar and Sandstorm emerged from the tunnel, the whole Clan was out in the open, yowling their greetings to their returning leader.

Graystripe felt a massive wave of relief at the sight of his friend. It was wonderful to see him, and Sandstorm too, safely back where they belonged. But also, he felt the tension in his body snap and give way at the thought of not being leader anymore. What a relief it would be to give back the responsibility to the cat who was so much better able to bear it!

"Where have you been?" Mousefur asked as the whole Clan crowded around the returning warriors.

"What have you been doing?" Speckletail mewed.

"Tell us what you've seen!" Brambleclaw added eagerly.

Firestar waved his tail for silence, though it took a while for the noisy questioning to die down. "Take it easy," he protested. "We haven't come home to get squashed!"

He didn't answer any of the questions, and Graystripe guessed there must be a story that the rest of the Clan wasn't allowed to hear. But if Firestar still didn't want to share where he had been with the whole Clan, he must have a very good reason.

Graystripe managed to work his way through the crowd until he came face to face with Firestar, and dipped his head to his leader and friend in deepest respect. "Welcome back," he meowed. "It's good to see you both."

"It's good to see you, too, Graystripe," Firestar responded. "How have things been while we were away? I hope you didn't have any trouble."

"Trouble!" It was Brambleclaw who replied, his amber eyes gleaming with excitement. "If it hadn't been for Graystripe—"

"That's enough." Graystripe silenced the young warrior with a stern look. He was grateful for the cat's praise, but he didn't want to worry his leader, especially now when he'd just returned to camp. "We had some problems," he told Firestar, "but nothing we couldn't handle, because you left behind a very strong, capable Clan."

Firestar's green gaze flicked from Graystripe to Brambleclaw and back again. "Well," he purred, "it's nice to know that I don't have to worry about you all the time! And now Sandstorm and I must rest," he added. "We've traveled a long way, and we both feel our paws are dropping off."

The Clan parted to allow the two cats to make their way to Firestar's den. Once they had disappeared behind the curtain of lichen, the rest of the cats began to disperse, excitedly discussing their leader's return as they headed to their duties. Seeing how deeply they respected Firestar, Graystripe felt even more certain that he wasn't meant to be leader. *I've been forgotten so fast,* he thought with a wry twist to his mouth.

But one cat hadn't forgotten him; Brambleclaw paused

beside him on his way to join Mousefur and Dustpelt for a hunting patrol. "Why didn't you want Firestar to know how well you did as acting Clan leader?" he asked.

Graystripe had to take a few heartbeats to think of a reply. "It was just instinct," he admitted at last. "It seemed like the right thing to do. Besides, Brambleclaw, you heard what Firestar said just now: He likes not having to worry. So why make him worry, if he doesn't have to?"

Brambleclaw pondered this for a moment before giving him an understanding nod; then he padded off to join his Clanmates, who were waiting for him at the entrance to the gorse tunnel. Graystripe drew in a deep breath, feeling truly relaxed for the first time since Firestar left on his quest. And he allowed himself a tiny prickle of pride.

After all, I'm the cat who guided our Clan through its troubles.

Sunhigh was past when Sorrelpaw came bounding across the camp to where Graystripe was enjoying a mouse beside the fresh-kill pile. "Firestar would like to see you in his den," she announced. The little tortoiseshell's eyes were shining and her tail was curled up.

"You look pleased with yourself," Graystripe remarked, gulping down the last morsels of mouse.

"My mentor is home!" Sorrelpaw gave an excited little bounce. "I've missed Sandstorm so much."

"No more Dustpelt, then?" Graystripe teased her. "You might get to keep your fur."

"No more Dustpelt." More seriously, Sorrelpaw added,

"But he's a terrific cat. I'm so lucky, to have learned from two great mentors!" She dashed off again, joining her littermates outside their den.

Graystripe padded across the camp to the Highrock and called Firestar's name at the entrance to the den.

"Come in," his friend called.

Graystripe entered to see Firestar crouched with his paws tucked under him, while Sandstorm was curled up in his nest. She opened her eyes to a green slit, then closed them again and let out a drowsy purr.

"It's good to be home," Firestar began, "and even better not to walk back into the middle of a crisis. I'm very proud of you, Graystripe." There was a glint in his eyes, Graystripe noticed uneasily. "What is it you're not telling me?" he continued.

Ruefully, Graystripe realized that his friend knew him too well. "There was a challenge from some of the surviving members of BloodClan," he confessed. At Firestar's sudden look of concern, he went on quickly: "There's nothing to worry about. They've been defeated, and they won't bother us again. Then there was an . . . issue with some foxes making a home at Fourtrees. I needed a bit of help from the other Clans on that one, but we drove them out, and all is well."

Firestar's green eyes widened. "I'm impressed," he meowed. "How did you unite the Clans to drive out the foxes? And how did you prepare the Clan to defeat BloodClan without any help, and without losing a single cat?"

"Well, I had to be clever," Graystripe replied. "And I made an agreement with a pregnant BloodClan queen. She told us when and where BloodClan was going to attack, and that meant we could make a battle plan."

"And she did all that out of the goodness of her heart?" Firestar asked, with a wry twist to his mouth.

"Well . . . no," Graystripe admitted. "I agreed to take her into ThunderClan—just until you came home, when you would decide if she could stay permanently. But she isn't here now. Cinderpelt was convinced it would be a hard kitting, and the queen was so concerned about her unborn kits that she chose to become a kittypet instead."

Firestar blinked thoughtfully. "You must have managed her well, Graystripe. In fact, between that and those pesky foxes, it sounds as if your leadership has been a great success. I obviously made the right decision when I chose you as my deputy!"

Graystripe had no words to answer that, and only licked his chest fur in furious embarrassment.

"You'll make a fine leader if anything happens to me," Firestar continued. "But I hope that will be a long time from now!"

Graystripe flicked his ears, pleased by his leader's praise, but uneasy at the same time. "That's the thing, Firestar . . . ," he began cautiously. "I think this experience taught me that I don't *want* to be Clan leader."

"Oh, come on, Graystripe . . ."

"It's not that I don't respect the position, or that I don't love my Clan," Graystripe interrupted. "It's just that I feel more comfortable supporting you than being the one to make the decisions. But I'll defend ThunderClan to my dying breath! I promise you, Firestar, I'll never leave my Clan! And maybe I will feel differently one day."

Firestar twitched an ear in surprise. "What do you think would make you change your mind?"

Graystripe looked down at his paws. "Well . . . you," he replied honestly. "I see how our Clanmates respect you, Firestar. I believe you were born to be leader, and believe me, having to do your job for a couple of moons helped me realize just what a hard job it is." He paused. "Maybe, if I have more time to learn from you, I'll feel one day that I *am* prepared. But right now, I don't."

Silence followed his words. Graystripe watched his leader through narrowed eyes; then, slowly and reluctantly, he meowed, "I'll understand if you want to choose another deputy."

He waited with his belly churning while Firestar seemed to be considering his offer.

"No," the Clan leader responded at last. "I hope you'll change your mind someday, but I'm still a young cat with plenty of lives left before you'll be tested."

"I hope so!" Graystripe exclaimed.

"And in the meantime," Firestar went on, "maybe there's no better adviser than a cat who doesn't want to be leader. Graystripe, do you promise to be honest with me always, and think of the good of the Clan before anything else?"

"Of course I do," Graystripe responded fervently.

Firestar nodded. "Then that's good enough for me."

Warm happiness enveloped Graystripe, as if he had stepped

out of his den into a patch of sunlight. He listened contentedly while Firestar continued to talk.

"There will be more challenges ahead, for all the Clans," the leader mused. "Simply driving back BloodClan, and eliminating the threat from Tigerstar, isn't enough to keep us safe. The world of the forest is big, and full of possible dangers. And now that I've seen the world *beyond* the forest, I know there are many, many more dangers out there."

Graystripe pricked up his ears at that. *Where did he go when he was looking for SkyClan? Did he find them? What has he discovered?* Looking more closely at Firestar, he thought that his friend seemed to have acquired a new air of experience, like an extra pelt. *Whatever happened, it wasn't all easy.*

"ThunderClan must always be ready," Firestar finished.

"We will be," Graystripe assured him. "After all, we have a whole Clan full of strong and capable warriors."

Firestar murmured agreement. "We do. And it's a relief to come back to such a happy Clan, with every cat safe and going about their duties."

As Graystripe left his leader's den, he pondered Firestar's words. Even if he didn't feel like a true leader, he'd kept the Clan he loved together. *And if there's one thing this experience has taught me,* he thought, padding across the camp to the warriors' den, *it's that I love ThunderClan more than anything. ThunderClan is my home, after all.*

CHAPTER 31

— *Now* —

Weariness threatened to overcome him as Graystripe padded toward the barn, his shadow stretching out beside him. It had been a very long day. He paused in the shelter of the hedge, warily tasting the air for any traces of dogs, but the only scents he could catch came from a safe distance. Graystripe bounded across the open ground and wriggled through the gap in the bottom of the barn door.

Beams of scarlet sunlight still angled down from the high windows and the holes in the roof, but most of the barn lay in deep shadow. Graystripe located Barley more by scent than sight, and slipped quietly through the piles of dried grass until he found the old cat curled up in a cozy nest. Gentle snores riffled the grass stems beside his muzzle.

"Barley?" Graystripe mewed quietly.

His friend's whiskers twitched and he blinked his eyes. "Ravenpaw, is that you?" he asked.

Graystripe felt his heart lurch with compassion. It wasn't hard to guess what Barley had been dreaming about. "No, it's me—Graystripe," he meowed.

Barley grunted, then sat upright, his eyes gleaming in the dim light. "Graystripe!" he exclaimed, fully awake now. "You came back."

Graystripe leaned forward to touch noses with him. "I did."

"And what about that young cat—what's-his-name, Fang? Is he with you?" Barley asked, glancing around.

"No, we managed to rescue the cats from his den, and he stayed on RiverClan territory with them," Graystripe replied. "Suppose I catch us a couple of mice, and then I'll tell you all about it."

It was good to relax in the soft grass, feasting on warm fresh-kill and telling the story of everything that had happened since he had left the barn two days before. Barley's eyes stretched wide with horror at Graystripe's description of the filth and stench of the Twoleg den, and of the starving, sick cats.

"I didn't think Twolegs could be so cruel," he murmured.

"She wasn't cruel," Graystripe explained. "She loved her cats, but she was sick herself, and she'd forgotten how to care for them properly. We should feel sorry for her."

"Hmm . . ." Barley still sounded doubtful. "So tell me how you managed to escape," he continued.

Graystripe described how he and Fang had managed to make a hole in the floor of the den to release the trapped cats, and how the older cats had sacrificed themselves to give the younger and stronger ones the chance to escape from the Twolegs who came searching for them. Barley let out a rusty *mrrow* of laughter as Graystripe told him about the part played by WarriorClan.

"I guess I'll have those young cats visiting me soon," he meowed, "to tell me all about it."

"Yes, and their whole adventure will get more dangerous and exciting every time they tell it," Graystripe agreed. "No, that's not fair," he went on a moment later. "We would have found it a lot harder without Monkeystar and the others."

"And I'd certainly miss their chatter if they never came to visit anymore," Barley added.

"I don't think there's much danger of that," Graystripe told him. "You might be getting some more company, too." At Barley's inquiring look, he explained, "Several of the cats who escaped have joined WarriorClan. But Monkeystar suggested that if they don't like Clan life, they should come live with you here."

Barley broke into a rumbling purr from deep within his chest. "They'd be very welcome." He paused for a moment, nibbling the last of the mouse that he had been eating while Graystripe told his story. "I suppose you'll be heading home tomorrow," he murmured at last.

Graystripe nodded. "Yes. If this journey has taught me anything, it's that my place is back home in ThunderClan."

"Then this is the last time we'll see each other." Barley's voice was sad but resigned. "I'm not ungrateful, you know. I never imagined I would see you, or any Clan cat, again." He paused again, then continued, "I started to think about the end of my life once I realized I could no longer do all the things I once did. Everything seemed pretty bleak after I lost Ravenpaw."

"I felt the same when Millie died," Graystripe mewed.

"And we were wrong. Because you turned up here, Graystripe, and that taught me that there's still the chance of wonderful surprises." With a lilt of amusement in his voice, he added, "Even for cats as *ancient* as we are, there's still something to look forward to."

"You're right, Barley." Graystripe felt warm with affection for the old, wise cat. "And from now on, I'm going to keep looking forward with every single heartbeat."

Graystripe scrambled up the steep, rocky slope and stood panting at the edge of the pool. In front of him the waterfall thundered down, throwing up a cloud of spray that soaked his pelt within heartbeats. Above the falls, the mountain peak was outlined against a scarlet sky as the sun went down.

"Hi there, Graystripe!"

At the sound of the voice, Graystripe looked up to see his son Stormfur standing at the end of the path that led behind the cascade. "Come up!" Stormfur called, beckoning with his tail.

Graystripe hauled himself up the rocks, terrified that his paws would slip on the slick surface, but determined not to show his fear in front of his son. When he reached the path, Stormfur led the way along it until both cats stood in the Tribe's cave.

"You knew I was coming?" Graystripe asked, stepping back to give his pelt a good shake so the water droplets wouldn't spatter his son.

"One of our hunting patrols spotted you," Stormfur explained. "It's really good to see you again."

"You too," Graystripe purred happily.

"Come and rest," Stormfur mewed, gesturing for Graystripe to follow him farther into the cavern. "I want to hear all about your adventures."

"I'll need some prey before I can tell that story," Graystripe responded. "I've traveled a long way today. My paws are sore, and my belly is flapping!"

"Well, the Tribe has eaten already," Stormfur began, "but I guess I can find you something."

He disappeared into the shadowy recesses of the cave, while Graystripe settled himself on the stone floor and started to give his wet fur a quick grooming. The wavering light that came through the waterfall was already dying, and the cavern was quiet; most of the Tribe seemed to have gone to their sleeping hollows.

Shortly, Stormfur returned, carrying a piece of prey that Graystripe guessed was part of an eagle's leg; it had obviously come from a bigger bird than anything ThunderClan caught beside the lake.

"Thanks," he mumbled, tearing into the succulent flesh.

Stormfur sat beside him and watched him while he ate. "I'm really glad you came back," he meowed. "I was worried about you. It's a long way to the old forest, especially—" He broke off, looking faintly embarrassed.

Especially for an old cat like you, Graystripe thought, supplying the words Stormfur had not said. It occurred to him that

Stormfur likely expected that he was going to come live with the Tribe, now that his journeying was at an end.

Blinking in concern, he looked up at Stormfur. The grim set of his son's jaw told Graystripe that he had already guessed his decision. "I'm sorry, Stormfur," he mewed. "I'm going back to ThunderClan."

Stormfur twitched his whiskers in alarm. "So you made contact with StarClan?" he asked.

"I wish I had," Graystripe replied, struggling with regret. "But no. I've realized that I don't need StarClan to tell me that my place is back in the Clan I love. ThunderClan is changing and moving on. Being back in the old forest made me realize how far we've come. Even StarClan has moved on."

"But how did that change your mind?" Stormfur asked, still bewildered. "Wasn't that part of your problem, that Thunder-Clan wasn't the Clan you grew up in?"

Graystripe hesitated for a moment, ordering his thoughts as he took another bite of eagle. "Yes," he mewed at last. "But now I realize that I need to move on, too. Because my love for ThunderClan wasn't just my love for one particular leader, or the warriors I fought and hunted alongside then. It was for everything ThunderClan is, and has ever been—and ever *will* be. For good or ill, as long as I have wisdom to share, that's where I belong."

Stormfur let out an annoyed snort. "I'm sure your Clan-mates haven't even noticed you've gone."

Graystripe stared at him, unable to believe the hostile tone coming from his son. At once, Stormfur looked regretful, stretching out a paw toward his father. "I mean because Clan cats are unfeeling, not because you're not important."

"I may be an elder," Graystripe meowed, remembering the self-respect he had gained after his successful rescue of the kittypets, "but I still have a lot to offer. Wisdom and experience."

"Then why don't you just stay here?" Stormfur suggested. "Your kin could use your guidance."

"I would like that," Graystripe admitted. "But I have kin in ThunderClan, too, and I have a duty to them now. I've given so much to my Clan, and they've given a lot to me."

"They can't expect you to go on giving forever," Stormfur argued.

"Maybe they can't," Graystripe allowed, "but I *want* to give something. When Stoneteller told me I still have a part to play, I thought he meant that I could be the hero. I could go to the Moonstone and bring back StarClan and we'd all have a clear answer for what ThunderClan is meant to do next." He paused. "What happened was nothing like that. Lightning struck the Moonstone and destroyed it. I reached out to Firestar, and I got no message back. For a while I was devastated."

Stormfur was watching him with wide eyes. "Of course," he said.

"But then I realized," Graystripe went on, "that I was still here. I was still trying to be a good cat, to help others. I was teaching younger cats the warrior ways."

"So you're okay with StarClan being gone?" Stormfur asked incredulously.

"No," Graystripe meowed, shaking his head. "No, it hurts terribly. I miss my kin. I miss my friends. But I know that if they don't come back, life hasn't ended. ThunderClan might struggle to keep itself together after all the strife we've been through. But it can still be a Clan. We're still cats working together, taking care of one another."

Even before he had finished speaking, Stormfur had sprung to his paws, his neck fur bristling with anger. "You actually *want* to return to a troubled place, instead of staying here?" he demanded. Shaking his head, he continued, "I'll never understand Clan cats, choosing conflict and battles over a peaceful life with your kin."

"You were a Clan cat yourself once," Graystripe reminded him. Impulsively, he added, "You could always come to ThunderClan with me."

Stormfur's anger didn't die away, but he seemed to consider that for a moment. Then he shook his head. "Brook and my kits would never leave the mountains. Besides, I'm too old to change."

"So am I," Graystripe responded.

At last Stormfur seemed to understand, dipping his head in acceptance. "I can't pretend I'm happy about it," he meowed. "But did Stoneteller really say you have a part to play?"

Graystripe nodded. "He did."

Stormfur's ears flicked up. "In that case, it's clear you must go back. Stoneteller is never wrong."

The pain and confusion Graystripe had felt during the argument with his son began to fade, until all that was left was a feeling of peace with his decision: that he truly belonged in ThunderClan, and that Stormfur understood why he had decided to go home.

But at the same time, he was grief-stricken at the thought of being separated from his son forever. He remembered how he had been brooding over the little time he had left; he'd already said good-bye to one old friend for what he knew was the last time, and now he realized that this could well be the last time that he ever saw Stormfur, too. The thought was like a heavy ball of fire, deep within his belly; Graystripe felt that he might throw up and start wailing in despair all at once.

With nothing more to say, father and son sat together in silence. Graystripe considered asking Stormfur to visit him in ThunderClan, if it was at all possible. *I want to see him as often as I can in the time that remains to me.* But something stopped him, and the words were never spoken.

Eventually, Stormfur asked, "Are you going to tell me about your adventures?"

Graystripe was relieved that there was something he could talk about other than the sadness of their parting. He described how he had found the old territories overrun with Twoleg dens, though Stormfur was pleased to hear that so far RiverClan's old hunting grounds had escaped. He told the story of his meeting with WarriorClan and Fang and his disastrous attempt to speak with StarClan in the cave of the Moonstone. He told Stormfur about his visit to Barley, and how he had freed the cats from the den of the old, sick Twoleg.

Mentioning Fang reminded Graystripe of his long-ago meeting with Gremlin, and how the BloodClan queen had saved ThunderClan.

"I never knew that!" Stormfur exclaimed. "Feathertail and I were in RiverClan then, and you ThunderClan cats never said very much at the Gatherings."

"Well, would you have told the other Clans that you'd risked your whole Clan's lives and made a deal with a Blood-Clan cat?" Graystripe asked.

Stormfur purred in amusement. "No, I suppose I wouldn't have."

Now Graystripe knew why he had stopped himself earlier from asking Stormfur to visit him. Once they'd gotten past their argument, this last evening had been perfect. If this was the last time he and his son would ever see each other, at least he would be leaving Stormfur with a happy memory.

Days after leaving the mountains, Graystripe was trudging up a steep, grassy slope, panting with the effort of putting one paw in front of another. The ridge seemed to draw no closer for all the effort he was making.

You're an elder, you stupid furball, he scolded himself as he halted for a breather. *You shouldn't be traipsing about on quests at your age!*

Toiling on, Graystripe finally scrambled up the last few tail-lengths and stood on the ridge with the wind buffeting his fur. The land fell away in front of him, and in the distance, tiny and glittering in the sun, he could see the lake. He almost felt that one enormous leap would take him right across the water and into ThunderClan's forest.

Happiness and relief surged over Graystripe. *I'm home,* he thought. *For better or worse . . . I'm here to help the Clan I love.*

EPILOGUE

— Then —

Rain had fallen earlier in the day, but now the sky was clear, and the full moon floated serenely above the treetops. The air was cool and fresh, and a breeze blowing from the direction of Fourtrees brought the scent of many cats.

Graystripe padded up the final slope in the paw steps of his leader, Firestar. His whole body tingled with relief that this time he wouldn't have to take his place with the other leaders on top of the Great Rock. Firestar had returned, and everything was as it should be.

When he came to the rim of the hollow, Firestar raised his tail for his Clan to halt. For a moment he stood still, gazing down into the meeting place. Looking over his shoulder, Graystripe saw the massed assembly of cats at the bottom, every one of them turning to stare. Their eyes gleamed as if the moonlight were reflected from countless tiny pools. From their position on the Great Rock, Tallstar, Blackstar, and Leopardstar broke off their conversation and stood rigid.

"Haven't they ever seen a cat before?" Firestar muttered.

Graystripe stifled a snort of amusement.

Then some cat called out, "Firestar!" As if at a signal the whole hollow erupted in yowls of mingled welcome and surprise. Graystripe guessed that some cats from other Clans, too, had believed that Firestar had returned to his kittypet life.

How wrong can you be? he thought.

When the clamor began to die down, Firestar waved his tail and led his cats down the slope to join the others. Raindrops clung to the ferns, soaking Graystripe's pelt as he brushed through them, but he was so eager to get to the Gathering that he scarcely noticed.

Firestar leaped up onto the Great Rock to stand with the other leaders, while Graystripe joined the other deputies below.

Tallstar stepped forward and dipped his head to the ThunderClan leader. "Welcome back, Firestar," he meowed. "I hope you're well again?"

Graystripe thought that the WindClan leader sounded sincere, but there was definitely an edge of sarcasm in Leopardstar's voice when she added, "Yes, Firestar, we've all been *so* worried about you."

"We thought you were never coming back," Blackstar put in.

"Well, I'm here now," Firestar pointed out. "Thank you for your good wishes. I admit I never expected that it would take me so long to recover from a bout of greencough. But I'm quite well now."

He certainly looked it, Graystripe thought. When Firestar

and Sandstorm had returned from their quest, they had both been thinner than usual, exhausted from traveling, their pelts ungroomed. But after a few days of rest and plenty of fresh-kill, they had both filled out; now Firestar stood strong and proud, his pelt shining in the moonlight.

Blackstar and Leopardstar exchanged glances, and for a moment Graystripe's muscles tensed with fear that they would challenge his leader. He guessed that they still believed there was something Firestar wasn't telling them.

But in the end Blackstar gave a curt nod, then stepped up to the edge of the rock and raised his head. "Let the Gathering begin," he called. Once the cats in the hollow had settled down to listen, he turned to Firestar and added, "Perhaps you'd better speak first, Firestar. I'm sure you've got a lot to report."

Graystripe could tell that the ShadowClan leader was hinting again that there was more to Firestar's absence than he had revealed to the rest of the cats. From the tilt of Firestar's head, the twitch of his whiskers, it was clear that he knew it, too. But he didn't let that bother him.

"I certainly do," he mewed briskly in response, moving to stand beside Blackstar, who dipped his head and took a pace back. "As you know," he continued to the assembled cats, "I've been too ill to carry out my duties as Clan leader. But, thank StarClan, I have an excellent deputy who took that responsibility on his shoulders."

Graystripe glanced down at his paws as murmurs of approval came from the crowd of cats around him.

"And not only that," Firestar continued, "but BloodClan chose this time to make trouble again. I think somehow they must have known that I was unable to fight them."

"Yes, what about BloodClan?" Tallstar raised his voice. "Graystripe told us they'd been spotted on your territory."

"BloodClan had a new leader called Fury," Firestar began. "A truly fearsome cat. She decided to do what Scourge failed to do, and take the forest for BloodClan. I suppose they thought that with its leader out of action, ThunderClan would be easy to defeat."

"No way, Firestar!" It was the apprentice Sootpaw who called out, then looked terribly embarrassed and slapped his tail over his mouth.

"No way, indeed," Firestar purred. "Because ThunderClan has a brave, quick-witted, and competent deputy. Graystripe soon showed BloodClan what a mistake they were making."

Graystripe leaned aside and muttered into Sandstorm's ear, "He doesn't have to make such a fuss about it. Any cat would have done the same."

"But 'any cat' didn't," Sandstorm mewed, giving Graystripe's shoulder a brief nuzzle. "You did."

One or two yowls of "Graystripe!" rose up from the Thunder-Clan cats, but at once Firestar raised his tail for silence.

"Think about this," he continued. "Do you believe for one moment that if BloodClan had managed to take over ThunderClan territory, they would have stopped at that? No, I'm guessing that they would have come for WindClan next, then ShadowClan and RiverClan. We would all have been driven out, reduced to living as rogues or loners, or even—StarClan forbid!—becoming kittypets. But we're not. We're at this Gathering here today, Clans in charge of our own territories. And you all owe that to ThunderClan—and to Graystripe's leadership."

Graystripe saw Tallstar nodding in approval, though both Leopardstar and Blackstar looked as though they had bitten into a piece of crow-food.

But they can't argue with Firestar, Graystripe thought. *Because what he said is true.* ThunderClan had stopped BloodClan before it could invade the rest of the forest. *ThunderClan, not me,* he added to himself.

Because no cat, not even Cinderpelt, would ever know how hard he had found it to make the decision to trust Gremlin. If he had been wrong, the Clan he loved would have been destroyed. Even now his belly cramped at the thought of how close they had been to disaster.

As Firestar stepped back, it seemed to Graystripe that every cat in the hollow had opened their jaws to yowl his name and the name of his Clan.

"Graystripe! ThunderClan! Graystripe! ThunderClan!"

He sat with his gaze fixed on his paws while the clamor buffeted his ears like a powerful wind. "I really don't deserve this," he murmured.

"Of course you do," Sandstorm mewed, narrowing her green eyes affectionately. "If it's any comfort, it won't last. The next time a rabbit runs across a Clan boundary, we'll be sliding our claws out again. But for now, shut up and enjoy it."

But I don't enjoy it, Graystripe thought. *I don't want to be the center of attention. That's one reason why I would never want to be leader.*

He was happy to be Firestar's deputy, and a loyal Thunder-Clan cat. *And for the rest of my life, until I travel to StarClan, I'll do my best to protect my Clan.*

READ ON FOR AN
EXCLUSIVE WARRIORS COMIC . . .

CREATED BY
ERIN HUNTER

WRITTEN BY
DAN JOLLEY

ART BY
JAMES L. BARRY

THOUGH...IF I'M BEING HONEST WITH MYSELF...I CAN'T TELL IF MY LEADERSHIP IS DOING THE CLAN ANY GOOD.

DON'T WORRY, BUGEATER. I'M SURE FIFTEEN TIMES WILL BE THE CHARM.

HMPH.

NOMINATING FANG TO BE MY DEPUTY WAS THE RIGHT MOVE. BUT...WHAT IF HE'D BE A BETTER LEADER THAN I AM?

WHAT IF HE DECIDES HE WANTS TO BE LEADER? WHAT WOULD I DO IF HE CHALLENGED ME? I DON'T KNOW.

ALL OF THIS WOULD BE A LOT EASIER IF MY MEDICINE CAT, PETUNIA, DIDN'T KEEP DISAPPEARING FOR DAYS AT A TIME.

EVERY CAT – LISTEN UP.

YOU ALL KNOW THAT PETUNIA'S BEEN LEAVING THE CAMP A LOT. AND I WANT TO RESPECT HER PRIVACY.

BUT SHE'S BEEN GONE FOR THREE DAYS THIS TIME, AND WE NEED TO MAKE SURE SHE'S NOT HURT OR TRAPPED SOMEWHERE.

SO WE'RE GOING TO GO FIND HER.

I'LL LEAD THE PATROL. BUGEATER, CLAWWHISTLE, LILY, YOU'RE WITH ME.

WHAT ABOUT ME?

I THINK WE MIGHT BE IN SOME OTHER CAT'S TERRITORY.

THAT'S RIGHT! YOU'RE IN OUR TERRITORY!

WHAT DO YOU WANT? COME TO TAKE OUR FRESHKILL? STEAL OUR HERBS?

NOT EVEN CLOSE. LOOK, WE'RE JUST PASSING BY.

WE DON'T WANT ANY TROUBLE, ALL RIGHT?

WELL THEN YOU SHOULDN'T HAVE PUT YOUR PAWS WHERE THEY DON'T BELONG! ATTACK!

THESE ARE KITTYPETS. NOT WARRIORS.

LUCKY FOR US, THEY FIGHT ABOUT AS WELL AS YOU'D EXPECT KITTYPETS TO. BUT...

WARRIORCLAN! THIS IS NOT WHAT WE CAME FOR! PULL BACK!

YEAH.

LET'S GO, THEN.

IT'S A HUGE RELIEF TO HAVE PETUNIA BACK...

BUT I CAN'T LET ONE OF MY CATS GO ON BEING THIS MISERABLE.

NOT IF THERE'S ANYTHING I CAN DO ABOUT IT.

AND MAYBE THERE IS.

ENTER THE WORLD OF
WARRIORS

Check out WarriorCats.com to

- Explore amazing fan art, stories, and videos
- Have your say with polls and Warriors reactions
- Ask questions at the Moonpool
- Explore the full family tree
- Read exclusives from Erin Hunter
- Shop for exclusive merchandise
- And more!

Check Out the New Warrior Cats Hub App!

HARPER
An imprint of HarperCollinsPublishers

www.warriorcats.com • www.shelfstuff.com

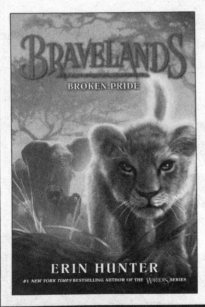

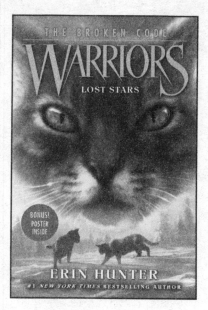

WARRIORS

How many have you read?

Dawn of the Clans
- ⭘ #1: The Sun Trail
- ⭘ #2: Thunder Rising
- ⭘ #3: The First Battle
- ⭘ #4: The Blazing Star
- ⭘ #5: A Forest Divided
- ⭘ #6: Path of Stars

Power of Three
- ⭘ #1: The Sight
- ⭘ #2: Dark River
- ⭘ #3: Outcast
- ⭘ #4: Eclipse
- ⭘ #5: Long Shadows
- ⭘ #6: Sunrise

The Prophecies Begin
- ⭘ #1: Into the Wild
- ⭘ #2: Fire and Ice
- ⭘ #3: Forest of Secrets
- ⭘ #4: Rising Storm
- ⭘ #5: A Dangerous Path
- ⭘ #6: The Darkest Hour

Omen of the Stars
- ⭘ #1: The Fourth Apprentice
- ⭘ #2: Fading Echoes
- ⭘ #3: Night Whispers
- ⭘ #4: Sign of the Moon
- ⭘ #5: The Forgotten Warrior
- ⭘ #6: The Last Hope

The New Prophecy
- ⭘ #1: Midnight
- ⭘ #2: Moonrise
- ⭘ #3: Dawn
- ⭘ #4: Starlight
- ⭘ #5: Twilight
- ⭘ #6: Sunset

A Vision of Shadows
- ⭘ #1: The Apprentice's Quest
- ⭘ #2: Thunder and Shadow
- ⭘ #3: Shattered Sky
- ⭘ #4: Darkest Night
- ⭘ #5: River of Fire
- ⭘ #6: The Raging Storm

Select titles also available as audiobooks!

HARPER
An Imprint of HarperCollinsPublishers

www.warriorcats.com • www.shelfstuff.com

SUPER EDITIONS

- ○ Firestar's Quest
- ○ Bluestar's Prophecy
- ○ SkyClan's Destiny
- ○ Crookedstar's Promise
- ○ Yellowfang's Secret
- ○ Tallstar's Revenge
- ○ Bramblestar's Storm

- ○ Moth Flight's Vision
- ○ Hawkwing's Journey
- ○ Tigerheart's Shadow
- ○ Crowfeather's Trial
- ○ Squirrelflight's Hope
- ○ Graystripe's Vow

GUIDES   FULL-COLOR GRAPHIC NOVELS

- ○ Secrets of the Clans
- ○ Cats of the Clans
- ○ Code of the Clans
- ○ Battles of the Clans
- ○ Enter the Clans
- ○ The Ultimate Guide

- ○ Graystripe's Adventure
- ○ Ravenpaw's Path
- ○ SkyClan and the Stranger
- ○ A Shadow in RiverClan

EBOOKS AND NOVELLAS

The Untold Stories
- ○ Hollyleaf's Story
- ○ Mistystar's Omen
- ○ Cloudstar's Journey

Tales from the Clans
- ○ Tigerclaw's Fury
- ○ Leafpool's Wish
- ○ Dovewing's Silence

Shadows of the Clans
- ○ Mapleshade's Vengeance
- ○ Goosefeather's Curse
- ○ Ravenpaw's Farewell

Legends of the Clans
- ○ Spottedleaf's Heart
- ○ Pinestar's Choice
- ○ Thunderstar's Echo

Path of a Warrior
- ○ Redtail's Debt
- ○ Tawnypelt's Clan
- ○ Shadowstar's Life

A Warrior's Spirit
- ○ Pebbleshine's Kits
- ○ Tree's Roots
- ○ Mothwing's Secret

HARPER
An *Imprint* of HarperCollins*Publishers*

www.warriorcats.com • www.shelfstuff.com